PRAISE FOR STEPHEN LEATHER

'A writer at the top of his game'
Sunday Express

'A master of the thriller genre'
Irish Times

'Let Spider draw you into his web, you won't regret it'
The Sun

'The sheer impetus of his storytelling is damned hard to resist'
Daily Express

'High-adrenaline plotting'
Sunday Express

'Written with panache, and a fine ear for dialogue, Leather manages the collision between the real and the occult with exceptional skill, adding a superb time-shift twist at the end'
Daily Mail on *Nightmare*

'A wicked read'
Anthony Horowitz on *Nightfall*

'In brisk newman's style he explores complex contemporary issues while keeping the action fast and bloody'

Economist

'Stephen Leather is one of our most prolific and successful crime writers…A disturbing, blood-chilling read from a writer at the top of his game'

Sunday Express on *Midnight*

'Lots of gunfire, tactical talk and imaginative plotting. Let Spider draw you into his web, you won't regret it'

The Sun on the *Spider Shepherd thrillers*

'He has the uncanny knack of producing plots that are all too real, and this is no exception. It is the authenticity of this plot that grasps the imagination and never lets it go'

Daily Mail on *First Response*

The Bag Carrier

Stephen Leather

Copyright © Stephen Leather 2019

The right of Stephen Leather to be identified as the Author
of the Work has been asserted by him in accordance with the
Copyright, Designs and Patents Act 1988.

All rights reserved.
No part of this publication may be reproduced, stored in a
retrieval system or transmitted, in any form or by any means,
without the prior written permission of the publisher, nor
be otherwise circulated in any form of binding or cover
other than that in which it is published and without a similar
condition being imposed on the subsequent purchaser.

All characters in this publication are fictitious and any
resemblance to real persons, living or dead, is purely
coincidental.

Prologue

The esteemed Imam climbed up the short flight of wooden steps, and stood tall on the third and final decoratively carved step, known as the minbar. He wasn't blessed with height, so he quite enjoyed standing head and shoulders above his congregation. It was Friday, and the crowd was growing and worshippers were politely jostling for space for the all-important *Salat al-Jum'ah* – Friday Prayer, held once a week at one-thirty pm. It was by far the busiest time of the week, not only at Central Mosque in Maida Vale, but at thousands of mosques all around the country.

Imam Abdullah Malik was a proud man and he was especially proud to be leading prayers at such a prestigious mosque. It'd very recently undertaken renovation, instigated by the Imam himself and reluctantly agreed by the Mosque Committee. The ladies prayer area, at the side of the building, had been vastly extended. New prayer carpets, red with cream border, had been stitched and laid throughout the mosque. CCTV had been installed. Out went the heat circulating ceiling fans, replaced by air-conditioning units. And a huge bespoke chandelier, imported from Iran, had been installed high within the glass dome. The high six figure sum necessary had been quickly raised, due largely to the generosity of the worshippers.

This was his home. These were his people. Malik's hard work and dream realised. Malik tugged at his beard and his eyes moved slowly over his congregation. Sat waiting in the front two rows were the mosque regulars, mainly elders. Some had been at the mosque since first light for Fajr Prayers, others had arrived an hour early to secure the sought after front row and just as importantly, secure the best parking spaces. The next set of eight to ten rows were taken up by those who were on a lunch break from the office or whatever life had them doing. The next couple of rows towards the back were taken up by fathers with young children, who didn't want their inevitably noisy kids disrupting the prayers and incurring the wrath of the elders. Finally, at the very back row, there were the youth, milling around, carrying out fist and chest bumps and talking in loud whispers and stifled laughs.

All in all, for Jum'ah Prayers, there were around five hundred standing in front of him, and half of that number upstairs. Another hundred in the ladies prayer area.

'Feet to feet, shoulder to shoulder,' Malik instructed softly, his voice easily emanating from the many speakers placed inside the mosque.

They all stood up and in doing so, spaces were created and filled until everybody was stood side by side, shoulders touching, elbows brushing.

The Imam glanced at his watch, and counted down the seconds until it reached one-thirty. He stepped down from the minbar, turned his back to the worshippers and faced the direction of the Ka'bah, Islam's most scared mosque, in the holy city of Mecca.

'Allahu akbar,' he began.

Every head bowed, every eye dropped and hands were raised to ears. Hundreds of voices echoed *Allahu akbar,* before the right hand clasped the left wrist, and placed it just above the naval. They observed the Imam recite the first chapter of the Qur'an. They followed it by bending down at the waist, straightening and then dropping down onto their hands and knees, foreheads touching the ground.

The Imam could not see them, his congregation, his brothers, but in his mind's eye he could picture each movement in perfect synchronization, as the weight of the world dissipated from their shoulders, if only for a moment.

Once Jum'ah prayers were over, those in a hurry left in a hurry, to get back to their busy lives. Those who stayed, prayed at their own pace. Malik watched as slowly the room started to empty, the noise levels rising as the worshippers exchanged small talk. He moved comfortably across the hall and mixed with his people. Malik wasn't a vain man, but it gave him a small thrill how the mosque-goers heartily shook his hand and afforded him great respect.

Malik said his farewells to those leaving, when he noticed a man still praying. He was in the back row, at the very end, in the corner of the room, a telltale sign of a latecomer. He was still in the prostrate position, kneeling down, forehead touching the ground, palms flat on the floor either side of his head.

The Imam watched him for a moment. It was not a position that one stayed in for any length of time. But it also wasn't out of the ordinary for somebody to complete their prayers in such a personal manner. Some rocked back and forth, some lifted their hands up high as they held a private word with Allah. Some cried. Others, like this brother, stayed down. So Malik averted his eyes and let him be. It was only after ten minutes passed and the man still hadn't moved that the Imam approached him.

'Brother,' he asked gently, to no reaction. '*Brother?*' He touched him on the shoulder.

The man didn't move.

The Imam smiled, *he'd fallen asleep;* it wouldn't be the first time someone had fallen asleep at prayer. He lightly shook him.

'Wake up, brother.'

That was when the Imam noticed the cream and red of the new prayer carpet darkening. He took a step back and frowned at the pool of glistening blood soaking into the prayer mat under the man's chest.

Chapter 1
(Harry)

It's never a good way to start the afternoon when your boss is standing at the door to his office and looking at his watch and you know you're fifteen minutes late. Not that we're clock-watchers in Homicide Command. We can't be, I'm an Inspector so I don't get paid overtime and murders happen around the clock. I went for lunch at 12.30 and I was supposed to be back at 1.30 and fair enough it was 1.45pm when I reached my desk, but do I complain when I work through the night for no extra pay? Well, yes, I do, but that's not the point.

'Harry, can I have a word?' said the Super, phrased like a question but really he meant 'in my office, NOW!' Superintendent Ken Sherwood. The Sheriff, they call him, which doesn't make any real sense because it was the Sheriff of Nottingham and Robin of Sherwood so really his nickname should be Robin but I suppose that's not much of a nickname and cops do love their nicknames.

'Right, boss,' I said. As soon as I walked into his office he told me to shut the door, which is never a good sign, but then he waved for me to sit down so I knew I wasn't going to get a bollocking because he makes you stand for that.

I dropped down into one of the two seats facing his desk and he sat down on his high-backed adjustable swivelling executive chair. Rank has its privileges, right? Superintendent Sherwood is a big man, but run to fat, the result of too many years sitting in a comfortable chair. Me, I'm whippet thin because I'm at the sharp end of policing, I'm out and about, running myself ragged on behalf of the Homicide and Serious Crime Command. Not many murders are committed inside Peel House so I'm out and about a lot.

The Sheriff leant back in his chair and pushed his wire-framed reading glasses up his nose. 'You ever come across a Mohammed Salim Nasri?' he asked.

The name didn't ring a bell so I shrugged. 'Terrorist or child-groomer, Sir?'

The Superintendent looked at me over the top of his glasses. 'He's a DC at Paddington Green, part of the Harrow Road policing team.'

I shook my head again. 'Not that I know of, boss,' I said, hoping he'd overlook my snap judgement. Or lack of it.

'Bit of a high flyer by all accounts,' said the Superintendent. 'He's going to be your bag carrier.'

I tried to keep my face straight because the Sheriff has read several books on body language and done all the interrogation courses. A guy called Mohammed is possibly the last possible person I'd want as my wing man. And that includes WPC Hitler if she's out there. 'I'm not sure I need an assistant at the moment, Sir,' I said. 'Louise is only on maternity leave for six months, right? I can get by for six months. Plenty of guys who can temp between jobs.' I maintained eye contact and kept smiling.

'Louise has been asked that she be reassigned elsewhere on her return to active duty,' said the Superintendent, which was news to me.

'Is there a problem?' I thought Louise and I always got on well. She was one of the better female officers, one of the lads. She always stood her round in the pub and could take a joke.

'She hasn't made an official complaint, no,' said the Sheriff. 'But then no one ever does, do they, Harry? You've had five partners in the last three years and none of them has had a bad word to say about you. They just ask for a transfer, which is their right, of course. Now from what I've been told, DC Nasri will be an asset to the squad and he'll learn a lot from you, obviously.'

That was not good news. And I wondered why The Sheriff was telling me and why it hadn't come from my direct boss, Detective Chief Inspector McKee. Homicide Command is part of the Specialist Crime and Operations Directorate, split into six units geographically, with a Detective Superintendent in charge. Each of the command units has four Major

Investigation Teams with fifty staff, led by a Detective Chief Inspector. In my case, it's DCI Ron 'Teflon' McKee but I guess the name is all the clue you need, right? I bet Teflon saw the problem looming and got The Sheriff to break the bad news.

Our Murder Investigation Teams are based on the top floor of Peel House, in Hendon, north London, part of the Hendon Police College complex. Peel House sits where the old Metropolitan Police swimming pool used to be and in 2014 most of the old buildings were knocked down and replaced with housing. The lower floors of Peel House are used to train new and serving officers but the top floor – the fifth – is where the Major Incident Room is, along with workstations for Police Intelligence and for Operation Trident, the unit set up in the late Nineties to tackle gun crime and murder in the city's Afro-Caribbean community. Or blacks, as we used to call them.

The Sheriff continued to look at me over the top of his glasses so I figured he still wanted to hear what I had to say. That didn't mean he would listen, but hopefully it wasn't yet a fait accompli. Or to put that in English, I haven't yet been tied up like a kipper. I was going to have to choose my words carefully because anything to do with ethnic minorities is a minefield in the politically-correct Met, so I smiled and nodded and frantically played around with various word combinations that would let him know I didn't want a partner called Mohammed without coming across as an actual racist or Islamophobe.

'The thing is, boss, I'm not sure that the assets DC Nasri brings to his post at Harrow Road would be transferrable to the MIT.'

He raised his eyebrows. 'Because?'

I felt like a mouse staring at a hunk of cheese. I knew it was a trap. It was definitely a trap. But I just couldn't walk away. The smart thing to have done would be just to have said great, happy to have DC Nasri on board, but it was probably my one and only chance to stop it happening so I had to say something. 'Because Harrow Road has a multi-ethnic population that would be more receptive to his background,' I said, choosing my words carefully. 'There are a lot of Arabs in that area, it seems a pity to move him out of his comfort zone into an area where his assets won't be utilised to such good effect.' That sounded quite good. Not in the least bit racist and actually concerned about DC Nasri's welfare. I smiled. Job done.

'He's not an Arab, Harry. His heritage is Asian, Pakistani, I think, but he was born in the UK. Speaks five languages, has a degree, and by all accounts is a first rate detective.'

'I'm sure he is, Guv,' I said. 'But I'm not sure how useful those skills will be in Homicide Command. The cases we investigate have less of an ethnic mix, to be honest. Pakistani, we'd be looking more at counter-terrorism, wouldn't we? For the sort of cases we handle, well, you know, Guv.'

'What do I know, Harry?' he asked, looking at me over the top of his glasses.

And that was that. I'd taken it as far as I could and when you've dug yourself a hole the time comes when you have to throw away your shovel so I just smiled and shrugged. 'Nothing, boss, we're all good.'

'Excellent, Harry,' he said, breaking into a grin now that he sees I'm going to play ball. 'And just to put your mind at ease, I'm pretty sure DC Nasri's skill set will come in useful for your first case together. We've just had a murder in a mosque. So you and DC Nasri are up and running.' He handed me a piece of paper with an address on it. So, I had a new partner, DC Mohammed Salim Nasri. Excellent. I stood up and let myself out of the office. The Sheriff was already tapping away on his computer. Probably filling out his expenses.

I saw DC Nasri as soon I got to my desk. Taller than I'd expected, and fairer, but at least he didn't have a beard. He was a couple of inches shorter than me and wearing a blue suit, a white shirt and possibly the worst tie I've ever seen. It looked as if there were cartoon cats wearing sunglasses on it. Who wears a tie covered in cats? Wearing sunglasses? What does that even mean?

He was grinning like he knew he'd been foisted on me and that there was nothing I could do about it. 'Alright Guv, I'm Sal.' His accent was pure East End. Almost Cockney. He stuck out his hand and we shook. No reason we can't be civilised, right? He's got a strong grip, which to be honest I wasn't expecting. I frowned. 'I thought your name was Mohammed.'

'Everyone calls me Sal, Guv.'

'But Mohammed is your Christian name?'

He looks at me like I've just broken wind. 'Obviously not, Guv. You know, with me being a Muslim. But yeah, my name is Mohammed Salim but everyone calls me Sal.'

'Or DC Nasri?'

'Or DC Nasri,' he said.

'Well, DC Nasri, we've got our first case.'

'Central Mosque in Maida Vale. I know, Guv.'

I frowned. I was just about to ask him how come he's so quick off the mark but then I realised that the Sheriff must have told him. I didn't say anything and I headed out. He followed. I was a bit annoyed, I have to say, because the Super had told him about the case before he'd told me and that's just plain unprofessional.

'We'll need a car,' I said.

He held up a set of keys and jangled them. 'Already sorted, Guv.'

'And a Book 194.' Even as the words left my mouth I realised he had the volume tucked under his arm. The Book 194 – also known as the Decision Log - is the major responsibility of the Senior Investigating Officer's assistant. Every decision the SIO makes is written down in the book so that senior officers can review the case at any time.

I forced a smile and nodded and said 'Good job' but I could see I was going to be having problems with this one.

Chapter 2
(Sal)

I'd made an effort, first day, first impressions, had to set the tone of what could be a long partnership, but I doubted that I'd be Detective Inspector Porter's bag carrier for more than a few months. From a cursory background check on my new Guv I'd discovered that he had gone through five partners in three years. That fact alone sent alarm bells ringing. But, you know, I'm not one to judge, even though I could see him doing exactly that when he first clocked me.

I could see him, blatantly take my measure. His eyes spending more time than necessary on my tie. Forgive me for brightening up what is otherwise a normally morbid day that this job tends to bring. I wasn't sure if he was frowning or if that was his natural resting face. I once dated a girl at Uni, stunning she was, made to perfection, with a personality to boot. She also had a strange resting face. She had to go.

He made his way to me, and from where I was standing DI Porter wasn't exactly a dedicated follower of fashion either. An unfitted blazer, too short for his tall frame, drainpipe trousers, too short for his long legs and clunky black shoes. It was a pretty sad sight, a middle-aged man who hadn't quite caught up and was stuck in another decade. But, as I said, I'm not one to judge, though I did wonder what kind of mobile phone he was packing. As he approached, I discreetly rubbed my palm on my trousers before shaking his hand, ensuring that my grip was tight. Nobody wants a partner with a limp, wet handshake. I introduced myself and straight off the bat he questioned me about my name, wanting to know why I didn't use Mohammed. *What's it to him?* It wound me up a little, but I shrugged it off with a smile.

He seemed surprised that I had already hooked up a ride, and even more surprised that I had a Book 194 ready to go. The Book 194 is a record of everything the SIO does on a case, everyone he talks to, every decision he makes. When it was first introduced a lot of the old school resented it. It gave the top brass the opportunity to go through every little detail the SIO had undertaken on any given case, giving them the chance to find fault and apportion blame when an investigation stalled. The way I see it, the 194 is key; a clean method of recording every step of an investigation and proving that all bases have been covered. Those who carry it are known as scribes or bag carriers, terms I'm not crazy about, but it was an important part of my duty to keep the book up to date and to make sure that both Porter and I sign and date each page.

Every few days the pages get ripped out and handed to a typist who inputs them into the HOLMES system. HOLMES is the computer system that's now used in all major crime investigations. Actually, following a major revamp it's HOLMES 2. Home Office Large Major Enquiry System, before you ask. Yeah, I know, *Major* and *Large* pretty much mean the same thing when it comes to an investigation. But the powers that be liked the idea of the *Sherlock* connection, so they shoehorned the L in and, voila, HOLMES was born. Well done. Pats on the back all around.

Porter and I walked out in near silence and located the pool car. It was nothing special, a grey Vauxhall Vectra. I glanced sideways at Porter as we took the short drive across town to Central Mosque. He hadn't put his seatbelt on and the seatbelt sensor started sounding off. No need for me to mention it, I ain't the seatbelt police, I'm *the* police. Homicide and Serious Crime Command. And I was raring to go.

He ignored the beeping and slipped out his mobile, flipping open the brown leather case to reveal a champagne coloured, new model iPhone. I was surprised that he didn't own one more suited to his wardrobe. He attempted to unlock the security screen, muttering something unintelligible after the second failed attempt, before finally cracking it. He checked his messages. The sensor continued to beep.

'SOCO have arrived,' he said, 'They want our ETA. Apparently there's a problem.'

'What kind of a problem, Guv?'

'Not sure. Didn't say.' He glanced out of the window, as we passed Kilburn Park Tube Station. 'I reckon about five minutes.'

The beeping was driving me crazy but he didn't seem to be aware of it. 'Yeah, I'll go with that,' I said, as he messaged back our ETA. 'So you know Central Mosque do you, Guv?' I could sense him fixing his glare to the side of my head. It was a poor question. I cleared my throat and continued. 'That's my local masjid.'

Another look, less glare, more puzzled.

'Mosque - masjid, same thing Guv. Just the Arabic term for it.'

'How about sticking with English?' he said. 'Seeing as how I'm not an Arab.' He smiled but his eyes didn't follow suit.

'Yeah, no, absolutely, Guv. I was. It's one of those words that isn't actually English but you'll find in the English dictionary, like, um...' Shit, I couldn't think of another example.

He turned away indicating that the subject was closed, just as it came to me.

Veranda! Karma! Bloody Chutney!

He finally got around to buckling his seat belt and the beeping stopped. 'How long have you been attending Central Mosque?' he asked.

'Since I was old enough for a clip around the ear but not old enough to do anything about it.' I smiled at the burst of memories. 'There's always been a good crowd there, hardly ever any trouble. Until now, obviously.'

I turned onto Jessop Street and the twin minarets of the mosque came into view, shining high and proud either side of the large green dome. A little guilt kicked in at the sight of it. I had slacked off attending recently. Once there was a time when I'd attended three times a week after school for Islamic Studies, and stay behind for prayers. As I got a little older and discovered sports and girls and video games, life got in the way and those visits were then reserved for only Fridays, for Jum'ah Prayers. When Uni beckoned, exams, parties, *more life*, my appearance was limited to twice a year, for Eid Prayers.

This was my first visit back in months, and it was work not worship that had brought me.

I knew the Imam a little, we shared a passing acquaintance, a *Salaam*, a few words exchanged, *Mashallah*, *Inshallah*, a pat on the back. He ran a tight ship and apart from one hate preacher occasionally setting up shop outside of the mosque and shouting the odds, it was a peaceful place, accommodated by good Muslims with good intentions.

I slipped the car into a parking space and killed the engine. 'Guv,' I said, 'how do you want to play this?'

'What'd you mean?' he said, unbuckling his seat belt.

'I just think that they may be more open with me, you know, brown skin and all that,' I showed him the back of my hand to demonstrate said skin. 'And I sort of know the Imam.' I wasn't trying to undermine him, but it was the obvious play. We had to tread carefully, I knew that this would be a sensitive situation, potentially leading to an explosive one.

He stepped out without saying anything and slammed the door. By the time I was out, he was approaching the grounds of the mosque. I quickened my pace and fell in step with him.

Chapter 3
(Harry)

I didn't say anything when DC Nasri said that he prayed at the mosque we were going to but it seemed weird. He's a cop, right? A detective. And Muslims pray five times a day. How's that going to work, that's what I want to know. If it comes time for him to pray, do we have to stop what we're doing while he gets out a prayer mat and does his thing? His crack about skin colour annoyed me, too. What was he suggesting, that only Asian cops should question Asian suspects? If I'd ever said that white suspects should only be questioned by white cops my career with the Met would be over before you could say 'racial discrimination'.

Anyway, as soon as we got out of the car I could see there's a problem. There was a squad car there, and a SOCO van, but no one seemed to be going inside. The two SOCO guys were all dolled up in their gear and carrying their cases, but they were standing outside while two uniformed cops talked to a group of

THE BAG CARRIER

Asian men, most of them wearing Islamic clothing - baggy trousers and tunics and long robes, topped off with skull caps. I've never understood why someone living in England would want to wear clothing more suited to the desert, but each to his own, I guess.

I walked over and Nasri hurried after me. One of the uniforms was a sergeant I've known for years. Michael Swaine. He was arguing with a large, bearded Asian who seemed quite agitated. Swaine looked over at me as I walked up, clearly relieved to be able to hand over to a senior officer. There were at least a dozen Asian men blocking the corridor and until they moved, no one was going anywhere. Swaine stepped to the side and I faced up to the bearded Asian who seemed to be the spokesman of the group. 'We've been told that someone has died,' I said. 'My name is Inspector Porter and you need to get out of the way, now.'

'We're bringing the body out,' said the man gruffly.

I thought I'd misheard. 'What?'

'The body is being brought out.'

'No!' I said. 'No one can touch it. It has to be examined where it is.'

The man shook his head. 'The body has to come out.'

I looked at Swaine and he shrugged. 'They just won't budge, Harry. What can we do? There's two of us, and even if we draw our batons they're not going to move. They're not being belligerent or violent so

I can hardly call for armed support. Besides – it's a mosque.' He shrugged again.

Strictly speaking he should be calling me Inspector, but Swaine and I go back a long way and we reserve titles for when the top brass are around. He was right. They weren't resisting, they just weren't moving. I could call out the Territorial Support Group and we'd have a couple of vans of back-up within minutes, but then what? I could hardly ask them to draw batons and start belting unarmed worshippers.

Nasri approached the man I'd been talking to. 'Brother,' he said. 'You have to let the police through.'

'Brother,' said the man, 'we are not stopping them from doing their job, but you must understand, first we must do ours.'

'How do you mean?' asked Nasri. 'What job, brother?'

'We are restoring the mosque to a state of cleanliness,' said the man. 'It must stay paak at all times, brother, surely you know that.'

The whole 'brother' thing was getting on my nerves. Cops shouldn't be calling civilians 'brother'. We're not their brothers, we're not related. We call people by their names or we say 'Sir' or 'Madam'. If you're a uniform trying to calm down a group of unruly drunks you might say 'mate'. But 'brother', that's just ridiculous. I took out my warrant card and held it up in the air, just in case they didn't know I was a cop. 'Please, gentlemen, I'm a detective and you need to let me do my job.'

To my surprise the men at the entrance parted. Swaine looked at me in amazement, but then we saw two Asian men further down the corridor placing another man down on the floor. The man's chest was wet with blood. It was the body.

I muttered under my breath, put my warrant card away, and pushed through the men.

'Guv!' shouted Nasri from behind me.

I ignored him and continued into the mosque. He ran after me and grabbed me by the shoulder.

'Guv, shoes! You need to take off your shoes.' I looked down and saw that he was now wearing just his socks on his feet. 'This is a place of worship,' he said.

'I'm not here to worship, I'm here to do my bloody job,' I snapped.

He looked at me earnestly. 'I get that, Guv, but this is *their* place of worship, and they're going to see this as a huge sign of disrespect.' He waved at the men standing in the corridor, most of whom were glaring at me with undisguised hatred. 'Take 'em off, trust me. Keep 'em on, and you're going to start a riot.'

He was right, of course. My bad, as they say. I kicked off my shoes.

'They have to be outside, Guv.'

'Why don't you do that for me, DC Nasri,' I said. 'I've got work to do.' I called over to the two SOCO men to follow me in and together we went to look at the body. It was a bearded man wearing Islamic clothing. As I got closer, I could see the chest was glistening with wet blood. I didn't get too close because I wasn't wearing gloves or overshoes.

The SOCO guys brushed past me and knelt down. He was clearly dead but they checked for a pulse anyway. Outside I heard the siren of an ambulance. Better late than never, I suppose.

Nasri reappeared and looked down at the body. 'Stabbed?' he said.

'Looks like it,' I said. There was a blood trail leading off to the main prayer room. I followed it.

The prayer room had a triple height ceiling with a massive ornate chandelier overhead. There were several dozen men milling around and then I spotted two men on their hands and knees, scrubbing the floor. There was a bucket of water between them and they had their heads down as they worked. I suddenly realised what they were doing and I ran over. 'Hey, stop that! Stop!'

They looked at me and sat back on their heels. They were both Asian, middle-aged and overweight with long beards and with knitted skullcaps on their heads.

'What do you think you're doing?' I shouted.

The two men looked at each other, shrugged, and then went back to cleaning the blood off the floor.

'Stop!' I yelled at the top of my voice.

Sergeant Swaine came running in. He'd taken his shoes off and was carrying his helmet.

'They're destroying evidence,' I said to him. Swaine grabbed the shoulder of the nearest man and tried to pull him away. Two younger Asians hurried over and pushed Swaine. Swaine fell back, slipped, and hit the ground hard. Half a dozen Asians stood around him, shouting at him in a language I didn't recognise. One of them kicked Swaine in the side. He was barefooted so he didn't do any damage but I yelled at him to stop and he backed away.

I pointed at the guy who was still cleaning up the blood. 'You! Stop that! Stop that now!'

He ignored me and carried on scrubbing.

Sergeant Swaine got to his feet but the Asians stood around him, not allowing him to move.

I looked around. Pretty much every man in the prayer room was moving towards us and it was clear they weren't happy. There must have been fifty of them, at least. I looked over at Swaine. 'Call for back up, Mike. Armed support.'

Before Swaine could reach for his radio, Nasri hurried over to me. 'Guv, please, a word.'

'Now what?'

'I'm not sure armed support is the way to go. Look... They're already riled up. Guns are just going to antagonise them further.'

'They're impeding an investigation into a murder.'

'Yeah, Guv, but this is their mosque, it's their place of worship, and they'll do whatever they have to do to defend it.' He moved closer and lowered his voice. 'Guns won't make them back down, Guv. The last thing we need is a Muslim to be gunned down in their place of worship.'

I cursed under my breath because while I didn't like what he was saying, he was right. 'What do you suggest?' I asked.

'Give me a minute, Guv. Let me talk to them. I'm sure I can make them see sense. If nothing else, I'll calm them down.'

'Okay, one minute.' I looked over at Swaine and nodded and he took his hand away from his radio. I looked back at Nasri. 'Don't screw this up.'

'I'll do my best, Guv,' he said. 'I mean, I'll do my best not to.'

'I know what you mean,' I said. 'Just get on with it.'

CHAPTER 4
(SAL)

My first day wasn't supposed to be like this.

Straight into the mix, on a case that I felt I might be too close to. I didn't express my concerns when the Superintendent first presented it to me and I didn't even entertain the idea of expressing it to Porter. I don't even want to think how that conversation would play out.

But, yeah, there were concerns.

I'm not religious, I mean... *I am*, but not textbook. Like most Muslims, it's grey.

I believe in an Almighty being, call him what you may, I call him Allah, but I don't worship *Him* as I should, or as I think I should, or how others think I should . I don't know. It's complicated. But whichever way you look at it, I *am* a Muslim, and these were *my* people, and this masjid was *my* place of prayer, regardless of the rarity of my attendance.

There was an emotional attachment.

I was there in the capacity of the law, with my copper's hat on and not my Paki hat, but it was frustrating. Watching my colleagues, not understanding, not even trying to understand how to conduct themselves in a mosque. Watching my brothers, relentless in their pursuit of trying to get the masjid back to a state of cleanliness, but in the process destroying the crime scene.

I believed that I could have been key to this investigation from the off, able to smooth relations, speak to key witnesses and ascertain pertinent details that my mainly white colleagues could not. But instead I was feeling like a spare part. I hadn't expected to slot straight into the team, but I wasn't expecting the coldness of my colleagues either. Porter didn't take to me for reasons I hadn't yet sussed out. And Swaine looked at me as if to say, *these are your fucking people, pal.*

Truth be told, the Jum'ah attendees, at least the fifty odd that remained, had made our life that much more difficult. The body had been covered by a white sheet and moved from where it had been found. This alone would set back the investigation, coupled with the fact that two men on hands and knees armed with a bucket of water and a sponge, were wiping away potentially crucial evidence.

But calling for armed support would've been catastrophic. Central Mosque was located in a heavily Muslim populated area, out of which operated an ultra-violent gang of youths who called themselves The Faith. It would be fair to say they did not like the police, with reason, if I'm honest. If they got wind that armed police had rocked up at their masjid we'd be looking at around thirty youths, with that number fast escalating, all wearing ghutrah scarves bound tightly over their faces, ready to go at it, blow-for-blow.

I approached the two men that had been cleaning the prayer mat. They had stopped to watch the commotion. I knelt down next to them so that we were eye level.

'Salaam, Uncle,' I said, just as one of them started to scrub again. I placed my hand gently on his and he stopped.

'We clean. Imam said we clean,' one said as he straightened his skull-cap. It was obvious from those few words that we would struggle to converse in English. By the look of them, they looked Pakistani, so Urdu, or possibly Punjabi. They were both in their seventies. I switched to Urdu.

'Uncle, you have done all you can. The body is away from the prayer area. This blood will not come out easily with water,' I said, in stuttering Urdu. I was out of practice.

'Police-walay, they show us no respect. Why do they have to shout? Why do they have to be aggressive?' Skull-Cap said. *'They will achieve nothing with this attitude.'*

'I understand.'

'Insects from a dirty drain.' The other spoke, citing a well versed insult. His forehead was slick with sweat under his Pashthun hat from the exertion of scrubbing. *'They come into our home and tell us what to do? No, Son, no.'*

'I understand, I do.'

I let them have their moment, as they went back and forth, venting. I glanced at the Guv who was cluelessly hanging onto every word, every insult. Pashtun in particular seemed to be enjoying himself, smiling sweetly as he viciously took aim. Amongst the colourful language was *Behanchood* and *Haram Salla* – Sister Fucker and Bitch dog!

'*Okay, that's enough, remember where you are,*' I said, sticking with Urdu. '*Mashallah, you have done your masjid proud. Now let the police do their work. I will personally speak with the Imam. He will understand once I explain.*'

They shrugged and stood up in tandem and moved away.

'What language was that?' Porter asked.

'Urdu, Guv. They probably speak English but it's easier to converse in their own language.'

I figured best not to mention that it was the language I spoke whenever I went back to see my mum and dad. English had always been a second language at home.

'I need to speak to the top man,' he said. 'What do they call him? The priest or whatever?'

'The Imam, Guv. The Imam here is Abdullah Malik.'

Before I could tell him that the Imam was standing at the far end of the prayer room, Porter raised his right hand and began clicking his fingers. 'Will Imam Abdullah Malik please make himself known!' he shouted.

The Imam was already walking towards us, his face remarkably neutral despite the blatant disrespect he'd just witnessed. The Imam was a small man, dressed in a long white thawb and a knitted skullcap. He stroked his trimmed beard and peered at us through round John Lennon glasses. Despite having met and briefly conversed with me on a handful of occasions, the Imam did not register recognition. It didn't surprise me, I was one of hundreds that he would have talked to at the mosque.

'I am Imam Abdullah Malik,' he said, softly. He turned to me, 'Aslamalykum.'

I could feel Porter about to blow a gasket. 'English please, Imam,' I requested respectfully.

'I'm DI Porter and this is DC Nasri,' said the Guv, flashing his warrant card. 'We believe it was you who found the body and phoned the police.'

Malik nodded.

'And it was at your request that the body be moved?' Porter asked.

'We are bound by duty. The body had to be moved.'

'You destroyed the crime scene,' Porter said, 'That's a criminal offence.'

The Imam looked at me, as if it fell to me to explain. 'Religious reasons, Guv,' I said. 'It's imperative that the mosque must always be spotless.' It wasn't exactly good cop, bad cop but breaking the Imam's balls wasn't going to get us his cooperation.

'You must know that you can't mess around with a crime scene,' Porter said to the Imam.

'For us, religion takes precedence,' Malik said, meeting Porter's eyes in defiance.

'In this country, the law takes precedence,' Porter countered. 'Now where's the knife?'

'Knife? We cleaned the masjid, Detective. We found no knife.'

'Someone here must have seen the knife,' said the Guv, getting loud again and catching the attention of the other worshippers. 'Now where is it?'

He wasn't going to achieve anything in this place with that attitude. I leaned in towards him. 'Guv,' I whispered 'Do you mind if I …?'

I expected a ticking off, but he blew out his cheeks and shook his head in annoyance. 'Just get him to tell us where the knife is,' he snapped.

'Right Guv,' I nodded. 'And Guv?'

'What is it?'

'I think he'll talk more if you … Y'know.' I inclined my head towards the door.

Porter tutted, sighed and nodded, then thankfully stomped out of the prayer hall in his socks.

I turned my attention back to the Imam but before I could say anything he began to speak. 'The good people of this masjid raised in the region of half a million pounds in the space of one year,' Malik said. 'For them to witness the utter contempt and disrespect that *they* displayed towards our holy place …' He shook his head sadly. 'Brother, I'm surprised that

THE BAG CARRIER

there was not more violence here today. You can only push us so far before we start to push back.'

'I apologise, truly. Today I was ashamed to be one of them.' I bowed my head, showing him the respect he thought he deserved.

'Brother,' Malik put his hand on my shoulder and smiled. 'Before you are one of them, you are one of us.'

I swear I felt like the Imam was trying to hypnotise me with his soothing voice. I had to remember that I was there in the capacity of a detective for the Metropolitan Police. A detective investigating a murder. 'The body should never have been moved,' I said. He dropped his hand from my shoulder as he quickly realised which side of the fence I was on. I smiled passively at him. Respect aside, I had to treat him like I would anybody else in a murder investigation. 'It's too late now, I just hope they don't charge you with obstruction.'

'What do you want, boy?' he asked, his tone now a little less soft and a whole lot colder.

'Did you personally phone nine nine nine?' I asked.

'Yes, I made the call, as soon as I realised that the brother wasn't moving.'

'And you say there was no knife?'

'There was no knife,' he said firmly. He frowned at being asked the same question again. He'd have to get used to it. It wouldn't be the last time he'd be asked.

'Right. I understand. But it may still be on the premises.'

'Why don't you just tell me what is on your mind, my ambitious brother?'

'Your co-operation, Imam.'

'Meaning?'

'A team will be searching the premises, from top to bottom. I can ensure that it is carried out with respect and minimum disruption, but I will need your help, Imam.'

'What do you need from me?'

'Access to all areas.'

'Anything else?'

'Everybody here is a suspect; nobody can leave the masjid until everyone has been questioned.'

Chapter 5
(Harry)

As I walked out of the prayer hall, the two SOCO officers were attending to the body. They were wearing blue covers over their socks. One was taking photographs, the other was patting down the body. 'I've got a wallet,' said the one kneeling on the ground.

'Got any gloves?' I asked.

He handed me a pair of blue latex gloves and I put them on, then he gave me a black leather wallet. There was a library card in the name of Mohammed Masood, and a Tesco loyalty card with the same name. There was a driving licence in the name of Sean Evans, but the picture didn't look much like the man on the floor. There was no beard on the man in the photograph and the skin was a lot whiter. I compared the driving licence with the face of the dead man. I really wasn't sure.

'What do you think?' I asked, handing it to the SOCO.

He studied the picture and the face, then nodded. 'It's him,' he said, passing it back to me.

'So we've got a name. Sean Evans. Twenty-four years old. And he lives in Bromley.' I used my smartphone to take a picture of the licence.

'He's been out of the country to get a tan like that,' said the SOCO.

'Any thoughts on the knife?'

'Not too wide a blade, I'd say, but you'll need a post mortem to be sure. Looks like it pierced the heart.' He held out an evidence bag and I dropped the wallet in and sealed it.

Nasri came out of the prayer room. 'The Imam insists there was no knife when he found the body, Guv.'

'Do you believe him?'

'No reason for him to lie, Guv.'

'There's every reason if he knows the killer and is trying to help him.'

'It was the Imam that called three nines.'

'That doesn't mean he didn't hide the knife.'

'Yeah, of course, Guv,' he said but I could see he was miffed that I'd insulted his precious Imam. I'm a cop first and foremost and I'd give the Archbishop of Canterbury the third degree if I thought it would solve a murder case. 'And he's amenable to a search,' said Nasri.

'Is he now? Amenable, you say?' I didn't try to keep the sarcasm out of my voice.

'All that I'm saying is that he's willing to play ball. If we approach this the right way, he could be useful.'

'There's what, fifty men in there?'

'About that. Most of the worshippers have left already.'

'So how many would there have been at the time of the killing?'

Nasri cleared his throat. 'About five hundred or so, Guv.'

My jaw dropped. 'What? Five hundred? FIVE HUNDRED?'

'Plus maybe another hundred women. They pray in a separate part of the mosque.'

My day was clearly going from bad to worse. 'So we have six hundred potential witnesses, most of whom have already gone?'

'Afraid so, Guv. *Salat al-Jum'ah* - sorry, Friday Prayers - is the busiest time of the week.'

'Shit. Shit, shit, shit.' I rubbed the back of my neck. The tendons there were as taught and hard as steel wire and I was getting the beginnings of a headache. 'Okay, we're going to need a full list of everyone who is here, and another list of everyone who was here who has since left.'

He looked over his shoulder. 'People are starting to leave, Guv,' he said. 'I'm going to need some help.'

He was right. All the worshippers were potential witnesses and had to be identified and questioned before they could go anywhere. 'Do what you can,' I said. 'I'll arrange for more uniforms.'

'Alright Guv, I'm on it,' he said. I waved him away. 'Well get on with it, lad.' He hurried back into the prayer room.

'He's with you?' asked the SOCO.

'Yeah, my new bag carrier,' I said.

'Good luck with that.'

I gave him the evidence bag and waved at the entrance to the prayer room. 'You've probably realised that the body was moved,' I said. 'It started off in the prayer room over there. The bad news is that for some reason they decided to start cleaning up. They've washed away a lot of the evidence already.'

The SOCO who was taking photographs lowered his camera. 'You are joking,' he said. 'Don't they watch CSI for fuck's sake?'

I assumed the question was rhetorical. 'Anyway, it was moved from there to here so the crime scene is already compromised. Just do the best you can. At the moment there's no sign of the murder weapon, if we don't find it soon I'll be organising a search of the surrounding area.'

I walked through to the entrance hall. There were dozens of pairs of shoes on the floor and on racks but mine were the only shiny pair of black brogues so they were easy enough to spot. I slipped them on, left the mosque and called the office on my phone. I could have used the radio but generally for one-on-one conversations the phone is better. To my surprise, Teflon McKee was at his desk. 'How are you getting on with the new member of the team?' he asked, and I could picture him grinning like the proverbial Cheshire cat.

'Like a mosque on fire, Guv,' I said, which probably wasn't the smartest thing to have said.

'What was that, Harry?'

'Like a house on fire,' I said. 'Look, Guv, this is definitely a murder, the victim is one Sean Evans, a 24-year-old IC1 male, killed with what appears to be a single stab wound to the chest. Several dozen potential witnesses but I'm fairly sure they'll be three monkeys.'

Three monkeys? Hear no evil, see no evil, speak no evil. Par for the course when a violent crime has occurred. But it probably wasn't the best expression to use with Teflon, because, well, racial discrimination, right? The days of being able to call a spade a spade in the Met are long gone, and monkey is one of several hundred words that police officers use at their peril.

If he had picked up on my use of the word, he didn't mention it. 'You can take SIO on this, Harry?' he asked.

SIO. Senior Investigating Officer. To be SIO you need to have the rank of DI or above but this case was a potential minefield, so if McKee had any sense of decency he'd step up to the plate and take on the SIO role himself. But there's a reason he got the Teflon nickname, obviously. If he sees any case that might be in the least bit controversial or tricky he'll do his upmost to sidestep it. And this case was going to be a minefield, no question, and it was my size tens that he wanted clumping around. He waited for my answer and there's only one answer I can give, of course. 'I don't see why not, Guv. I've a lot on my plate but who hasn't?'

'Good man. What do you need?'

'SOCO are here. There's a bit of a wrinkle in that the worshippers have moved the body.'

'What the hell for?'

'Religious reasons, I'm told. And they cleaned up the blood.'

'They what? For fuck's sake, Harry, get a grip.'

'Guv, this all happened before I got here. I've explained to SOCO, they're on it.'

'Potential suspects?'

'We've got a dead white guy in a mosque full of Muslims, Guv. You tell me. But there's no sign of a murder weapon. If one doesn't turn up we'll need a search of the surrounding area. And we have several dozen potential witnesses. Fifty maybe. I don't see that it's going to be practical to bus them all back to the station so I'm proposing we do the preliminary interviews here.'

'So what do you need?'

'Several dozen uniforms to secure the scene and make sure no one leaves. And I'm going to need bodies who can handle interviews. Ideally CID.'

'Five be enough? We're stretched at the moment.'

'Ten would be better, Guv.'

'Eight. Final offer.'

'Eight it is, Guv.

I smiled to myself because I'd been expecting six so I was ahead of the game. 'We'll need interpreters, too. Some of them don't speak English. Or at least they claim not to.'

'Okay, I'll get that sorted for you. What languages?'

'I don't know, Guv. What do they usually speak? Urdu, right? Indian? Pakistani? Arabic?'

'I think you'll find they all speak English, Harry. English is the national language. But okay, I'll talk to Translation Services and see what they suggest. DC Nasri's a language expert so make full use of him.'

'I plan to, Guv. Now what about a Deputy SIO?' Every major investigation has a Senior Investigating Officer and a Deputy Senior Investigating Officer. I had the feeling that DCI McKee would like to use Nasri as my deputy but the role has to be filled by a Detective Sergeant or higher.

'What about Dave Roffe? He's just back from leave.'

I gritted my teeth. DS Roffe is a lazy arsehole and the last person I'd want as my deputy. He's also screwing around with a married CPS lawyer and that shit is sure to hit the fan at some point. The thing is I'm pretty sure that Teflon knows that. 'Maybe someone with a bit more experience, Guv. This is going to be a tough one.' He knows that it's going to be a tough one, of course, that's why he side-stepped the SIO role.

'Have you got anyone in mind, Harry?'

That came as a surprise. Maybe he realised how he'd screwed me over on this and wanted to make amends. Or maybe he just wanted me to make a suggestion so that he can shoot it down. 'What about Stuart?' I asked. 'He's just winding up that multiple rape-murder case.' DS Stuart Turley is my age, pretty much, and old school. His wife divorced him and took the kids to stay with her and her new husband so he doesn't have any family demands on his time, he drinks but not to excess and he knows his stuff. He's a Chelsea supporter but you can't have everything.

'That makes sense, Harry, let's run with Stuart. I'll get him started on the incident room. David Judd is also coming off that rape team so we'll use him as Office Manager.'

'Good choice, Guv.' It was, too. DC Judd is young – barely out of his twenties – and he decided very early on in his career that he didn't enjoy working with the Great British public. Some guys enjoy walking a beat or driving round in fast cars, but Judd was born to sit behind a desk and the thing is he does a bloody good job. The job of Office Manager is exactly what it says on the can. Basically he keeps his eye on everything that's happening in the investigation and makes sure that the SIO is always up to speed. He's in charge of proofreading all documents, making sure that everything is filed away where it should be, liaises with the force media department about press and TV coverage, makes sure that all officers carry out the relevant risk assessments and makes sure that the investigation has all the resources it needs. And about a hundred other things. It's mind-blowingly boring and you need an eye for detail that most coppers just don't have, but Dave took to it like a fish to water. He works all the hours that God sends and doesn't really care, though to be fair, as a DC, he gets paid overtime which is one of the reasons he drives a very tidy BMW sports car.

'Stephen Courtney's also coming off that murder-rape case, so I'll lock him in as Finance Manager,' said McKee.

'Another good call, Guv,' I said, and I wasn't blowing smoke up his arse. Finance Manager is always one of the first appointments to any investigation because these days policing is all about money. Every single expenditure has to be accounted for and approved, and it's the Finance Manager's job to do that. Basically he – and in my experience it's always a man – has to maintain a running total of the current expenditure of the enquiry, so that means tracking the hours worked including overtime, rest days cancelled, public holidays worked and expenses claimed. He looks at the cost of transport, forensics, pathology, consultants, everything that is needed to progress an enquiry. Every week he has to provide a report on costs so that the powers-that-be can see how much has been spent.

A good Finance Manager – and DS Courtney is one of the best – can massage the numbers so that the SIO isn't constantly looking over his shoulder. I'd worked on a few Major Investigation Teams with him and he always had my back. Some Finance Managers act more like bean-counting accountants and quibble every hour of overtime but Courtney was a good cop when he walked a beat and he's never forgotten his roots. Sometimes coppers who have worked two shifts back-to-back deserve a pizza and maybe a cab home and Courtney knows how to bury stuff like that.

'I'll have a look to see who's available as Receiver and Action Manager, hopefully I'll have that fixed up before you're back in the office.'

'Cheers, Guv. Can I suggest Pete Davies as Receiver?'

'I'll see what he's up to. When does he retire?'

'Another three months, Guv.'

Receiver was another vital role on any MIT and it's important to get the right guy – or girl – in play. The Receiver's role is to read every single document that enters the Major Incident Room. Everything. He's the go-to guy – or girl - for a state of play briefing because he more than anyone knows what's going on. He also has to decide which Actions should be fast-tracked. What's an Action? The official definition of an Action is 'any activity which, if pursued, is likely to establish significant facts, preserve material or lead to the resolution of the investigation'. That's what it says in the manual. Whoever writes those things really loves the sound of their own voice, obviously. Basically an Action is any written instruction to carry out a task. I kid you not. Everything is written down. If you want a PC to knock on a door, you need a written Action and the Receiver has to read it and check it. An enquiry will generate thousands of Actions. The Action Manager hands out the Actions and checks that they are carried out. He's an administrator and to be honest you could get a trained monkey to do it. The monkey probably wouldn't need much training either. But the investigation generally goes smoother if the Action Manager is on the ball. 'Plus I'll need someone pretty sharpish to gather CCTV. Two would be better. I'll get the uniforms to gather details of parked vehicles. And can I request DS Paul Rees as Investigative Team Leader, Guv? I need someone out here who can get these interviews organised.'

'As part of the eight?'

'I was thinking in addition, Guv. He's going to be in a management role.'

McKee sighed. 'So you need nine, including DS Rees? Plus two for CCTV?'

'Yes, Guv. And in view of the complexity of the crime scene I'm going to need a Crime Scene Manager and a Forensic Manager now. And as we don't have a suspect I'm going to need an Outside Enquiry Manager fairly soon.'

'I'll get that sorted straight away, Harry. I'm pretty sure Alan Russell is available.'

'And my recommendation would be that we have Press Liaison here as soon as possible, Guv. There are no journalists here at the moment but there's a lot of people aware of what's happened so I think it's only a matter of time before the TV and papers turn up.'

'I'll talk to the press office,' said McKee. 'Anything else that we need to fast track?'

'Those are my immediate requirements,' I said. 'A lot depends on whether or not we turn up the murder weapon. If we don't find it with an initial sweep we're going to need to widen the search area.'

'Let's cross that bridge when we get to it,' said McKee.

'And there's an added problem in that the mosque was full when the murder occurred. That means there could be up to six hundred potential witnesses.'

'I thought you said fifty?'

'Fifty by the time we got here. Most of them had already left.'

I could hear him groan. If the killer had been one of the worshippers then he – or she – would have probably left immediately. And six hundred was a huge number to deal with.

'Will we have names?' he asked.

'I hope so, Guv. I figured we'd question the fifty we have here and see where that leaves us. But unless we get an ID or a murder weapon, we're going to have to be looking to interview those six hundred sooner rather than later.'

He groaned again and I'm fairly sure I heard him swear. 'So this mosque, it's in Maida Vale?' he said.

'It's called Central Mosque, Guv. Jessop Street.'

'I'll send you the back up, the detectives and the translators now. And Harry, tread carefully. The Mayor will be watching, guaranteed. Don't put a foot wrong.'

'I hear you, Guv.'

I put the phone away and ran through my mental checklist. There are five principles to any murder investigation. The building blocks, they're called. Number one is the Preservation Of Life. You have to make sure that no one else is at risk. That was easy. One victim. Dead as a door nail. The second block is to preserve the crime scene. Well, I'd done that, pretty much. Better late than never. But even though the crime scene had been tampered with big time, it was now in the hands of the experts. The third block was to Secure Evidence. SOCO were working on that. The murder weapon would be key, and I was pretty sure one of the men in the prayer room had taken it. The building would need to be searched, and so would the worshippers. If that didn't turn up the weapon then we would have to extend the search. The fourth block was to identify the victim, and I'd done that. At least I had a name and address. The next step would be to find out exactly who he was and why someone would want to stab him in the chest.

The fifth and final block? Last but not least. Identify Suspects. And I had more than six hundred of them. Game on.

CHAPTER 6
(SAL)

I had to ensure that I could keep all the worshippers, or at least as many as I could, contained in the masjid. Porter was arranging for uniforms to assist me, but I wanted to gather as many as I could before the uniforms arrived and spooked the hell out them. Muslims and uniformed cops tended not to be a comfortable mix. I secured the overspill room at the side of the main hall as a holding place and guided them in. I was polite and respectful, and most did as they were asked, especially the older ones and most of the women. They didn't mind being kept behind, it got them out of an afternoon of work and chores, plus they'd have a great after dinner story to tell.

But, as expected, there was some opposition.

'Nah, bruv,' a track-suited Pakistani youth said, as I tried to guide him from the main hall to the overspill area. 'I got things to do, people to see, you get me.'

'Bruv,' I said, it's not a word I used, but sometimes you have to adapt and improvise. 'Just stick around for a bit, yeah. They're just going to ask you some questions and then you can be on your way.'

'You're jokin' right?' Another youth, Somali, smiled, the light from the chandelier reflecting on his gold tooth. 'If the cops don't like the look of you, they'll pin whatever they damn well want on us.'

'He's right,' Tracksuit said. 'I've got a record, yeah, GBH, from time back. That comes out and I'll be back drawing tally charts inside of four walls.'

'No,' I shook my head. 'That's not going to happen.'

'The hell you know about it. You're on the other side, bruv,' Tracksuit continued. 'The way I see it, cops walk into a room full of Muslims, it's like Christmas come early for them. Pointing fingers and interrogating us, treating us like shit from their shoes.'

'It's not an interrogation. Just a few questions, is all,' I said, knowing that I was quickly losing them. Others had started to gather around me, all around the same age, late teens to early twenties.

'Questions? Yeah, alright, mate,' one spat from behind me, bumping his shoulder into mine. 'Are you thick, bruv? Or do you think that we are?'

It was clear that they saw me as police first and Muslim second. 'Look, I'm on your side, really. I just want this over with as quickly and as peacefully as possible. If you could just co-operate with ...'

'*Peacefully*. Think this Paki tripping.' There were five around me now, and others approaching. All now talking over each other.

'Never thought the day would come where I'd see this many pigs in a masjid.' Another voice, rising anger.

'They're not going to allow you to leave until they've spoken to all of you.' I said, trying to keep the shake out of my voice.

'I like to see them try and stop me,' Tracksuit said, waving his phone in my face. 'One phone call, and there'll be fifty pretty pissed off Pakis waiting for us outside.'

I didn't doubt it. I was surprised The Faith hadn't already shown up.

'We have rights. We know our rights. You can not stop us, Detective.' This voice was equally as angry but it was the voice of a female. Immediately, it quietened everybody down. I couldn't see her as I'd been swallowed by the youths. 'Let me through,' I heard her say.

The youths parted, and she walked confidently between them until she was standing in front of me. Her eyes darted at me from under her red headscarf, her lips parted as if she was about to let rip. Her eyes were coal black and her skin a flawless olive. The hijab did nothing to hide her beauty. And when a beautiful woman has something to say, men tend to listen.

'Aslamalykum, Sister,' I said, respectfully and for some reason dropped my eyes.

'It's *Sister*, now. Is it? Tell me, are you a *Brother* right now, or are you a Detective?'

While I searched for the answer, she continued. 'And can you please look at me when I am talking to you.'

I met her eyes and tried not to get lost in them.

'This is my masjid,' she said sternly. 'We have the right to enter and leave as we please.'

I glanced over her shoulder at the far end of the hall. The Imam had disappeared. I scanned the prayer hall and caught a glimpse of him making his way upstairs as the door slowly closed behind him. I didn't want to lose sight of him, he was a key witness and a potential suspect, but I couldn't follow him until I'd calmed the youths.

I looked back at the woman but before I could say anything she turned on her heel and walked towards the exit, leaving me open mouthed. The youths who'd been giving me a hard time, looked at me smugly as though I'd just had my balls handed to me on a hot plate before following her.

I took my phone out as I hurried after them and made a call I didn't want to make. 'Guv,' I said. 'I couldn't keep them all in. A group of them are insisting on coming out.'

Chapter 7
(Harry)

I put my phone away, kicked off my shoes and hurried back into the mosque, just in time to see Nasri trying to keep back the flood of worshippers who now seemed intent on leaving the building. I had given him one simple job to do – to keep the worshippers in one place until they had been processed – and he'd screwed it up.

Two of the men blocked my way, one in a tracksuit, the other a tall, lanky black man with a gold tooth. Both of them were clearly angry. 'Get the fuck out of my way, man,' said Tracksuit.

'I'm a police officer and this is a crime scene,' I said.

'Yeah, well we already told your boy that we got places to be,' said the guy in the tracksuit.

'Step off, cop,' said Gold Tooth. 'Manz make moves, you get me.'

I didn't understand the wording but I got the drift. 'Not until we've spoken to you,' I said. 'This is a crime scene and you are potential witnesses.'

'Yeah your boy said that too but situation here ain't got jack to do with us,' said Tracksuit. 'We out!'

'You can't go, not until you've been questioned,' I said, using my authoritative voice and giving him my very best cold stare.

'You can't force them to stay,' said a woman. I looked around but couldn't see who had spoken, then Tracksuit and Gold Tooth moved apart and I saw her. She was barely five feet tall, her head covered with a blood red scarf, wearing a navy blue sweater and dark denim jeans. She had a large designer bag over one shoulder.

'I'm not forcing anyone,' I said.

'You said they had to stay, and that's not true,' she said. 'They're not suspects so under the Police and Criminal Evidence Act you are entitled to ask them for identification but that is all. Am I correct?'

I looked down at her. Coal black eyes, long eyelashes, smooth olive skin and perfect white teeth. She was lovely and I smiled but her eyes were cold and contemptuous and there was no way I was going to be winning hearts and minds here, no matter what I said. 'Are you a lawyer, Miss?' I asked.

'No, but I work with lawyers,' she said. 'At the Citizens Advice Bureau in Harrow Road. And I am very familiar with the Police and Criminal Evidence Act of 1984. As are you, I am sure.'

'Indeed,' I said, still smiling but knowing that it wasn't going to get me anywhere with her.

'Then you are aware that interviewers must treat all witnesses with sensitivity, impartiality and respect for their culture and rights, while maintaining an investigative approach.'

'Absolutely,' I said. She knew her stuff. I doubt that I could have quoted that from memory.

'If a murder has indeed been committed on the premises, anyone here could be suffering from shock,' she said. 'They might need counselling or therapy.'

One of the youths laughed harshly. 'Yeah, man, I'm well shook up, innit.'

She ignored him and continued. 'What they don't need is to be detained against their will and subjected to aggressive interrogation.'

I held up my hands but realised immediately that might look threatening so I clasped them instead and continued to smile, but by now my face was aching. 'I absolutely agree with you, Miss,' I said. 'And anyone who wants to leave can identify themselves and having confirmed their identity they will be free to go.'

Tracksuit looked at Gold Tooth. 'I ain't feeling that. Let's duss.'

Again I didn't understand the vocabulary but I got the intent. I smiled at Tracksuit. 'But, just so we are clear. We have the authority to interview anyone who is a potential witness. If he – or she – doesn't want to be interviewed here then we will visit them at their home or their place of work. I can't guarantee when that will be. Would you prefer a couple of uniforms to come around to your home one evening? Or as you're getting out of your car at work? Maybe they might check your car details while you're there? Or see something in your home that you'd rather they didn't see?'

'That sounds like a threat,' said the woman.

She was feisty, all right. She couldn't be much more than five feet tall and she had to tilt her head back to look me in the eyes. There was a confidence in the tilt of her chin as if she was used to getting her own way. I smiled down at her. 'I'm not in the business of threatening anybody, Miss,' I said. 'I'm here to investigate a death that looks as if it might well be murder. I'm sure you are as keen as I am to find out what happened and who killed one of your worshippers in your place of worship. If you and everybody else here would help us by just waiting for a few minutes and telling our officers what you know, we can get this resolved very quickly and not have to bother you again.' That wasn't strictly speaking true, of course. Yes, they were all potential witnesses, but they were also potential suspects. They needed to be searched as well as questioned and for that we needed manpower. Until that manpower arrived we weren't in the strongest of positions because if they all decided to leave there was no way we could restrain them all.

'Where will you do the questioning?' asked the woman.

'We'd prefer to do it here,' I said. 'I certainly don't want to take everyone to the station.'

'Ain't no way I'm setting foot in a pig sty,' said Tracksuit and from the way he said it I figured he'd probably been there several times already.

'That's what I'm saying,' I said patiently. I looked over at Nasri. 'Is there somewhere here we can do the interviews?'

'On the ground floor, there are several rooms designed for overspill for when there's a religious occasion. Plus the Imam has an office. I'll ask him if we can use that.'

'Sounds like a plan,' I said. 'I've asked for interpreters but I want as many conducted in English as possible.'

'Understood, Guv.'

I really wasn't happy about having to use interpreters. We needed to get them interviewed as quickly as possible and interpreters were going to slow things up. Plus, truth be told, I don't trust a lot of the interpreters. A lot of them have their own agenda. We had a case a while back when we had a Polish guy we were sure was a serial rapist. He said he couldn't speak English so we got him an interpreter. What they didn't know was that one of our DCs had a Polish mum and spoke enough to overhear what the interpreter was saying. The bastard was giving the suspect legal advice, telling him what to say and what not to say. That's not their role, they're just supposed to be translating what our detectives say and then translating the response. That's why it's always better to have interviews conducted in English.

'This joker chatting about interpreters,' Tracksuit said. 'What? You don't think we can speak English, bruv.'

'I got GCSE English, blud,' said a fair Asian youth, a tight skull cap pulled down low over his eyebrows. 'I coulda gone to Uni, yeah.'

'It's not for you, brothers,' said Nasri. 'There are some elders who may require assistance.'

I smiled down at the woman again. 'Can I ask your name, Miss?'

'Ayesha Khan,' she said. 'And can I see your warrant card?'

'Yes, of course.' I took out my wallet with its silver Met crest and flicked it open so she could see the warrant card inside. She leant forward to get a better look, then smiled. 'Harold Potter? You are Harry Potter?' She laughed. 'You don't look like the boy wizard.'

'Porter,' I said. 'Like the guy who carries your bags in a hotel. Detective Inspector Porter.' I put my warrant card away. 'Miss Khan, you're obviously used to dealing with people in crisis so could I ask you to help me here? We need to get everyone interviewed as quickly as possible. It won't take long, I promise, and we'll do everything we can to make the process as painless as possible.'

She nodded graciously. 'I will be happy to assist you, Inspector Porter,' she said. She turned to face the group of youths. 'Brothers, we should wait. It won't take long. They do have the right to ask us to identify ourselves, so we should cooperate. Let's not forget that a man died here today and the police need to find out what happened.'

'Also, we will need to search you, as we still have not found the murder weapon,' I said.

'Search!' Gold Tooth shouted. 'No pig be putting their trotters on me.'

'Thought you said we were witnesses not suspects,' Tracksuit shouted.

'Listen, please.' Nasri raised his voice and held his hands up in the air. 'The search is just procedural.'

'Check out this Paki, with his big words,' said Skull Cap mockingly. 'Maybe we should get an interpreter in.'

'Please, if we could just have your cooperation it won't take long,' I shouted, but they were starting to get loud again, voices overlapped, faces masked with pent up aggression.

'You think you're on the streets, copper? Be talkin' to us about cooperation!'

'Yo, cop? Show me a search warrant or show me the door.'

'You step in our house, you best come prepared, copper!'

'We're walking and ain't shit you can do about it. I'd like to see a pig stop a lion.'

'Please, brothers, just calm down and listen!' shouted Nasri but no one paid him any attention.

Ayesha held up her hands and shouted something in Urdu. The crowd fell silent immediately. She spoke for a minute or so and they listened without interruption. It was clear she had their respect. Eventually she turned and looked at me. 'They will cooperate, Inspector Porter,' she said. 'But I suggest you get it done as quickly as possible. And with respect.'

I nodded. 'Thank you,' I said.

'No need to thank me,' she said. 'The last thing I want is violence in my mosque.' She forced a smile as she realised what she had said. 'Any more violence,' she said.

The worshippers began filing back into the prayer room. I heard shouting from outside, at the front of the mosque. I nodded at Nasri. 'I'll leave you with my colleague, DC Nasri,' I said. 'And again, thank you.'

I hurried out of the prayer hall and along the corridor. The SOCO team had stopped work and were looking towards the entrance, wondering what was causing the commotion.

As I stepped outside, I saw that two vanloads of uniforms had arrived and half a dozen men in baggy tunics and skullcaps were gesticulating and shouting at them.

A sergeant was trying to reason with them while a dozen constables in hi-viz fluorescent jackets stood behind him.

'What's the problem?' I shouted, trying to make myself heard over all the noise.

'They won't let us in, Sir,' said the sergeant. He was in his thirties, his hair prematurely grey with broken veins across his cheeks.

'It's probably your shoes,' I said. 'They have a thing about shoes.'

I turned to face the angry worshippers and held up my hands. 'Okay, okay!' I shouted. 'They will remove their shoes before they go in. We understand.'

One of them with a straggly grey beard that reached his stomach waved his finger at me. 'No kaffir women!' he shouted, peppering my face with spittle. 'No kaffir women!'

Three of the uniformed constables were women, so I guess that's what was upsetting them. 'Fine, I said, 'the women officers will not enter the mosque, is that okay?'

'No kaffir women!' he shouted again and this time his finger jabbed just inches from my face. I had half a mind to grab it and break it but, you know, community relations.

'No women,' I said, and turned back to the sergeant. 'We need a cordon around the mosque to make sure that no one leaves, so the female officers can handle that,' I said. 'The guys are going to have to take their shoes off.'

'I hear you, Sir, but you know there are health and safety issues if they take off protective footwear.'

'I'll fill in the risk assessment,' I said.

'What about using the protective overshoes that SOCO use?' asked the sergeant.

I nodded. That sounded like a plan. I went back over to the worshippers. They still didn't look happy. I gave them my most reassuring smile. 'Would it be okay for my men to wear covers over their shoes?' I asked.

The guy with the straggly beard was back in my face, yelling. 'No women!' he shouted. 'No women!'

'The women aren't going inside, Sir,' I said.

'No kaffir women!'

I didn't know what a 'kaffir' was. 'Sir, do you speak English?'

'No kaffir women!' He jabbed me on the shoulder.

'Sir, can you understand what I'm saying.' Jab, jab, jab. 'Do any of you speak English?' I shouted.

I was faced with angry faces that seemed to be getting angrier by the second.

Two of the uniforms reached uneasily for their Tasers and I could understand why. The Asians were all shouting now and waving their fists and they clearly weren't going to listen to reason.

The sergeant looked over at me, wanting to know how to proceed. He had enough manpower to control the crowd outside but I knew there were a shed load more in the prayer hall and if they kicked off there was no way we'd be able to keep a lid on it.

I pulled out my phone and called Nasri. 'There's a guy here keeps telling me that kaffir women can't go into the mosque,' I said. 'What does he mean?'

'Kaffir means unbeliever,' he said. 'Basically non-Muslims, Guv.'

'He says they can't go in the mosque.'

'Not strictly true, Guv. Men and women pray separately, but women can go into the mosque, no problem. They use a side entrance. They have to cover their heads and dress modestly, but other than that there are no restrictions.' I thanked him and put the phone away.

The Asians were getting angrier by the second and one of the constables pulled his Taser from its holster. I looked at him and shook my head. I could see the lad was scared but Tasering wasn't going to make things any better.

The uniforms started to move back towards their vans and the Asians took that as a sign of weakness and surged forward, shouting and waving their fists.

'Gentlemen, can we please remain calm!' I shouted.

'Shall we draw batons, Sir?' asked the sergeant.

'No,' I said. 'Not yet.'

The police were still backing away which I knew was a mistake. They needed to hold their ground. The mob was sensing victory now and the shouts were louder and more aggressive. Several had started spitting at the officers.

'You all need to calm down!' I shouted at the top of my voice but even as the words left my mouth I knew I was wasting my time. Nobody was listening to me, I was like a teacher who had lost control of an unruly class except if this ended badly it wouldn't be detention it would be bodies on the ground.

Chapter 8
(Sal)

I slipped my phone back into my pocket, aware that Ayesha had been hovering around as I spoke with Porter. The word, *that word*, would have pricked her ears and I knew that she'd come at me. Like Paki, *Kaffir* has two very different definitions and ultimately boils down to intent. Paki can be a term of endearment, dependent on context which usually tends to get forgotten about in our politically correct world. But if three skinheads step to me uttering that word, believe me, it's on. *Context* and *intention*. Kaffir, as I loosely explained to Porter, means non-believer, which to an extent is true, but it's not a definitive explanation and Ayesha was itching to enlighten me.

'Kaffir,' she said, 'means more than just non-believer.' She smiled but there was something in her eyes that I didn't like. Something that she suggested that she thought she was a lot smarter than I was.

'I know that,' I said.

'You should tread carefully in your response. The intention does not have to be derogatory.'

She was right, but I didn't like the way she was lecturing me in front of the worshippers. I pushed open the double doors and the tone of untapped aggression from the streets spilled into the prayer hall. 'I think the intention is clear,' I said as the doors slowly closed and blocked out the sound. I glanced over her shoulder. The youths were calming down now.

'You should go help,' said Ayesha, as if she had read my mind. 'Go and dig your boss out of whatever hole he has gotten into. I'll hold the fort for you here.'

I looked down at her. She really was a little thing. Fair play, though, she wasn't fazed even though she was the only female in a room full of men, in the men's prayer area. She stood her ground and then some. Call it a cynical mind, but personally, I think she was milking the attention. The way that she quoted sections of the Police and Criminal Evidence Act of 1984, yeah, she's sung that tune before. She knew that it would only serve to rile up the youths. Or maybe she was just laying out the law, *in front of the law*, so all were aware of their options. I don't know. Ayesha Khan would take some sussing out.

I considered her offer. It was pretty clear if the lads wanted to walk, they were going to walk, regardless of the presence of the law or what the law states. Experience has taught me that some, if not all, of these youths had previously been in police custody or encountered police harassment at some point in their young lives. Whether that had been imprisonment, false accusation or just pulled over for driving a Honda and being the wrong colour.

Yeah, I know. It's happened to me on more occasions than I like to remember. Being tailed for a couple of miles, sweating me as they breathe down my neck, waiting for me to make a mistake. If that doesn't happen, they'll pull me anyway. Blues on, the short sharp burst of a siren, just in case I hadn't noticed that they were behind me. Check my documents, raise their eyebrows as they read the Prophet's name on my licence. Search my car for anything that would give them an excuse. Scrutinise each tyre for wear. Bombard me with questions as they radio back to HQ to confirm that I was the owner and that the vehicle is insured.

I never told them that I'm on the job. There was no point. It wouldn't stop it happening again. And again.

Now, these lads, who felt they had been wronged in the past, understandably had a chance to return the favour. So they were going to make it a priority to be as difficult as possible. I could feel them, frustration bordering on aggression, itching for us to make the wrong move. A golden opportunity to get one back on the man.

'Fuck that,' Gold Tooth exclaimed. 'I'm bouncing.'

I put my hand out and stood in his path. As is the way of the world, Tracksuit pulled out his phone and started to film. I had to let them pass, I couldn't risk another episode unfolding within the prayer hall, metres away from where a dead body was found. It would have done the rounds on social media and burned through the Internet within minutes. If we had to be careful before, we had to be doubly careful now.

Gold Tooth and Tracksuit slipped past me and out of the door. 'Can you try and keep the rest behind,' I said to Ayesha.

'I'll do my best. Now go,' she said, the worry at what was transpiring outside her masjid apparent on her face. I hurried out of the prayer hall, jogged along the hallway and back outside to a wall of noise. Half a dozen middle-aged men dressed in shalwar kameez and a handful of youths were spitting venom, aggressively trying to get their point across to the uniformed officers. The officers were being careful not to use any force, but even a guiding touch would have them screaming hell. I noticed Gold Tooth, head down, pacing quickly away from the scene, only for a sergeant to rush over to him and attempt to guide him back in.

'Hands fucking off!' Gold Tooth shrugged the cop's arm away and continued to walk. Tracksuit walked away too, in a different direction. A constable hurried after him and gently raised his hands to stop him.

'Touch me, Blud,' Tracksuit spat holding up his phone camera. 'Fucking touch me, I dare you.' The constable took a step back and looked anxiously at his sergeant who seemed to be equally as perplexed as he dealt with Gold Tooth.

A fair Asian youth, skull cap low down over his forehead, tried to shoulder past two uniforms but they held firm and he ended up tripping at their feet. From another view, the worshippers' view, it looked as though he had been forced to the floor by the police. A couple of elders moved in, shoving the uniforms out of the way and helping the youth to his feet.

'Gentlemen, can we please remain calm!' shouted Porter, waving his arms in the air. His voice was easily drowned out. The crowd were getting angrier and more vocal by the second. To my right, two worshippers stepped with intent towards a constable. He took a step back into the bumper of a parked car and in a moment of desperation he reached for his Taser and started to pull it from its holster. I ran the few metres cursing to myself and was on him quickly. I grabbed his arm before he could release the Taser and shot him a look. 'It's okay,' I said. 'They're cool.' He moved his hands away from his holster. The two worshippers did nothing more than scowl.

This was no longer about the right to walk away or the right to be detained. Apart from Gold Tooth and Tracksuit, the rest of the youths had stayed, mixed in with the elders, women and children. In their eyes this was about the sheer lack of respect of their masjid, of Islam. The heavy handed approach, the insensitivity, and years of the police condemning and treating Muslims like they're about to go BOOM.

'Guv,' I said to Porter. 'We need to ride this out. They're not getting physical, they're just venting. It's just noise.'

The uniforms had backed up against their vans and the crowd surged forward, faces screwed in wrath, hands closed in tight fists, pinning the police to their vans. But not once was a hand raised with intent.

'We have to separate them,' said Porter striding towards the vans.

'Let me have a go,' I said, stepping into line with him. Porter slowed and allowed me to approach them.

'Go for it.' he said.

'Brother,' I said, and put my arm on the shoulder on a tall bearded elder, who I vaguely recognised as a regular. He turned towards me, his red stained eyes flashed with anger. I put my hand up. 'Please... This is not what we represent.' He didn't know whether to regard me as a policeman or as a Muslim, but I did have his attention. 'The world sees our Deen as destructive. This is our opportunity to show them the real Islam. To show them peace. Otherwise we are what they say we are.'

He blinked and I could see in his eyes that the fight had dissipated. A few of the other elders had noticed me now. They stepped away from the van and stood around me as though I had all the answers.

The youths realising that they were now light on numbers also stepped away. Porter approached the relieved uniforms and spoke with them. Between us we seemed to calm everyone down. The elders, as they do, took the moral high ground and started to guide the youths back into the mosque. That's the thing with Asian youths, they would respectfully listen to an instruction of an elder rather than the instruction of the Police.

I bent forward and rested my hands on my knees and took in the scene around me. If a baton had been lifted or a Taser had been fired, it would have been all-out-war. Porter had made the right decision, and I liked to think that I had played a part in the peaceful resolution. I glanced over at Porter around the same time that he glanced over at me and we shared a look of pure relief.

Behind Porter, three cars were approaching at speed. Three hatchbacks, one blue, two black, heavy tint on the windows, screeched to a halt about a hundred metres from the mosque. Doors flew open and from the three vehicles out poured twelve young men, baseball caps low and tight over their heads. Each face covered with a ghutrah scarf. Every one of them brandishing a weapon. Any chance of a peaceful resolution quickly faded.

The Faith had arrived.

Porter reached for his radio and barked for Armed Support as he eyed them. A Vectra drove slowly towards us. There were three people in it, two women and a man, detectives by the look of it, though the car was a giveaway.

One of The Faith pointed at the car and half a dozen broke away towards it. They surrounded the vehicle, forcing it to come to a stop and began pounding on the roof, shouting and waving their bats, bars and knives. I flinched at the unnerving sound of metal rubbing against metal as one of them scraped his machete down the side of the Vectra.

As part of police training we had practised using batons against knives but there was a world of a difference between practising in a gym with your mates and facing a pretty pissed off individual comfortably wielding a machete.

I instinctively took a step towards them, but Porter held me back. 'Wait for the ARVs,' he said. Armed Response Vehicles. Cops with big guns.

The small Vectra was now being rocked back and forth as The Faith tried to upturn it. In the front, the two women looked scared and the guy in the back opened the door and attempted to slip out just as a rock shattered the window on his door. He cowered back inside the car, shutting the door as cubes of glass showered him.

Porter signalled to a couple of uniforms to join him and hurried over to the Vectra. I followed closely behind. Two of The Faith spotted us approaching and they moved away from the car and moved threateningly towards us, their machetes swaying gently by their sides.

'Who the fuck's in charge?' one asked, red and white chequered scarf tightly wrapped around his jaw.

'I'm in charge. Detective Inspector Porter. What's the problem?' Porter said, his voice steady and authoritative. I had no idea how he could display that amount of calm, my heart was ready to burst out of my chest.

'Wrong answer. I think you'll find that we're in charge,' said one of The Faith. His scarf was black and had the skeleton of a jaw covering his mouth. He brought his machete up from his side and in front of him. Easy enough to buy on any High Street, a machete can cost less than a tenner and selling them is lawful. But carrying one in public is very much against the law, with a maximum penalty of four years and an unlimited fine. Not that The Faith seemed to care about jail time or financial penalties.

'This is our masjid!' Red Checked screeched. 'Pack up your shit and bounce.'

'Try to understand,' said Porter, still with a measure of authority in his voice. 'This is currently an active crime scene and we are investigating a murder.'

There was the sound of smashing glass off to my right and I looked over to see that one of The Faith had smashed in the rear window of the Vectra.

A sergeant tried to force his way towards the car but he was pushed back. Three of the uniformed constables had drawn their Tasers but they looked around uncertainly, clearly scared at the implications of pulling the trigger. Each Taser could only be fired once and they were facing machetes plus other hand-held weapons.

'Let's do them!' screamed the youngster, raising his knife and waving it around. 'Let's gut the fucking pigs!'

I opened my mouth to shout but I had no idea what to say. They weren't going to listen to me. The younger worshippers had already made it clear how they'd felt about a brother on the Force. This lot? Forget about it.

It was complete chaos and once Armed Support turned up, it was going to be complete carnage. I ran as fast as I could, past the two petrified looking uniforms that I had stand sentry at the mosque gates. I entered the grounds and pushed through the doors into the main prayer hall. It was bare, not a soul in sight. I clocked a uniform standing sentry at the door of the overspill room where the worshippers were waiting to be questioned.

'Keep the door closed. No one leaves,' I shouted, as I flew up the stairs two steps at a time and burst through the office doors. The Imam's office.

'Imam,' I said. He was sitting behind a large desk, his eyes on two widescreen monitors.

He nodded gravely as he adjusted a small microphone on the collar of his kameez and stood up. I held the door open for him. As he went by I caught a glimpse of his screens – he had been watching live feeds from outside the mosque.

I hurried him down the stairs with a gentle hand on his back. We rushed out of the mosque and onto the street.

To my left, three BMW SUVs had arrived, doors opened and nine cops stepped out and took up position, armed to the teeth. To my right, The Faith not deterred by the change in dynamic, not fazed by the automatic weapons, organised accordingly. They stood shoulder to shoulder, shuffling feet, a bundle of energy, wound up and ready to release.

I was concerned that the Imam, who wasn't blessed with height, would be drowned out before he'd been noticed but I was wrong. He stepped out calmly into the middle of the two warring factions and stood perfectly still. He glanced across taking the measure of the armed police and nodded slowly to himself. He turned his attention to the other side and, like a Jedi, he placed his hand out and gently lowered it.

The Faith immediately lowered their weapons and fell silent.

The Imam began to speak, his voice transmitted by the radio microphone through the sound system within the mosque and out of the speaker placed within the high, shining minarets.

'Brothers,' Malik said. The bass lending his voice a deep baritone. I swear it felt like our masjid had come alive. 'On this Jum'ah, this auspicious day, we should be standing side by side and praying to Allah and thanking Him for all that he has given us ... In its place, our mosque, our Deen, has been blackened.'

The worshippers mumbled in agreement.

'Who's this Deen, then?' Porter was at my shoulder.

'Deen, double E,' I replied. 'Means religion.'

'As I look amongst you now, I am proud of every single one of my brothers for protecting our masjid,' the Imam continued. '*They* will never understand like we understand. *They* will never experience what we experience. They lack respect for our culture and for our way of life. Their refusal to be educated will mean that they'll forever live in ignorance.'

'Give me a break,' Porter mumbled under his breath, only serving to validate the point that the Imam was trying to make. I edged away from him, maybe he noticed, maybe I didn't care at that point.

'However they are a necessity… For today we have seen murder.' Malik emphasised and paused at the last word. 'And I will not allow any more bloodshed in the presence of the House of Allah. So, I ask you, please, go back to your homes and leave the police to complete their tasks. And pray that they never darken our door again.'

The Imam walked into the embrace of the crowd, and slowly but surely The Faith started to disperse, with menacing eyes on us for good measure.

'Good call, bringing out the Imam,' said Porter.

'Thanks, Guv.' My first compliment. Hopefully not my last, but only time would tell.

Chapter 9
(Harry)

As soon as the mob had dispersed, I hurried over to the Vectra. DS Jacqueline Beard was behind the wheel and DC Lorraine Sawyer was in the front passenger seat. DC Alan Russell was sitting in the back. Beard was a top-notch crime scene manager and Sawyer was a forensics manager; both would be assets to the investigation, and I was glad that McKee had kept his word and given me Russell as outside enquiry manager. He was a hard worker and got on with most people and I'd worked with him on more than a dozen cases. They were all shaken up, though Beard seemed more angry than frightened.

'What the fuck, Harry?' she said, which wasn't how detective sergeants normally spoke to SIOs, but Beard and I go back a long way. She had her dark hair clipped back and she adjusted her glasses as she glared at me,

'Sorry, Jacqueline. Tempers got a bit frayed.'

'A bit of advance notice might have helped,' she said. 'We could have parked and walked here.'

'It all blew up quickly,' I said.

'I'm just glad we were in a pool car.' She climbed out and brushed cubes of glass from her coat and threw me another withering look.

Sawyer also got out. 'SOCO are inside?' she asked. She was already pulling on latex gloves.

'Yes. Just so you know, some of the worshippers moved the body and started cleaning up.'

She sighed. 'Terrific.' Before she could say anything else, one of the armed officers jogged over to us.

'Who's in charge?' he asked.

'I am,' I said. 'DI Harry Porter.'

The sergeant grinned. 'The boy wizard? Why didn't you wave your magic wand and make them all disappear?'

'It's Porter. Not Potter, But you can call me Inspector. Or Sir.'

The sergeant shrugged. I guess he felt his big gun took precedence over my rank and in some situations that was probably true. 'So what was that all about?' he asked. 'Who were those guys?' He was a big man with a shaved head and dark glasses. I don't know the make of gun he was cradling but it looked impressive, as did all the equipment hanging from his webbing belt.

'The Faith,' said Nasri.

'The Faith? Who the hell are The Faith?'

'Local crew,' said Nasri. 'They were protecting their turf.'

The sergeant looked at me. 'And we're letting them go? They had fucking knives. Big knives.' As an afterthought he added a 'Sir'.

'They were over-reacting,' I said. 'It's sorted now.'

One of the cars sped away, burning rubber.

'Last time I checked carrying a blade in public was still an offence,' said the sergeant.

'It was a storm in a teacup, sergeant' I said. 'A misunderstanding.'

'In their eyes, their place of worship was being disrespected,' said Nasri.

The last of the cars left. The sergeant nodded at the mosque. 'Is there a problem in there?'

'A man was stabbed,' I said.

'Dead?'

I nodded.

'I have to say I'm a bit concerned that we've just let a gang of knife-wielding thugs ride off into the sunset.'

'We could say the knives were ceremonial,' I said. 'If that helps.' I flashed him a sarcastic smile.

'That's Sikhs, Guv,' said Nasri.

'What?'

'It's Sikhs that carry ceremonial knives. Kirpans, they're called.'

'I was being ironic, DC Nasri.'

Nasri grimaced and looked away. I nodded at the sergeant. 'All's well that ends well, we ended a potentially violent situation without a shot being fired and no one was hurt.'

'So we just forget the knives?'

'I intend to,' I said.

'There's a precedent,' said Nasri. 'Remember the 2011 riots in Southall? Sikhs were defending their Gurdwaras and businesses with swords and knives and they were never charged.'

'You're defending them?' said the sergeant. 'Why am I not surprised?' he muttered under his breath.

'What's that supposed to mean?' said Nasri but I put up a hand to quieten him,

'This whole Muslim thing is a minefield, isn't it?' I said to the sergeant.

'Not really,' muttered Nasri. 'Not if it's handled properly it's not.'

'All right, we'll head off,' said the sergeant.

Russell had climbed out of the Vectra and was shaking cubes of glass off his coat. 'Give me a minute Alan,' I said, 'and I'll bring you up to speed.'

'No problem, Guv,' he said.

The firearms officers piled into their SUVs and drove off. As the final vehicle disappeared down the road, another van of uniforms turned up, along with Paul Rees in his battered old Toyota. Rees lit a cigarette as soon as he got out of his vehicle, then he waved at me and ambled over. He was a big man, closer to seven feet than he was to six, but really he was a gentle giant. In his spare time, he ran a boxing club for local kids near his house in Ealing and he was a bit of a local hero. He was one of those men who inspire respect in pretty much everyone he met, not just because of his size but I guess that helps, but because he has a quiet authority about him. He made DS after just six years in the job but made it clear he didn't want to go any higher. The thing about Paul is that he's a people person, he genuinely likes people and being around them. I think he'd be happier walking a beat like Dixon Of Dock Green but that style of policing went out with black and white televisions. He was perfectly suited as Investigative Team Leader because the troops enjoyed working with him and he was good with the public.

'The cavalry's arrived,' he said, grinning and flicking ash onto the pavement.

'Better late than never,' I said. I gestured at DC Nasri. 'This is DC Nasri, he's...'

'I know who Sal is!' boomed Rees. He put his arm around Nasri's shoulder and hugged him. 'How the hell are you, Sal?'

'Yeah, you know, all good, Paul.'

Rees grinned down at him. 'They put you with Harry, did they? What the hell did you do wrong?'

'Nah, I've always wanted to be with Homicide Command.'

'Yeah, but Harry churns through his bag carriers, don't you, Harry? What's the average? Three months?'

'It's not for everyone,' I said.

Rees laughed and hugged Nasri again, like a grizzly bear playing with its young. 'Sal here is a diamond, Harry. A real diamond. Remember that rapist we were after, the one who worked as a food delivery driver and then went back to rape and pillage after he'd delivered? We'd been on the case for months. Bloody months. It was Sal here who gave us the name. We put the bugger under surveillance and three nights later we caught him in the act.'

'Nice one,' I said. 'The rapist was...' I was going to say 'Muslim' but I realised that was going to sound racist and then I thought of saying 'Asian' but that would have been just as bad and I could see from the glint in his eyes that Rees knew I was struggling so he finished the sentence for me.

'Sent down for ten years,' he said, giving Nasri a final hug before letting him go. He pointed at Nasri. 'You watch this one, Harry. He'll be running Homicide Command before long, you mark my words.' He took a final drag on his cigarette, dropped the butt on the pavement and stamped on it with one of his size thirteen brogues. 'Right, what do you need from me, Harry?'

'Two things as priority,' I said. 'There are fifty worshippers in the main prayer hall. We need everyone spoken to, we need their ID and ideally they need to be searched. McKee has promised us eight bodies for the interviews. But they're witnesses not suspects so be careful. There are interpreters on the way but let's try to keep them to a minimum, use English wherever possible. The Imam is being co-operative so any problems and you can talk to DC Nasri – Sal – and he'll liaise with him. Also there's a woman around who works for the Citizens Advice Bureau in Harrow Road. Ayesha Khan. She's being helpful too. Just so you know, our women can go into the mosque but they have to use the side entrance and they need to keep their heads covered. To be honest, best to keep the number of women down to a minimum, use them for the outside jobs.'

'Got you,' said Rees, throwing me a mock salute.

'And everyone needs to be photographed,' I said, which earned me another sarcastic salute.

Rees was an experienced investigator so he wouldn't need hand-holding. Basically he would be implanting a TIE strategy – Trace, Interview, Eliminate. Initially everyone at the mosque would be in the TIE category, and one by one they would have to be eliminated, either through having an alibi or through forensic evidence. Those that couldn't be immediately eliminated would be investigated further. His interviewers would be following the PEACE interview model – Preparation and Planning, Engage and Explain, Account Clarification and Challenge, Closure and Evaluation. The Met does love its acronyms.

'Guv, might be worth making it known that only female officers should question the female worshippers,' said Nasri.

'Good point,' I said. I looked at Rees. 'Let's do that, okay?'

'Not a problem,' said Rees.

'And I need you to organise a full search of the mosque for the murder weapon,' I said. 'We'll use uniforms for that. And again, be tactful. It's a place of worship. The search has to be respectful and make sure everything gets put back the way it was.'

'I'm on it, Guv,' said Rees and he ambled away.

I turned to look at DC Nasri. 'Okay, at some point you and I need to question the Imam. Let's do it back at the station.'

'With all due respect, Guv, you might want to rethink that. We take him away, it'll look as if he's been arrested and it wouldn't take much to set them off again.'

'He's not being arrested. It's just an interview.'

'I know that, Guv, but around here when cops put a Muslim in a car and take him to the station it's not usually for a cup of tea and a samosa, if you get my drift.'

I nodded slowly. I got his drift. 'Okay, point taken. Have a word with him and see if we can interview him in his office. You said something about him watching events on CCTV?'

'They've got a CCTV system, but it's mainly covering the outside of the mosque. Cameras were placed after the London Tube bombings in 2005 after a spate of revenge attacks, if you recall. Mosques were vandalised, Muslims were attacked, so the Imam decided to beef up security.'

'We need any CCTV footage he has.'

'I'll ask him,' said Nasri.

'We're the police, DC Nasri,' I said. 'We don't ask him, we tell him. His mosque is now a crime scene and the CCTV footage is crucial evidence.'

'Right, Guv.'

I took out my phone and showed him the picture of the driving licence. 'The victim was carrying this. Along with a library card and a loyalty card in the name of Mohammed Masood. I need you to do an electoral roll check on the licence address. We're looking for two things, where the victim lives and who his next of kin are. Then talk to the loyalty card people, see what address they have for Mohammed Masood and do an electoral roll check on the name while you're at it.'

'Evans, he's a convert, right?'

'That's what I'm thinking. Also do PNC checks on both names.'

He nodded. 'I'm on it, Guv.'

I headed back to the battered Vectra to talk to Alan Russell. Russell was still tense from being trapped in the Vectra by the angry mob but he was starting to calm down. Someone had given him a cup of coffee and he was sipping it gingerly. 'You okay, Alan?'

'Yes, Guv,' he said. 'Bit shaken, but yeah, ready for action.'

There was blood on his right hand. 'You sure you're okay?' I asked, nodding at the blood.

He looked at the scratch and grimaced. 'I got covered in glass when they smashed the window.'

'Sorry about that.'

'Can't believe you gave them a pass, Guv. Possession of a knife, destruction of property, threatening behaviour.'

'Tempers were frayed, Alan. And at the end of the day no one was hurt.' I realised what I'd said and I winced. 'Sorry. That's a wound, no question. If you want to press charges...'

'I'll live, Guv. And I take your point, trying to arrest them would only make things worse. But, you know...' He shrugged and left the sentence unfinished.

Yeah. I knew. We both knew but the simple fact was that neither of us could say out loud what we were thinking. If a gang of white youths had started brandishing knives in public their feet wouldn't have touched the ground and they would have been in the cells faster than you could say 'breach of the peace'. But a group of Muslims wave machetes around and we pat them on the head and let them go home. It isn't fair but it's the way of the world and if I had tried to arrest them and it had turned messy, then I'd be the one taking the blame.

'Thanks, Alan,' I said. 'So, here's what I need from you as priorities. Let's get a team of six uniforms canvassing all the houses overlooking the mosque, asking if they had seen anything unusual before, after or during the one-thirty service. I also need you to identify any CCTV cameras overlooking the main routes to the mosque. McKee has promised me two bodies for that but we can use uniforms and I'll slot the two detectives in elsewhere. The victim didn't have any car keys on him so he had either walked, taken public transport or travelled with someone else. We need to examine CCTV footage from the Tube stations close to the mosque and any buses that had travelled there that morning, looking for Sean Evans. There's a CCTV system in the mosque and I'll make sure we get the video from that.'

'Any idea where he was coming from?'

'There's an address in Bromley on his driving licence but that was issued five years ago so it might not be current.'

'Have we got a picture?'

I showed him the photo of the driving licence on my phone. 'I've got this but he's got a beard now.'

'Convert?'

'Maybe. He's got bank cards in a Muslim name, we're checking on that now. But there's no point in using this picture. I'm hoping we'll get a new picture from the next of kin but if not we'll have the body photographed. That's a last resort, obviously.'

Obviously. Because when you photograph the face of a dead person it looks like a dead person and no one likes looking at a corpse. We needed a picture of happy, smiling, living and breathing Sean, not stabbed and dead Sean.

'At this stage start identifying the CCTV footage that's available and hopefully I'll have a useful photograph for you early tomorrow.'

Russell gave me a thumbs-up and sipped his coffee as he walked away. I took a deep breath and ran through my mental checklist. We were coming to the end of the Initial Investigation phase. I had managed the scene, identified and preserved it. I had identified potential evidence, though to be fair there wasn't much, just the body. I had initiated interviews of witnesses. Interviews of the victim or the offender was obviously not on the cards. And I had organised an initial search of the premises and access and exit routes. I was on the ball. So far, so good. There was still a lot to do, but I had the basics covered.

When we get a murder in London the Met throws serious resources at it, if it's necessary. In a good year we get about eighty. In a bad year, double that. In a really bad year – say 2003 – we had more than 200. But that doesn't mean we go into full MIR mode every time. Most murders are solved almost immediately. A family member snaps, a neighbour is pushed too far, a long-standing feud erupts into violence. Gang-related killings are harder to crack, but usually if you know who the victim is you have a reasonably good idea who pulled the trigger or stabbed the knife. At the present moment there are fewer than twenty unsolved murders from last year. Most were done with knives, four with guns. Hand on heart, if they're not solved within three months we're probably not going to solve them, not by detective work anyway. A DNA sample might come good when someone is put into the system for the first time, or someone might talk, but that's not really solving a crime, that's having it solved for you.

In fact, most murders aren't really solved at all, not in the sense of dealing with a puzzle. Which is why when we do get a genuine mystery, the full weight of the Met's resources are thrown at it, initially at least.

An Audi sports car came to a halt in the road and then did a perfect reverse park into a gap that was only slightly large enough to accommodate it. A small dark-haired woman climbed out and waved over at me. Donna Walsh. Press Officer. Number three in the Press Office in terms of job title but by far the best operator they had. I figured McKee had asked for her knowing how sensitive the investigation would be. She was a little over five feet tall and always wore impossibly high heels to compensate and they clicked on the pavement as she walked over to me. She was in her late twenties and had been divorced twice. She was tough and confident and a bit brash and journalists loved her. They respected her, too, and that was important. She never lied to them, and if she couldn't give them the information they wanted it was always because there was a good reason.

'Harry, darling, sorry I'm late.'

'You're not late,' I said. She went on tip-toe, put a hand on my shoulder and air-kissed me, twice. I got a whiff of an expensive perfume.

'I missed all the fun, apparently,' she said. She reached into her handbag and took out a blue and white headscarf.

I tilted my head on one side. 'What fun?' I asked.

She grinned and her eyes sparkled as she tied the scarf over her hair. 'Exactly,' she said.

I wasn't surprised that she knew about the near-riot. She had sources throughout the Met and the Media so someone must have called her and tipped her off. The fact we hadn't had TV cameras and photographers turning up probably meant the former.

'Storm in a teacup, just a cultural misunderstanding that was soon resolved,' I said. 'The Imam is cooperating fully.'

'It's definitely murder?' She tucked a few locks of stray hair under the scarf.

'The victim was stabbed.'

'Racially motivated?' She used her phone to check that all her hair was hidden by the scarf.

'Difficult to say. The victim's white but wearing Islamic clothing so we're thinking convert.'

She pulled a face. 'The Press will love that,' she said.

'We haven't released a name yet,' I said. 'We haven't informed next of kin.'

She nodded and put her phone away. 'Make sure we get the Family Liaison people in ASAP. We're going to have to keep the parents away from the Press until we know where we stand.'

I took out my phone and showed her my picture of the driving licence.

'Text it to me,' she said. 'I'll take a look at his social media to see what we're dealing with. If there's anything worrying I'll see about getting it taken down.'

'You can do that?'

'Sometimes,' she said. 'What about an appeal for witnesses?'

'We've got about six hundred, give or take, so no.'

'Then at the moment it's more about keeping it as quiet as possible,' she said, 'A man was killed at a mosque, not thought to be a racial attack, police are investigating, blah blah blah.'

'Have you had any calls yet?'

'No, so far so good,' she said. 'I'll get a Press Release drafted but we won't put it out until we're approached.' She looked around. There were uniforms at the entrance and groups of Muslim men smoking and talking. 'Who's Office Manager at the MIR?'

'David Judd.'

She grinned. 'Good choice. Okay, I'll head to the MIR and set up a desk there. Obviously if any journos turn up, give them my mobile number if they don't have it already.'

'Will do.'

She blew me a kiss and click-clacked back to her sports car. A group of worshippers turned and watched her go. One of them said something in Urdu and the others laughed. It wasn't a pleasant sound. My phone rang and I took it out. It was Nasri. 'The Imam's happy to be interviewed in his office, Guv,' he said. 'First floor.'

'I'll be right there.'

Chapter 10
(Sal)

Imam Abdullah Malik looked every bit the man in charge. He was sat behind a busy but organised desk. A PC with two 22 inch widescreen monitors to his left. An open laptop to his right. His fingers busy tapping away on his iPad.

Back in the day, when the old Imam ran things, I'd occasionally been in this very office for an occasional clip around the ear. It had never looked this slick. It seemed Malik liked to keep up appearances. Even the seat of his chair was lifted giving the impression that he wasn't a small man.

'Bear with me,' Malik held up a finger. 'Let me just finish sending out this circular informing the worshippers to use the hall upstairs for the day's remaining prayers.'

Porter and I stood in front of his desk like a couple of schoolboys who'd been summoned before the headmaster.

'Imam, can you hold sending it just yet?' I said. 'The whole mosque is currently an active crime scene. We have to discuss access, obviously.'

The Imam wasn't wearing his Lennon glasses, but if he was he'd be peering over them about now.

'Obviously,' he said.

'We'll come to that later,' Porter said. 'But first, let's go from the beginning.'

Without taking his eyes off us, Malik swipe-locked the screen and took his time placing his iPad flush on the corner edge of the table, as though buying time or simply demonstrating his position of power.

We had to be careful, even though he seemed to be cooperating, deep down he must have been seething at our earlier heavy-handed approach and the near riot.

Porter nodded at me to speak. 'First of all,' I said, 'we'd like to extend our gratitude. You have helped us immensely in what must have been an extremely demanding day for both you and your congregation.' I wasn't blowing smoke up him, the sentiment was sincere, he really did pull us out of a spot. But it didn't hurt for him to hear it either, it would serve to keep him onside. Malik did not react to the compliment and just steepled his fingers under his beard. I cleared my throat.

'As I understand, you were the first to find the victim?' I said as I opened my notepad.

'Yes.'

'When exactly?'

'After prayers had finished. The brother was on the floor. I thought he had fallen asleep.' He shrugged. 'It happens.'

'And prayer finished at what time?'

'One forty. One forty-five.'

Porter was staring at the Imam but the Imam wasn't letting it affect him and he continued to stare back at him. He was holding a string of amber prayer beads.

'Imam, would you like a glass of water?' I asked. 'I know I would.'

'Very well,' Malik replied.

I looked over at Porter, hoping that he would realise what I was up to. I needed to be alone with the Imam for a few minutes. We locked eyes and for a moment I thought he was going to tell me to go fetch my own water but then realisation dawned and he flashed me a tight smile before standing up. 'I'll get it,' he said.

'There is a kitchen on the ground floor, to the right of the entrance,' said the Imam.

Porter left the office. It was obvious that Malik was acting a certain way around Porter. I wasn't sure if he was trying to impress him or challenge him, or if he just enjoyed seeing the bemused look on Porter's face when he started using terms that he would not understand. I'd make more progress without Porter. Especially now I had shown the Imam that a *brother* had some clout over the white man. I hoped that would serve to form a trust between us. It's a useful interrogation technique, one I had used to good effect in the past, especially with cases that involved Asians. The result was immediate, the hardness in his eyes replaced by a glint. He removed his steepled fingers from under his chin and began fingering his prayer beads.

'Please,' I said. 'In your own words, tell me what happened.'

'After all had completed their prayers, I walked around the hall greeting some of the regulars. In the far corner, I saw him, he was kneeling on his hands and knees, his forehead touching the ground. I didn't think anything of it. It is perfectly natural for one to finish a prayer in a personal manner.'

He paused, waited for me to ask a leading question. I didn't want to influence or direct his account so I said nothing and gently nodded for him to continue.

'I continued on my rounds around the hall. You have to understand there were still thirty or forty people, maybe more, all vying for my attention.' He smiled. It was becoming obvious that he was a vain man. The way that the mosque was kitted out and the money that had been spent on his office reflected his personality. He enjoyed the adulation and respect, and as genuinely distraught as he was at the near riot outside the mosque, it was clear he took pride in the way that he had handled The Faith in front of an audience. The Imam was not a modest man. It was fine, I could use that vanity against him. I mirrored his smile and he continued. 'I could see that the brother was still down, I excused myself and approached him, standing respectfully behind him and waited for him to get up. I thought maybe he had gone to sleep. It would not be the first time for one to nod off. So I nudged him gently. That is when I noticed the blood on the prayer rug and realised something terrible had happened.' The Imam paused, and then blinked as if to clear his vision. 'I called the police immediately,' he said, softly.

It sounded rehearsed, right down to the blink, though it didn't mean he was lying. He would have expected that at some point he'd be questioned so he'd prepared himself and had probably run the story around in his head a few times.

'Why did you move the body?' I said.

'As a Muslim, you must know,' he replied.

'In your words, please, Imam.'

'I could not have a dead man bleeding all over the prayer mats, it was imperative that the masjid is forever in a state of cleanliness. I had to prepare for Asar Prayers a couple of hours later. So I had to act fast.'

'I see,' I nodded, a show of understanding. 'But you must have known that you were ruining a crime scene.'

'Of course, but we were careful with the body. Respectful. It was not my intention to make your task difficult... But as Imam of this great masjid, I did what I believed was just, not in the eyes of the law, but in the eyes of Allah.'

Okay, all right, the damage was done, there was no use me banging on about it. 'Did you recognise him? As a worshipper or otherwise?'

'I did, yes,' he said, immediately. 'As a worshipper.'

'Can you recall when he was here last?'

'Most Fridays, for Jum'ah. I don't recall seeing him at any other times.'

'Did you find the knife in or near the body?' I asked, my questions coming quicker now, and purposely out of chronological order.

'I told you, there was no knife.'

'And you were by yourself when you found the body?'

'Yes. There were others in the prayer hall but they were otherwise engaged.'

'The victim,' I said. 'Does he usually attend alone?'

'He was usually with others. He seemed popular.'

'Anyone in particular?'

He shrugged. 'Not really. Not one person, I mean. He was usually with a group, some of the more vocal members of the congregation.'

I frowned. 'Vocal?'

'I am sure you know what I mean, brother. Some Muslims are more forceful about their religion than others.'

'So they were poppy-burners?'

The Imam smiled thinly. 'I never saw them burning poppies, but yes, they were the type.'

'His name was Sean Evans, did you know that?'

'I never knew his name.'

'He also might have used the name Mohammed Masood.'

The Imam shrugged but didn't say anything.

'When you phoned the emergency services, how did you make the call?'

'My mobile.'

'Which was where?'

'Excuse me.'

'Your mobile phone. Was it on your person? I assume you don't carry it with you when leading prayers.'

'No, I had it in my office.'

'So did you go to your office to make the call?'

'No. I asked somebody to fetch it.'

'You stayed with the body?'

'Yes. I stayed with the body.'

'So who fetched the phone?'

'One of the students who stays behind for Islamic classes.'

'His name?' I said, pen hovering over my pad.

'I don't recall.' he said, his voice for the first time, catching. He was lying. But he might just be trying to protect a younger member of his congregation. Or perhaps he didn't want to become known as an informer. It was still very much them against us. So was I 'them' or was I 'us'? That was a tough question to answer.

'Okay. At some point you will have to give an official statement, and we're going to need the name of the student.' I stopped. He let out a small breath, I smiled respectfully. It wasn't reciprocated. I sat back, looked at my notes carefully, considering there wasn't much that I had jotted down. He wasn't the only one that could play on appearances. I looked up from the notebook. 'There is something I should mention, before DI Porter returns,' I said. 'He wants you to supply him with any CCTV footage from the mosque.'

The Imam grimaced. 'My congregation would not be happy with that,' he said.

'It might provide evidence as to what happened.'

'This is a place of worship, Mohammed.' His use of my name was deliberate, I knew. He wanted to put me in my place. He was my Imam and he wanted me to pay him the respect he deserved. I was also a policeman, a detective constable investigating a murder, but so far as he was concerned, that was irrelevant. 'Our brothers and sisters come here to pray and to worship, they should be free to practise their religion without the fear that every moment is being scrutinised by the police.'

'There are no cameras in the prayer hall, are there?'

'No. But there are cameras at the entrance. And covering the outside, obviously.'

'It would help our investigation to see who Sean Evans arrived with.'

The Imam nodded. 'But that would mean everyone who was at the prayers being scrutinised by the police.'

'With the greatest respect, that will happen anyway. We need to compile a list of suspects.'

'And therein lies the problem, Mohammed. The brothers and sisters are worshippers, why should they be regarded as suspects?'

I took a deep breath and let it out slowly before speaking. 'Well, Imam, because someone who attended the mosque today killed Mr Evans. Stabbed him to death and left him to die. That person is almost certainly on your CCTV footage. I understand your reservations, but DI Porter will insist and he will have the power of the law on his side.'

'The law does not overrule our religion,' said the Imam. 'Allah the merciful stands above all earthly laws.'

'I understand that, but if you refuse to hand over the CCTV footage he will get a court order.'

'Which we will ignore,' said the Imam.

I smiled. 'I was hoping that there might be a less confrontational way of resolving the matter.'

He frowned. 'How so?'

'It is within DI Porter's power to have the mosque closed for the duration of the investigation,' I said. 'It remains a crime scene. But it seems to me that if you showed that you were cooperating, he does have the leeway to allow services to continue.'

'Your DI Porter has no power over me,' said the Imam.

I shrugged. 'I was merely pointing out your options.'

'There would be a riot.'

'Which would be dealt with. And no one would profit from that. But an offer from you to release the CCTV footage would show that you are eager to help, and that offer to help could be reciprocated by him allowing the mosque to remain open.'

The Imam was still nodding thoughtfully as the door opened and in walked Porter.

'This is all I could find.' he muttered, plonking down on the table two small cartons of Sunny Delight. He sat down and looked at me expectantly.

'Guv,' I said, piercing a hole in the juice carton. 'We were just now discussing access to the mosque.'

'Mr Malik,' Porter said. 'I'm aware that you have more services throughout the day.'

'Yes,' Malik replied. 'Asar Prayers are due imminently, then when the sun sets, Maghrib and soon after, Isha. It is imperative that there is access to the mosque. I think we can provide a limited service in the upstairs prayer hall. We have a second stairwell by the side entrance, so we won't be interfering with your... crime scene.'

'With all due respect, Mr Malik,' Porter said. 'A murder has been committed, we have to cordon off the whole of the mosque. It may be a few days before we complete the...'

'A few days?' Malik hissed. 'Impossible, Inspector.'

'Keeping the mosque open might be the way to go, Guv,' I said. 'It could work to our benefit.'

'In what way?'

'We've got about fifty witnesses to interview here,' I replied. 'But there would have been closer to five hundred potential witnesses in the prayer room. I'm assuming that some, probably not all, would return for the later prayers. They could be questioned on their return.'

Porter made the right sounds and faces and finally agreed. I looked at the Imam for his reaction to the compromise. He nodded, his eyes narrowed as to where I was going with this.

'You've helped us out greatly already,' I continued, 'and I'm embarrassed to be asking you for more.'

'You don't seem embarrassed.' Malik smiled tightly. He took a breath and sighed. 'What do you want?'

'The CCTV cameras covering the entrance to the mosque, would you allow us access to the footage? It would assist us in our enquiries.'

The Imam stared at me stone-faced, then slowly nodded. 'I don't think that will be a problem,' he said. 'I shall have my assistant put the footage on a hard disc drive for you.'

'Thank you for your co-operation,' I said, standing up. 'Really, very much appreciated.' And it was.

'So what did the good Imam have to say for himself during my absence?' Porter asked as we stepped outside. DS Paul Rees was organising the search for the murder weapon, and a dozen uniformed officers were making their way through the ground floor. Interpreters had been drafted in and the witnesses were being gently searched and questioned.

'He's smooth, Guv. And very calculating.'

'He's definitely smooth. Tell me why he's calculating.'

'When it all kicked off earlier, with The Faith, he was watching the whole thing on CCTV. And not only was he watching, he was preparing.'

'Do you think Malik called them in? Set the whole thing up?'

'Not sure, Guv. But he certainly took advantage of it. He knew that sooner or later we would require his help. When we first spoke with Malik, I didn't notice a microphone on his collar. He would have taken it off after prayers. But when I burst into his office, it was attached to his collar and connected to every speaker in the mosque, including the external speakers within the minarets. Trust me, Guv, he was set and ready to address his audience.'

'Risky though. How did he know that The Faith would take any notice of him? It could easily have back fired and embarrassed him.'

'That's the other thing, Guv,' I said. 'I'm pretty sure The Faith are on the payroll.'

Porter frowned. 'In what way?'

'Protection,' I said. 'Mosques are vulnerable these days and who better to protect the place than your own worshippers?'

'Why do they have to be paid?'

I couldn't help but smile. 'Guv, nobody does anything for nothing these days, you know that.'

Chapter 11
(Harry)

It was almost nine-thirty and dark by the time I had everything pretty much under control. SOCO had done their job and the body had been taken away to the mortuary. We had allowed the Imam to carry on with services, the first one at just after five o'clock and again at just before nine. There was one more service to be held – Nasri had described them as Isha prayers – at a few minutes after ten.

Jacqueline Beard wasn't happy about her crime scene being compromised by several hundred worshippers, but there were two main reasons for allowing the prayer sessions to go ahead. First, I really didn't want a repeat of the near riots earlier in the day and refusing the worshippers access to the mosque would be sure to get tempers flaring. But second, it meant that a lot of the worshippers who had been at the earlier session would return, giving us a chance to identify them. The Imam agreed to help, standing at the entrance with a couple of our detectives and speaking to the men as they arrived. It was the Imam who asked if they had been at the one-thirty prayers. I didn't expect the killer to return to the scene of the crime, but after the two prayer sessions we had close to a hundred names and addresses of worshippers who had been in the mosque when Sean Evans had been killed.

When an investigation kicks off, witnesses and forensics are your main sources of leads. Everyone needs to be identified and interviewed to find out what they saw and, just as importantly, who they saw. The killer must have been in the mosque at some point so someone must have seen him. The sheer number of people who had to be spoken to was intimidating, but be it five or five hundred the principle was the same. Not all potential witnesses would have been inside the mosque, of course.

What made this investigation that much harder was the number of witnesses who claimed to have problems speaking English. Translation services cost the Met close to £10 million a year and every time we used one it would be billed to the investigation. McKee had arranged for a dozen in the first instance, eight spoke Urdu, two Somali and two spoke Hindi. Two of the Urdu speakers and both Somali speakers also spoke Arabic. It turned out we didn't need the two Hindi speakers but they had been promised six hours work minimum so they sat in their car smoking until their time was up.

I sat in on a few of the early interviews and I was pretty sure that most of the worshippers spoke perfectly reasonable English, at least well enough to answer the questions they were being asked. It wasn't rocket science. We needed ID and we needed them to turn out their pockets, and then we just needed to know what time they arrived at the mosque, if they saw Sean Evans, and where they were when they prayed. Nothing too hard there, right?

The first interview I sat in on was a Pakistani man in his fifties. He was wearing one of those dishdasha robe things and a skullcap and had a grey beard that reached down to his stomach. He sat with his fingers interlinked and started shaking his head the moment the detective said that he wanted to pat him down. He didn't say anything but there was a lot of head-shaking and clearly he wasn't happy at being searched. When the interpreter explained what the detective wanted, the man spoke quite aggressively and there was more head-shaking. I was pretty sure he'd understood every word the detective had said.

Part of me wanted to just send the interpreters home and let the detectives get on with it, but Miss Khan had been right, the police had a duty to treat all witnesses with sensitivity, impartiality and respect for their culture and rights, and part of that respect meant talking to them in the language they were most comfortable with.

The man eventually agreed to a patting down. He told the investigator that he was close to the front of the mosque and had arrived half an hour before the service. He hadn't seen the body, and hadn't been aware that there was a problem until two men carried it out and another two began cleaning up the blood. He started speaking aggressively for the best part of thirty seconds and then sat back with his arms folded. I looked expectantly at the interpreter. He was in his twenties, clean shaven and wearing a Ralph Lauren polo shirt, one of those with a big horse on it. He shrugged. 'He's just sounding off about the police being in the mosque,' he said. 'In his opinion, the police should have waited outside.'

'Well, everyone is entitled to their opinion,' I said. Even idiots who are too stupid to trim their beards and wear proper clothes is what I thought, but obviously I didn't say that. I've no doubt the day will come when I'll be sacked for just thinking it, but hopefully I'll have retired by then.

The interview took the best part of half an hour with all the to-and-froing with the interpreter. The detective was a young guy I hadn't come across before but he was good, patient and polite and respectful. Before he patted the man down, he explained exactly what he was going to do and that if at any time he felt uncomfortable he was to say so. And when he'd finished the interview he thanked the man for his help and shook his hand.

The second interview I sat in on was a lot less productive. It was a Somali teenager who according to his driving licence had been born in the UK but who pretended to speak not a word of English. He sat with his arms folded and scowled at the detective who was interviewing him. The detective was Willie McLeish, a crusty Glaswegian who'd moved down to the Met from Strathclyde Police ten years earlier. McLeish's wife was a doctor, a kidney specialist, and when she took up a post in a London teaching hospital, he came with her and always gave the impression that the move was very much against his will. He was a constant complainer about all things English – the food, the weather, the people – but he was a good, solid copper and he stood his round in the pub. I could see McLeish was having a tough time controlling his temper, his eyes were hard and he kept gritting his teeth as the Somali teenager got progressively more belligerent.

McLeish kept insisting he wanted to search the teenager, the translator translated, the teenager replied in Somalian, the translator translated. The translator was a middle-aged women with a black headscarf and a pleasant smile and I could see that even she was getting frustrated with the teenager. Round and round they went with McLeish's blood pressure on an upward trajectory. Eventually I caught McLeish's eye and nodded at the door. He had the good grace to wait until we were in the corridor before sounding off. 'I'm sorry, Guv, this is doing my head in,' he said. 'He understands every word I'm saying. A good clip around the ear, that's what he needs.'

'No argument here, Willie. But we need to keep things moving. We've got his ID, we'll get someone to pay him a visit in a day or two. Don't sweat the search, his jeans are tight enough to show he's not hiding a knife. I'm guessing he's got drugs on him which is why he's being so defensive. Just find out where he was when he was praying and chuck him out.'

'Thanks, Guv.'

'And relax, Willie. I'm not one for assumptions but I think it's safe to assume that the killer wouldn't have hung around. We just need to process the witnesses and then we can get down to looking for the killer.'

Willie headed back into the office and I took a walk through the mosque. There was a quietness about the place, belying the fact that it was a murder scene. The walls seemed to absorb any noise and the lights were all soft and warm giving it a dream-like feel.

Forensically everything had gone very well under the watchful eye of Lorraine Sawyer. The body and the area around it had been photographed and examined. One of the worshippers who had moved the body had taken the SOCO team to where it had been originally. More samples and photographs had been taken.

We'd had less success looking for the murder weapon. Let me rephrase that. We'd had zero success. I'd put Paul Rees in charge of the search for the weapon and assigned him a dozen uniforms, all male. They'd worked their way through the ground floor rooms, searching everywhere but being careful not to cause any damage. There were dozens of knives in the kitchen and they were all sealed in evidence bags and put on one side for forensic analysis. Once they had searched the ground floor they had moved upstairs. They had even gone through the Imam's office while he watched them, stony-faced. They turned up nothing and Rees was certain that the knife had been taken from the mosque, probably by the killer, but I was going to insist on a more thorough search the following day. Most murderers wanted to dump the murder weapon as soon as they could. It was a psychological thing. Taking a person's life was a big thing, it was stressful, it got the heart pumping and had adrenaline coursing through the veins, and that psychological pressure meant that often the perpetrator would toss the weapon close to the crime scene. You've got to have ice in your veins to stick a knife in a man's chest and then walk away with the bloody knife in your pocket. I figured there was a good chance the killer had either hidden it in the mosque or dumped it close by.

The Imam was still there and he had agreed to stand at the entrance again and talk to the late-night worshippers. There were usually a hundred or so, he said, and only men. He gave me a portable harddrive onto which he'd loaded all the CCTV footage from first thing in the morning until the point when the body was discovered and asked me to return it when the investigation was over.

I left Paul Rees with three detectives to take names, stationed uniforms at the entrances and called it a night.

Chapter 12
(Sal)

Porter finally left the mosque at about ten. I drove him back to Hendon, dropped off the Vectra and picked up my own car, an Audi. After my wife and daughter, it's my pride and joy. I drove to the nearest cashpoint, parked and hurried over to it, saying a silent prayer to Allah. I'd applied for the overdraft online but got knocked back and then I'd applied on the phone and had a long chat with a very nice lady called Sheila. I'd explained that I was a detective and that the case I had just been assigned to meant that I would be earning lots of overtime over the next few weeks. She pointed out that I already had an overdraft of five thousand pounds, which was true, and she asked what I had used that money for. It was a trick question because they'd asked me that before they gave me the first loan and I'd said it was for a new kitchen so that's what I told Sheila. A brand spanking new kitchen. So what was the new loan for, she asked, and I lied and said that the boiler needed replacing and while we were doing that we thought we might as well put in a new shower and get the bathroom retiled and that my wife and I thought that two grand would cover it. Sheila asked a few more questions and said okay, she would agree the additional overdraft, and promised that the money would be in my account by close of business. I hadn't been able to check all day so I slotted the card in the cashpoint, said another silent prayer to Allah the beneficent, the merciful, then tapped in my PIN number and requested the balance of my account. I grinned when I saw the two thousand pounds was in my account. I withdrew five hundred, kissed the notes and put them in my wallet. I was free and unfettered. Miriam, my wife, was currently in a Travelodge somewhere in Bath. A work conference or training, I wasn't quite sure which. She was due to return tomorrow evening. My daughter, five-year-old Maria, was staying with her grandparents, Miriam's side. I didn't fancy going back to an empty house and besides, I had an itch to scratch.

I got back in the car and headed towards Uxbridge to the nightclub. It was Friday night so it was jumping and the car park was full so I had to park on the street and walk a couple of hundred yards. The building was a featureless concrete block with a flat roof, the entrance at one end and a fire exit at the other. The name of the club was up in neon, flanked by giant cocktail glasses with umbrellas.

I walked past the queue mainly comprised of good natured students, punctuated with a few creepy old men who'd invariably spend the night trying and failing to pull girls half their age and having to settle for perving from a distance.

'Who do you think you are?' said the Bouncer. I had to crane my neck to make eye contact. 'Did you not see the queue?'

'C'mon, mate.' Shit. I couldn't remember his name. I frowned. 'It's me. Sal.'

'Nah, the Sal I know is a jovial sorta fella. Always smiling. You look kinda grumpy to me. House rules, can't let any of the seven dwarfs in. Especially Grumpy.'

'It's been a long day.'

'Apart from Happy. We'd let that motherfucker in.'

I grinned at him.

'Oh, shit, Sal! It is you. Didn't recognise you for a minute.' He winked at me and unhooked the velvet rope.

'Nice one, Marcus,' I said, his name finally coming to me.

'You here to party or play?'

'I'm here to play.'

'Good luck.'

'Don't jinx me, Marcus.'

'Okay then, break a fucking leg.'

He was still chuckling as I walked through the door and into the club, all flashing lights and thumping bass and lyrics that might have rhymed or made sense but the sound system was shit and anyway I wasn't there for the music. At the far end of the club next to the toilets was another bouncer in a black suit, even bigger than Marcus. This one's name I remembered straight away, his nickname anyway. They called him Everest, because he was a mountain. Or because he used to sell double glazing. Who knows where nicknames come from?

Everest grinned at me as I approached. 'Fucking hell, Sal, are you a glutton for punishment, or what?'

'What do you mean?'

'I heard you were on a losing streak.'

'Who told you that?'

'Walls have ears, mate.'

'I've had a couple of bad nights but my luck's gotta turn at some point.'

'If you say so, Sal.' He turned and opened the door for me. 'Good luck,' he said.

There were six men sitting around a circular table and I knew five of them. The man sitting directly opposite me was the dealer, an Irishman by the name of Declan O'Brien who had spent two decades dealing in Las Vegas. He was grey-haired and overweight and by the end of the night his face was usually bathed in sweat, but he was one hell of a dealer and as straight as an arrow. On his left Brandon Judnarine, a doctor from Barbados. Brandon rarely spoke and was a tight player, I'd never caught him bluffing in the five or six times I'd played with him. He nodded when he saw me but didn't smile.

To Brandon's left was a Russian, Boris Popov, which everyone thought was a hilarious name. We always tried to get 'I'll Popov now' into the conversation and he took it in good spirits. He was a big man, but whereas O'Brien was all fat, Popov was muscle, with bulging forearms and a Desperate Dan jaw. He turned to flash me a grin and then went back to staring at the cards on the table. King of clubs, jack of hearts, jack of spades, and three of diamonds. Texas Hold 'em. One more card to come. The river.

The man on Popov's left had his back to me but I recognised his dyed blond hair and lucky leather jacket. Grieg Landers was a car salesman, or so he told us all, but I'd run a PNC check on him after I'd first met him and he was more of a car thief, arranging for luxury sports cars to be stolen in London and shipped over to South East Asia. That was the intel anyway, he was a clever bugger and had so far eluded the clutches of the Met's finest. He and Popov seemed to be the only two left in the game.

Popov reached up and tugged his left ear. He did that a lot, but it was more of a nervous tic than a tell.

The guy I hadn't seen before was on the left of Landers, a West Indian who showed me dazzling white teeth when he smiled. From the look of the chips in front of him, he was the table leader which could be good news or bad. If he was winning because he'd had a run of good luck then his luck could change and I could take some of his money but if he was winning because he was a shit hot player then I could be in trouble. The only way to know for sure was to play.

The Bag Carrier

The final member of the game, sitting between the West Indian and O'Brien was another regular, a middle-aged Iraqi who'd been granted asylum in the UK during the Saddam Hussein years and who now ran a chain of kebab shops in south London. Pretty good kebabs, too, it has to be said. His name was Ali Saleem and I was really pleased to see him because he was a crap player, always played loose and had a tendency to go full tilt at least once each night. He was another big man, fat like O'Brien, and the armpits of his shirt were already stained with sweat. Saleem looked over at me and smiled. 'As-salamu alaykum,' he said. Peace be upon you.

I smiled back. 'Wa alaykumu as-salam.' And upon you, peace.

We're both Muslims but we both take the view that while the Koran says that games of chance are haram, forbidden, poker isn't a game of chance, it's a game of skill, and the Koran is perfectly happy with people challenging each other in games of skill. I wouldn't bet on a horserace or a game of chance like Blackjack or roulette, but poker is about skill and technique and usually, in the long run, the better player always wins. I was going through a dry spell, which wasn't a pleasant experience, but I knew what I was doing and in the long term I was sure I'd be in the black.

Sitting in the far corner of the room, next to a table loaded up with drinks and snacks and a coffee-maker, was the man who ran the game, a Bangladeshi by the name of Ray Chottopadhyay. He was a Buddhist, stick-thin with deep set eyes that stared unblinkingly over the game. Chottopadhyay was a big-time money lender and probably a launderer, too, who ran poker games as a profitable sideline. The games moved around but the Friday night game at the nightclub had been a regular event for more than six months. There were games most nights and we all received daily text messages telling us where and when.

Ray looked up at me and smiled like a snake contemplating its next meal. 'Good to see you, Sal,' he said. 'I hope you've got something for me.'

I took the five hundred quid from my pocket. I owed him two hundred that he'd loaned me from two nights earlier. Well, two hundred and fifty because Chottopadhyay never lends for free. 'Here's the thing, Ray,' I said. 'I've got five hundred but I'd really like to play with it all.'

'You owe me two fifty, Sal. Remember?'

'Sure, yes, of course. And I'll pay you back. You know I will. I always do, right? I've got two grand in my account but my card will only give me five hundred.'

He licked his lips. 'So you want to let the debt ride?'

'I want to play with the five, yes. Then when I win I can pay you back the two fifty.'

'If you don't pay me back tonight you'll owe me three, you realise that?'

I smiled through gritted teeth and nodded. 'Sure, Ray. It's all good.'

He shrugged then held out his hand. I gave him the notes and he ran them through his electronic counter before handing me a stack of chips. 'Be lucky,' he said.

'I wish everyone would stop wishing me luck,' I muttered. I went over to the table and took the chair between Saleem and O'Brien. The West Indian nodded at me. 'How ya doing?'

'So far so good,' I said, arranging my chips.

Popov was pulling the pot towards himself. He'd won with a full house, jacks over threes. Nice.

The West Indian held out his hand. 'Name's Jasper.'

'Sal,' I said. We shook hands.

I played tight for half a dozen hands, paying to see the flop twice when I had pairs but dropping out as soon as anyone raised. I played it casual but I was watching Jasper like a hawk. He was the unknown quantity and I needed to get his measure. He seemed pretty loose and I saw him lose a hundred after paying to see the flop with a six seven unsuited which was either ballsy or stupid depending on how you look at it. But I also saw him win two hundred by filling an inside straight on the river so my theory that he was just lucky seemed to be holding up.

Popov won two hands on the trot, then lost a big pot to Saleem, then Landers had a run of good cards, a pair of tens followed by a pair of aces. Perversely he won with the tens but lost with the aces when Brandon landed a flush with the river card.

My chance to make a move came after I'd been there an hour and was about seventy quid down. I got a pair of kings, paid to see the flop and kept a straight face as I saw a third king. I didn't raise, but Jasper did so I tried to look like it was a tough decision before calling. Popov stayed in and pulled his ear again but like I said, I'm pretty sure that's just a tic.

I had the king of hearts and the king of spades and I was looking at the king of diamonds flanked by the six of spades and the queen of spades. I couldn't see that either of them could have had the last king so I reckoned that maybe they both had a queen each.

O'Brien dealt the turn and it was a jack of hearts so no real help to anyone unless one of them was going for a straight. I looked at Jasper. He seemed fairly confident so maybe it was a straight he was after. Could he have nine ten or ten ace and already have the straight? If he did then I needed to drop out and drop out quick. Unless I felt lucky and banked on getting a full house with the final card. A full house would be nice. Very nice.

Popov didn't bet. Jasper put in fifty which suggested he was looking for something on the final card so maybe it was a straight he was going for. Though a flush was a possibility. Either way I'd need a full house but it was still worth paying fifty to see the river. I put in fifty and then Popov grins and raises. Raises. What? He puts in a hundred. Jasper immediately throws in another fifty and now I am annoyed. I've now got seventy quid in the pot and have to put in another fifty just to see the river. If I fold then that's seventy quid down the drain plus the seventy I'd already lost which is a hundred and forty quid. They were both looking at me and I smiled to cover my uncertainty. My head was telling me to cut my losses but I had three kings and unless one of them had already filled a straight or a flush I had the best hand. I threw in another fifty.

O'Brien placed the river card on the table and it was only a queen smiling up at me. The queen of clubs which made a flush even less likely and gave me a full house, kings over queens. Allah be praised.

Popov was looking pained now and he tugged his ear again and didn't bet. Jasper threw in fifty which felt to me like he was just trying to push Popov away. I was sure I had the best hand so it was just a matter of maximizing my profits. If I raised there was a good chance that I would scare Popov off so I made a play of looking at my cards, grimacing, and reluctantly throwing in another fifty.

I forced myself to stay calm but I wanted to jump out of my seat and punch the air. I had a full house. Popov grinned. 'All in,' he said.

All in? Did I hear him right? All in. Thanks be to Allah and his prophet Mohammed. All in? He must have made his flush because he wouldn't have been that confident with a straight.

Jasper threw his cards in immediately, muttering under his breath.

'How much is it?' I asked.

'You need to put in another three hundred,' said O'Brien.

'Three hundred,' I nodded in thought. With one last look at the cards I pushed my chips in knowing that in a few seconds it's all coming back to me.

'Show,' O'Brien said.

Keeping his eyes on mine, Popov turned one card over. A queen. Then he slowly, really slowly, turned his other card over.

Another queen.

His two queens, plus the two queens already out gave him...

'Four of a Kind.' I whispered the words.

'That's right, Sal.' Popov grinned.

I looked down at my cards. My mighty full house could do nothing but kneel down, lower its eyes and surrender against his four of a kind.

'Are you serious?' I said.

His grin widened. 'As cancer.'

I tossed down my cards. He reached for them but I swatted his hand away. 'Don't you dare,' I said, and pushed them towards O'Brien who quickly gathered them up.

I stood up and went over to Chottopadhyay. 'Ray, I hate to ask but I don't want to walk away when I'm down,' I said. 'Can you spot me five?'

He grimaced like he had a bad taste in his mouth. 'Five on top of the three? That's eight.'

'I'm good for it, Ray. I told you, I've got a grand in the bank. I'll pay you the eight tomorrow.'

'You'll pay me nine tomorrow.'

'Okay, right, fine. Nine tomorrow.' I held out my hand. 'Just give me the five.'

He picked up five hundred quids worth of chips and gave them to me. 'Nine tomorrow,' he said.

'Ray, I'll win it back tonight, don't worry.'

'Oh, Sal, I'm not worrying. I haven't a care in the world.'

Chapter 13
(Harry)

I arrived at the station at just before seven-thirty in the morning and went along to the canteen on the first floor to get a coffee and two bacon rolls. When I got to the MIR, David Judd was already at his workstation. He had his jacket over the back of his chair and his shirtsleeves rolled up, and had flicked his tie over his shoulder. It was his thing. I don't know why he did it, he just did. Whenever he was looking at his screen, his tie was over his shoulder. Whenever he got up, he flicked it back. 'Morning, Guv,' he said.

'How's it going, Dave?'

'Not much further forward since you left last night,' he said. 'All the interviews of the worshippers at the mosque are done and dusted but not much help. They were all photographed with the exception of about a dozen who got bolshy but as they had driving licences we've downloaded mugshots from the DVLA. Nobody questioned saw anything. We have a list of names of worshippers who left the premises before the body was discovered but it's long, Guv. Three hundred so far.' As office manager it was his job to keep his finger on the pulse of the investigation and to make sure that I was always up to speed. Nothing happened without him knowing about it, and he would pass all the important stuff to me.

'They all need to be spoken to,' I said, dropping down onto my chair.

'We're going to need more interviewers,' he said. 'Say two hours each including travel time, ninety minutes if we're lucky, we're looking at three hundred-man hours, Guv. If you want that done in three days, then even with overtime we're going to need ten guys. Twenty if you want to double up, and considering the case that's probably best.'

'Go ahead and organise it, Dave,' I said. 'And yeah, twos-up.'

Carrying out interviews with just one investigator was just about possible with a straight-forward fact-gathering exercise, but turning up on a Muslim's doorstep and asking what he was doing and who with at his local mosque was asking for trouble. Two detectives were a lot less likely to be accused of racism than one flying solo.

'Tell everyone we'll have morning prayers at nine prompt,' I said, then made a mental note to refer to the briefing as just that in future. I didn't want to go upsetting anyone who actually did pray first thing in the morning. I looked at my watch, wondering what time DC Nasri planned on putting in an appearance.

'I don't suppose you've any good news for me regarding the murder weapon?'

Judd shook his head. 'We're starting the outside search in about an hour. We'll have twenty bodies and we've been promised as many cadets as they can spare.'

'What's the name of the investigation?'

'Salford,'

'Salford?'

'Don't look at me like that, HOLMES gives us the name.'

In the good old days of murder investigations, the SIO was the one who gave the investigation a name, but there were several cases of inappropriate titles being used – not the least being Redrum – and so now HOLMES issued a name at random, usually a place name and with the same first letter being used each year. This year was S, and we got Salford.

'Where's Alan?'

'In the CCTV room. They've already got footage from a couple of council cameras in the streets leading to the mosque.'

I patted him on the shoulder and went over to Pete Davies. Davies was only a few months from retirement but he definitely wasn't coasting. Davies had been divorced two years earlier and his ex-wife had taken the house, their two dogs and half his pension fund. Now he lived in a rented flat with noisy neighbours so he spent most of his time working, plus the overtime was a Godsend his financial situation being what it was.

He looked up from his terminal as I walked over. 'Hi Harry, how's it hanging?' He was in his late fifties and since the divorce he'd taken to dying his hair a brilliant chestnut brown and had grown a moustache, dying it to match.

'All good, Pete.'

He looked pleadingly at my bacon rolls so I held out the plate. He grinned and took one. 'You're a star, Harry.' He bit into it and chewed happily.

'Actions coming through okay?' I asked. It was early days but the witness interviews, weapons search and CCTV requests had resulted in several dozen Actions being initiated and they all had to pass through Davies in his role as Receiver. Once the Action Results started coming in, one of his tasks was to underline anything in the Action that needed to be indexed on HOLMES 2. It was the indexing that was key to keeping a track on the investigation. As SIO it would be my first port of call each morning and the last thing I'd check at night. I also have a portable copy on my laptop that I can tap into if needed when I was away from the MIR. But like most computer systems, the quality of the information you could get from it depended on the quality of the data that was put in. The IT guys had an expression for it – GIGO. Garbage in, garbage out. With Pete on the case, the amount of garbage would be kept to a minimum. He had a good eye for detail and he rarely screwed up. On the few occasions he did mess up, he'd work tirelessly to put it right.

'Slow and steady,' he said, and took another bite of his roll.

'Yeah, well just so you know, there are likely to be upwards of four hundred witness statements,' I said. I sipped my coffee.

He nodded. 'Yeah, about that. We're having some issues already with names. Can you get the troops to be extra careful with spellings? And remind them that HOLMES won't take apostrophes. If there's an apostrophe in the name they need to use a hyphen.'

'Will do, Pete, thanks.' I went over to my workstation, dropped my briefcase on the floor and put the coffee and bacon roll next to my keyboard. I had three screens on the desk and they were all on, showing the Metropolitan Police badge on a dark blue background. I logged on and sipped my coffee as I went through the Action reports. It was going to be a busy day and at some point the Sheriff would want to know how we stood. He had access to HOLMES, as did all senior management, but he'd be sure to want it from the horse's mouth. And yes, I'm the horse.

The hard disc drive that the Imam had given me was in the briefcase. I took it out and I walked along to the room that Alan Russell was using to get the CCTV footage reviewed. There were three civilian workers with him and they were already at work.

Russell was sitting at a desk tapping updates into HOLMES.

'How are you doing manpower-wise for the CCTV?' I asked him.

'Just the three bodies at the moment. We've got two council downloads and we're hoping to get footage from two ATMs in the street that should give us a view of pedestrians. But you know how shitty ATM footage usually is.'

I gave him the hard disc drive. 'This is from the mosque. Treat this as priority, obviously. Once we know what time Sean Evans arrived at the mosque we can work backwards and look for him in the street.'

Russell nodded and took the hard drive.

'How did Paul get on last night?' I asked.

'Sixty worshippers turned up. The Imam was quite helpful and they all provided ID and gave statements. We've got close to three hundred names now that need to be interviewed. I'm having the Actions issued this morning.'

'And what about another search of the mosque? We really need the murder weapon.'

'You really think it's still there, Guv? If the killer legged it, he probably took it with him.'

'People panic, Alan. And when they panic they react instinctively and if you're holding a bloody knife in your hand your first thought is to get rid of it. Did we search upstairs?'

Russell nodded. 'The Imam wasn't happy but he let us up there eventually.'

'Good to know we're not letting the Imam set the parameters of our investigation.'

'I know, I know. But there's the cultural sensitivities to consider, right?'

'If it was a Catholic Church we wouldn't be pussy-footing around,' I said.

'True, but if we upset the congregation of a Catholic Church the worst we'd get is a few angry looks and a bit of tutting. Fuck off the Muslims and they'll come at you en masse waving machetes.'

'You heard about yesterday?'

He grinned. 'You can't keep something like that a secret, Guv.'

'Yeah, well I just hope it stays out of the papers,' I said. 'Okay, we're going to have to have another search of the mosque, upstairs and downstairs. More thorough this time. Let's start lifting drains and pulling back skirting boards if we have to. Give the kitchen a real good going over this time, backs of fridges, ceiling spaces, the works. Same with the Imam's office.'

'You think he's involved?'

'Who knows? But I get the feeling that he's not a big fan of the police. Do I think he'd hide the murder weapon to protect one of his flock?' I shrugged. 'I don't see why not. If DC Nasri ever puts in an appearance I'll get him to talk to the Imam and make sure he's OK. But we need to be absolutely sure that the weapon isn't somewhere in the mosque.'

'No problem, Guv.'

I went back into the MIR. There was still no sign of Nasri. Lorraine Sawyer was at her desk unscrewing the top off a bottle of paracetamol. 'You okay?' I asked.

'Migraine,' she said. 'Coming in on a Saturday isn't helping.' She swallowed two tablets and washed them down with coffee.

'How did it go yesterday?' I asked. As Forensic Manager she was in charge of collecting and analysing all the forensic evidence at the scene, though with the worshippers cleaning up before we got there, I was guessing there wouldn't be much in the way of evidence for her to collect.

'The only blood we found was the victim's,' she said. 'The fact that they moved the body means we're not sure whether the blood trails we found are pre or post mortem. No defence wounds on the hands, no fibres that shouldn't be there. Not great, Harry. Sorry.'

'What about the knives that were taken from the kitchen?'

'They were all clean. Literally. They'd all been through the dishwasher.'

'The dishwasher wasn't running when we were there.'

'No, it was used earlier that morning. Of course that doesn't mean that a knife from the kitchen wasn't the murder weapon, just that it wasn't put back.'

'Can you put the details of all the knives into HOLMES and I'll see what the coroner has to say about the blade?'

'Already done,' she said.

DC Nasri still hadn't turned up by nine o'clock so I started the briefing without him. By that stage the MIR was packed. There were more than fifty investigators and support staff in the room and that wasn't the whole team by a long shot. Murder is a serious business and in the initial stages at least the Met doesn't hold back on resources. If you get your information on murder investigations from the TV then you'll think it's like Morse and Lewis, or Lewis and whoever he had as his bag carrier when Morse died, or whoever those two are in Midsomer Murders. They wander around and interview suspects and spot clues and then solve it over a pint in the local. Crime books aren't much better. They always have a dynamic duo with lots of banter and maybe a hint of will-they-won't-they romance and they do all the work and get the credit. Either that or it's the lone maverick cop with a chip on his shoulder and a bottle of whisky in his bottom drawer. Truth be told, fictional cops like Rebus wouldn't last a day in a real-life murder investigation. Not these days, anyway. Back in the days of Dixon Of Dock Green I dare say CID detectives did work unsupervised and had a fair bit of leeway, but those days are long gone. I'm not saying that some cops weren't larger than life in the Seventies and early Eighties but long before I joined all that had been cleared out. Everything we do – every single thing – is recorded and analysed. Everything we do is accompanied by a written Action and that Action has to be either carried out or an explanation given as to why it wasn't carried out. Every piece of evidence is recorded and accounted for from the moment it is discovered until the moment it is presented in court. Every interrogation is recorded, on tape and written down, and more often than not with a video to go with it. Even though I'm Senior Investigating Officer on this case, I have Teflon McKee looking over my shoulder and the Sheriff watching over him, and they've got senior officers above them and every one of them is nit-picking and second-guessing and waiting for someone to make a mistake so they can show everyone what clever bastards they are. Every minute of my time is accounted for, everything I do is recorded and I have to justify every single decision I make in writing so that it can be queried later.

Murder investigation is a team game these days, and I guess I'm the equivalent of the manager which means I can be given the boot at any time if the powers-that-be reckon I'm not doing a good job.

I looked around the assembled throng, nodding and smiling and waiting for them to stop what they were doing and get into a position where they could see and hear me. I knew pretty much everyone by name but it was their titles that mattered. Deputy SIO, Crime Scene Manager, Forensic Manager, Outside Enquiry Manager, Office Manager, Finance Manager, Receiver, Action Manager, Investigative Team Leader, two SOCOs, Search Co-ordinator, Press Officer and Community Awareness Specialist.

The only one I hadn't spoken to was the West Indian lady who was the Community Awareness Specialist. Her name was Sophie Lanning and she would be responsible for drawing up the Community Impact Assessment, something that all the chief officers would be concerned about bearing in mind where the murder had occurred. I'd worked with her a couple of times and while she was a civilian rather than a cop she was definitely a team player. I needed that because the near-riot at the mosque hadn't been mentioned and I wanted to keep it that way.

If the number of job titles sounds like overkill, it really isn't, not when we have to follow the manual religiously, no pun intended. Anyway, everyone seemed to be pretty much ready so I cleared my throat. 'All right ladies and gentlemen, let's get started,' I said, and gave them a few seconds to put their phones away. 'I'll keep this brief, partly because that's my style but mainly because there isn't much to say. For those of you that don't know, the investigation is codenamed Salford. The deceased is one Sean Evans, though it appears he has also been using the name Mohammed Masood. I'm not one to jump to assumptions but we are obviously looking at the possibility that he was a Muslim convert. The next of kin are the deceased's mother and father. They live in Bromley at the address that is on the deceased's driving licence. They were informed of their son's death by two uniforms from Bromley and Mr Evans identified the body yesterday evening. I'm going down to

Bromley with DC Nasri later today to talk to them, assuming that DC Nasri decides to turn up.'

There were several guffaws from around the room. 'We'll also check out the post mortem. So, priorities today. We have now interviewed all the worshippers who were at the mosque at or around the time of the murder and who remained behind. No one saw the killing but several remember seeing the victim on the floor. The fifty-two we have interviewed have given us another two hundred or so names. They all need to be spoken to. We have another hundred or so names of worshippers who came back to the mosque for services later yesterday evening. But we need to have the details of everyone who was in the mosque yesterday. And we need to speak to them all. Obviously we need to know what they saw but we also need to know exactly where they prayed. The victim was at the back so we are most interested in those who were also at the back. So far no one has admitted to being on the back row.' I shrugged. 'I suppose it makes sense that those at the back would be first to leave. And I have to stress that just because they left with a dead man on the floor isn't significant, I'm told it's not unusual for worshippers to stay prostrate after prayers have ended.' I saw Paul Rees grin and I pointed at him. 'Prostrate,' I said. 'It means lying down.'

'Right, Guv,' he said and there were a few chuckles around the room.

'Ideally I'd like a map of the prayer room with every person marked on it but I appreciate that's a big ask. But I am asking so let's aim for that. We're not sure yet whether the victim was stabbed in the prayer hall or outside but either way there is a very good chance that the killer is one of the worshippers.'

I paused a few seconds to let that sink in. There were several nodding heads but at least a dozen were bent over their smartphones. I just hoped they were listening while they were Facebooking or texting or whatever. There was no way I could tell them to stop without sounding like an arsehole so I had no choice other than to let them get on with it.

'Right, second priority is the murder weapon. An initial search of the mosque didn't turn anything up and Stuart is going to work with DC Russell to organise a more intensive search this morning in between prayer sessions. As you know the mosque is staying open, even though it's a crime scene. As some four hundred or so worshippers left the mosque before the body was discovered, we are today initiating a search of the area around the mosque. Drains, skips, gardens, the full Monty. We've arranged with the council to hold off on all rubbish collections for the next two days, so that's our window.'

I let that sink in before continuing. 'DC Russell organised a house to house last night around the mosque but no one reports seeing anyone running away after the service, or anything unusual. We'll go back today with a photograph of the victim to see if anyone remembers him arriving at the mosque. We're also scooping up transport CCTV plus any other cameras, ATMs and the like, on the routes to the mosque. We need to know what time Sean Evans arrived at the mosque and who, if anyone, he went with. The Press Office will be releasing a photograph of the victim for Monday morning's papers asking for anyone who saw him on Friday to come forward. Right, any questions?'

I looked around but there were no raised hands. Not that I expected any, not at this stage. They were all professionals but they also didn't want to look stupid by asking a question in public. Anyone who needed a heads-up would have a quiet word with me or David Judd or Paul Rees afterwards.

'Great,' I said. 'So, onwards and upwards. And I'm sure I don't need to remind you of the sensitive nature of the investigation. We almost had a riot at the mosque yesterday and tempers are still pretty frayed. Let's treat everyone with respect, let's think about every situation we go into and how our actions will be perceived by the public. And I know most of you know this, but shoes off when you go into a Muslim home unless you're told otherwise by the occupants. It's a small thing but speaking from experience it can lead to problems up front. If you have any worries or questions about cultural sensitivity, Sophie Lanning should be your first port of call. And again, you all know this but no one, absolutely no one, talks to the Press. The Press Office and only the Press Office will be dealing with the media. You all know Donna Walsh. She is our main - and at the moment only - point of contact with the Press Office. If anyone from the media wants information, you pass them on to Donna.'

Donna smiled and raised her hand but the team were already drifting back to their workstations or studying their phones. Briefing over. Which is when DC Nasri decided to put in an appearance.

Chapter 14
(Sal)

I walked into the MIR just as the officers were walking out. Not only was I late in, I had missed the briefing. Porter was the last man standing and he did not look pleased. Rather than waiting for a bollocking I got in first. 'Sorry about getting in late. Guv, but I had a flat. Some joker, piss-head probably, had dropped a glass bottle just outside my drive.'

'You drove over it?'

'Yeah,' I said. 'I drove over it.'

'Right,' Porter said.

'I've never had to change a tyre before, Guv.' I ventured a smile. 'Wouldn't know where to start, so I had to give the AA a shout.'

Yeah, it wasn't my best work and Porter wasn't buying it, but it was plausible.

'I was in at seven,' Porter said.

'And I'll be in at seven tomorrow, Guv.'

'I know it's the weekend, but it's all hands to the wheel at the moment. The first few days are crucial.'

'I had a flat tyre, Guv. It won't happen again.'

'Okay, well get your act together. We're due at the mortuary at midday. Fix us up with a car.'

'Right you are, Guv.'

'And I need you to put a call in to the Imam. The preliminary search didn't turn up the murder weapon so we need to go through the whole building again, including the Imam's office and the rest of the upstairs rooms.'

I frowned. 'The Imam's not going to be happy about that.'

'Which is why you're the one telling him.'

'Ok, Guv.'

'You got him to hand over the CCTV footage easily enough, just work your magic again.'

'Work my magic, Guv. Right. Will do.' I smiled and held back the Harry Potter joke that sprang to mind. I know, I know, his name's Porter but when he says it, it sounds like Potter.

'Once we've spoken to the pathologist we'll head down to Bromley to speak to the parents of the victim. Did you get anywhere with an electoral roll address for Mohammed Masood?'

'I'll get right on it, Guv.'

'You saw the Action I raised on that?'

'Yes, Guv,' I said. 'I'm on it.'

He threw me a withering look and walked out of the MIR. It was the second lie that he had let slide. I took no pleasure in it but the truth would have been worse.

The Bag Carrier

It had been a bad night that turned disastrous. What was I going to say to Porter? *I was up until four in the morning at an illegal poker match.* Yeah, think I'll stick with the flat tyre story, thanks. Don't get me wrong, I don't usually let my poker habit impact on my work, in fact last night was a first and I'll make damn sure it's the last. I'm certainly not proud of myself. But there's no way I could tell Porter, not on my second day as his bag carrier.

Chottopadhyay had spotted me five hundred without much persuasion and I had lost it without much persuasion, too. My game and instincts were off last night. It wasn't that I was getting crappy cards, on the contrary, I was getting some killer cards which was pushing me into betting. My two pairs were beaten by a three of a kind. My high straight was beaten by a low flush. Even when I bluffed with an ace high, it was taken apart by a low pair. Yeah, there was a pattern to the downfall of my night. I had walked out with Chottopadhyay in my ear reminding me that I now owed him nine hundred. The three plus the five plus the interest.

I walked back to my desk and logged onto HOLMES and checked the Actions I'd been assigned. I figured the Imam was a priority so I put in a call to him at Central Mosque and asked to be put through to him. He took my call immediately.

'Aslamalikum, Mohammed,' he said, his voice coated in sugar. 'How are you this fine day?'

Calling me Mohammed was as subtle as taking a hammer to my head. The Imam was trying to wind me up. I didn't mind. Actually it was nice, nobody really called me Mohammed anymore. It's my name and I am proud of it but I just preferred to be called Sal because I preferred not to be judged by the ignorant.

'Walikum-Aslam,' I said. 'I just wanted to thank you for your help and co-operation yesterday,' I said.

'Do you find out who killed the brother?' he asked.

'The investigation is ongoing,' I said. 'Which is why I'm calling. We would like to carry out another search of the premises today.'

'The masjid?'

'Yes. The masjid.'

'For what reason, if I may be so bold?'

'We are still concerned that the murder weapon might be located within the mosque.'

'You searched yesterday, did you not?'

'We did. But they want to check more thoroughly.'

There was a long pause. 'Thoroughly?' he said eventually and evenly. 'Would you care to elaborate?'

'The search would be in more obscure places,' I cleared my throat. The Imam was not going to like this, I was banking on it. 'They want to bring in sniffer dogs.'

'No dogs,' said the Imam sharply. I sighed, 'Mohammed, you are aware that dogs are unclean and cannot be allowed inside the masjid. Did Gabriel himself not tell the prophet that angels do not enter a home in which there is a dog?'

'I understand,' I said and sighed and hesitated. 'Look, Imam, I'll tell them that you are not allowing dogs into the mosque and that they must carry out the search without them. Would that be all right?'

'Very well,' he said.

'Again, I apologise for the inconvenience.' I thanked him and ended the call then gave myself a pat on the back for pulling a fast one on the esteemed Imam. Using sniffer dogs was never an option, but by playing on the Imam's vanity and letting him think that he'd got his way, I had got him to agree to a second search.

Chapter 15
(Harry)

I logged onto HOLMES and began flicking through the statements taken at the mosque. They all followed the same format. The name of the person being identified, the identification number of the person issued by the system, along with their date of birth and their address. Then a brief statement saying when they had arrived at the mosque, where in the prayer hall they had been, and whether or not they had seen anything out of the ordinary. They were also asked whether they knew the victim. Finally, they were asked for a list of anyone else they saw at the mosque that day who had left before the police had arrived. Hopefully we would eventually be able to identify everyone who had been there. I went through a dozen statements and they all denied knowing Sean Evans and they had only realised that something was wrong when the Imam had discovered the body. It was only to be expected, if anyone had seen the murder they would have sounded the alarm.

I still didn't quite understand how a man could be stabbed to death surrounded by hundreds of people without anyone seeing anything. I suppose it was possible that he had been stabbed elsewhere and then made his way to the prayer room to die but that would depend on the type of wound and how quickly he bled out. Hopefully the post mortem would answer that question.

I did a search for Ayesha Khan but she wasn't in the system. I frowned. That couldn't be right. I checked the spelling and tried again but still nothing. All the statements had been indexed and everyone had been issued with an identifier number. How was she not in the system?

Alan Russell was back at his terminal. As Outside Enquiry Manager he was ultimately responsible for making sure that everyone at the mosque was interviewed. I didn't want to shout across the room so I went over and dropped down on the seat next to him. 'I don't see Ayesha Khan among the mosque interviews,' I said.

'Remind me again who she is?' he said.

'She was the woman who helped control the worshippers when we first got there. They were ready to bolt but she calmed them down. Asian woman, red scarf, blue sweater.'

Russell scratched his neck. 'I don't remember seeing her.' He reached for his phone. 'Let me call Alison Dyke, she was collating the female interviews.' He made a call and gave Dyke the name and description. He listened, then held out the phone to me. 'Might be better to talk to her yourself,' he said.

I took the phone. Alison Dyke was a DC who had been working murder investigations for more than five years. She was a good copper, one of the lads. 'Guv, I don't remember an Ayesha Khan,' she said. 'There were only twenty or so women to be interviewed at the mosque and I don't remember one by that name.'

'She's not in HOLMES. Which means she wasn't even mentioned. But I'm not imagining her. She was small, dark skin, she had a blue pullover, jeans and a red scarf.'

'Doesn't ring a bell, Guv. Sorry.'

'No problem, she must have slipped away.' I ended the call and gave the phone back to Russell.

'Problem?' he asked.

'I don't think so,' I said. 'It's no biggie, I know where she works.'

Nasri walked over, holding the Book 194 and twirling his car keys. 'Ready when you are, Guv,' he said.

'Did you smooth things over with the Imam?'

'All good, Guv. And I checked the electoral rolls for Mohammed Masood. There are a dozen or so in Greater London but none matches our victim.'

'That's a pity,' I said. We went outside and got into the car. It took just over half an hour to drive to Westminster Public Mortuary in Horseferry Road, not far from Lambeth Bridge. The mortuary is the biggest in the country and can handle just over a hundred dead bodies at a time, but I was only interested in one, the guy who had been stabbed in the mosque. The Iain West Forensic Suite cost almost a million quid and is state of the art. It even has a CCTV set up so that cops can watch the bodies being cut up without suffering the smell. The first thing you notice and the last thing you forget about mortuaries – the stench of death.

'So who's this Iain West character?' asked Nasri as we walked into the building.

'Before your time,' I said. 'He died back in 2001. He was a living legend, cut up all the rich and famous. He did Robert Maxwell, Jill Dando, Yvonne Fletcher, all the famous ones.'

'Sorry, Guv, none of those names mean anything to me.'

'Well if nothing else the last one should,' I said. 'WPC Yvonne Joyce Fletcher was shot and killed outside the Libyan Embassy in St. James's Square in April 1984.'

'Guv, I was a twinkle in my mother's eye in 1984.'

'That's not the point. She was one of ours. She deserves to be remembered.'

Nasri nodded. 'Point taken, Guv.'

The post mortem on Sean Evans had been carried out by Lucy Wakeham, a plain-speaking Geordie with dyed blonde hair cropped short. It was so short that I wondered why she bothered with the dye job but I never mentioned it because, well, sexual harassment. I checked in at reception and a bored security guard phoned through to say I was there. Five minutes later she burst through a set of double doors wearing surgical scrubs and a hairnet, a mask loose around her neck.

'Good to see you, again, Harry,' she said. 'Another partner I see? You can't keep them, can you?'

'Louise is on maternity leave.' I nodded at Nasri. 'This is DC Mohammed Nasri,' I said.

Nasri grinned at her. 'They call me, Sal,' he said, and held out his hand. Then he saw the blood-spattered glove and he pulled his hand back. 'Sorry.'

'I've just finished sewing Mr Evans up,' she said, by way of explanation. 'Come on through.'

She pushed through the set of double doors and we followed her. Mr Evans was naked and lying on a metal tray with grooves so that any blood could drain away. I knew from experience that pathologists have their favourite ways of opening up a body. The most common is the Y-shaped incision where deep cuts are made at the top of each shoulder and running down the front of the chest to the sternum. Quite a few prefer to make it a T, moving horizontally across from the collar bones and then down through the sternum.

I knew one pathologist who made a point of doing only one cut from the throat and straight down the chest. His post mortems always seemed a bit messy to me. And once I saw a guy, Scottish he was, I think, do a U-shaped cut straight down from the shoulders, down the chest to the bottom of the rib cage. He said he did it that way because the deceased was a woman with very large breasts but I'm not sure if he was winding me up or not. Pathologists do have a bloody strange sense of humour at times, I guess because they spend so much time with dead bodies.

Lucy is a traditional cutter and she had done a first class job of stitching up the Y. 'So, Mr Evans is a 24-year-old male, with excellent teeth,' she said. 'No fillings, and he'd never worn braces.'

Nasri raised his hand as if he was at school and Lucy smiled at him. 'You don't have to put your hand up, Sal. Just spit it out.'

'What told you he was 24? Just wondering.'

She smiled. 'His driving licence, Sal.'

Nasri looked uncomfortable so I didn't say anything, but I winked at Lucy.

'Mr Evans was in excellent health, notwithstanding the fact that he is obviously dead. He was killed by a single stab wound to the heart. The blade of the knife was long and thin, and at least four inches long. I've put the dimensions in the file. The blade went in between the third and fourth rib and into the upper right ventricle. One blow, in and out. It was a neat cut and at rest probably wouldn't have bled much, but each time the heart pumped, blood would leak from the ventricle. If he wasn't exerting himself he could have taken several minutes to bleed out.'

'So whoever killed him knew what they were doing?' asked Nasri.

'In what way?' asked Lucy. 'You don't have to have a medical degree to realise that stabbing someone in the heart is a good way of killing them.'

'I mean that it's not easy to stab someone in the heart,' said Nasri. 'Not with a single blow. You have to know where it is, for a start, then you have to know how to get the knife between the ribs, and keep it moving in the right direction. Most killers who use knives use them again and again, up to half a dozen blows in the hope that one will hit the mark. Same if they go for the kidneys. Multiple stabs are usually what they go for. You have to have a lot of confidence to just stab once.'

Lucy nodded. 'I see what you mean. I suppose he could have been lucky with the first stab.'

'Yes, but then if he hadn't expected to kill with the first blow he would have carried on, wouldn't he? That suggests he knew what he was doing. He was confident. He knew that one stab was enough.'

Lucy looked over at me. 'He's got a point.'

'It could have been an accident,' I said. 'The killer has the knife, jabs at Evans to get him away, accidentally stabs the heart.'

'I don't know, Guv,' said Nasri. 'It's hard to get a knife into the heart accidentally.'

'Any defensive wounds?' I asked Lucy. 'Any signs that he put up a fight?'

'Nothing,' said Lucy.

'So either he knew his killer or he was taken by surprise,' Nasri said, which is exactly what I was going to say.

'There are a couple of other interesting things I spotted,' said Lucy. 'Have a look at his tan line.'

They both looked at the body. In the mosque he'd been wearing a long tunic and baggy trousers, so most of his body was covered. Now that it was naked they could see that while face, hands and feet were tanned, the rest of the body had the paleness of uncooked chicken.

'He's been somewhere where the sun was fierce but he was covered up,' said Nasri.

I looked at the feet and spotted the white marks of sandals. 'He was wearing sandals.'

'I'm guessing he wasn't sitting on a beach somewhere,' said Lucy. 'The tan line suggests he spent all the time covered up.'

'What else?' I asked.

'You'll need to help me roll him over,' she said.

I took two gloves from the box on a shelf and put them on, then helped Lucy turn the body onto its front. There were more than two dozen small scars on his back, just above the waist. I bent down to peer at them.

'They look like shrapnel scars,' I said.

She nodded. 'But plastic rather than metal. He was fairly close to something that exploded, but whatever it was it wasn't designed to kill.'

There were cuts over some of the scars. 'You took some out?'

She nodded. 'That's how I know they were plastic. I had them tested and we found traces of explosive.'

'Do you know what type?'

'I'm having it analysed as we speak, but the lab's backed up.'

'So, a bomb? An IED?'

'A practice IED, I'd say.'

I nodded and straightened up. 'So he was somewhere hot and sunny learning how to make IEDs?'

'That's what I'd be thinking,' said Lucy.

'So if he's a jihadist, who stabbed him?' I asked.

'I'm assuming that's rhetorical,' she said, and I suppose it was. But it was a question that needed answering.

CHAPTER 16
(SAL)

Linda and Clive Evans lived in a tidy three-bedroomed semi a couple of hundred yards from Bromley city centre. Clearly, they were house proud, neatly-trimmed rose bushes around a tidy lawn in the middle of which stood a stone bird bath devoid of any bird shit. The windows sparkled and in the middle of the door there was a brass door knocker in the shape of a lion's head that appeared to have been recently polished. A three-year-old shiny Toyota Prius sat in the drive looking as if it was scrubbed behind the ears more often than necessary. What did this all tell me? Not much. Just that they had time on their hands.

'They already know what happened, right, Guv?' I asked as we approached the front door.

He nodded. 'They've had a visit from a Family Liaison Officer,' Porter said. 'But they said they didn't need any support.'

'That's middle class stiff upper lip for you,' I said, and then silently cursed myself.

'You say that like it's a bad thing,' he replied tersely.

I could see he'd taken offence. 'That's not what I meant, Guv.'

'You'd rather they were wailing in the street?'

'Guv, I just meant that they were dealing with their grief in their own way.'

'Everyone does,' he said.

I lifted the weighty brass door-knocker and let it drop heavily just as I noticed the doorbell. The thud reverberated louder than I'd expected, rudely breaking the silence. From the corner of my eye I could see Porter shaking his head. I stared at the door, at the smudge of fingerprints I'd left on the shiny lion's head.

After a moment or so we heard a soft footfall behind the door and it opened slowly. A small, grey-haired man looked out at us. He was in his fifties and wearing steel-framed glasses, a green cardigan with brown leather patches on the elbows and brown corduroy trousers. He looked like my old geography teacher. I showed him my warrant card, he took his time reading it.

'Mr Evans?' I asked to confirm. But, really, just from the hidden grief in his face, it was clear that he was the father of Sean Evans.

He nodded. 'I'm Clive Evans.'

'I'm Detective Constable Nasri,' I said. 'This is my colleague, Detective Inspector Porter. We're here to talk about what happened to your son. Can we come in?'

We stepped into the hall. I crouched down to remove my shoes but Mr Evans waved his hand. 'You can keep your shoes on, son,' he said and just from the mention of that word, I felt emotionally attached. He closed the door and led us along a narrow hallway to a kitchen. 'My wife is in the garden,' he said. Through the kitchen window we could see a woman on her knees clipping roses. 'She spends a lot of time there, since... It keeps her mind occupied.' He nodded at an open book of Sudoku puzzles. 'With me it's numbers.' He smiled ruefully. 'Anything so that you don't have to think about... Would you like a tea or a coffee?'

'Please. Tea thanks,' I said, not because I was desperate for a brew, which I was, but because he'd be more comfortable if he had something to do. He flicked on the kettle and gestured at a pine table. 'Please, sit down. I'll get my wife in.'

'If we can have a chat first, Mr Evans. We're looking for information about Sean, what he was doing in the days and weeks leading up to his death.' I sat down and Porter joined me at the table as Mr Evans placed two matching mugs on the worktop. I wasn't sure why Porter was letting me take the lead, he hadn't said anything to that effect on the drive south.

'I'm not sure I'll be much help there,' said Mr Evans. 'Sean moved out and we just didn't see much of him.'

'Where was he living, do you know?' I asked.

'Kilburn,' He opened the fridge and took out a carton of milk.

'On his own?'

Mr Evans shrugged. 'I really don't know. I don't think he ever said and we never asked. We didn't like to pry.'

'When did he move out?'

'Oh, it would be around four years ago, but really it felt longer. He stayed away at university before that. My wife always kept his bedroom for him but a couple of years ago she finally realised he wouldn't be moving back in and she turned his bedroom into a sewing room.'

'And when did you last see Sean?'

'It'll be two weeks tomorrow,' said Mr Evans. 'He came for Sunday lunch.'

'And he was using the name Sean?' asked Porter. His first question since we'd entered the house.

'How do you mean?' asked Mr Evans, frowning. 'Why would he not use his name?'

'Did his appearance seem different, Mr Evans?' asked Porter.

'A little unkempt, perhaps,' Mr Evans replied. 'He wore a beard. Why would you ask about his name?'

'He had been using the name Mohammed Masood,' said Porter.

Mr Evans laughed harshly. 'Nonsense.'

'He didn't ask you to call him Mohammed?' asked Porter.

Mr Evans looked over at me. 'What's he talking about?'

I opened my mouth to speak but Porter lifted his index finger off the pine table, a small gesture, but one that spoke volumes. Porter was taking over.

'We were under the assumption that he was at the mosque to worship,' said Porter.

'Mosque? Sean is a Catholic.' Mr Evans' smile didn't match his tone.

'But the beard,' said Porter. 'Didn't you think the beard was strange?'

The kitchen door rattled and Mrs Evans pushed it open. Like her husband she was grey and wearing glasses, but she was almost twice his weight. She was wearing a thick quilted jacket over a blue denim dress and had protective pads on her knees. She slipped off her gardening gloves and squinted at Porter and me.

'They're detectives, dear,' said Mr Evans. His face had turned traffic light red, most likely due to Porter's revelation that their Catholic son could possibly be a Muslim convert.

'Have you found out anything?' Mrs Evans asked, facing us.

'We're very sorry for your loss, Mrs Evans,' I said. 'Nothing of note as yet. We are still exploring all avenues.'

She nodded but there was a faraway look in her eyes as if she hadn't registered what I had said. She closed the door and placed the gloves on a shelf before going over to the sink to wash her hands.

'They were saying that Sean had … had … become a *Muslim*,' said Mr Evans.

'A Muslim?' Mrs Evans frowned. 'I'm afraid I don't follow.'

'The beard,' Porter said. 'He'd grown a beard, hadn't he?'

The beard, Porter kept on about the beard as though that was the convert criteria. It was clear that Mr and Mrs Evans had not been told that Sean was in a mosque when he died.

'Guv,' I said, but he ignored me.

'Lots of young men have beards these days,' said Mr Evans. He nodded at his wife. 'What do they call them?'

'Hipsters,' said Mrs Evans. She shrugged. 'I actually thought he suited a beard. My father had a beard. I always remember the way it scratched my cheek when he kissed me good night.'

'But Sean had converted to Islam, hadn't he?' Porter asked.

'Guv,' I said, but again he ignored me.

Mr Evans narrowed his eyes. 'Why do you say that? Because he had a beard?'

Porter tried to hide his confusion but made a pretty poor job of it. 'He died in a mosque, Mr Evans. And he was wearing Islamic clothing. Weren't you told?'

'The officers said he was stabbed in Maida Vale, they didn't say anything about a mosque,' said

Mr Evans. He looked at his wife. 'They didn't, did they?'

She shook her head. 'They didn't say anything about a mosque. Definitely.'

'He was in the prayer room,' Porter said. 'Praying.'

'That doesn't make any sense,' she said. 'We're Catholics. Sean was baptised.'

'When did you last see him?'

'I told you, the Sunday before last,' said Mr Evans. 'He came for Sunday lunch.'

'Did you go to church?' asked Porter.

Mr Evans shook his head. 'We don't go that often, truth be told,' he said. 'Christmas, of course. And Easter. But not every Sunday.'

I could see Mrs Evans nervously wringing her hands. The last thing we needed was for them to get on the defensive so I interjected. 'So. Sunday lunch? I suppose he missed your cooking.'

Mrs Evans dropped her hands to her side and took a seat at the table. 'That's what he said.' She smiled. 'He said he missed my cooking, but we hadn't seen him for, maybe, three months?' She looked over at her husband and he nodded.

'What did you prepare for lunch?' I asked.

Porter looked over at me, annoyed that I'd hijacked his questioning, but when she answered he realised that I was ahead of him. 'His favourite,' said Mrs Evans. 'Roast pork, with crackling and apple sauce.'

'He's always loved his crackling,' said Mr Evans.

'Washed down with red or white?' I asked.

Mrs Evans smiled at the memory. 'We could never agree on that. I always say red for meat and white for fish but Sean liked white with his pork.'

Mr Evans nodded in agreement. 'Me too,' he said.

I looked over at Porter and could see that he was thinking the same as me. It made no sense that a converted Muslin was tucking into pork and knocking back wine with his parents. I nodded and Porter took back the lead.

'Did Sean have any enemies? Any problems that he was worried about?'

Mr Evans shook his head. 'He was happy. Happier than I've seen him for a while.'

'Did he have a job?' asked Porter.

Mr Evans nodded. 'He was working for a minicab firm.'

'Uber?' Porter asked.

'No, a regular taxi company. In Kilburn, I think.'

'Waste of a good university education,' said Mrs Evans.

'Sean was a graduate?'

'He got a 2-1 at Reading University,' said Mrs Evans. 'Economics. We always assumed he would go into the City. I never thought he'd end up driving a taxi.'

'Was he looking for another job?' Porter asked.

'He seemed happy driving a taxi,' said Mr Evans.

'How could he be happy, doing a job like that?' snapped his wife. 'He could have done so much more with his life.' She sighed and shook her head. 'I just wish he had more get up and go.' She sighed again. 'And now it's too late.'

Mr Evans moved behind his wife. He tried to put his arms around her but she shook him off. 'I don't need a hug, I just want my son back,' she said quietly. She sat down and put her head in her hands.

Porter stood up. I followed suit. 'We'll perhaps come back some other time,' Porter said. 'And again, we are very sorry for your loss.'

Mr Evans sat down opposite his wife and reached out for her hand. This time she didn't reject the physical contact as tears fell from her eyes.

'We'll see ourselves out,' I said. 'Thank you for your time.'

Mr Evans forced a smile but his eyes were brimming with tears. We left them to mourn in peace.

'What made you think of asking about her cooking?' Porter asked as we stepped out of their house.

'Just a hunch,' I said. 'I noticed some decent wines in the rack on the counter.'

'What do you think it means?' he asked.

'A Muslim who eats pork and drinks alcohol?' I shrugged. 'It's not unknown. Guv,' I said. 'Plenty of Christians convert their neighbours.'

'What does that mean?' Porter said.

'It means that not all Christians follow the Ten Commandments, right? There are plenty of Christian thieves and murderers. Similarly not all Muslims slavishly follow the five pillars of Islam.'

'Pillars?'

We reached the car and I unlocked it. 'All good Muslims are supposed to practise all five pillars. The first is Shahada. Faith. You have to believe that there is only one God, Allah, and that Muhammad is his messenger. Then there's Salat. Prayer. You have to pray five times a day.'

'And you do that?'

'I do what I can, Guv,' I said. 'Then there's Zakat. Charity. You have to give a percentage of your wealth to the needy. That's an easy one. Then there's fasting, going without food and water during Ramadan. That one is a little tricky, obviously. Especially in the summer. And the final one is Hajj, where you make a pilgrimage to Mecca.'

'I didn't hear anything about pork or alcohol in that list,' he said.

'That's covered in the Koran,' I said. He climbed into the driving seat. I got in next to him. 'A lot of Muslim ways are in the Koran which means they can be open to interpretation,' he said. 'But pork and booze is pretty much verboten to most Muslims.'

'But is it possible that Sean Evans could have been a Muslim who enjoyed pork and a crisp Cabernet Sauvignon?'

I started the engine. 'Unlikely, Guv. Don't get me wrong, there are Muslims that drink alcohol and even eat pork, but Evans was wearing full Islamic gear when he died, skullcap and all. Seemed devout, right? Pork and wine don't add up, Guv.'

'What about you? Do you drink?'

'Alcohol? No, Guv.'

'Never?'

I chuckled. 'Yeah, you know. Tried it when I was a kid. Not for me, Guv. Don't like not being in control.' I tapped my head. 'Know what I mean?'

'And pork? Ever eaten bacon?'

I shook my head. 'No, come on. Never.'

'Because you don't think God wants you to?'

'It's in the Koran, Guv.'

'And because it's in a book, you won't eat bacon? Sal, you don't know what you're missing. So, what do you think we do next, victim-wise?'

Porter was testing me, obviously. It's fine. I knew the answer.

'Grab a shovel and keep digging, Guv,' I said. 'He didn't seem particularly close to his parents, not anymore anyway, so doubt they would know if Sean had any friction. So, we speak to his cab firm and the other drivers, find out who he's been knocking about with.

'Sounds like a plan. Can't be too many minicab firms in Kilburn.'

'Think we should look at his university background, too, Guv?'

'His university?'

'Maybe he started life at university as Sean Evans and left as Mohammed Masood. It's worth a shot, Guv. Possibly track down his tutor, could be that someone noticed a change in his appearance, his behaviour.'

Porter nodded. Course he nodded, I was right. We needed to step in his shoes and look back in time and find out when and what sparked the change. We suss that out, we'll be a little closer to a motive for his murder and a little closer to identifying his killer.

'Yes to both,' Porter said. He glanced at his watch. It was just after two. 'Let's do a bit of a detour, Sal. I want to swing by the Citizens Advice Bureau in Harrow Road.'

'Got a problem you need help with, Guv?' I asked, though I knew right away what he was up to. It was where Ayesha Khan worked and I knew he was interested in her. It made no sense for the Senior Investigating Officer to be interviewing a witness, especially a female one.

'Very funny,' said Porter. 'I need to talk to Ayesha Khan. Remember, the woman who helped us at the mosque?'

Remember? Yeah I remember. I remember the way she'd twisted Porter around her little finger. 'Yes, Guv. You don't think we should send a female officer?'

He looked across at me, clearly not happy with my suggestion. 'She seemed perfectly at ease talking to male officers at the mosque,' he said.

'Right, Guv,' I said, knowing there was no point in pressing the issue. He was SIO and I was the bag carrier so in the grand scheme of things my opinion carried no weight.

I used to work the Harrow Road area and I knew the Citizens Advice Bureau. I'd been in a couple of times for the odd skirmish and their offices were always bustling. Most of the residents of the area were immigrants or asylum seekers or on benefits, or all of the above and there was a stream of people going through the doors needing help with their benefit paperwork or asylum applications.

I found a parking space close to the office and walked with Porter, threading our way through the crowded pavements. It was a short walk but I heard four different languages spoken, saw three women wearing the full burkhas, two Jamaicans with waist-length dreadlocks, and a group of men in turbans standing around a motorbike. Par for the course in the multicultural melting pot that was the Harrow Road. Porter was the only white guy in the vicinity. I wondered if he felt a little of what I go through.

The Citizens Advice Bureau was between a charity shop and a bookmakers, the windows plastered with posters offering advice and contact numbers on a range of subjects – benefits, housing, debt and fraud among the most prevalent. I pushed open the door. There was a buzz of conversation with people sitting at tables being helped by half a dozen advisers, two were black, four were Asian. Ayesha Khan was one of them.

She was sitting at the table to the far right of the room, running through a printed form with an elderly Asian couple. She was talking to them in Urdu, then filling out the form for them in English. They looked as if they hadn't been long in the country and from the time she was having to take to explain things to them, I figured they spoke next to no English themselves.

She was wearing a dark blue headscarf, a light blue polo neck pullover and jeans. She had more make up on than she'd had at the mosque, pale pink lipstick and mascara. She looked up and caught me looking at her, for a fraction of a second her eyes hardened but then she clocked Porter and smiled. I turned to see Porter smiling goofily back at her. She gestured for us to wait while she finished with the elderly couple.

I walked over to the water cooler and by the time I had filled two cups, Ayesha had finished and Porter was already approaching her desk. I quickly joined him and we sat down. He looked at me as though he had just realised that I was there.

'Hello, Inspector Porter,' Ayesha said, through the widest of smiles. 'How is the case progressing?'

'It's early days, Miss Khan,' Porter smiled. 'We're just getting all our ducks in a row.' Ayesha nodded and it took a second for Porter to continue. He cleared his throat. 'Can I ask, were you interviewed by the police at the mosque yesterday?'

'You mean you don't remember, Inspector Porter?'

Porter frowned. 'Excuse me?'

'*You* interviewed me. *You* asked me for my name and I told you where I worked. Which is presumably why you're here.'

'That wasn't an interview, Ms Khan.'

'Well, actually, it was.'

'Not an official interview. You were supposed to have been interviewed at length by a detective.'

She bit down on her lower lip, giving her the look of a schoolgirl who'd been accused of handing in her homework late. I got the distinct feeling that she was playing Porter and it was clear from the look on Porter's face that it was working. 'I'm so sorry,' she said. 'I misunderstood.'

'It's okay, not a problem,' said Porter hurriedly.

It *was* a problem. A big problem. Everyone at the mosque was supposed to be interviewed and searched and somehow she had slipped through the net. What made it worse was that Porter had spoken to her at the mosque, so he couldn't claim not to have known she was there. As SIO it was his responsibility to make sure that everyone there was questioned and clearly he hadn't done that. Strictly speaking that should be written up in the Decision Log and if it was it would be sure to be picked up on by any senior officer reviewing the case.

'But you're going to have to be interviewed,' continued Porter.

'Absolutely,' she waved at the chairs full of people waiting to be helped. 'Though, as you can see, we're snowed under at the moment. Can we possibly do it some other time?' She flashed him a little-girl-lost smile. How could Porter not see through her? It was obvious she was playing him.

Without taking his eyes off her, Porter took out his wallet and slipped out a business card. He slid it across the table in front of her. 'Give me a call when it's quieter and we'll arrange something,' he said, in a voice I did not recognise. Ayesha reached across the table, her fingers brushed his as she picked up the card. She took her own business card from a stack on her desk and handed it to Porter.

'Or maybe you can call me?' she said, eyes fixed on him and nothing else.

What is going on here?

I felt very uncomfortable at that moment, as though I'd just caught my father flirting with the neighbour's hot daughter over the garden fence. I pursed my lips but I kept quiet. It wasn't my place to query the decisions of a senior officer, just to record them in the Decision Log – but I could see that he was bang out of order. There was only one reason he was being so soft on her and that was because she was a pretty girl who kept batting her Bambi eyelashes at him. If she'd been a middle-aged man with a pot-belly and a wart on his nose, Porter would have had him down the station faster than his feet could touch the ground. Put simply, Ayesha had left the mosque without being searched and interviewed, which compromised the whole case.

Porter looked over at me and smiled. 'Best we get back,' he said.

'Right, Guv.' I said, not returning the smile.

Porter gave Ayesha a last look and a Clint Eastwood nod.

Chapter 17
(Harry)

As soon as we got back to Peel House I went along to The Sheriff's office. He looked up from his terminal and flashed me a tight smile. 'How's it going, Harry?'

'Slowly, Guv,' I said. 'You wanted me to bring you up to speed on the victim.'

'Still dead, right?' he said and I smiled at his attempt at humour.

'Very much so, Guv. The thing is, from the post mortem it looks as if he has been through some terrorism training. Scars on his back that looked like he might have gotten too close to an IED at some point.'

The Superintendent sat back in his chair. 'So we're talking home-grown jihadist?'

'Possibly. He's not known to SO15, but there are plenty of them below the radar. I'll check with MI5. There is something that's a bit weird. We went to see the victim's parents and they weren't even aware that he'd become a Muslim.'

SO15 – the Counter Terrorism Command – was tasked with handling terrorism investigations. It was set up in 2006 when the Anti-terrorist Branch (SO13) and the Special Branch (SO12) were merged. Now it had a staff of more than 1,500 but was still struggling to cope with its workload.

'What, he was ashamed? Wanted to hide it from them?'

'He had roast pork with them. And wine.'

He frowned and rubbed his chin. 'Did he now? That doesn't make sense, does it?'

'It might if someone found out that he was having second thoughts.'

'About his choice of religion?'

'About all the choices he'd made. If he was having second thoughts about being a Muslim he'd be unlikely to continue as a jihadist.'

'So another jihadist might have killed him, is that where you're going with this?'

'It's a possibility. We're still putting together a list of everyone who was at the mosque and we're running all those names through SO15. We've had a dozen matches so far and we'll do more intensive interviews with them at some point.'

'And still no sign of the murder weapon?'

'Afraid not.'

'Is it worth another search?'

'It's in hand. We're starting to search around the building, too.'

'We need the murder weapon, Harry.'

I tried not to get upset at his attempt to teach me to suck eggs. 'I know, I know. My first thought was that the killer hid it in the mosque but now I'm starting to think he took it with him. It's probably long gone and if it isn't I don't see that we are going to get search warrants for several hundred homes.'

'No, but there'd be probable cause for anyone on SO15's watch lists,' said the Superintendent. 'We are sure he was stabbed where he died?'

'The body wasn't carried in to the mosque, if that's what you mean,' I said. 'Somebody would have seen it, the prayer hall was packed. But he could have walked in under his own steam. There was one stab wound which nicked the heart, so he would have bled out slowly. That means he could have been stabbed anywhere in the mosque, maybe even outside.'

He raised his eyebrows. 'You think he walked in and then died?'

'It's possible.'

'What about a blood trail?'

'There wouldn't have been much blood externally, not initially. And what little there was would have soaked into his clothing. Plus the worshippers cleaned up a fair bit before we got there.'

'CCTV?'

'There are cameras in some areas of the mosque but they are mainly for security against break-ins and vandalism rather than keeping an eye on the congregation, but Alan Russell is getting the footage checked.'

'Sounds like you've got all the bases covered,' said Sherwood. He'd done his own base-covering, too. He'd be able to note in his diary everything he'd told me to do, so that if it did turn to shit down the line it would be raining down on my head.

My phone started to ring. 'I'll take this outside,' I said, pulling the phone from my pocket. Sherwood waved me away and went back to studying his terminal. I didn't recognise the number but I took the call anyway. 'Inspector Porter?' It was a woman.

'Yes?'

'It's Ayesha Khan.'

I couldn't help smiling and I wasn't sure why that was. It was crazy but I was just happy to hear her voice. 'Yes Miss Khan, how can I help?'

'You said to call you to arrange a follow up interview. I'll be finishing work at six, I wondered if we could do the interview near where I work.'

'That should be okay. I'll send a female officer.'

'To be honest, I'd prefer to talk to you,' she said. 'I feel we have a connection and I know I can trust you.' She chuckled. 'Don't worry, I won't bite.'

She had a nice laugh. I think it was the first time I'd heard it. 'I wasn't worried,' I said. 'I just thought that under the circumstances you might prefer to be interviewed by a female officer.'

She laughed again and this time I felt a tingle in my stomach. 'The circumstances being that I'm a Muslim woman?'

I struggled to find the words to explain what I'd meant, but yes, she had pretty much nailed it.

'I'm fine talking to a police officer such as yourself,' she said. 'If you come to the office at six, that would be fine.'

'I'll see you there,' I said. She ended the call. My heart was beating fast, I realised. And my cheeks were flushed. I looked at my watch. It was almost five. I planned on taking my own car and driving home afterwards so I'd have to leave soon as I'd be hitting rush hour traffic.

I went back to the MIR. Nasri was standing by a typist who was inputting pages from the Decision Log into HOLMES. I was going to tell him where I was going, but as he looked up I had second thoughts. I had seen the disapproving way he'd looked at me when I was talking to Ayesha in the Citizens Advice Bureau. I didn't say anything at the time, but it was clear from the look on his face he resented the fact that she was talking to me and that I gave her my card. I don't know, it feels as if he thinks he should be doing all the interacting with Asians and that I should stick to my own people, and if that's not racism then I don't know what is. Or it might be that he fancied her. She was pretty and smart and had a confidence about her that anyone would have found attractive. I didn't know anything about Nasri's personal situation but I wouldn't have been surprised if he wanted her for himself and was jealous of the attention she was paying me. 'Yes, Guv, do you need something?' he asked.

'Nah, I'm heading off early,' I said and he nodded and went back to looking at his screen.

I headed downstairs and got into my car. The traffic was as bad as I'd anticipated and I arrived in Harrow Road a few minutes before six. Ayesha was standing outside the Citizens Advice Bureau wearing a beige raincoat with her designer bag over one shoulder. I remembered the bag from the mosque. She smiled when she saw me and waved. I walked up. I wasn't sure how I should greet her but she solved the problem by holding out her hand. We shook. A metal shutter had been pulled down over the window. 'I thought we were meeting in your office?' I said.

'We close at six. Have you eaten?'

I frowned, not sure what she meant. 'Have I eaten?' I repeated.

'Food? Dinner? Evening meal. Have you had dinner yet?'

'Err, no,' I said, embarrassed by my confusion. It had been a simple enough question, why had I fumbled with an answer?

'Neither have I, so why don't we do the interview while we're eating. There's a really good curry house around the corner and I'm starving, I had to work through lunch.'

'Sure,' I said. Part of me knew that interviewing a witness was a formal process and it wasn't something to be done over dinner, but I hadn't eaten since breakfast and like coppers the world over I did like a curry.

She smiled and led me along the pavement. 'How's the investigation progressing?' she asked.

'Slowly,' I said.

'So there's no suspect? No clues?'

I laughed. 'It's not like it is on television, I'm afraid. Murder investigations usually go one of two ways. We know immediately who did it and we arrest them straight away. Or we don't know who did it in which case we launch a major inquiry and that takes time and manpower.'

'You've investigated a lot of murders?'

I shrugged. 'A few dozen, over the years.'

'And do you always solve them?'

I shook my head. 'Again, it's not like the television where every case is tied up before a commercial break. Sometimes a case never gets solved. Or sometimes it goes cold and years later new evidence comes to light or the killer slips up and tells someone. Murder isn't always cut and dried.'

She flashed me what I assumed was a sympathetic smile. 'So you might never solve this one?'

'I hope we do. But you never know. The fact that we haven't found the murder weapon is a big worry.'

'Why?'

'Because there's a good chance there'll be forensic evidence on it. But more importantly, the fact that the knife wasn't there suggests that the killer took it with him. Which means the killer wasn't at the mosque by the time we got there.'

'So that's why you're asking everyone who they saw at the mosque. So that you can find out who had left by the time you got there?'

'Exactly,' I said.

We reached the Indian restaurant and I opened the door for her. As she walked past me I noticed again just how small she was, she couldn't have been much more than five feet tall. The manager was a middle-aged Indian with a bald head and a thick moustache and thick-lensed spectacles. He clearly recognised Ayesha and spoke to her in her own language before taking her coat and ushering her to a corner table. Menus arrived and she asked me how well I knew Indian food.

'I'm a big fan,' I said. 'Most cops are.'

'Why don't you order, then?'

'I'm sure you're a better judge than me,' I said.

'Because I'm Asian?' I wondered if I'd offended her but she laughed before I could answer and I got that tickle in my stomach again. 'Okay, then. I'll order.' She waved the manager over, spoke to him in whatever language it was, then he took the menus. 'I've ordered water, do you want a beer?' she asked.

I'd have loved a Kingfisher or a Cobra but I was working and I was going to be driving home so I told her I'd be happy with water.

The manager headed to the kitchen with our order. 'So the food here is halal, right?' I asked her.

'Here yes, but not all Indian restaurants are. Well we say Indian but almost all the chefs are from

Bangladesh. And the ones here are Muslims so of course the food they handle has to be halal.'

'I don't really understand what halal means.'

She laughed. 'Then I shall enlighten you,' she said. 'Basically halal is an Arabic word that means permissible. It's the opposite of haram, which means forbidden. So pork is absolutely haram. The Koran says we mustn't eat pork, under any circumstances.' She smiled, showing perfect teeth. 'Actually, that's not true, come to think of it. If a Muslim was starving and the only way to save their life was to eat pork, then under those circumstances it would be okay. But so far as halal goes, anything with blood in it is not halal, and alcohol is not halal.'

'But I still don't understand what halal means when it comes to food. It's to do with how the animal is killed, right?'

'It's complicated, Harry. Basically anything we eat has to come from a supplier that uses halal practices. And part of that comes down to how the animal is killed. They have to use a razor-sharp knife to cut the throat as the head is aligned towards Mecca and at the moment the animal is killed it has to be blessed.'

'So it's cruel, right?'

'Not really, usually the animal is stunned first in the same way that it would be in a non-halal abattoir. The only real difference is that the animal is blessed and all the blood is drained from the body. You hear people saying that halal is cruel but really it's no different to what happens in a normal abattoir, it's just the method of killing that's different, Western abattoirs fire a bolt into the skull of the animal, I don't see how that's any more humane.'

Our water arrived and she offered to clink glasses with me, which I thought was cute.

'So you were born here?' I asked.

She looked around the restaurant, her mouth open in mock surprise. 'Here? Why would you think I was born in a restaurant?'

I grinned. 'I meant in England.'

'Why do you ask?'

'Your accent I guess. You sound…' I struggled to find the right word.

'British?' she said helpfully.

'Local,' is what I was going to say. 'You sound like a Londoner.'

'Which is exactly what I am,' she said. 'Yes, I was born here. My parents came here in the summer of 1972, from Uganda. The President back then, Idi Amin, gave all the Asians in Uganda ninety days to get out of the country. Almost thirty thousand came to the UK, and my parents were among them. They arrived with only what they could carry in four suitcases. My mother's jewellery was confiscated at the airport as she left. They took my father's car, his business, their house. Everything. They had to start again, from scratch. But they did it. And they've given me and my brothers and sisters a good life. '

'You're from a big family?'

'You're asking that because I'm Asian?'

I looked at her closely, trying to work out if I'd offended her, but her face broke into a grin. 'I'm only teasing you, Harry. I'm sorry, I really shouldn't. To answer your question, three brothers and two sisters. I'm the youngest. What about you?'

'One brother. We're not close.'

'And your parents?'

'Both dead,' I said.

'I'm sorry.'

'It's okay, they had almost sixty years together, good lives both of them.'

'And are you married, Harry?'

'Divorced.'

'Children?'

'Just one. And we're not close, either.' I shrugged. 'I was working too long and too hard and my wife got fed up. She remarried pretty quickly.'

'And you didn't?'

'I'm married to the job.' I smiled. 'You'd have made a good detective, the way you ask questions.'

She narrowed her eyes. 'Is that a compliment?'

'Of course.'

She reached over and patted me on the hand, just twice. 'I'm sorry if I seem inquisitive, it's just that you interest me.'

Her hand moved back to her side of the table and part of me wished that it would reach out again. 'In what way?'

'You're a policeman doing a job which can't be easy at the best of times and which probably brings you into contact with a lot of not very nice people, but you seem very easy going and relaxed.'

I laughed. 'I'm like a swan,' I said. 'Calm on the surface...'

'...but paddling like crazy under the water,' she finished for me. She laughed. I really was starting to love her laugh and the way she looked me in the eye when she did it. 'Well, if you are under pressure, you do a good job of hiding it.' She sipped her water. 'Worst possible scenario and you don't solve the case, what happens then?'

'After a month they'll bring someone in from outside to review the case, basically to see if we missed something.'

'A fresh pair of eyes?'

'Exactly. Usually someone with extensive experience of murder investigations and if we have missed something, they'll spot it.'

Our food arrived. Ayesha had chosen a Malai Kofta, vegetarian meatballs served with naan bread, a Palek Paneer, spinach and cheese in a curry sauce, and a Rogan Josh, a lamb dish that is always one of my favourites. It was good Indian food but I'd had better. I didn't tell her that though, just complimented her on her choices. We chatted about her family as we ate, and her work at the Citizens Advice Bureau. Advisers worked for free and she was there five days a week, pretty much full time. She had a law degree from the University of London and was a director of several of the property companies her parents ran.

She didn't have to work for her parents for more than a few hours a week and while they weren't happy at the fact that she gave her services for free, she had convinced them that it was what she wanted to do, in the short term at least.

'It sounds like a cliché, but I really do get a kick out of helping people,' she said. 'Especially dealing with bureaucracies and government departments. They tend to treat people very badly, especially immigrants, and I get a kick out of overturning stupid rulings and decisions.'

'David and Goliath?'

'I never thought of myself as a David, but yes, I guess so.'

We finished the meal and a waiter whisked our empty plates and dishes away. I really wanted a beer but I was there on duty and I was driving so drinking was out of question. 'So, we need to go through what you saw that day in the mosque,' I said, and took out my notebook and pen.

'Wow, you really do have police notebooks,' she said. She held out her hand. 'May I?'

I gave her the notepad and she examined the Met crest on the front. Her nails were painted bright red, matching her lipstick. 'I assumed you'd be all high-tech and use digital recorders and such,' she said. She gave me the notepad back.

'We tape all interviews in the station but we still write things down,' I said. 'So, what time did you arrive at the mosque?'

'A little before one.'

'With?'

She frowned. 'I don't understand.'

'Who did you go with?'

She smiled. 'Oh, I see. 'My friend, Yalina. Yalina Wazir. We got the bus and walked the rest of the way.'

'Did you know the victim? Sean Evans?'

She shook her head. 'No.'

'He was also known as Mohammed Masood.'

'I didn't know him.'

'We think he was killed just before prayers started. Where were you at the time?'

'I was in the women's prayer hall. We came over when we heard the commotion.'

'Can you give me the names of the people you were with?'

'Why is that necessary?' she said.

'As we talked about before, we need to know who left and so we need to know the names of everyone who was there initially. It's not as if the Imam takes a roll call. So we're asking everyone who they were with and who they saw. Hopefully by the time we've finished we'll have all the names. So, inside the mosque, where did you go?'

'Just the woman's prayer hall, really.'

'You can go anywhere in the mosque, is that right?'

She nodded. 'Men and women pray separately, but we're not banned from certain areas. As soon as I heard that something was wrong I went through to the prayer hall, which is where I met you and DC Nasri.'

'When we got to the mosque, there were only nine women there. Well, ten including yourself. How many were there for the service?'

'Fifty or sixty, I suppose. Maybe more. I wasn't counting.'

'But a lot of them left before we got there?'

She nodded. 'Sure. That usually happens after the service has finished. The men will often stay and chat but the women have homes to run.'

'And what was your first inkling that there was a problem in the main prayer hall?'

'When I heard the commotion. DC Nasri was trying to get the worshippers to stay.'

I smiled at her. 'And thanks for your help with that.'

She smiled back at me, held my gaze and then lowered her eyes. 'It was a pleasure.' My stomach turned over.

'You really should have stayed until you were interviewed.'

She tilted her head on one side and smiled sweetly at me in a way that made my stomach turn another somersault. 'But if I had stayed, we wouldn't have had this meal, and it has been quite good fun, hasn't it?'

I couldn't help but grin back at her. 'It's been a lot of fun,' I said. I tapped my pen on the notepad. 'So can you give me as many names as you can remember?'

'Of course.'

She gave me twenty-seven names in all, twelve were women. When she had finished, I put the notepad and pen away, then asked for the bill. 'Can I give you a lift anywhere?' I asked.

'I'm okay, I'll call for an Uber,' she said.

The bill arrived and I paid it as she tapped away on her phone. She put on her coat and we walked outside. It was dark now, and chilly. 'Thank you so much for coming all the way out here,' she said.

'It's not a problem,' I said. 'You're on my way home.'

'Really?'

'Well, a bit out of my way, but not much. And you're right, it was fun. I might start doing all my interviewing in Indian restaurants.'

A small blue hatchback came down the road. It slowed and the tinted side window wound down. At first I thought it was her Uber but then a young Asian man with a beard and dark glasses snarled over at us and shouted something. Ayesha flinched as if she'd been slapped. Then the rear window opened and another Asian, this one younger and lighter-skinned, glared at her and shouted something, then spat into the street. The car's engine roared and it sped off down the street.

Ayesha was shaking and without thinking I put my arm around her. 'Are you okay? What was that about?'

She shook her head. 'Nothing.'

'It was obviously something. What did they say?'

'Harry, really. Nothing. They're just kids.'

'No, they were grown men and they had no reason shouting at us like that.'

'It was addressed to me. And I'm a big girl. Please, Harry, let it drop.'

I took my arm away and she smiled up at me. 'Let's just say that some men in our community are less liberal and understanding of cross-cultural relationships than others.' Despite the smile, I could see that she was upset.

'It was because they saw you with a white man?'

'Of course. What else?'

I turned to look down the road but the hatchback had gone. No matter, I'd memorised the number. And despite what Ayesha had said, I wasn't going to let it drop. I thanked her for her help, and as I did her Uber arrived. We shook hands formally, I thanked her again for her help, then I watched her get into the Prius and be driven away.

My radio was in my car and I used it to do a vehicle check on the hatchback. It was owned by a Mr Waseem Chowdhury who lived in Wembley, a couple of miles away. I did a PNC check on Mr Chowdhury and came up with a couple of fines for cannabis possession and three breaches of the peace, involving anti-Israel demonstrations. Part of me wanted to go home, the part that knew that what I wanted to do was a bad idea. A very bad idea. But the other part of me, the Alpha male part, wanted to confront Mr Chowdhury and show him the error of his ways. I drove to Wembley and parked close to his house. It was a small semi and the PNC gave his age as twenty so I figured he lived with his parents.

It was just after midnight when Chowdhury turned up, hip-hop crap blaring out from his stereo. He switched off the engine and I walked over as he climbed out. He was wearing a long-sleeved shirt in a blue paisley pattern and jeans that looked as if they had been sprayed on. His hair was slicked up in a quiff and it glistened under the streetlights. He heard me coming and turned to face me, his lip curled back in a snarl.

'Waseem Chowdhury?' I said.

'Don't say my name like you fucking know me,' he snarled. He was a couple of inches shorter than me, whippet-thin with spindly arms, but he glared at me with no fear, just contempt.

I put my hard face on and glared back at him. I took out my warrant card and flashed it. 'You were screaming abuse in the Harrow Road earlier tonight.'

He grinned. 'What and somebody called thee nines for that? Shouldn't you be out catching fucking criminals?' He stared closely at the warrant card. 'Harry fucking Potter?' he said and he laughed. 'The boy fucking wizard got old, did he?'

'It's Porter, and racial abuse is a criminal offence,' I said, putting my warrant card away.

'Nothing racial about it.' He squinted at me. 'Wait a fucking minute, you were the old geezer walking with the sister.'

'That's right, and if you don't watch your mouth, I'll arrest you for breach of the peace. It won't be the first time, right? You've got a bit of a reputation for screaming and shouting in public.'

He stared up at me, then grinned again. 'You fucking old pervert. You need to keep away from our women, you kafir fucker. Go sniffing around your own dogs, leave our sisters alone.'

'So you admit it,' I said. 'That's good because I can arrest you for that.'

'Go ahead, see if I give a fuck.' He held out his hands and put them together, palms up. 'Go on, cuff me and throw me in the back of your pig mobile, Oh wait, you don't have a cop car, do you? Just a piece of shit Volvo. So maybe you're not here officially.'

'Officially or not, that doesn't matter,' I said. I still had my game face on but it clearly wasn't working. The little shit didn't care what I said. He was totally unfazed and totally without fear. 'When you got out of your vehicle I could smell cannabis.'

'Yeah, well you're not in uniform so you can go fuck yourself.'

'Possession is still an offence.'

'Yeah, and so is racially abusing a Muslim.'

'What the hell are you talking about?'

'You've been calling me a fucking Muslim for the last five minutes, telling me that all fucking Muslims are the same and that I should go back to my own country.'

'I did no such thing.'

He held out his arms and looked around theatrically. 'I don't see any witnesses. Which means it'll be my word against yours. And no matter how it turns out it'll stay on your work record and you know how the cops don't like promoting racists.'

'You are insane.'

'Not as crazy as you, Pig. Coming to my house. Threatening me. You think I can't find out where you live, little piggy?' He leaned towards me, his eyes burning with hatred. 'You want me to creep up on you one night with half a dozen of the brothers? Is that what you want, little piggy?'

I stared back at him, lost for words. There was no fear in his eyes, none at all, and there was no doubt he meant what he said. Which meant one of two things – I had to up the ante or walk away. And upping the ante meant either arresting him or getting physical. If I arrested him, he was right, no one would give a toss about a small amount of cannabis. And if he did make allegations of racial abuse they might not stick but they would be investigated and they'd stay on my file. Getting physical was what the Alpha Male part of me wanted to do, but that wouldn't end well. He was younger than me but I was bigger and stronger but even if I did knock him around, what then? If he called the police then there was a good chance my career would be over for good. It wasn't like the old days when a cop could get physical and be backed up by his colleagues. If I were to lay a hand on him Professional Standards would be on the case quicker than you could say 'assault and battery'.

'What's it going to be, little piggy?' he said, and prodded me in the chest. 'You want to go to war with The Faith?'

The Faith? The heavy mob from the mosque? Had he been one of the men who'd turned up with knives and machetes? I held up my hands and took a step back. He grinned in triumph. 'Yeah, I thought so. Fuck off, then!'

I turned and walked back to my car, his jeers and catcalls ringing in my ears. I climbed in and drove off. I knew that I'd made a big mistake, but what was done was done and there was no going back.

CHAPTER 18
(SAL)

Different night, different table, different opposition. The same game. A touch past midnight and a hundred up. Well, a hundred pounds more in front of me than when I'd walked in, but not enough to make a dent in the money that I owed.

I was sitting on a plastic chair around a foldaway plastic table in a room at the back of a dry cleaning shop in Wembley. It wasn't a Chottopadhyay table, there was no way he'd let me participate until my debt was cleared, so I had to play elsewhere. It wasn't a problem, the gambler in me knew a handful of illegal tables dotted around London, and the gambler in me also knew that it wouldn't be long before my pockets were lined with gold.

There were four at the table, three were new to me and the other was Domonika, a Russian woman who I'd come across a few times over the past year and knew that she had an aggressive game. Her father, Serge, a black-suited menace of a man, ran the game. He was sitting on a stool, a heavy arm on the makeshift bar, watching us all. An old scar ran from just above his cheek bone and out above his dark impenetrable sunglasses.

It was Popov who'd introduced me to the dry cleaner game but he rarely came, I think he'd had a falling out with Serge at some point.

I focused on the three cards laid out on the table. Seven of clubs, ten of diamonds, queen of spades. In my hand, the ten of clubs and the jack of clubs. First impressions, I had the second best pair, two tens. As it stood, anyone with Her Majesty would have the upper hand but I had the possibility of a straight or a high flush.

The dealer, a tough old woman with a leathery face, grey hair tied neatly in a bun and bright lipstick over and beyond her lips. Her name was Betty and she was the regular dealer at this table.

She flipped over the turn and all eyes fell on the eight of clubs.

I focused on my cards as though desperately searching for a combination, but the combination was screaming out at me. I was one card away from a straight and I was one card away from a flush.

I'd folded early the last four games, betting heavy now would give my hand away, and really, I was only sitting on two tens, at least until the last card was turned. The minimum blind was fifty quid, so I fed the pot a fifty chip, making the total on the table £250.

To my right, Trevor, I think his name was, sighed heavily. 'Not for me.' He placed his cards face down on the table and folded. Next to him and opposite me, Domonika dropped a hundred onto the table confidently and without hesitation, raising the blind by fifty. The way she did it sent alarm bells ringing. She wasn't one to bluff so I was certain she was holding the queen.

Trilby-wearing Samuel smiled ruefully at her. 'Why'd you have to do that? You're taking the fun out of it.'

'You want fun. You come see me afterwards.' Domonika smiled sweetly at Samuel as he folded. She turned her attention to me. I tried to muster up similar confidence but if she had the queen then I was relying heavily on the last card. I matched her fifty and then raised another fifty just to wipe the smile off her face.

Trust me, Domonika was a dirty player, only just staying within the rules. She liked to talk and goad, her heavily thick Russian accent delivered profanities as though literal threats.

'I will fuck you up, Sal, until you learn to love me,' she said, dropping another fifty onto the table. I didn't quite know what that meant, but I noticed uncertainty in her eyes.

The pot was now worth £500. One card had yet to be turned. The river.

Serge leant forward onto his stool to watch the game unfold. Samuel and Trevor looked relieved to be out of it. Betty looked to us both and slowly her hand reached out to the final card. A nine for a straight or a club for a flush, I could see it. Call it gamblers intuition. Betty turned the card and it wasn't what I had hoped for.

Ten of Hearts.

Three of a kind. I didn't see that coming. Three of a kind. Domonika's pair of queens would have to bow down to my three tens. I didn't want to get carried away but my emotions were getting the better of me. I checked. I only realised that she was pulling on a cigarette when she blew smoke in my face.

'Don't be pussy, Sal. Put money down.'

'Nah, you're alright,' I said. 'I'm happy with five ton.'

'Well, I am not.' She looked at my chips, I was down to my last two hundred. Domonika picked out four fifty chips and placed them on the table.

'Two hundred,' I said. 'It's all I've got.'

'You want to play man's game, Sal. Then play like man.' Her accent thick, her tone taunting.

My hand hovered uncertainly over my remaining chips. I looked across at Trevor, he shrugged at me.

'Let it go, man,' advised Samuel and Domonika shot him a furious look.

I picked up the last remaining blue fifty chips and dropped them one at a time onto the pile. The pot now a tidy £900. The room fell silent, only the whir of the tumble dryer adding to the tension.

'Show,' said Betty.

I was left of the dealer, so I had to show first. I took my time, I milked it. I showed my first card, jack of clubs. I locked eyes with Domonika and placed down my second card.

The ten of clubs.

Her face. Oh man, her face when she clocked my three tens. All her features touched in bemusement.

'Boy finally become man, huh,' she said.

'I am wearing my big boy pants,' I risked a look up at Serge and smiled passively at him. I had taken his daughter for a ride and I could imagine, behind his dark shades, his eyes lasering into me.

'Brave move,' Domonika clapped slowly, the sound echoing around the small room.

'Fortune favours the brave,' I said, I'd read that earlier on my Facebook timeline.

'You waited until the last card,' she said, her eyes sharp like slits.

'Yup.'

'You shouldn't have.'

She laid down her first card. Queen of clubs. Then she laid down her second card.

Queen of hearts.

I watched in a daze as she raked the nine hundred towards her. Her three queens had taken my three tens to school. I slumped back in my chair and dug the heels of my hands into my eyes.

My phone vibrated in my pocket. It was Miriam.

I stood up and hurried over to the door and let myself out to echoes of mocking laughter.

I took the call. 'Where are you, Sal?' she asked.

'Miriam. Hi. Still at work. This case has got me working.'

'It's Saturday night, Sal. Actually, it's Sunday morning.'

I glanced at my watch and sighed. 'I did say I'd be late. The first few days of a murder investigation are always frantic. The bright side is that there'll be loads of overtime.'

I hated myself for lying to her. There's no way I could tell her I was at the bottom of a hole and the only way out of it was trying to win it back in an illegal game of poker in the back of a bloody launderette. 'How's Maria?' I asked.

'She waited for you until ten, clutching onto a story book that she only wants Daddy to read to her.'

I sat down on a wooden bench and leaned my head back against a washing machine and closed my eyes. My body felt heavy as all the earlier adrenaline seeped away.

'What do you want me to say, Miriam?'

'Nothing, Sal,' she said softly. 'I don't want you to say anything.'

Miriam ended the call and right at that moment it was so clear to me. I could be home in thirty minutes. Kiss Maria on her head and watch her smile in her sleep. Get into bed with Miriam and hold her tightly as she tells me about her day and I don't tell her about mine.

It was time to go home. I'd screwed up. Repeatedly. But whatever problems I had, we'd get through them together as a family.

I stepped into the back room to fetch my coat and call it a night.

On the table, where I had been sitting, stacked neatly in neat rows, there were five hundred pounds in chips. I looked across at Serge at the bar.

'You want?' he said. 'It's yours.'

I sat back down at the table.

Chapter 19
(Harry)

Sunday is always a quiet day, even in a Murder Investigation Room, because most of the civilian staff get to work regular hours unless they're on overtime. I got in at half eight and DC Nasri was already there, munching on a croissant and studying his HOLMES screen. 'Morning, Guv,' he said, as if he wanted to drive home the point that he'd got in before me.

I nodded and put my briefcase down. 'How did the search go yesterday?' I asked.

'No joy, I'm afraid. The mosque was clean.' Sal cleared his throat. 'They searched every rubbish bin, drain and flower bed within a couple of hundred yards. I spoke to Lorraine and she's sure that it wasn't one of the kitchen knives.'

'And there are no knives missing from the kitchen?'

'Paul Rees had the staff questioned and there doesn't seem to be, no.'

'Which means the killer brought the knife with him. Which means it was either premeditated or the killer was prone to carrying a knife.' I rubbed the back of my neck. I had the beginning of a headache. 'We really need to know if anyone had it in for Sean Evans. Any joy with his tutor?'

Nasri shook his head. 'It's the weekend, Guv, skeleton staff at the uni. I'll be on it first thing tomorrow. Alan Russell is after you, think he's still in the CCTV room.'

My stomach growled. 'I need a bite,' I said. 'Do you want a bacon sandwich from the canteen?'

He looked at me in surprise. 'Guv...'

'What?'

'Why do you keep forcing pork products on me?'

'Oh shit, I forgot. Cheese sandwich, then? You can eat cheese, right?'

'Yes Guv, Muslims can eat cheese.' He held up his half-eaten croissant. 'But I'm good. I wouldn't mind a coffee, though.'

I went down to the canteen and bought three coffees and two bacon rolls. I gave Nasri his coffee and then carried the tray through to the CCTV room. Russell looked up from his terminal and grinned when he saw I was bearing gifts. 'You're a life-saver, Guv, he said, grabbing a bacon roll and a coffee.

I sat down next to him and bit into my own roll. 'So what's happening?' I asked.

'So, we have Sean Evans arriving at the mosque just after one o'clock.' He tapped on his keyboard, clicked his mouse, and footage from one of the CCTV cameras in the mosque started to play. A stream of Muslim men, mainly wearing Western clothing but with several in long robes and skullcaps, were threading their way through the entrance towards the prayer room. The picture quality wasn't great but it was possible to make out the faces.

Sean Evans appeared at the doorway and bent down to remove his shoes.

'Here he is,' said Russell. He took a bite of his roll.

Evans straightened up and put his shoes in a rack. I recognised the man standing next to him. 'Freeze it, yeah,' I said and Russell clicked his mouse.

I leaned forward to get a better look but I was already sure I knew who it was. Waseem Chowdhury. The piece of shit who had been hurling abuse at me and Ayesha Khan. The guy who I'd confronted and then had to back off. This was not good news. Not good news at all. 'They're together?' I said. 'Evans and that guy?'

Chowdhury looked pretty much as I'd seen him outside his house, with gelled hair and an arrogant thrust to his chin. He was wearing tight trousers and a baggy jacket.

Russell nodded and clicked the mouse. Chowdhury took off his shoes and then he and Evans headed inside. Russell clicked the mouse as another figure came into view. It was the Imam.

'That's interesting,' I said.

'He knows the victim,' said Russell. 'At least he acknowledges him. You'll see the Imam nod and then Evans says something as they walk by.' He clicked the mouse and the video started again. Russell was right. The Imam did seem to nod at Evans. Or at least nodded in his direction. The video quality wasn't great and it was hard to be sure.

'I think I need to pay the Imam a visit,' I said.

'What about the guy who came in with the victim?'

'I know him,' I said. 'Waseem Chowdhury. He's one of The Faith.'

'The Faith?' he repeated.

'Those nutters who came around with knives when we were first at the mosque. Sal thinks they're on the payroll. Hired security. Is Chowdhury in HOLMES yet?'

Russell opened HOLMES and tapped in Chowdhury's name and then shook his head. 'No. Which means he wasn't there after Evans was killed.' He looked over at me. 'Do you think we've got a suspect, Guv?'

'They seem friendly enough on the video,' I said. 'Let's see what Stuart gets out of him.'

'Do you want me to enter Chowdhury into HOLMES now and assign him a Nominal?'

Every person involved in the investigation – detective, witnesses and suspects – was assigned a Nominal Number for each investigation so that everything they said and did could be cross-referenced. The victim was always Nominal 1 and HOLMES assigned all the numbers automatically each time a new name was entered into the system. On this investigation I was Nominal Eight and DC Nasri was Nominal Nine. 'Might as well,' I said. I took out my notebook and gave him Chowdhury's address and date of birth, details I'd obtained from the PNC. 'How are you getting on with the rest of the mosque footage?' I asked.

'Slowly but surely,' said Russell. 'There are five cameras, four outside and the one covering the entrance hall. We've looked at most of the footage up to the start of the prayers. What we'll do now we've found Evans arriving is to check the rest of the footage.'

'Be nice if we could see someone running out with a bloodstained knife,' I said.

Russell laughed. 'Hell, yeah. But with the camera pointing the way it is, all you'll see is the back of their head.'

I patted him on the shoulder and left him to it. I took my coffee and roll over to where Nasri was sitting. 'We need to have another word with the Imam,' I said. 'Face to face. Fix up a car.'

'Right, Guv. What's the story?'

'Seems he did know the victim. At least he said hello to him before prayers on Friday. Give me ten minutes and then we'll head out.'

I went over to my terminal and typed my Ayesha Kahn interview notes into HOLMES. She was in the system now and had been assigned a

Nominal – 348 – as several worshippers had reported seeing her in the mosque. All the names that Ayesha had given me were already in the system and had been assigned nominal identifiers. I checked the name of Yalina Wazir, the girl that Ayesha had gone to the mosque with. Yalina had been given the identifier Nominal 136. I called up the interview she'd given at the mosque. Her account agreed with that of Ayesha, they had travelled together on the bus to the mosque. Yalina had also provided a list of more than a dozen men and women she had recognised. Some of them matched names in Ayesha's list, some didn't. That was to be expected, they would presumably know different people. Yalina's interview had been put into HOLMES earlier that morning. There was usually a delay between interviews taking place and them appearing on the system, and the workload of the typists had a lot to do with that.

I checked the combination of Ayesha and Yalina and they appeared together in more than a dozen witness statements. They had been seen either entering the mosque or in the women's prayer hall. Several witnesses saw them with Nominal 86. Fazal Wazir. I frowned as I saw the name. A relative of Yalina's? A brother maybe? So why was there no mention of him from either Yalina or Ayesha?

I called up the statement made by Fazal Wazir. He was twenty-years-old, eight years younger than Yalina and they shared the same address so they were probably siblings. Fazal said that he had walked to the mosque and had been close to the front of the prayer hall. He had stayed behind to talk to friends and was in the prayer hall when the Imam discovered the body. He had stayed in the mosque and had been one of the first to be interviewed. He had provided the investigating officer with two dozens names of worshippers, all male, and several matched names on the lists provided by his sister and Ayesha. No red flags. I checked Fazal Wazir on the Police National Computer and he was clean. As an afterthought I ran Ayesha Khan's name through the PNC database and she was also clean.

Stuart Hurley arrived at nine o'clock, bright-eyed and bushy-tailed. He seemed happy enough to be in the office on a Sunday morning but then he was a sergeant so was earning overtime. As soon as he flopped down onto his chair I went over and gave him the picture of Waseem Chowdhury. 'I've raised an Action on this guy, Stuart, can you take care of it?'

'Sure.' I'd written the Wembley address across the bottom, and Chowdhury's date of birth.

'He arrived at the mosque on Friday with the victim. There's no record of him in HOLMES so no one reported seeing him.'

Hurley frowned. 'How could that happen?"

'I'm guessing because Chowdhury is a nasty piece of work. One of The Faith, those nutters who turned up with knives.'

'Do we get a search warrant?'

'Let's just interview him first. Find out how he knew the victim, where they had been before the mosque and more importantly why he didn't hang around after Evans was killed. Who are you going to take with you?'

'Mark Bryant's coming in.'

I nodded. Bryant was a safe pair of hands, a former Military Policeman who had done two tours in Iraq before leaving the Army and joining the Met. He'd be useful just in case Chowdhury turned nasty.

Nasri came over holding a set of car keys. 'Ready to go when you are.'

We went down to the car park. This time we had a blue Vectra and whoever had been in it last had obviously been smoking. I opened the window to let in some air.

Chapter 20
(Sal)

We arrived at the mosque just as Zuhr prayers were winding down. Again I felt a touch guilty, second time at the masjid in three days and both times I was there to work and not pray. A higher power is furiously making notes somewhere. *Yet again, Salim missed another prayer.* Yeah, I'll be judged, what am I going to tell Him; that I was busy? Maybe catching a murderer would win me some points. When I'm eventually put to bed with a shovel, I like to think I'd have done enough good not to be banished to hell for not following my Deen, but on the flip-side, I doubt I'll get a seat on the head table.

Zuhr prayer is the noon prayer but the actual time is a moveable feast. Today it's at twelve-thirty. Zuhr prayers during the week aren't usually well attended because despite what you read in the Daily Mail, most Muslims aren't benefits freeloaders, they're hard-working husbands and fathers working their nuts off to support their families.

Porter made a point to take off his shoes first. He had laces which meant he had to kneel and untie them. We got quite a few hostile looks as we moved towards the stairs, as many aimed at me as Porter. I was being seen as one of the enemy, and it wasn't a nice feeling. I was used to whites glaring at me like I was planning to behead them with a machete, but it was unnerving to have my own people stare at me with undisguised hatred on their faces. I acknowledged them with a curt nod anyway and tried to ignore the whispers designed loud enough for me to hear.

I knocked on the door to the Imam's office. He waited a good few seconds before his voice came through for us to enter. He was at his desk. He didn't acknowledge us, instead he busied himself on his laptop. He stopped in his own time. I could sense Porter getting fed up with the passive aggressive power struggle. This interview was going to be hard work, and despite my three strong coffees, the events of the night before were catching up with me.

'Good to see you again, Inspector Porter, and you too, Mohammed. Please don't tell me you want to search our place of worship for a third time.'

I smiled back. I was getting tired of this nonsense back and forth with the Imam, as if I have a problem being called Mohammed. He's misguided if he thinks he's winding me up.

The Imam picked up his string of amber prayer beads and ran them through his fingers as he waited for us to start.

'I wanted to thank you for assisting us in our search,' began Porter.

The Imam shook his head and wagged his finger. 'No, no, no, Inspector Porter, I did not assist you. I acquiesced to your request for a search, and agreed to allow your men to search again. That is not assisting. I would have much preferred that your men had not desecrated our mosque.'

'No disrespect was intended and my men – and women – were instructed to be especially sensitive when carrying out the search. My apologies if they in any way caused offence.'

The Imam waved away Porter's apology with a languid hand and gestured for us to sit. 'What would you like from me today?'

I sat down on one of the two chairs facing the Imam's desk. Porter stayed standing. His decision to not sit down felt disrespectful and I couldn't work out if that was his intention or a play to make the Imam uncomfortable. 'Guv?' I said. He looked at me. I nodded at the chair. Porter stood his ground for a moment before taking a seat. The Imam visibly relaxed.

'You said you didn't know the victim, Sean Evans,' said Porter. 'Known to you as Mohammed Masood. That is what you told DC Nasri.'

'This is true, Inspector.'

'But we have video of you greeting him at the entrance to the mosque.'

The Imam frowned but said nothing.

Porter reached into his jacket and took out two sheets of paper. He made a show of slowly unfolding them flat onto the desk. I leaned over to get a better look. They were print-outs of the CCTV feed from the camera in the mosque's entrance lobby.

It was winding me up the way Porter was approaching this. If he was going to pull a white rabbit out of the hat, he should have told me. Producing the pictures was tantamount to accusing the Imam of lying. It's not how I would've played it.

The Imam took them and studied them carefully, before handing them back to Porter as though they were yesterday's news. He shrugged, aiming for and hitting nonchalance.

'You can see why this confuses me a little,' said Porter, looking anything but confused. 'You said you didn't know Sean Evans but here you are nodding and smiling at him.'

'You are right, Inspector Porter, it is highly suspicious for an Imam to warmly address his congregation in this manner.' The Imam ran his fingers in the underside of his beard as though trying to determine if it required a trim.

'It looks to me as if you said something to him.'

'Yes, possibly a greeting.'

'You don't remember?'

'There were six hundred people at the mosque. Do you think I remember what I said to everyone?'

'I think if that person ends up dead just a few minutes after you spoke to him, yes, you might remember.'

'I greeted many people that day. You asked me if I knew him. I did not know him, not by name. Did I recognise him? Yes, I had seen him at the mosque but other than to greet him, I said nothing to him.'

'In the video, it looked as if you made a special effort to talk to him.'

The Imam held out his hand for the print-outs and Porter gave them to him. The Imam studied them again for several seconds. 'I think it was not Mr Evans I was talking to. It was his companion.'

'Waseem Chowdhury?'

'Yes. I know Waseem.' He gave the sheets back to Porter. 'If I said anything, it would have been to Waseem.'

'So you know Waseem?'

'I just told you that I do. Young Waseem has been a regular at the mosque for several years.'

'And you know that he is a member of The Faith?'

The Imam's eyes hardened, then flitted across at me. He wasn't happy. He turned his baleful stare back on Porter. 'I am not sure what you want me to say, Inspector Porter.'

'The men who turned up at the mosque on the day of the killing. They were The Faith, were they not?'

'They were a group of concerned worshippers who were angry, and rightly so may I add, at the way the police were treating their masjid.'

'And they call themselves The Faith?'

'I don't know where you got that name, Inspector.'

Porter's head turned towards me and I winced. Does the man know nothing about body language and non-verbal cues? The Imam grinned but it was more like a snarl. He looked at me and raised his eyebrows and I looked away, my cheeks burning.

'I think it's generally known that they go by that name,' said Porter. 'Do you have any idea why Sean Evans would be involved with them?'

'Of course not,' said the Imam. 'My relation begins and ends with the worshippers within the confines of these walls. Now, Inspector Porter, I have told you, repeatedly, I did not know Mr Evans other than to perhaps greet him with a Salaam.'

'Salaam?' Porter repeated, like a parrot trying to copy a word it had heard for the first time.

The Imam snorted and looked at me in disbelief.

'It is a short form of Aslamalykum, the Arabic greeting for Peace,' I said, my voice sounding out of place after their game of mental chess.

Porter frowned. 'I'm sorry, I don't understand.'

'Peace be unto you,' said the Imam, like a teacher addressing a particularly stupid student. 'Or as you would say, hello.'

'What can you tell me about The Faith?' Porter asked.

'Inspector, I have already told you, I do not recognise that name.'

'On the day of the murder, they came with knives to confront my officers. Did you call them?'

I swear I was this close to elbowing Porter in the ribs. What was he playing at? The Imam had already proved himself to be difficult, he wasn't exactly going to play ball faced with Porter's hostile confrontation. The Imam had co-operated, allowed the officers to search the mosque, helped send The Faith away and handed over the CCTV tapes. All because we, *I*, had handled him. And now Porter was running the risk of getting the Imam's back up and losing his co-operation.

The Imam stared silently at Porter, seething, fighting to control his temper. 'I did not call them, Inspector Porter,' he said through gritted teeth. 'If you recall, I dealt with them when you couldn't. It was I that persuaded them to leave. Peacefully.'

I glanced across at Porter. I could read his reasoning in his face. He was going to suggest that the Imam had called The Faith for exactly that reason – to send them away so that the police would know where the real power lay. The thing was, Porter was probably right. But to say it out loud would be to accuse the Imam of lying and that wouldn't go down well. I guess what Porter doesn't know is that lying isn't actually a sin for Muslims, not when it comes to dealing with non-believers. The Koran calls it Taqiyya - righteous or pious – basically it states that lying to non-believers is okay so long as you are protecting your own. The Imam wouldn't appreciate being called a liar but as he had the backing of the Koran, it would be sticks and stones.

My mind was in overdrive as the interview was getting away from us fast, on horseback, in the opposite direction. 'Guv?' I said, hoping that Porter would recognise in that one word, in that one syllable, that he should calm down and lay off the antagonising. He spent a moment longer making eyes at the Imam before looking across at me.

'DC Nasri?' he said coldly.

'We, um...' I cleared my throat, 'We should update the Imam on the progress of the crime scene.' Porter leaned back into his chair and nodded at me to continue.

I faced the Imam and started with a smile. He didn't follow suit.

Crime Scene Manager DS Beard had done all she could at the mosque. The kitchen had been locked and sealed with crime scene tape, and four bollards and tape had been used to keep people from walking across the section of the floor where the body had been found. The Forensic Manager, Lorraine Sawyer, had confirmed that she had got all she could from the scene so DS Beard had decided that it was time to release it.

'The good news, Imam, is that we no longer need to restrict your masjid.' I hesitated, then corrected myself. '*Our* masjid.' I could feel Porter firing off laser beams at me. 'I'll organise someone to clear away the crime scene tape and again I want to express my gratitude for your co-operation.' I stood up. Porter was already on his feet. 'Thank you again for your help, and we will be sure to keep you informed of any progress we make in the investigation.'

I expected the Imam to stand up, I expected him to take and shake my outstretched hand. Instead, from his seat he looked up at me, only me, as though it was I who had allowed for his position and his *izzat* – his honour - to come into question. An Imam is nothing without respect.

I hurried down the stairs and into the shoe area. I slipped on my shoes and stepped out of the masjid, greedily sucking the fresh air, glad to be out of the Imam's office. I turned back and watched Porter take his time creaking down to fasten his laces and creaking back up again.

We walked away from the mosque and to the car in silence.

'I could do with a drink,' said Porter, closing the car door. 'Are you okay to go into a pub?'

'Yeah, Guv, course.' I said, his inane question not helping to ease my frustration.

'Excellent. And I promise not to offer you any smoky bacon crisps.'

'Artificial flavouring, Guv,' I sighed as I started the car. 'There's no pork in smoky bacon crisps.'

'Really,' he said, looking bemused, not for the first time today. 'Smokey bacon crisps are halal?'

'As a vegetable samosa, Guv.'

'The world is getting way too complicated.' Porter shook his head as I manoeuvered out.

Porter was quiet on the journey. I knew that he was replaying the interview with the Imam in his head, searching for any tell-tale signs. I headed towards Hendon and stopped off at a pub in Brondesbury, one of those big double-fronted buildings that often close due to lack of business and end up being converted into mosques. Work out the irony in that.

There were blackboards outside offering pub lunches and cheap tequila shots between 6pm and 9pm. Porter ordered a pint and fish and chips and I asked for a Coke and the same. Porter paid despite my protestations.

I excused myself and found a quiet spot and phoned Miriam. By the time I'd got home last night, she was asleep and she'd woken up early this morning and taken Marie out before I'd opened my eyes. The call went through to voicemail. I figured she was still sour from the night before.

Porter had found a table by the window and the fish and chips had just arrived. I pocketed my phone and sat opposite him.

'So what do you think about Imam Malik? Is he lying?' Porter asked.

'About what, Guv? If he knew Sean Evans or if he was the one to call The Faith?'

'Let's start with the victim.'

'I don't know, Guv. If there is any sign of extremism at the mosque, I really don't think the Imam would hold back.' I took a sip of my Coke as he started his pint. 'Five hundred men at the mosque and probably another thousand who use the mosque on an irregular basis, he can't be expected to know everybody.'

'He remembered you?'

'Must be my sunny disposition, Guv.' I smiled. He didn't return it. 'Probably because I'm a cop.'

'Right. He remembers you because you are a police officer. By the same token, he should remember Sean Evans.'

'Because he's a convert?'

'Yes. Like you he sticks out.' Porter tucked into his chips. 'Could it be a racial thing? Evans was white so below his radar?'

'A racist Imam?'

'Not necessarily racist, but maybe not worth his attention.'

'I'd have thought the opposite. There are only a few non-Asian Muslims at the mosque. They're a rarity. I'd notice them and I'm sure the Imam would. The question is whether or not he would make the effort to get to know them.'

'And?

I took another sip of my Coke, playing for time. He continued to look at me, waiting for an answer. I was starting to get the feel for what it would be like to sit opposite him in an interview room. 'Yeah, you're right. It would make sense for him to have gotten to know Evans.'

'That's what I thought. So he was lying to us. Which begs the question, why?'

The answer that sprang to my mind was that the Imam just wanted to avoid getting into trouble with the police. If he admitted that he knew Evans, he'd maybe become a suspect or at the very least would face a lot more questioning. As a Muslim, the last thing he would want is to be on the police radar, where suspicious eyes and suspicious minds were quick to judge.

'He might just be stretching the truth, Guv. Might have just had a few words with him at some point but doesn't want you to read anything into it. The Imam's not on any watch lists, is he?'

'True. But then there are plenty of jihadists we don't know about. They're getting cleverer at hiding their true intentions. You can see where I'm going with this? Sean Evans becomes a Muslim, wears the gear and calls himself Mohammed Masood. He is pally with at least one member of The Faith. The Faith carry knives. So could The Faith have killed him?' While he waited for me to respond he sipped his pint.

It was a little too ABC for my liking. I could see his logic, but for me, it didn't click. It would be unbelievably stupid for a Muslim to commit a murder in their mosque. I mean, it's not just the Bible that says "*though shalt not kill*". The Koran is equally clear. *Whoever kills a human being… it shall be as if he had killed all mankind, and who saves the life of one, it shall be as if he had saved the life of all mankind.* Alright, I'm paraphrasing a little, but the point is murder is a sin in both religions, but killing in your place of worship compounds that sin.

I shook my head as I finally tucked into my cod. 'Doesn't make any sense, Guv. I can't see it playing out like that.'

'He could have taken him to the mosque and other members of The Faith did the dirty deed.'

'It would have been easier to do it away from the mosque,' I said through a mouthful. If they were friends, which we assume they were, Chowdhury could have gone to his home and killed him there...And plus, what's the motive?' I shrugged.

'Maybe The Faith don't like converts?'

I scoffed at that. Then I held up one hand in apology and wiped the grin off my face. 'Guv, it's like this. Muslims, Asian-Muslims, love converts. Don't you see? It's like we've taken one of yours.'

Porter sighed. 'Maybe,' he said. 'So where does that leave us? If it wasn't The Faith who killed Evans, who was it? And what were they doing with a knife in the mosque?'

'Plenty of gang members carry knives,' I said. 'Most Somalian gang members carry a blade, and most of them are Muslims.'

'And they'd take the knives into the mosque?'

'It's possible, but honestly, Guv, I don't think so.'

'I've got to be honest, I'm getting a bad feeling about this,' said Porter, as he tucked into his lunch. 'Hundreds of potential witnesses but no one saw anything. No murder weapon and as things stand no chance of finding it. And with the murderer doing a bang up job of covering his tracks, I don't see there's any likelihood of him confessing any time soon.'

'It's only been forty-eight hours, Guv.' I was trying to sound optimistic but he was right. The majority of murders aren't actually solved as such. A wife stabs her abusive husband; a homeowner takes an axe to a nightmare neighbour; two guys get in a ruckus and one lands a final and fatal blow; the cops rock up and walk the killer out in bracelets. Job done. Crime solved. No actual detective work required. If it's gang-related, it gets tougher because the cops might know which gang is involved but not the gang-member and you know no one's going to sing to a cop. The simple fact is that a quarter of murders in the United Kingdom are never solved, and if the cops don't have a suspect within the first twelve hours then there's a good chance they never will.

I wasn't sure what was troubling him more – that a murderer might get away with his crime, or that he would look bad for not solving it. Porter was SIO which meant that the buck stopped with him.

'We need a motive,' said Porter. 'And at the moment we just don't have one.'

We ate in silence for a while, but there was something that had been bugging me ever since I'd been assigned to be his bag carrier. I figured now was as good a time as any to broach the subject. 'Can I ask you a question, Guv?'

He looked at me and narrowed his eyes. I guess he assumed the fact I had to ask obviously meant he wasn't going to like the question. 'I guess so. So long as it's not maths. I was never good at maths.'

'It's about the name thing.'

'You being called Mohammed, you mean?' he shrugged. 'It's not a problem. I'm happy to call you Sal.' He grinned. 'Or DC Nasri whenever you piss me off.'

I shook my head. 'Not my name, Guv. Yours. Why does that whole Harry Potter thing annoy you so much?'

'Are you serious?'

'It seems to really annoy you. I don't get why. It's not even your name. Porter, Potter. Tomato, potato.'

'Everyone hears it as Potter. They just do. Every time I introduce myself I get the same sly smirk. And the same bloody jokes, time after time. Where's Ron Weasley? Where's Hermione? I had to go to Brixton prison a few days ago and a warder there asked if I was there to see the Prisoner of Azkaban. Do you have any idea how annoying that is?'

'We had a DS at Harrow Road, name of Tony Colegate. Everyone called him Toothpaste. It never seemed to upset him. And you know Inspector John Holland, right? He's been called The Dutchman for donkey's.'

He shook his head in annoyance. 'I've lost count of the number of times I've had "Expelliarmus" shouted at me,' he said. 'It's just not funny any more.'

'The thing is, Guv, I can see the inconvenience of being called Harry Porter, but compared to me you've had it easy. You want to try going through life with Mohammed as your first name.'

'Most common boy's name in the UK, is what I heard.'

I nodded. 'Yeah, it is. Muslims reckon it's a blessing to give their kid the name of the prophet. But when I fly to the US, how do you think it goes down? They held me for over three hours last time, and even my warrant card didn't make it any easier. You get a smile and a joke when they hear your name, I get the rubber glove treatment. And it's not just the US. You think anyone other than a Muslim wants to rent a flat to a guy called Mohammed? I try not to use it, truth be told. But when they do ask for ID and they see I'm called Mohammed they think I'm a bloody jihadist.'

He thought about what I'd said as he chewed and swallowed. 'You know what, Sal, you're right. We're in the same boat, you and me.'

No, Guv, I thought, we're really not.

Chapter 21
(Harry)

We got back to Peel House at just after two o'clock. The fish and chips had hit the spot and it was an eye-opener that Sal could go into a pub. But I guess it's not that surprising, plenty of teetotalers still go into places that serve alcohol.

Hurley and Bryant were already back in the MIR. Hurley was drinking coffee while Bryant entered the results of their interview with Waseem Chowdhury into HOLMES. 'How did it go, Stuart?' I asked.

'He's a belligerent bugger,' said Hurley. 'One of the "I know my rights" brigade. I told him we could do it the easy way or the hard way, and the hard way meant bringing him here and that quietened him down. He admitted to driving Sean Evans to the mosque. Said that Evans had spent the night at his place.'

'Why?'

'They were studying the Koran, he says.' Hurley grinned. 'I don't believe that for one minute, either. More like watching jihadist videos together.'

'Who was with them?'

'He says he doesn't remember.'

'Anyone else in the car when they drove to the mosque?'

'He says no. Just him and the victim.'

'What do you think?'

Hurley rubbed the back of his neck. 'Do I think he's a suspect? I think we can cross him off the list straight away. He's a nasty piece of work, but if he wanted to kill Evans he could have done it in his flat and no one would ever have known. It wouldn't make any sense for him to have driven Evans to the mosque and then to have killed him.'

Unfortunately, I had to agree with my deputy. Waseem Chowdhury was a nasty piece of work but almost certainly not the killer we were looking for. 'When you're done here, run Chowdhury by SO15, will you? If he's not known to them already, make sure he is now.'

Hurley nodded. I went through to the CCTV room. Alan Russell wasn't there but there were three officers studying footage. 'Who's looking at Waseem Chowdhury?' I asked.

A young PC raised his hand and turned to look at me. He had unruly ginger hair and a sprinkling of large freckles across his nose and cheeks. 'No joy yet, Sir,' he said.

'I'm particularly interested in seeing if there was anyone else in the car with him other than the victim when they arrived,' I said.

'No problem, Sir,' he said and went back to looking at his screen.

I went back into the MIR and sat down at my terminal and spent the next couple of hours going through HOLMES. Chowdhury had been assigned the identifier Nominal 145. Hurley's interview wasn't in yet but Chowdhury's name came up more than fifty times, usually mentioned in passing by worshippers. Plenty of people remembered seeing him at the mosque but there were no reports of him doing anything untoward.

I sat back in my chair. One of the problems I had was that I still didn't know how to classify the murder. The most common types are domestics, involving a spouse or former spouse, or a parent or a child, or in-laws. About half of all murders are domestics, but that almost certainly wasn't the case with Sean Evans. Then there was murder in the course of a crime – robbery, or burglary or a sexual attack. Again that didn't seem likely and the fact that Evans had his wallet on him suggested robbery wasn't the motive.

Then there was gang homicide which was a possibility, him being a white guy surrounded by Asians, but the fact that he was friendly with one of the leading lights of The Faith made a racial attack unlikely.

Other motives include jealousy and revenge which I hadn't ruled out, but again, the setting made that unlikely. If it was a revenge attack, why carry it out in a mosque where some six hundred worshippers were all potential witnesses? Reckless acts caused deaths but I couldn't see how anything reckless could have happened in the mosque. Then there was racial violence which again was a possibility but didn't make much sense in view of his connection to The Faith. And that was pretty much it so far as motives were concerned – all that was left were serial murder, mass homicide and terrorism, none of which seemed to apply here. I stopped running through my mental checklist as I got to terrorism. I sat back in my chair. Sean Evans was a convert to the religion, was he also a convert to terrorism? The scars on his back suggested that he had been in the vicinity of an exploding IED and the suntan suggested he'd been somewhere hot and putting two and two together it was realistic he'd been out in the Middle East, most likely Iraq, Afghanistan or Syria.

I leaned forward and tapped on the keyboard, raising an Action to get Sean Evans's passport checked. Border Force generally didn't check the passports of people leaving the country, but everyone flying back had their passports scanned. I also raised an Action to get flight manifests checked but there were dozens of flights to and from the Middle East every day so I knew that was a tough ask.

I sat back in my chair and ran through my mental checklist, trying to think if I'd missed anything. It felt to me that the investigation had stalled and I needed to do something to get the momentum going again. But what? Being SIO was a double-edged sword. If I got a result and caught the killer then I'd get the credit. But if the case remained unsolved then that would be down to me. The role of SIO is very clearly defined. Basically there are five responsibilities and I smiled at the thought that I might start calling them the Five Pillars, just to piss off DC Nasri.

The first pillar is to perform the role of officer in charge of an investigation as described in the Code of Practice under Part Two of the Criminal Procedure and Investigations Act of 1996. Basically it means I get to manage detectives.

The second pillar is to develop and implement the investigative strategy and I'd done that. I'd arranged for witnesses to be interviewed, carried out a search for the murder weapon, had CCTV footage reviewed and was in the process of collecting information about the victim. So far so good, except that it hadn't got me anywhere.

The third pillar was to develop the information management and decision-making systems for the investigation, and that basically meant feeding HOLMES on a daily basis and reviewing all the information that went in.

The fourth pillar was to manage the resources allocated to the investigation, which really followed on from the second pillar. You put the resources where you needed them. We'd done the search, now we needed manpower to interview everyone who was at the mosque and check through all the CCTV footage.

The final pillar is to be accountable to chief officers for the conduct of the investigation. Which basically means my neck is on the chopping block, and so far nothing has happened that will stop the axe from chopping off my head.

Had I missed something, that was the question I kept asking myself. Was there some other strategy I could implement that would crack the case? 'Inspector!' I looked up to see the ginger PC hurrying towards me. 'I've got Evans and that Chowdhury character getting out of their car. And there's another guy with them.'

'Excellent,' I said, pushing myself out of my chair. I followed him back into the CCTV viewing room. The PC had paused a CCTV feed. It showed the blue hatchback. Chowdhury was standing at the driver's door. Sean Evans was already on the pavement standing next to a middle-aged bearded Asian with a straggly beard and thick-lensed glasses. 'What's your name, lad,' I said. 'We haven't spoken before.'

'John Reynolds,' he said.

'Right John, run it for me, will you?'

Reynolds clicked on his mouse and started the video as the car pulled into a parking space. The passenger door opened first and the man with the glasses got out, followed by Evans. Then Chowdhury climbed out and locked the car.

'Nice one, John,' I said.

I watched the screen as the three men walked away from the car. The pavements were thronged with Muslims making their way to the mosque. There was no sound and the video quality wasn't great but it was definitely Chowdhury and Evans. Suddenly the three men all looked across the road as if something had happened to attract their attention. No one else had turned to look at the source of the noise so I figured someone had shouted something to them. There were two girls and a man on the other side of the road. I recognised the red scarf and navy blue sweater of one of the girls. Ayesha Khan.

The three men hurried away and the girl with Ayesha opened her mouth, shouting I guess. Ayesha put an arm around her shoulder and then they moved out of the camera's range of vision. Evans, Chowdhury and the man wearing glasses hurried towards the mosque and out of the camera's view.

'Replay it, will you, John?'

He did as I asked and I watched the clip again carefully. It definitely looked as if the woman with Ayesha was shouting at the three men and they were rushing to get away.

'Do me a favour and give me stills,' I asked. It took him a couple of minutes before he produced a handful of stills showing the whole camera view and close-ups of the individuals. The close-ups weren't great, blowing up the images had emphasised just how grainy the images were. I could recognise Ayesha well enough but that was more to do with her clothing.

I took the pictures out into the MIR. Alan Russell had arranged for all the photographs of the worshippers who had been interviewed to be stuck onto four large whiteboards. There were more than three hundred so far, mainly taken at the mosque with just a dozen or so downloaded from DVLA. I scanned the pictures, row by row. The man wearing glasses was on the third board, close to the bottom. His name and date of birth were underneath the head-and-shoulders shot. I made a note of it and sat down at my HOLMES terminal.

The man was Nominal 231, his name was Gohar Abbasi and like Chowdhury he lived in Wembley. Abbasi had supplied half a dozen names of worshippers he had seen at the mosque but in his statement there was no mention of Chowdhury or Evans. I sat back in my chair and wondered what the hell was going on. People lie. Ask any copper and they'll tell you that. People lie all the time but that doesn't necessarily mean they've done anything wrong. A lot of Asians don't trust the police and it might just have been that Abbasi might have thought he was opening himself up to a world of trouble by admitting that he had travelled to the mosque with the victim.

I checked Chowdhury's statement on HOLMES. He made no mention of Abbasi being in the car with him and Evans, but that could just have been because Abbasi asked him to keep his name out of it.

I raised an Action for Stuart Hurley to re-interview Chowdhury in light of the CCTV footage, and another to interview Abbasi. They had both lied, but the fact remained that it would have made no sense for them to have driven Evans to the mosque to kill him.

I took the print-outs back over to the whiteboards. All the female worshippers – eighty so far – were on one of the boards. Twenty had been interviewed at the mosque, the rest at home. Ayesha's picture still wasn't on the board and I realised that was my fault. I hadn't taken her photograph when I'd interviewed her. The girl she was with in the CCTV footage was Yalina Wazir and her picture was up.

I went back on to HOLMES to check the name of the man with the same family name as Yalina and quickly found it – Fazal Wazir. His picture was on the second whiteboard. The blown-up picture was grainy but good enough for me to confirm that he was the man with the two women. I checked with DVLA to see if I could get a photograph of Ayesha Khan from them but she didn't have a licence.

I sat down and put my feet on the desk. I always think better with my feet up, maybe because it gets more blood to my head. From what I'd seen on the CCTV footage, Ayesha and Yalina were with Fazal on the opposite side of the road to Sean Evans and his two friends. Yalina had shouted something and the three men had hurried off. So what had she shouted? And why had Ayesha comforted her? And why hadn't Ayesha mentioned seeing Sean Evans outside the mosque? It would surely have been an obvious thing to tell me.

In theory I should have raised Actions to have them all re-interviewed, but if I did that then questions would be asked about why Ayesha's picture hadn't been taken. Then it struck me I could kill two birds with one stone if I interviewed her again and this time took her picture. Once I had asked her about what had happened I could decide whether or not Yalina and Fazal Wazir needed to be interviewed again. I took out my mobile and called her, explaining that I needed another quick interview.

'It's Sunday,' she said.

'I know, but there's a couple of new leads that I need to talk to you about, and I'd prefer to do it in person.'

'I'm at home, and I'm going out in a couple of hours,' she said. 'I tell you what, what are you doing this evening?'

"Nothing,' I said. A Marks and Spencer ready meal, a can of beer and a night in front of the television was how I planned to end my Sunday.

'How about this, Harry? I'm going to see a movie tonight at the Vue in Shepherd's Bush. I was going to see it with my friend but she can't go so I have a spare ticket. Why don't I see you there and we can talk before or after the movie?'

I almost asked her if the friend was Yalina Wazir but bit my tongue. She'd realise that I had been checking up on her. 'Sounds like a plan,' I said. 'I'll see you there.' I ended the call.

My mobile rang almost immediately. It was Donna Walsh. 'Harry, just thought I should let you know that the Deputy Commissioner is about to give a press conference on the mosque murder.

'Must be important for him to be working on a Sunday,' I said. The Deputy Commissioner was a career officer, with the emphasis on career. He had walked a beat, but many years ago and not for long, and once he had been promoted to sergeant and started up the greasy pole he had pretty much given up on real police work. He knew what courses to take, how to excel at interviews, and which arses to lick. It had taken me ten years to get from sergeant to inspector, but he had been promoted after just two, and was a chief inspector after another three. He was still under fifty and if he didn't land the top job on the Met there was no doubt that he'd be running a force somewhere in the country within the next couple of years.

'Several Muslim groups have been critical of the investigation, claiming that their religion has been disrespected, so he wants to nip the criticism in the bud,' said the press officer.

'You'd think he might have spoken to the SIO first,' I said.

'He's not planning on going into specifics,' said Walsh. 'He's thinking more broad brush strokes.'

'Yeah, well good luck with that,' I said. She ended the call and I put one of the big screens onto Sky News. The press conference was being held in the main press interview room at New Scotland Yard. The Deputy Commissioner had on his best tunic and had his cap under his arm. His teeth were gleaming white and his hair clearly benefited from Grecian 2000, though he had allowed his temples to stay grey.

The Bag Carrier

I knew a couple of things before the Deputy Commissioner started to speak. He would say community a lot. Probably every thirty seconds. They're told to. You don't get to climb the greasy pole without learning 'PC-speak' and 'Community' is right at the top. When something goes wrong, 'lessons will be learned'.

The top brass in the police aren't coppers. They might have been once, but a real copper wouldn't get to the top of the organisation. You have to be a political animal, you have to play the game, balance budgets, say the right sound bites and back your political masters.

Most of the rank and file have zero respect for the top brass, and that contempt seems to be reciprocated.

Remember the Manchester bombing? Son of a Libyan refugee set off a nail bomb at a kid's concert, killed 22, mainly youngsters? Three days after the suicide bombing, the Chief Constable called a press conference. I remember watching it live on the BBC. In his uniform with his badges and his buttons and his peaked hat and his little row of medals. We thought he was going to announce a break in the case, but no, he wanted to talk about an increase in hate crime. I kid you not. Hopkins, his name was, I think. Chief Constable Ian Hopkins. That's what he wanted to talk about, the fact that there had been 56 hate crimes, double the rate the Manchester cops normally see. Now, you might think that by hate crimes he meant people had been killed, or at least attacked. No, that's not what he meant. Feelings had been hurt, and that to him was a hate crime. A Muslim bank teller had been called a terrorist. An Asian woman was approached in a supermarket and verbally abused for the bombing. Another Muslin woman in a supermarket was told not to wear a niqab. Racist graffiti had appeared on a wall.

That was it. End of. The dead hadn't been buried, there were still 66 men, women and children in hospital, almost a third in the ICU, and Manchester's top copper was worried about hurt feelings in the Muslim community. And yes, he used the word 'community' four times in two minutes.

And they wonder why the public is so quick to bash the police these days? Why should they help us, why should they respect us, when they see how we behave towards them? And here's what sticks in my gut. A police officer died in that Manchester blast. One of our own. One of his own. Elaine McIver was a copper with Cheshire police. She was killed and her partner was injured and still in hospital yet the chief constable was more concerned about hurting the feelings of the Muslim community. Any respect I might have had for the man went out of the window, and I know a lot of coppers felt the same.

But it's par for the course, that's the problem, and there's nothing we can say about it, not without being branded as a racist and thrown out of the job. Like when those Muslim youths had turned up at the mosque, waving knives and machetes. We had no choice other than to pat them on their heads and send them on their way. Can you imagine what would have happened if a group of white lads had turned up armed to the teeth? We'd have cracked heads and taken them in and they'd have been charged and probably spent time inside. Why? Because if we beat up white thugs, all is well and good. If we beat up Asian thugs, we're racist. It's unfair, of course it is, but then life is unfair.

The Deputy Commissioner made his way to the podium. He spoke for just over five minutes and Walsh was right, it was very much a broad brush briefing in that it contained almost nothing in the way of factual information. He made no mention of the gang of armed Muslims who had confronted us at the mosque, and he only used the Muslim name of the victim – Mohammed Masood. There was no mention of the fact that he was a convert, and no picture of the victim flashed up on the screen. He spoke about the horror of the crime, and how the full resources of the Metropolitan Police had been put behind the investigation. The Muslim community could rest assured that the culprit would soon be in police custody and that everything was being done to make sure that the mosque – all mosques – were safe places where worshippers could carry out their religion free from harm.

An appeal for witnesses would have been nice, along with a photograph of the victim, but the press conference wasn't about moving the investigation forward, it was about showing how the Met understood the fears of the Muslim community. Personally I cared more about the fear that the knife-waving thugs had inspired in the unarmed cops who had been trying to maintain order at the crime scene, but that's probably why I'm still just an inspector and why the Deputy Commissioner is the one being interviewed by the capital's Press.

There were a few questions which the Deputy Commissioner deflected with oily well-rehearsed charm. I tried to keep the look of contempt of my face as I listened, but I didn't do a particularly good job. I turned to look at Nasri who grinned and flashed me a thumbs-up. I smiled and nodded. Nasri was clearly lapping it all up, but then he was on the fast-track himself so the Deputy Commissioner was preaching to the converted.

CHAPTER 22
(SAL)

It had been a while since I'd gotten home from work before seven pm. As I drove up to my house I clocked a lead grey Lexus SUV, full body kit sitting on low profile black graphite rims. It was facing me. Two pairs of eyes locked onto mine. Whatever was going to happen, I could not allow it to happen at my door step. I carried on past my home, giving a curt nod to the two figures through the windscreen as I passed and parked a distance away from them. I glanced up at my rearview as the two doors opened in tandem. A pair of sandy Caterpillar boots out of the passenger side and a pair of what looked like steel toe-capped boots out of the driver's side. I committed their number plate to memory as the figures loomed in my rear view. One substantially taller, wider, just outright bigger than his short companion. Talker and Enforcer, I presumed. They were both white, the smaller one wearing a blazer with an open neck lairy red Hawaiian shirt. The bigger decked out in a bomber jacket, cargo pants and, yeah, they were definitely steel toe-capped boots.

I waited until they were closer to me and further away from my home, and then I stepped out.

'Can I help you, lads?' I smiled at the less threatening one.

'We'd like a word, Sal,' said Hawaiian Shirt.

'What's this about?' I said, glancing very quickly at the bigger of the two. He had cauliflower ears and a nose that had been broken with regularity, which coupled with his rugby player physique made me quickly want to avert my eyes.

'It's about a little something that you owe.'

'Oh, Ray sent you.' I said. 'That's a bit dramatic, he could have just called.' Cauliflower Ears loomed over me like a storm about to break. I worked out what he had for dinner when he bared his teeth at me. I took a step back, my car bumper digging into my leg. 'Tell Ray not to sweat it, he'll get his money.' I tried to slip by but a big hand on my chest kept me pinned against my car. I put my hands out in an appeasing manner. He swatted them away and continued to bear down on me.

'Eleven hundred, Sal,' said Hawaiian Shirt. 'Or my friend here goes to work.' Cauliflower Ears made a show of curling his hand into a fist and I could see his red raw cracked knuckles immune to pounding flesh.

'Alright! Okay!' I said. 'I'll sort it, I swear.' Cauliflower took a step back. 'Obviously I haven't got it on me right now, but Ray and I go way back, he knows I always pay my debts. I just need a little time.' I pushed against him but he was as hard as a rock so I stopped. 'You know I'm a police officer, right?'

Cauliflower loomed over me, his thick lips curled back in a snarl. 'Not to me you're not,' he said, his mouth so close to my face that I could smell the garlic on his breath. 'To me you're just a Paki who owes us eleven hundred quid. So are you gonna give us the cash now or shall we go inside and ask your pretty little wife for the money?'

'You leave my family out of this,' I said, and shoved him in the chest. It was like thumping a tree. He didn't move. Not for a second or two, anyway. Then he pulled back his hand and smacked me in the chin. He was fast, so fast that I didn't see it coming and by the time I realised what was happening I was flat on my back seeing stars.

Hawaiian Shirt kicked me in the ribs but I was so stunned from the punch I barely felt it.

Cauliflower Ears bent down and went through my pockets. He pulled out my wallet and flicked through the contents. 'Eighty quid?' he sneered. 'Eighty fucking quid? Is that all you've got?' He tossed the wallet on the ground and pocketed the notes.

Hawaiian Shirt knelt down and pulled out my warrant card in its nice leather case with the Metropolitan Police crest on it. 'We'll keep this until you've paid what you owe,' he said.

'You can't take that,' I moaned. 'It's more than my job's worth.'

'Yeah? And how much are your fucking legs worth, Paki?' said Hawaiian Shirt. 'Because if Mr Chottopadhyay doesn't get his eleven hundred back within twenty-four hours you'll be spending the rest of the year on crutches.'

'It's nine hundred.'

'Plus two hundred for interest and expenses. Eleven hundred, Paki. Twenty-four hours. Deal or no deal?'

Hawaiian Shirt drew back his foot to kick me again. 'Deal,' I gasped.

He grinned and kicked me anyway. This time it hurt like hell and I felt something crack inside. 'Twenty four hours,' he said.

I lay on my back, gasping for breath as they walked away. I heard them get into the car and drive off. I rolled over onto my front and carefully got up. My side hurt like hell but it didn't feel as if anything was actually broken. I looked around but didn't see anyone and the curtains were still drawn at my house so my attack seemed to have gone unnoticed.

I fixed my tie, patted my hair down and tucked my shirt in before driving the short distance to my house. By the time I was letting myself in I was looking halfway decent. Maria came running down the hall in her dinosaur bathrobe and I scooped her up and held her tightly, ignoring the pain running down my side.

'Welcome home, daddy!' she said. I buried my face in her neck and breathed in her scent.

'I love you, princess,' I said, tears pricking my eyes.

'I love you, daddy.' She beamed when she saw my tie with its cartoon cats. 'You're still wearing my tie,' she said.

'Of course, it's the best tie ever,' I said. 'Everyone at work is so jealous.'

'I spent ages choosing it,' she said.

'I know.' I put her down, wiped my eyes, put on a brave smile and held Maria's hand as I walked through to the kitchen where Miriam was cooking something that smelled really good. Probably a French recipe. Maybe Italian. The one thing it wouldn't be was curry, because neither of us are fans. I let go of Maria and hugged my wife. 'Bad day?' she said.

'How could you possibly know that?'

'You look tense. Why don't you run a bath and have a soak before dinner? I'll be a while yet.'

'It smells good.'

'It'll taste good, too. Now go on with you, half an hour in a Radox bath will relax you.'

I forced a smile and hugged her. It was going to take more than a bubble bath to relax me, but there was no way I could tell her the trouble I was in. She didn't know I gambled and she sure as hell didn't know that I was in debt to a guy who thought nothing of sending a couple of heavies to my home. She patted me on the backside. 'Go,' she said.

I went upstairs. My laptop was in the bedroom. I sat on the bed and booted it up, then went through to the PokerStars website. I was down to my last fifty quid on the site. I took out my wallet. At least they'd left me with my credit cards. One of the cards had arrived in the post a few days earlier and I hadn't used it. I tapped in the details and added another two hundred quid to my account, then went looking for tables.

In my experience the top tables are best avoided because that's where the professionals are hanging out so playing there is asking for trouble. There are too many idiots playing on the cheaper tables, guys who'll go all in with a pair of threes because they're stupid or drunk. The best tables are midway, there are guys who know what they're doing but there are plenty of fish too, waiting to be caught and gutted.

I started playing on four tables, Texas Hold 'em, because one table was just too slow; there's always someone who is over-thinking or having connection problems. I played pretty-much non-stop until I heard Miriam calling me from downstairs. I looked at my watch. An hour had gone by.

'I'm coming!' I shouted. I looked back at the screen I was a hundred and fifty quid down. How the hell had that happened? I took off my suit and tie and hung them in the wardrobe and pulled on a pair of jeans, then had a quick wash in the bathroom.

Miriam and Maria were sitting at the kitchen table waiting for me. 'You didn't have a bath?'

'I'll do it before bed,' I said, sitting down. I nodded at the bowl of whatever she had cooked which she had set in the middle of the table. 'Stew?'

'Beef bourguignon,' she said. 'It's from an internet recipe but I fiddled with it.' She lifted the lid off a bowl. 'And garlic mashed potatoes.'

I grinned. My wife is one hell of a cook. She spooned stew and potatoes onto my plate while I poured water for the three of us.

'Daddy, can you help me with my homework after dinner?' asked Maria.

'Of course, Princess.'

'Daddy's tired,' said Miriam. 'He's had a busy day.'

'Catching killers?' asked Maria.

'Princess! Where did you get that from?' I asked.

'I heard you and mummy talking,' said Maria. 'That's what you do now, isn't it? Catch killers?'

'I'm in Homicide Command,' I said.

'What's homicide?'

Miriam flashed me a warning look.

'I catch bad guys,' I said.

'How many did you catch today?' she asked.

I nodded at her plate. 'Eat your dinner,' I said.

I tucked into my food and made small talk with my wife and daughter but all I could think about was getting back to the internet poker tables. I still had a hundred pounds in the account and if I had a good few hours I could turn that into a thousand or so. Maybe more. At the moment internet poker was my only hope because I didn't have any cash to buy my way into a real game.

Chapter 23
(Harry)

I wasn't sure what the parking situation was going to be around the cinema so I caught an Uber cab and got there ten minutes early. I stood outside the cinema looking at a poster for the movie we were going to see. I couldn't make sense of it, but the main character seemed to be a very beautiful Indian woman who was surrounded by men who appeared to be dancing with spears and swords.

'Her name is Padmaavat, she was a Queen in medieval India,' said Ayesha behind me.

Her voice was so soft that it didn't make me jump. I turned and smiled at her. She had on a pale purple headscarf and a bright red trenchcoat with black buttons and black boots and over her shoulder was a black bag that looked expensive. 'You could creep up on the devil himself,' I said.

She shrugged and smiled prettily. 'I'm small. I don't make a lot of noise.'

I laughed and resisted the urge to give her a hug. 'I was just thinking that maybe the movie wasn't a good idea.'

'It's sub-titled,' she said. 'You'll be fine.'

'I meant job-wise. I'm supposed to be here officially. I'm not sure that watching a movie is official.'

'Okay,' she said thoughtfully. 'How about this? You're not very familiar with my way of life, are you?'

'In what way?' I asked. 'Because you're female, Asian or Muslim?'

She laughed and quickly covered her mouth with her hand. Her tiny hand. She was wearing three intricate gold rings and her nails were painted a bright pink. 'I suppose the last two, you've come across women before, I'm sure. What I meant was you could consider it research. It was obvious at the mosque that you were a fish out of water, a Bollywood movie might help you on your learning curve.'

I grinned. 'I hope my bosses see it that way.'

'I won't spoil the plot for you, but it's a love story. Most Bollywood movies are. Padmaavat lives in a Kingdom in the north west of India. A sultan in a neighbouring kingdom sets his sights on her and lays siege to the fortress where she lives.'

'I'm looking forward to it.'

She laughed and again she covered her mouth with her hand. 'You don't sound like you mean it.'

'I mean it.'

She looked at her watch, a gold Rolex. 'Let's go in,' she said. 'I want popcorn. And a fizzy drink. And some chocolate.'

'You are here for the movie, right?' She laughed again. She seemed to be laughing at pretty much everything I said.

We went in and I bought her sweets and her drink and felt a little as if I was a father taking out a daughter. I knew her date of birth, of course, and that she was twenty-six years old. Hell, yes, I was easily old enough to be her father.

'Are you okay, Harry?' she asked, catching me deep in thought.

I wondered if I should correct her and insist that she called me DI Porter but that would have sounded churlish so I just smiled and nodded. 'I'm good.'

'If you really hate it, we can leave early.'

'I'll be fine,' I said. And actually I was. As it turned out, Bollywood movies are fun, even if you have to read the subtitles. Though to be honest the plot was easy enough to follow, there was a lot of singing and dancing, some slapstick comedy, a lot of bare-chested men running around on a beach, and some love scenes that left a lot to the imagination. I'm pretty sure I was the only non-Asian in the cinema, and we did get quite a few curious looks, but all in all the two and a half hours passed quickly.

'So, are you hungry, Harry?' she asked when we were back outside on the pavement.

'Sure. But I need to finish the interview and get a picture.'

'A picture?'

'We're photographing everyone at the mosque that day, it makes identification easier. I should have done it when I first interviewed you.'

'Well why don't we combine business and pleasure and do it over a pizza?'

I couldn't help but smile. 'Sure. Why not?'

She took me along the road to a Pizza Express and we were given a table in the corner. We ordered pizzas and bottled water. 'Have a beer, Harry,' she said. 'Don't think you have to stick to water for me.'

'You're sure?'

She laughed and again her hand flew up to cover her mouth. 'I'm the Muslim, not you. If you want pepperoni on your pizza and a beer that's totally fine with me.'

'I would like a beer,' I said. I ordered a Peroni. While we were waiting for our pizzas I used my phone to take a photograph, close up so that it wasn't obvious that she was in a restaurant. She had an amused smile on her face and there was a spark in her eyes that had nothing to do with the flash.

'How is the investigation going?' she asked as I put my phone away.

'Slowly but surely,' I said.

'But you don't have a suspect?'

I shook my head. My beer arrived and I took a sip. 'If we don't have a suspect within a few hours then generally it's down to a long haul,' I said. 'It's about interviewing witnesses, establishing alibis, and analysing forensic evidence.'

'Is there any in this case?' she asked. 'Forensic evidence?'

'Not really,' I admitted. 'No strange fibres on his clothing, no bloody footprints leading away from the body. We have a pretty good idea of the shape of the knife that was used but of course that doesn't help us find it.'

'So what do you do now?'

'We just keep plugging away. Interviewing witnesses. Examining CCTV. And we have a computer system that cross-checks everything.' I took another sip of my beer. 'So, you told me you got the bus to the mosque with your friend Yalina.'

'That's right.'

'But you didn't mention Fazal.'

She frowned. 'Fazal?'

'Her brother.'

'Why would I mention Fazal?'

'Wasn't he on the bus with you?'

She shook her head. 'No.'

'Are you sure?'

Her eyes widened. 'Well, I'm not a hundred per cent sure. We were sitting downstairs, I suppose he could have been upstairs. What's wrong, Harry? Am I in trouble?'

'I just need to make sure that your statement reflects what actually happened. A lot of people reported seeing Fazal at the mosque. And indeed he was interviewed there. It seems a bit strange that you didn't mention arriving at the mosque with him.'

'But I didn't,' she said.

I kept smiling at her but behind the smile my mind was racing. That was a lie. An absolute lie. And I had the photographic evidence in my pocket. But if I showed it to her, what then? I'd be confronting her in a direct lie. In an interview room that could work to the investigator's advantage because her reaction would be caught on video, but I was in a pizza restaurant and I had a bottle of beer and if I wasn't very careful this could all come back and bite me in the arse. She had lied. She had been with Yalina and Fazal Wazir, and someone had shouted over at Sean Evans. She had mentioned none of that to me. That could only be because she was hiding something and while that didn't necessarily mean she was a suspect, it certainly raised a bloody big red flag. 'It's okay,' I said, picking up my glass. 'It's just his name came up and I assumed he might have travelled in with his sister, that's all.' I took a sip of my beer.

'They don't live together,' she said.

I put down my glass. 'It's okay, there's no need for you to have mentioned him if you didn't see him.'

She sat back in her chair, frowning. 'Oh my gosh,' she said. 'I did see him. Oh my gosh.' She picked up her glass of water and took a couple of gulps. 'He wasn't on the bus, but we bumped into him on the pavement.'

I leaned towards her. 'Did you go into the mosque together?'

'No, we just said a few words and then he went on ahead. As you know, the men and women pray separately.'

I nodded.

'Harry, I'm so sorry. Is this a problem?'

'Of course not.'

'I don't know how I forgot.'

I held up my hand. 'It's absolutely no big deal. I'll just add what you've said to the original interview.'

That wasn't true. It was a big deal. She'd admitted to seeing Fazal because she knew that I already knew. She had either realised I had seen them on the CCTV footage or that a witness had reported seeing them together. Either way she had clearly decided that it was better to come clean rather than to persist in her lie. But she hadn't admitted to seeing Sean Evans because I hadn't raised it, and now I didn't intend to.

Our pizzas arrived and she clapped her hands in delight, like a little girl getting ready to open her Christmas presents. I smiled at the image. Did Muslims give each other Christmas presents? I had absolutely no idea. But I did know when someone was lying to me, and Ayesha Khan was definitely being less than truthful.

Chapter 24
(Sal)

I got up really early Monday morning. It was still dark but I needed to get to the Islamic Centre for the first prayers of the day. It was a popular mosque, converted from a cinema in the Nineties. I'd taken the gold in the middle of the night while Miriam was fast asleep. She kept it in our safe in the wardrobe, along with important documents and our passports. It was the gold she had worn on her wedding day, my present to her so it didn't seem that unreasonable that I should borrow it for a while. There were several bangles and rings and a filigreed necklace, all of almost pure gold. She kept the pieces in three red velvet bags with gold drawstrings.

I kissed her on the forehead and told her I had been called in early. Just one lie to add to the many I'd told her over the last few months. I still felt ashamed at lying to her, but the shame was decreasing with every lie. I told myself that the lies were a means to an end. Once I'd gotten my financial situation under control I'd never gamble again, that was the promise I'd made to myself. But one step at a time – my priority was to get Chottopadhyay's thugs off my back.

I drove to the Islamic Centre in Maida Vale, getting there at just before five, in plenty of time for early morning prayers. The pavements were busy, but not packed; a lot of Muslims preferred to do the first prayer of the day at home. I did, though truth be told I tended to sleep through it more often than not.

I parked a short walk away. It wasn't my regular mosque and I didn't recognise many people, but I was only looking for one man. Uncle Siddiqui, they called him. He wasn't my uncle. He wasn't the uncle of anyone I knew, though I'm sure he had plenty of nephews and nieces. He owned more than a hundred flats and bedsits in Kilburn and the shabbier parts of Maida Vale, mainly rented out to asylum seekers and families on benefits who for whatever reason weren't able to get council accommodation. He was also a money-lender, rumoured to have more than a million pounds on the street at any one time.

I took off my shoes, put them in a rack, and went through to the massive prayer hall. It took me a while to spot him. He was close to the front, deep in conversation with two elderly Asians. His hair was grey and slicked back, his skin a dark brown and peppered with small black spots that some said was a form of incurable skin cancer, but as he'd had the marks for all of the ten years or so that I'd known him, I assumed that was an inaccurate diagnosis.

The Bag Carrier

The gold was burning a hole in my pocket but I knew it would be bad form to even attempt to discuss business in the mosque. I stayed at the back throughout the prayer session, and waited for him outside. He came out on his own wearing a long camel coat with a black-trimmed collar over a suit that was almost certainly Savile Row.

'Uncle Siddiqui?'

He turned to look at me and beamed. 'Sal!' he said. 'Long time no see.' He grabbed me, hugged me and kissed me on one cheek. 'How is little Maria? How old is she now? She must be five now.'

'She is, Uncle. She's fine.' You had to admire the man, he was in his seventies but had a mind like a steel trap. He'd met my daughter once. Maybe twice. But always asked after her, by name. 'Uncle, I need to talk business with you, if you have the time.' I patted my pocket and he understood immediately

He put his arm around me and squeezed. 'Then come into my office,' he said, leading me down the road.

We walked across the car park and towards his office, an almost new gleaming white Mercedes AMG E-class. I climbed into the front passenger seat and gave him the red velvet bags. He opened one and looked inside. 'How is Miriam?' Siddiqui asked knowingly.

'She's fine, Uncle.' I replied, looking out of the passenger side window, not wanting him to catch the shame on my face. I didn't really want to be talking cosy about my wife right then. I nodded towards the velvet bags. 'What do you think?'

He opened the bags and took his time picking up and appraising each piece individually. Bracelets. Earrings. Rings. Bangles. All gold. And a thin gold chain that Miriam had set aside for my Maria. He smiled knowing how much trouble I was in. 'Two grand.'

'It's worth five, at least, Uncle. I've had them appraised.'

'Yes, of course, but these are second-hand and no one wants to wear used jewellery. Especially a bride. Look, Salim, you've paid a premium for the decorative work but the gold itself...' He shook his head. 'If I end up getting stuck with it, then it's scrap value and that means two.

'Uncle, please, hear me out.' I said, trying to keep the desperation out of my voice, but it was clear that I wouldn't be sitting here with my wife's gear if I wasn't desperate. 'Firstly, it's worth twice that. And secondly, it's my wife's jewellery and you know I'm coming back for it.'

'Two, two,' he said. 'Final.'

I threw my hands up in the air, '*Two thousand, two hundred! C'mon Uncle!* Two seven, at the very least.'

'You can chase me around the park all day, Salim, and when you catch me, I'll still only be handing you two two.'

He put the gold back into the bags, then took out his wallet and counted out the money in fifties.

'And when I buy it back, what's the interest?' I asked, pocketing the two and a bit.

'Five per cent a week, Sal. Same as always.'

Yeah, I know. I realise that I'm borrowing from Peter to pay Paul – or strictly speaking borrowing from Siddiqui to pay Chottopadhyay – but there was a big difference. Uncle Siddiqui never leant money without collateral, which means that he didn't have to use thugs to collect, he'd simply confiscate the assets and not give it a second's thought. We both knew that my gold, my *wife's* gold, was worth a lot more than the money he'd be lending me but not more than my life's worth if Miriam ever found out.

'I'll be back for it next week,' I said, reaching for the door handle.

'Sal, a quick word,' he said, lowering his voice.

'What's that?' I said.

'I've seen gambling ruin more lives than almost anything else. It's a sickness. Most part, I couldn't give a damn what a client does with the money, but you, Salim. I like you. Growing up, you were a good kid and now you're a good cop. One of very few. Continue down this road you're going piss away your career.' He smiled. 'Cops like you help me sleep well. I wouldn't want anything to happen to you.'

'All right, Uncle,' I said. 'Appreciate you saying. But I'm not addicted to gambling. I've just had a run of bad luck.' I opened the car door with one hand and put out my other for him to shake. He took it and held firmly.

'Especially with all the nasty business at Central Mosque.' He met my eyes. 'I hear you are investigating the murder.'

It was a statement of fact rather than a question. I closed the car door and faced him. 'How would you know that?'

'The streets are noisy, Salim,' he said, as a way of explanation as he released my hand.

'Yeah, I'm on the case.'

'Any joy?' Siddiqui asked.

'It's ongoing. Why?'

He leaned across his seat closer to me until I could smell his expensive cologne. 'The victim's name, Sean Evans?'

'And?' I wasn't giving anything away.

'Or I should say, previously known as Sean Evans,' Siddiqui said. 'Until his untimely demise, he went by the name of Mohammed Masood.' He looked out of the window towards the prayer hall. 'He used to hang out here, before he became a regular at Maida Vale.'

'Is that right?'

Uncle Siddiqui nodded. 'He tried hard to ingratiate himself with a bad crowd. They didn't want to know, he was too keen.'

'Bad crowd? What do you mean?' My interest was piqued.

'Those brothers who are of a different mindset to us. Those that prey on the weak. Those that indoctrinate, persuade and groom.' Siddiqui laughed, but there was nothing in it. 'This Mohammed Masood was doing all the running, coming across as a little...desperate.... and they didn't want to know. The last I heard he moved to Maida Vale Central Mosque and started mixing with The Faith.'

'So what? They thought he was a plant?'

Siddiqui shrugged his big shoulders. 'Plant, bush, tree, who knows? But it wouldn't be the first time the police or the spooks have sent in an undercover agent.'

'Thank you, Uncle,' I said. I knew more about the victim from a five-minute chat with a loan shark than I did from 48 hours of police investigation.

'Thanks?' He raised his eyebrows. 'For what, Sal? I told you nothing. I'm not one to fraternise with the police.' He smiled. 'Now get the hell out of my car.'

Chapter 25
(Harry)

I was in the MIR bright and early Monday morning. I wanted to catch up on HOLMES before morning prayers, but I also wanted to update the interview with Ayesha Khan. I printed off the head and shoulders photograph that I'd taken on my phone and stuck it to the whiteboard containing the female worshippers who had been at the mosque. Then I sat down, logged onto HOLMES and called up Ayesha's witness statement. I sat back and considered my options. Strictly speaking I should enter the details from the second interview as exactly that, a re-interview that had been separate from the first one. But that would mean explaining why the interview had taken place at a pizza place after a Bollywood movie. The only information that had come out from the second interview was that she had seen Fazal Wazir. I hadn't raised the subject of Sean Evans being on the other side of the road from her group, nor had I told her about the CCTV footage.

So strictly speaking I didn't have to enter that into HOLMES. I had the picture up on the board and there was no requirement to say when it had been taken. So I could probably just leave things as they were.

I was still wondering what to do when Alan Russell arrived. I went over to him as he was taking off his jacket. 'Alan, do me a favour. Can you get John Reynolds to pursue Ayesha Khan for me on the video front? He had footage of her on the pavement outside the mosque, see if he can find out when she left. She wasn't among those questioned so she must have left before the interviews started.'

Russell frowned. 'Ayesha Khan?'

'She's Nominal 348.'

'I'll get him on it,' said Russell.

'Bacon sandwich?' I asked.

'You read my mind,' he replied. 'Brown sauce.'

I went down to the canteen and bought two coffees and two bacon sandwiches. By the time I got back to the MIR, Nasri was at his desk. Russell had gone into the CCTV room so I joined him and we ate our sandwiches together as he brought me up to speed on what little the Outside Enquiry Team had achieved over the weekend.

Nasri looked up as I went back into the MIR. 'Guv, when did you do the interview with Ayesha Khan?' He looked up from the terminal, his face a blank mask but I just knew he wasn't happy. I was starting to suspect that Nasri was taking a personal interest in her and if that were the case I'd have to nip it in the bud.

'Are you looking at HOLMES? It says, doesn't it? Or did I forget to put in the time and date of the interview, because that's not like me.'

'No, Guv. It says Saturday, 6pm.'

'Then that's when I conducted the interview. Do you have a problem with that?'

One of the typists turned to look at me and then quickly turned back to her terminal. Nasri got out of his chair and walked over to me. He lowered his voice. 'I don't have a problem, Guv, but I recall you saying that you were going home early Saturday night.'

'Miss Khan phoned me and said she could be interviewed Saturday evening.'

'Right, all right.' Nasri nodded and followed it with a frown, 'All due respect, Guv, it should have gone through DS Rees? And also, shouldn't the interview have been conducted by a female officer, you know... As per your instructions?'

I kept a smile on my face and my voice level, but I was struggling to contain my anger because Nasri is only my bag carrier, he's not my deputy and he's certainly not my superior so he had no business querying my decisions. But he did update the Decision Log and I'd have to sign off on it and I didn't want to be arguing with him about what he should or shouldn't write about the Ayesha Khan interview. 'She had no problems talking to male officers at the mosque if you recall, and I did make the suggestion that I send a female officer but she said she was quite happy for me to do the interview. As you'll see from the record of the interview in HOLMES, she didn't go into the main prayer hall until after the body had been discovered, she didn't know the victim, and she gave me almost thirty names including half a dozen names of people she'd seen there who weren't already in the system. So I think you could say the interview was a success on several levels.'

'That's great, Guv,' He was smiling but the smile was as false as mine. 'By the way, where'd you interview her? The Citizens Advice Bureau closes at six at weekends.'

The smile was still on his face but his eyes were hard, weighing me up. It would be easy enough to lie but lies had a habit of coming back to bite you in the arse and if I did lie and he wrote it up and I signed off on it and then I was caught in the lie then it could well cost me my job.

'We went for a meal,' I said quietly. 'At an Indian restaurant.'

His eyes widened. 'You took her out on a bloody date?'

'Watch your tone, Detective Nasri,' I said.

He looked around as if he feared being overheard. 'You can't be seen in public with her, Guv. If The Faith find out, they could get really nasty. Muslim girls can't be seen out with….' He hesitated and I knew he was going to say 'white' but he bit back the word because he knew how racist that would sound. 'A non-Muslim man' is how he finished the sentence.

'I was a police officer interviewing a witness,' I said.

'Appearances, Guv. Come on! You know better... Word gets out, they won't come after you, yeah. You understand what I'm saying?'

'We had a curry. It took less than an hour which is how long a regular interview would have taken. It wasn't social, like you seem to think. It was work.'

He opened his mouth to reply but then stopped himself and held up a hand and shrugged. 'I just thought I should mention it, Guv, that's all.'

'You have done, DC Nasri, and your concern is noted.'

He took a deep breath, then forced a smile though he was obviously still far from happy. 'Right, Guv. In other news, I've spoken to Sean Evans's tutor at Reading University and he's happy to talk to us. I've got a car sorted so ready when you are.'

Chapter 26
(Sal)

It was an hour's drive to Reading University, but it felt like twice that. Apart from Porter grunting the odd direction or muttering disagreement under his breath at the radio, the journey was pretty much in silence. Not the usual silence with Porter mentally pondering the case, this was different, he was still pissed off. With reason? No, I don't think so. I had every right to question his handling of Ayesha Khan. Chain of command does not come into it. I'm not trying to be a stickler here, trust me. But it's these very, sometimes small details, which can be the difference between a collar and a murderer let loose to commit again. And if it went to court, and this procedural oversight came to light, then we're looking at a mistrial and shit hitting the fan, with most of it flying at the SIO.

I glanced at Porter and pictured it.

'What?' He said.

'Nothing, Guv,' I said.

The thing is, put aside the case, what he did was just plain witless. He didn't get it. He should have. The Faith are no joke. They make it their business to get into yours. Loitering outside supermarkets and harassing any brothers who dare walk out with any liquor. Screaming abuse at sisters who dress a touch less than what they perceive as modest.

And if they see a Muslim in an interracial relationship; particularly a *sister*, with a white guy? Then, believe me... It's On. The white guy will get the shit kicked out of him, but the girl? I don't even want to think about it. It's exactly this mind set which lands us in the media. Porter should have known better. What was he playing at, taking her out for a Jalfrezi and a couple of poppadoms right in the heart of Maida Vale's Muslim community?

Porter should have known better. More so, Ayesha should have known better. She must have known the risk of being seen out in public with him. Where's the up side? What? She's attracted to him?

'What?' he asked again.

'Nothing, Guv.'

She definitely ain't attracted to him. So what's her game? A free curry? She didn't look as if she was short of money. She was wearing a gold Rolex, discrete and understated but nevertheless a gold Rolex, and her clothes didn't look cheap. Most of the advisers at the Citizens Advice Bureau were volunteers so she either had another job or family money. Either way she didn't need to be poncing free meals off a middle-aged detective. And I'm only saying middle-aged on the assumption that the old fart lives to be 110.

We arrived at Reading University, a sprawling campus to the South East of the town. The Department of Economics had its own car park and Clive Jenner's office overlooked it. He had been Sean Evans's tutor during his years at the university and he was expecting us so we were ushered straight in.

Jenner was tall and bookish with thinning hair and he blinked at us through a pair of black-framed spectacles as he shook our hands.

'I'm DC Nasri, we spoke earlier,' I said, hoping that he wouldn't ask to see my warrant card. 'This is DI Porter. As I said on the phone, we'd like to talk to you about Sean Evans.'

Jenner walked behind his desk and sat down. He waved at two chairs on our side of the desk. 'Please, sit.' He waited until we were settled before he asked. 'So it's confirmed... Sean was murdered?'

'I'm afraid so,' I said.

Jenner took off his glasses, squeezed his eyes closed and pinched the bridge of his nose. I let him have that moment and scoped his tidy desk. There were two framed photographs, a wedding picture taken a decade or so earlier - judging by the fashion - he was holding hands with a pretty brunette, and a formal picture of Jenner with his wife and two young sons, all smiling toothily. The perfect family. I wondered how many takes it would have been to capture such a priceless moment.

'What happened?' Jenner asked, glasses on, composure regained.

'He was stabbed,' said Porter. 'We don't have a description of his killer so we're trying to put together a profile of Sean, see if we can find out who might have wanted to hurt him.'

'So it wasn't a random attack?'

'We're not sure,' said Porter. 'The circumstances are a little strange so at the moment we're pursuing several avenues of enquiry.'

'I assumed when you said he had been stabbed that it had been a mugging or a…' He hesitated, not sure how to finish the sentence.

'No,' I said, 'Sean was targeted.'

'At the moment we don't have a motive for his killing,' said Porter. 'How was he here? Was he popular? Well-liked? Or did he have issues?'

'Issues?'

'We know almost nothing about Sean. We've spoken to his parents, but obviously they're biased. Was he the sort of person who might get into a fight? Did he have a temper? Was he aggressive?'

'No more than any other teenager,' said Jenner. 'I'd say he was popular, yes. Hard working, took university life very seriously. A lot of students go a bit crazy their first few months away from home, but Sean was very grounded. Always did well in exams, well-liked, a member of the mountaineering club, contributed to discussions. I always said I'd wish we had a class full of Seans.'

Yeah, right. Bet he never once said that.

'No problems at all?' Porter asked. 'No issues?'

'Not during the first two years, no,' said Jenner. 'But things changed in his third year.' His eyes landed on mine and quickly looked away again before shuffling uncomfortably in his chair. I was sure now that Sean Evans had first dipped his head towards Mecca during his time at Reading University.

'You know about his conversion, I suppose?' Jenner said, 'About him converting to Islam.'

'You're sure about that?' Porter asked, 'That he became a Muslim?'

Jenner frowned. 'You didn't know?'

'We're a bit confused about that, to be honest,' said Porter. 'His parents don't believe that he was a Muslim, but he was wearing Islamic clothing when he died.'

'Oh, he was a Muslim, no question about that,' said Jenner. 'It happened during his final year. He had an Asian girlfriend, a Pakistani girl. Beautiful little thing, her name escapes me but Sean fell head over heels. He converted to Islam, started wearing Islamic clothing, and insisted that we call him by his Islamic name.'

'Mohammed Masood?' I said.

'I can't remember,' said Jenner. 'I know the university turned down his application for an official change of name because he hadn't done it by deed poll. He wanted his degree issued in his Islamic name but that didn't happen.'

'You don't remember the name of this girl?' asked Porter.

'Sorry, no. I might be able to find out. She was involved in the Islamic Society, I remember that. He joined, I think, to get closer to her. Then in the Christmas break of his final year she arranged for him to do volunteer work at an orphanage in Pakistan. Peshawar, I seem to remember.'

'And she went with him?'

'A group went, quite a large group. It's a common thing, they arrange sponsorship and pay their own way and they get a few weeks' holiday. But when Sean came back he'd changed.'

'How so?' I asked, and Jenner had no option but face me. His face carried a pinched pained expression.

'He'd grown a beard, started wearing a dishdasha all the time. Insisted that we call him by his Islamic name.'

'Yes, you said that already,' I said.

'No, I mean to the extent where he would bluntly refuse to acknowledge his birth name.'

'Surely it's his right to be called whatever he likes.'

'DC Nasri,' Porter interjected.

I cleared my throat, 'Please, continue.' I said, smiling tightly at him.

'He was behind a campaign to get the canteens and shops to serve halal options and he led several pro-Palestine demonstrations. I tried talking to him but he wouldn't listen.'

'You wanted to talk him out of being a Muslim?' I said, this time Porter flashed me a warning look. I leaned back in my chair and crossed my arms.

Jenner put up his hands defensively. 'No, no, of course not. Religion is a matter of choice. But when it started to interfere with his studies then as his tutor I have a duty to bring it up.'

'So his work suffered?' Porter sensibly took over.

'Well, he was on target for a First before he went to Pakistan, and he ended up with a 2-1. So yes, I would say it suffered, but it was still a good pass.'

'Did he have any close friends here, other than the girl?'

'Before his conversion, yes. As I said, he was very popular. But afterwards?' He looked pained. 'I got the feeling he had cut himself off from all his non-Muslim friends. He referred to them as kafirs. Said it means unbelievers and that a kafir is lower than an animal. One time I asked if that meant I was an animal and he said that if I didn't believe in Islam, then yes, I was lower than an animal.'

'Was he aggressive at all?'

Jenner grinned. 'To me, no. Forceful in his beliefs, yes, but not aggressive towards me. But there were occasions when he was aggressive on campus. Towards the end of his final year he was warned several times about shouting at female students for not covering their heads or for dressing immodestly.' He picked up a bottle of water, unscrewed the top and drank. 'Can I ask you something, Inspector? Did Sean gain employment?'

'He was driving a cab.'

Jenner shook his head. 'Such a waste.'

'His parents thought he would end up working in the City.'

Jenner nodded. 'He could have done, no question. He knew his subject, he'd have been snapped up by one of the banks or brokers. Before his conversion, anyway. Religion has a lot to answer for, doesn't it?'

I wasn't sure if his question was rhetorical or not but we weren't there for a theological discussion.

'Would it be possible for me to have a list of the members of the Islamic Society while he was here?' Porter asked.

Jenner looked pained. 'If it was up to me, of course. But I can't see the university would be happy about giving you that information.'

'It would help in our investigation,' Porter said.

'I can see that,' he said. 'But you can see how the students might worry about their names being on a list that was being scrutinised by the Metropolitan Police.'

'It's more a matter of speaking to students who knew him,' Porter said.

'Well, yes, you say that. But playing devil's advocate, the students might worry that you might compare that list against a list of terror suspects and if there were any matches then they might all become tarred by the same brush. You can see how that would be a worry, right?'

He was right, I'll give him that. It was exactly what we intended to do, because Sean Evans hadn't just converted to Islam, the scars on his body suggested that he'd been working towards some sort of terrorist activity and we needed to know who if anyone had been helping him.

'I'll try through official channels, obviously,' Porter said.

'Good luck with that,' said Jenner. 'Do you have any idea who might have killed Sean?'

'The investigation is ongoing,' Porter said.

'But you have no suspects?'

'As I said, it's ongoing. But between you and me, no, we don't have a prime suspect at the moment. Which is why we need to know more about Sean and what he was doing prior to his death.'

'I wish I could be of more help,' he said. 'But even if I could get a list, if anyone found out I had given it to you my job would be on the line.'

'I understand,' Porter said. He took out his wallet and gave him a business card.

'What do you think?' Porter asked me as we walked back to the car.

'You really want to know what I think about Jenner?' I said.

'About Sean's conversion? Do you believe he would become a Muslim because of a girl?'

'It happens, Guv.' I kicked a pebble along the way. 'It's more common for women to convert for their husband but it's not unheard of for a man to convert for love.'

He shrugged. 'Seems like a big step, just for a relationship. Maybe they used her to pull him in. A honey trap, that's what they call it. They get a pretty Muslim girl to pull him in and then they radicalise him.'

I blew out my cheeks. 'That's a big assumption, Guv.'

'Yeah, and not one I need to see in the Book 194.'

'Absolutely, Guv.'

I understood why Porter didn't want me putting his honey trap theory in the Decision Log - it was the sort of assumption that might come back to haunt him down the line. But it didn't mean he didn't have a point.

Sean Evans might well have been interested in the Pakistani girl, enough to go through conversion, and yeah, it's possible that she could have used that infatuation to draw him in. Either way, we had to find her.

But what Porter doesn't see is that the same thing applies to him and his relationship with Ayesha Khan. He seems to think that she's interested in him, but that's simply impossible, as likely as a camel passing through the eye of a needle. He met her in a mosque, she had her head covered and was surrounded by brothers – did he think for one moment that she saw him as anything other than a symbol of Christian authority that had invaded her place of worship? And having met the way they did, how was it even possible that she could have any sort of romantic interest in him? What did he think, he was Romeo and she was Juliet and somehow everything would end up happily ever after? Well this wasn't a Shakespeare play, this was the real world and in the real world Muslim girls didn't get wet for non-Muslims and in the very unlikely event that they did, the brothers would step in pretty smartish and point out the error of their ways. So if Ayesha Khan was cosying up to Porter she was doing it for a reason and that reason had nothing do with romance. I could see that but he clearly couldn't. What is it they say? Love is blind? Yeah, and they also say that there's no fool like an old fool, but I figured that Porter wouldn't want to hear that so I kept quiet as I drove back to London. But he had a point about Evans and the girl he'd met, and that point was that a respectable Muslim woman fancying a non-Muslim man was about as likely as a mongoose cosying up to a snake. That's not racist, that's just a fact. A Muslim woman from a good family wouldn't even consider entering into a relationship with a non-Muslim man. What I said about Muslim men marrying non-Muslim women was bang on – it happens, and it happens quite a lot. One of my good mates, Hari, married a blonde and they've got three kids and are the perfect family. Her parents weren't happy about her marrying a Muslim and even less happy when she told them she was converting, but once they saw how well Hari took care of their daughter they came around. It didn't hurt that Hari is a good-looking bugger and his family own more property than you can shake a stick at.

I know it sounds sexist but there is a difference between a Muslim man approaching a non-Muslim girl, and a non-Muslim man trying to chat up a Muslim girl. Chalk and cheese.

When a Muslim guy approaches a non-Muslim girl, chances are she'll give him a chance, especially if like Hari he's got movie-star looks. If he makes her laugh and treats her good then she might well open her legs for him. And you never know, maybe he falls in love and decides to marry her. It happens. It's easy enough for the girl to convert and if she really loves him she'll do it.

But when a Muslim girl is approached by a non-Muslim man she's going to hear all sorts of alarm bells going off. It doesn't matter how good looking he is or how charming he is, the fact that he's from a different religion means she won't be interested. And even if she was interested, her friends and family would put a stop to it straight away. Muslim men are very protective about their sisters, and if it looked like a non-Muslim man was hassling a sister then they'd be in like Flynn.

The traffic wasn't too heavy and mercifully Porter was a little more chatty on the ride back to Kilburn.

'Did you check the company out?' Porter asked as we stepped out of the car around the corner from the minicab office that Sean Evans drove for.

'It's run by a couple of Pakistanis, Hamid and Hashim Nawaz. They employ around fifty drivers but they're all self-employed and bring their own vehicles. I checked with Companies House and they pay their taxes. Nothing on the PNC. No red flags.'

'What about their drivers?'

'Like I said they're all self-employed so no details on line. Hopefully the Nawaz brothers will be more forthcoming than Mr Jenner.'

We rounded the corner onto Kilburn High Road. The minicab office was perched above a hairdressers. The street-level door was open and above it was a sign saying Top Hat Cabs and two phone numbers. 'Guv, maybe I should take the lead here.'

'Sure,' said Porter. 'It makes sense.'

I climbed the narrow stairs with Porter on my heels. At the top there was a door with a small glass window that had been reinforced with metal bars. There was an intercom to the left and I pressed the call button and almost immediately the door lock mechanism buzzed. I pushed the door open. An Asian man wearing a lightweight headset looked up from a computer. 'Cab?' he said. He waved at a line of plastic seats up against a wall. 'Be fifteen minutes, OK?'

'Detective Constable Nasri,' I said. I nodded at Porter. 'My colleague, Detective Inspector Porter. We need to talk to you about one of your drivers.'

'Mohammed Masood?' said the man. He was in his late fifties, slightly overweight and wearing a fake yellow Lacoste tee. I knew it was a fake because it had

TOP HAT CABS emblazoned across the chest over a logo of a dancing cartoon top hat holding a cane. Classy.

'You heard what happened?'

'Of course. One of my drivers gets knifed in his mosque, how could I not hear about it?'

'Are you one of the owners?'

The man nodded. 'Hamid Nawaz. Would you mind showing me your warrant cards?'

Porter took out his warrant card wallet and flipped it open. I patted my pockets as if I was looking for mine but, thankfully, Hamid seemed happy enough with the one. 'What about your brother? Is he around?' I peered over his shoulder. 'Be good to speak to you together.'

Hamid twisted around in his seat. 'Hashim!' he shouted at a closed door behind him. 'Can you come out here?'

The door opened and the brother appeared. He was an identical twin, also wearing a yellow company *Lacoste* shirt. Unlike Hamid he was wearing glasses, wire-framed with round lenses. 'What's wrong?' he asked.

Hamid waved at me and Porter. 'They're police, here about Mohammed Masood.'

Hashim peered at me, and then at Porter. It was Porter he spoke to, obviously. I'm assuming that he assumed that Porter being the older was the more senior officer but I'm cynical enough to believe that even if I was older he'd still talk to the white officer. 'Did they catch the guy?' he asked.

'The investigation is ongoing,' said Porter.

'Brother was stabbed in a mosque, on a Friday. How difficult can it be to find the killer?' asked Hashim.

Porter looked over at me. I wasn't sure if he wanted to duck the question or if he just wanted me to continue to lead, but either way the ball was back in my court. 'We're following a number of lines of enquiry,' I said. 'Did Mr Masood have any problems that you were aware of?'

Hashim laughed harshly. 'He had a fucking attitude problem, that's what he had.'

His brother looked at him admonishingly. 'Hashim, you show the dead some respect.'

'He was lucky he wasn't stabbed in his cab,' said Hashim. 'If anyone was looking to get stabbed, it was that fool.'

'Why do you say that?' I asked.

Hamid held up his hand to silence his brother. 'He had a bit of an attitude when it came to his religion.'

Hashim snorted but turned away when his brother glared at him. It was clear which twin came out into the world first.

'You're a Muslim, right?' Hamid asked me.

I nodded but didn't say anything.

'Right, and we're Muslims too. But do you thrust the Koran in the face of everyone you meet? Do you tell every woman you meet that they are immodest if they don't cover their head? Well he did. He refused to take passengers who'd been drinking and that was just madness.'

'Most of our customers are usually drunk,' Hashim added, helpfully.

'And he was always stopping to pray.' Hamid continued, 'Nearest masjid, side of the road, anywhere. Didn't care if he had a passenger or not, if it was time to pray he would pray.'

'So he was a radical Muslim?' Porter asked.

I glanced across at Porter. *Praying five times a day doesn't make you a radical. Why would he say that?*

'He was a fucking nutter,' sneered Hashim, folding his thick arms.

'Hashim, please,' said Hamid. He clasped his hands together. 'I apologise for my brother, but yes, we did have a lot of complaints about Masood. In fact if what happened hadn't happened we would probably have had to let him go. Drivers are hard to get these days but it was getting to the point where he wasn't worth the hassle.'

'Was he the only driver who was so fundamentalist?' Porter asked.

'Unfortunately not,' said Hamid. 'We have half a dozen who seem to think that driving a cab entitles them to lecture people on how to behave. They don't seem to get that we are a service industry. The customer is always right, even when he is wrong.'

'The other like-minded drivers,' I asked, choosing my words with a little more care than Porter. 'Were they friends of Masood?'

Hamid nodded. 'They would pray together, and when they weren't working they would be in here discussing the Koran. They did my head in, to be honest, but what can you do?'

'Could you give us the names of these friends?' I said, pad in hand, pen hovering.

Hamid looked over at his brother who waved dismissively. 'I've no problem with that,' he said. 'If the cops start knocking on their doors they might fuck off. Win-win.'

'Give me a minute,' said Hamid. He tapped on his keyboard.

Hashim looked over at me. 'So you're a detective?'

I nodded but wasn't sure what to say.

'How is it? Being a detective?'

'Hard work. Long hours. Not much in the way of appreciation from the public.'

Hashim laughed. 'Sounds the same as driving a cab. What do they pay you?'

I wasn't happy about being asked personal information but they were being decent about giving us the names. 'Not far off thirty grand.'

He raised his eyebrows. 'That's it?' he laughed. 'Our drivers earn more than that.'

'Don't forget overtime,' Porter said.

'Yeah,' I said, wondering if they would offer me a job. 'Plus overtime.'

'It's not about the money, though,' I added.

Hashim laughed again. 'Obviously,' he said.

The printer behind Hamid kicked into life and spewed out a printed sheet. He handed it over to me. There was a list of six names, each with an address, a phone number and a National Insurance number. I showed it to Porter and he nodded his approval.

'Please, do not mention where you got that list from,' said Hamid.

'Goes without saying,' I said, tapping the side of my nose.

'Do you know anything about his personal situation?' asked Porter. 'Wife? Girlfriend?'

Hamid shook his head. 'Seemed to me that when he wasn't working he was at the mosque.'

'Always the same mosque?' I asked.

Hamid shrugged. 'I don't know. He was a regular at the one where he died, the one in Maida Vale, but most of the drivers go there.'

'He also went to the Finsbury Park mosque a lot,' said Hashim. 'And I did see him with a girl a few times. In the coffee shop across the road.'

'You did?' said his brother. 'You didn't tell me.'

Hashim nodded. 'He was holding her hand one time.'

'Dark horse,' Hamid mused.

'Asian?' I asked.

'Of course, he thought white women were scum,' said Hashim. He looked over at Porter and shrugged apologetically. 'No offence.'

'None taken,' said Porter. 'Any idea who the girl was?'

Hashim shook his head. 'Pakistani. Early twenties maybe. They were there last week. I think they were arguing. She didn't seem happy anyway.' He laughed. 'Maybe he wanted her to go full burka.'

'Hijab?' I asked.

'Yes, Hijab. But with Western clothing.'

Porter walked down the stairs, I stayed a moment longer to thank the brothers. They both shook my hand enthusiastically, as though happy to have been in the limelight.

'Fancy a coffee?' Porter asked, as I joined him outside. He was staring at the coffee shop across the road that the twins had mentioned.

We crossed the road and went inside. It was busy and most of the tables were occupied by Asians. Porter went to buy the coffees while I grabbed a table by the window. I could hear Urdu being spoken, and Arabic, but no English.

Porter came over with the coffees and sat down. He'd bought a couple of sandwiches and let me choose, which was nice. One of them was cheese and pickle. The other was a ham salad.

'So, that was a surprise,' said Porter.

I took a bite of my sandwich. I'd taken the cheese and pickle one. Obviously. 'What was?'

'The fact that the brothers were so helpful. With the list. I was expecting more resistance.'

'It's no skin off their noses,' I said. 'And they want to help.'

'I know, but after the way that university lecturer got all pissy over giving us the names of the members of the Islamic Society, I thought...' He shrugged and didn't finish the sentence but I caught his drift. If the nice white middle class man wouldn't help the police, why would the nasty Muslims? He'd never have said that, of course, but that's what he was thinking. It doesn't matter to him that Hamid and Hashim were born in this country and that they were as British as he was, he didn't see that, all he saw was their colour. Racism, pure and simple. I didn't say that to him, of course. For a start he's my boss and I need to make a good impression, but in my experience no racist has ever stopped being racist because their racism is pointed out to them. Porter wouldn't see it as racism. He'd say that his views are based on his experiences and that in his experience Asians cooperated with the police less than white people. That maybe true, but then I'd say that in my experience Asians get treated a hell of a lot differently than whites by cops. There's a whole different attitude. I saw it in the way Porter treated Jenner at the university. He was polite and deferential, maintained a lot of eye contact and shook hands at the start and the end of the meeting.

'We got the names, and that's what matters,' I said. 'I'll check them against the PNC and the SO15 watch list.'

Porter nodded, then took a bite out of his sandwich. 'So what do you think about Sean Evans?' he asked. 'I'm picking up mixed signals.'

I sipped my coffee. 'Good middle class boy meets pretty Muslim girl and starts to learn about Islam.

Goes over to Pakistan to help out in an orphanage and learns more about the religion, decides that he wants to become a Muslim. Like a lot of converts, he goes over the top. Dresses in Islamic gear and goes all evangelical.' I shrugged. 'That about right?'

'And decides against a career in the City because what, Islam says banking is a sin?'

I smiled at his sweeping generalisation and wondered where he was getting his information on Islam from. 'It's not banking that's the sin, it's the charging of interest,' I said. 'There are plenty of Islamic banks he could have worked for.'

'His degree was good enough to get a decent job, so why does he start driving a cab?'

'Good money, according to the brothers,' I smiled. 'Maybe he liked the freedom, didn't want to be tied down to a nine to five.'

'Except that he clearly wasn't a happy camper, was he? Picking fights with his customers.'

'His non-Muslim customers,' I said. 'Maybe that's why he chose the job. He wanted to convert non-believers.'

'There's a difference between converting and confrontation.'

I nodded. 'Maybe he started out trying to explain his religion to people and when they weren't receptive he began to get frustrated.'

'So why didn't he quit?'

'Maybe he'd run out of options. It's hard enough for a Muslim to get work these days, never mind a convert.'

Porter put down his sandwich. 'Are you serious? In London? Haven't you heard, whites are a minority now, have been for a while.'

'Come on, Guv, whites still hold the power. Pretty much everywhere. Look at the top brass, you can count the number of Asians and blacks on one hand, pretty much. My name's Mohammed, right. Most common boy's name in the UK. Most of my mates are called Mohammed but none of them use it when applying for jobs. You put Mohammed on a job application and you might as well toss it in the bin, unless you're planning on working in a kebab shop.'

'Did you have to do that?'

'I applied as Salim Nasri. Which is my name. The Mohammed bit is really to honour the prophet, lots of Muslims don't use it as their only name. It's not because they're ashamed. They're just getting by.' I smiled as a memory of playing with my friends came back to me. 'Playing five aside with my mates back in the day, it was all *Cross it in, Mohammed! Make some space, Mohammed. No, not you, Mohammed, the other Mohammed...* Simpler times. Nowadays...' I left it at that, my smile disappearing as quickly as it had arrived.

'The Met wouldn't discriminate, surely? Not these days?'

'Guv, being a Muslim is one thing. Being a Muslim called Mohammed is something else.'

'So why would Sean choose Mohammed as his name?'

I shrugged. 'Maybe because he wanted confrontation. A lot of converts are like that. They're far more likely to get in your face than someone who was born into the religion. In my experience, anyway.'

'So was that what was going on? He'd chosen Islam as his religion and confrontation did what, made himself feel better about his choice? And he chose to be a cab driver because that would bring him into contact with more potential converts?'

'Except he didn't seem to be converting, did he?' I said. 'He was arguing rather than persuading. And stopping the cab to pray is a bit much.'

'You have to pray at set times, don't you?'

I laughed at his naivety. 'What, we're in a squad car chasing some bad guys and a bell goes off and I have to pull over and pray? Do you hear about ambulance drivers stopping and switching their sirens off to pray? Yeah, there are regular prayer sessions at the mosques and yeah, good Muslims are supposed to pray five times a day, but there's a window. You don't have to drop everything and do it on the dot.'

'You pray five times a day?'

'No, Guv. But I know some of the other Muslim officers do. There's a prayer room. In Peel House.'

'I didn't know that.'

'Why would you?'

'And they just go off and pray?'

'It takes about the same time as a cigarette, and some smokers nip out ten times a day. More.'

He looked at me thoughtfully, then nodded. 'I hadn't thought of it like that,' he said. 'You're right. But Sean Evans AKA Mohammed Masood was stopping his cab to pray, so what was that about?'

'Like I said, maybe he wanted confrontation.'

'But why?'

'Maybe he wanted to seem like the big man to the other Muslims.'

'Could he have provoked his killer like that? Somebody who hated Islam and Muslims.'

'He was stabbed in a mosque, Guv. There wouldn't have been any members of the National Front there. He was among friends.'

'The nature of the wound being what it was, he could have been stabbed outside and got inside before bleeding out. Let's take a closer look at the CCTV footage we have and see when he arrived at the mosque.' He took a bite of his sandwich. 'That business at his parents, him eating the pork and drinking wine. How does that fit into his conversion?'

'It doesn't, Guv. You can't be a committed Muslim and eat roast pork. Not the sort of Muslim he was making himself out to be.'

'So some Muslims eat pork?'

'Sure. The same way that some Jews eat shellfish. Some people pick and choose what parts of their religion they go with. I mean, Catholics are supposed to eat fish on Fridays, but how many do? So yes, there might be some liberal Muslims out there who drink alcohol and eat pork, but Sean Evans wasn't that sort of Muslim.'

'It's only a sin to eat meat on Ash Wednesday, Good Friday, and on the Fridays during Lent.'

'Are you Catholic, Guv?'

'Lapsed,' said Porter. 'But I take your point. Knowingly eating meat on those days is a mortal sin, but lots of Catholics do.' He frowned. 'Maybe he was having second thoughts about his choice of religion. Maybe one of his fundamentalist friends found out and they stabbed him. Is that a possibility?'

I thought about it for a few seconds and then nodded. 'I guess so, yes. But if he was having second thoughts, why not just cut and run? He could have shaved his beard, changed back into Western clothes and gone to stay with his parents while he works out what to do next. If he was in danger, why go to the mosque?'

'He probably didn't think he was going to get stabbed because he'd enjoyed a Sunday lunch,' said Porter.

'You're forgetting the scars on his body, Guv. He'd been close to an IED. If he had been trained in bombmaking or whatever, he was more than a convert, he was a jihadist. And a jihadist having second thoughts could well be a fatal change of heart.'

'But again we come back to the fact that he was killed in the mosque. Why wouldn't they kill him somewhere quiet? Somewhere where they could interrogate him first? And wouldn't they try and make it a propaganda coup? There hasn't been anyone claiming responsibility. But yeah, it's something to think about.'

'There's something else, Guv.'

'Yeah?'

'A contact of mine told me that Evans had been getting busy at another mosque, trying to get in with some of the mosque's militant groups. They sent him packing and that's when he turned up at Maida Vale.'

Porter's eyes narrowed. 'Who is this contact?'

I tried to keep my face relaxed as I lied to Porter. I didn't want to have to lie to him, but I couldn't very well tell him who Uncle Siddiqui was and why I needed to see him. 'Just a guy I know, Guv,' I said. 'But he was quite definite that Evans was sniffing round the militants.'

Porter nodded thoughtfully. 'Are you thinking what I'm thinking?'

'It adds up, Guv,' I said. 'Signs up as a Muslim at university and starts getting cosy with militants, but at the same time is eating roast pork and knocking back wine with his parents over Sunday lunch? Yeah, could have been working for one of the agencies that we don't talk about. Undercover.'

Porter sighed and put down his coffee. 'Keep all the supposition out of the Decision Log for the moment,' he said. 'All we need is the fact we got a list of his friends from the taxi firm which we will check against the SO15 watch list.'

'When you say *we* you mean me, Guv,' I said.

'You're catching on,' he said, and grinned.

Chapter 27
(Harry)

Just as Nasri and I walked back into the MIR, my mobile rang and I took it out. I didn't recognise the number but I took the call anyway. It was Clive Jenner from the university. 'I spoke to the Vice Chancellor about getting a list of the members of the Islamic Society when Sean was here but I'm afraid he's not receptive to the proposal,' said Jenner.

'That's unfortunate,' I said.

'He cited the Data Protection Act and said that any official request for the information should be passed on to our legal department.'

'I'll take that on board,' I said. The Met had its own lawyers and while it might take time to get the list I was pretty sure we'd get it eventually.

'He was actually sympathetic to your request on a personal level, but the Islamic Society is very vocal and he doesn't want to upset them.'

'I understand,' I said, and I did.

'I can be more helpful on the matter of the girl that Sean was infatuated with,' he said. 'Her name is Rahmi Indra. I have her date of birth and her home address if that would be of any help.'

'It would, thank you,' I said. He gave me her details. I thanked him again and asked Nasri to tap her details into the PNC. Nothing. While he did that I checked the electoral roll but there were no Indras at the address.

I went over to the Intelligence section with Nasri following. Sergeant Andy Parkins was sitting at his workstation, his jacket over the back of his chair. He was a big guy and his fondness for full English breakfasts and pints of Guinness meant he had been on blood pressure medication for the past five years. I flopped down next to him and gave him Rahmi Indra's name and date of birth. 'Bloody hell, Harry, you've got a live one here,' he said as her details flashed up on screen. He scanned the information, then grinned. 'I take that back, she's dead. They got her with a drone three months ago in Syria.'

'What's the story?' I asked.

'She was a big time ISIS recruiter,' said Parkins. 'She was arranging for home-grown jihadists to go to ISIS training camps and then on to Syria. They reckon she sent dozens over. She also ran several social media groups encouraging British girls to go over to Syria and become wives to the jihadists there.'

'Why wasn't she arrested?'

'Lack of evidence,' he said. 'Then they discovered she was sending money to fighters overseas. They had hard evidence of that but just before they moved in to arrest her she took a Eurostar to Paris and flew to Syria from there. Probably best. If she'd stayed here there'd have been a trial and all the publicity that goes with it. As it is, she was blown to bits with two jihadists from Birmingham, so all's well that ends well. What's your interest?'

'The guy who was stabbed in the Maida Vale mosque, he converted to Islam because of her.'

'Yeah, she'd be good at that,' said Parkins. There was a picture on the screen and he pointed at it. 'Pretty girl. A regular honey trap.'

'Our guy met her at Reading University.'

'You can see why a guy might think about switching religions to get into her pants,' said Parkins. 'How's the investigation going?'

'Bloody slowly,' I said. 'No obvious motive, no murder weapon, no witnesses to the killing.'

'Suspects?'

'There were six hundred people in the mosque and in theory any one of them could have been the killer.'

Parkins whistled softly. 'Rather you than me, Harry.'

On my way back to my desk, David Judd looked up from his terminal. 'The Sheriff just called, says he wants you in his office as soon as you're back.'

'Did he say what he wanted?' Judd shook his head. 'Just said straight away.' I wondered why the Superintendent hadn't called me direct instead of talking to the office manager. I took out my phone. I'd had it set to silent while I was with the victim's parents and I'd forgotten to reset it. Three missed calls, all from the Sheriff. I cursed under my breath.

'Problem, Guv?' asked Nasri.

It was a stupid question, how the hell would I know what the Sheriff wanted or whether or not it would be a problem? I'm a detective, not a bloody psychic. I ignored the question and gestured at his workstation. 'Put the details of the interview into HOLMES,' I said.

I headed to Sherwood's office. His door was open and there was another man there, grey haired, late fifties maybe, wearing dark brown trousers, gleaming brown brogues and a greenish tweed jacket. My first thought was that he was a member of the public making a complaint, which just goes to prove that I am not in the least bit psychic.

'Hi Harry, you not answering your phone?' asked Sherwood. He didn't offer me a seat but then he was standing and so was the man with him.

'Sorry, Sir, I had it on silent during an interview.'

'Where were you?'

'Reading University. Talking to the victim's tutor.'

Sherwood nodded. 'Close the door, Harry.'

I did as I was told and looked at him expectantly. We were all still standing and weighing each other up, like guests at a cocktail party who hadn't yet been introduced.

'Something's come up regarding the investigation that makes it somewhat...complicated.' He looked over at his visitor but the man just smiled and nodded, leaving it to the Superintendent to say whatever it was that needing saying.

'This is...Simon,' said the Superintendent, with just enough hesitation to suggest that that wasn't the man's real name. 'He's with another agency.' He looked pained as if he was uncomfortable being so vague. But I knew what he meant. 'Another agency' meant MI5 or MI6 or sometimes GCHQ or Defence Intelligence. In other words, he was a spook and I wasn't to be told what sort of spook he was.

'Unfortunately our investigation into the death of Sean Evans has cut across a long-running investigation at the Central Mosque and if we are not careful there is a good chance of our investigation endangering national security.'

I nodded but didn't say anything. Simon the Spook nodded too. He had dandruff, I noticed, there were flecks of white on the shoulders of his jacket. And he was a nail-biter. I hadn't met many people who worked for the intelligence agencies but all the ones I'd met were nail-biters. Just an observation. Simon seemed to be weighing me up, too. I wondered how I looked to him? A hard-working detective who was trying to do his best in a police force that was being starved of resources? A meddling incompetent who was putting an intelligence operation at risk? At least I didn't have dandruff. We both smiled and it was clear we were both faking it. He held out his hand and we shook. He had a firm grip and I matched it. I knew how to play the handshake game. 'Harry, you don't mind if I call you, Harry, do you? It always seems to get things off on the right foot, using first names.'

'When they're genuine, yes,' I said and I saw the Sheriff's eyes harden at my lack of respect, but I could tell that Simon the Spook was playing me and I hated being played. I let go of Simon's hand. He ignored my dig and continued to smile amiably. 'The thing is, Harry, we have a number of assets in place at the mosque, and your investigation causes problems, not the least being that if your detectives start questioning our assets too closely then their cover stories could start to unravel. And obviously if that happened we'd have to pull them out.'

'Have we questioned any of your assets yet?' I asked.

Simon shook his head. 'Not yet, no.'

That meant Simon had been given access to HOLMES, which was fair enough, though it was never a pleasant feeling knowing that the spooks were looking over your shoulder.

'No offence, Simon, but do you know who killed Mr Evans?'

Simon looked at me for several seconds before answering. He voice was flat and emotionless and he looked me in the eyes without blinking. 'No, Harry, I do not.'

Like the Super, I've done all the interrogation courses and read a few books on body language but there was no way I could tell if he was lying or not. 'And was the mosque under observation when Mr Evans was killed?'

There was a slight tightening of the eyes, just a fraction. 'I'd have to check,' he said.

'You don't know?'

'Harry,' said the Sheriff, just a quick tug on my lead.

'No, no, it's a fair question, Kenneth,' said the spook, and calling the Sheriff Kenneth showed how fake the whole first name business was. No one called him Kenneth, not even his wife. He held up his hand. His left hand. There was a thin wedding band on his ring finger and I wondered if that was any more real than the name he'd given us. 'The reason I'm not sure is because I'm not familiar with the surveillance rota in place. I know there was a time when the mosque was under 24-hour surveillance but that might no longer be the case. But I can assure you, Harry, that if our observers had seen a murder committed I would very much have been made aware of that.'

'And what about visual or sound surveillance inside the mosque?'

'So far as I know, there is none.'

'So far as you know?'

'Harry.' Another tug on the lead from the Sheriff.

'Last time I checked, no. And I think I would have been told if either had been put in place.' He chuckled. 'Actually, Harry, I didn't come here to be questioned.'

'I understand that, Simon. But the quicker I can solve this murder, the quicker we can leave the mosque and take any pressure off your assets.' I rubbed my chin thoughtfully. Play-acting, but what the hell. 'How about you supply us with a list of assets and we handle their questioning with kid gloves. I could do them myself.'

Simon shook his head. He was still smiling but his eyes had gone cold. 'I don't really think that would work, Harry.'

Neither did I, but with the way the Sheriff was yanking my chain I thought it only fair that I gave Simon's a tug. 'Can I bother you with another question, Simon?'

His smile tightened. 'I don't see why not.'

'Harry, Simon has a lot on his plate at the moment,' said the Sheriff. 'I'm not sure we should be tying him up like this.'

'Oh, it's all right, Kenneth,' said Simon. 'Harry's only doing his job. Ask away, Harry.'

'Was Sean Evans an asset of yours?'

Again, the slight pause. The measured look. The even tones. 'Why would you think that?'

'A number of reasons, mainly the fact that Sean Evans appears to have undergone jihadist training but seems happy enough to eat pork and drink wine with his parents. All the signs are that he converted to Islam while at university and when he came to London seemed quite happy to work as a minicab driver. Now, that would make sense if he was a genuine convert, but it would also make sense if he had been recruited by MI5 at university and tasked with infiltrating potential Islamic terrorist cells.' I shrugged. 'Me, I'm thinking the latter.'

Simon looked at the Sheriff, then back to me. 'What I tell you stays within these four walls, obviously.'

'Of course,' I said. 'We've all signed the Official Secrets Act.'

Simon nodded. 'Sean Evans was indeed an MI5 Officer, recruited while at university and signing up when he graduated. As you say, he was tasked with infiltrating jihadist groups, starting with the university's Islamic society. He was instrumental in helping us neutralise one of their leading recruiters.'

'Rahmi Indras?'

He fixed me with a steely look for several seconds and I could see that I'd gone up in his estimation. 'Now how would you know that, Harry?' he said eventually.

'She recruited Evans at university,' I said. 'At least she thought she did. Obviously he was the one doing the entrapping.'

Simon nodded. 'Sean was very successful at identifying extremist groups and infiltrating them,' he said.

'Do you think that's why he was murdered?' I asked. 'Had someone discovered who he really was?'

'We don't know. Sean was careful. Very careful. He knew the risks involved and if he had any inkling that he had been discovered he would have pulled out.'

'My feeling is that if he had been discovered then they wouldn't have killed him in the mosque.'

'My feeling exactly,' said Simon. 'And again, I need to stress that only you and Kenneth are privy to the fact that Sean Evans was an MI5 officer.'

I thought it best not to mention that Sal had already floated the idea that Evans had been working for MI5.

'We'll need to tell DCI McKee,' said the Sheriff. 'He's overseeing the case and Harry reports to him.'

'Just the three of you, then,' said Simon. 'No one else must know.'

'So we're all good, Harry?' said the Sheriff, obviously keen to get the meeting over with. Over-keen, if you ask me.

'Sure, but I'm going to need some guidance as to how we move forward,' I said. 'We obviously have to keep interviewing everyone who was at the mosque because at the moment we believe that the killer left the mosque, possibly with the murder weapon, before the body was discovered.'

Simon frowned. 'I understood the body was in the prayer hall?'

'It was, in full view of everyone, but no one realised Mr Evans was dead until some minutes after the service ended. Most of the worshippers had left before the Imam had even called nine nine nine. There is a very good chance that the murderer was one of the worshippers.'

Simon nodded. 'And obviously they all need to be identified. So, name, address, date of birth, and positive ID. Where they were at in the mosque and where they went afterwards are all reasonable and fair questions,' he said. 'But I wouldn't want your men to be pressing them on immigration status, for instance, or how long they have been in the UK. The questions should be confined to what happened in the mosque.'

'I understand,' I said, and I did. But I wasn't happy about what he was suggesting.

'Excellent, then we're on the same page,' said Simon.

'So we're done?' I asked. I looked at the Sheriff and he nodded. He didn't seem happy either, but I couldn't tell if it was Simon or me that had pissed him off.

'Just one more thing,' said Simon. 'Your colleague, DC Nasri?'

I nodded. 'He's in the MIR. Do you want him in here?'

'No, no,' said Simon. 'I was just wondering if you knew he was at the Islamic Centre in Maida Vale yesterday morning for sunrise prayers at just after five? The early bird, as they say.'

I knew the Islamic Centre. It was a large mosque in Maida Vale that had opened in 1998. It had originally been a cinema and after that a Mecca Bingo Hall. I know, ironic, right? But jokes about Islam and Mecca are pretty much forbidden in the Met so I just nodded. 'He's a Muslim so I guess he prays regularly.'

'Of course, of course,' said Simon. 'He's as entitled to go to early morning prayers at the Islamic Centre as you are to pop into morning Mass at St Patrick's. Was he there officially?'

I looked Simon in the eyes. Part of me wanted to cover for Nasri because it looked as if Simon was gunning for him, but I didn't know Nasri well enough to take a bullet for him. Simon smiled as he looked back at me. He was waiting for me to lie, I could sense it, so I shrugged and told the truth. 'He didn't mention it, no, but then he's a Muslim and they pray five times a day, right?'

'Indeed they do.'

'So do you have the Islamic Centre under surveillance?' I asked. 'Or just DC Nasri?'

'Harry, enough,' said the Sheriff, his voice hard. He looked across at Simon. 'Do we need to detain Inspector Porter any longer?' he asked.

'Well, actually there is one thing that I need to bring to your attention, in connection with DC Nasri.' He took some folded sheets of paper from his inside pocket. 'We have an ongoing operation at the

Islamic Centre and as a result of that operation we saw DC Nasri in what appears to be somewhat of a compromising position with a man we believe to be an Islamic State fundraiser.'

'What!' I exclaimed, probably louder than was necessary.

'We've been looking at a man called Sameer Siddiqui. He's a property-owner and a bit of a financier, who we believe helps ISIS move funds around the world. Your DC Nasri met with Siddiqui yesterday.'

'I'm sure he would have met a lot of people at the mosque, they seem to be very busy places.'

He flashed me a thin smile. 'Give us some credit, Harry,' he said. He passed the sheets of paper to me. They were printouts of surveillance photographs. They were very good shots, clearly the work of a professional. One was of an elderly Asian in a camel coat walking with his arm around Nasri's shoulder. Another of them getting into a white Mercedes. Another of the two men deep in conversation. And in the final one, the Asian handing a wad of fifty pound notes to Nasri. The photograph had been taken through the windscreen so both men were clearly visible.

'And as you can see, DC Nasri accepted a large amount of money from Mr Siddiqui. We don't know why the money was handed over, but obviously it is a worry.' He held out his hands for the printouts.

'Can we keep these?' I asked.

The Sheriff was craning his neck to get a better look so I passed them to him.

'I'm afraid that's not possible,' said Simon. 'The surveillance operation is ongoing and if those pictures became common knowledge then everyone at the mosque would know. So we'll be keeping them in-house at the moment.'

'I don't understand,' I said. 'You're not passing them on to SO15 or Professional Standards?'

Simon held out his hand and the Sheriff gave him back the printouts. 'As I said, low profile.'

'What are we supposed to do with the information?' asked the Sheriff.

'That's up to you,' said Simon. 'I just thought you should be forewarned, that's all. Now, I must be going.'

'Harry, you can pop off,' said the Sheriff. 'I just need a word with Simon.'

Simon smiled but didn't offer to shake my hand, which was fine, so I headed back down to the MIR. Five minutes after I'd sat down at my terminal, my phone buzzed. It was a text from the Sheriff. MY OFFICE. NOW. No please or thank you but then he wasn't much for pleasantries.

I went back and this time he was sitting behind his desk. He didn't ask me to sit but he was smiling, so swings and roundabouts. 'Fuck me, Harry, what are you like?' he said.

'Sorry, Boss, but who does he think he is? He swans in here, gives us a false name and starts telling us how to carry out a murder investigation.'

'They're a law unto themselves.'

'Yeah, well they shouldn't be. Every time we meet the public we identify ourselves. People know who we are. He walks in here and we know nothing about him. That's just insulting. He's saying what, that we can't be trusted? Why can't he tell us who he is and who he works for?'

'It's their way. There's no question he works for MI5, I got the call from the Commissioner's Office paving the way.'

'So the Commissioner knows who he is, I hope. In case there's a problem down the line.'

'Not necessarily,' said the Sheriff. 'But our hands are tied, Harry. He calls the shots.' He waved me to sit down. 'Look, between you and me and these four walls I'm as pissed off as you are. But if it's terrorism-related then their cards trump ours.'

'And it's starting to look as if it is, right?'

The Sheriff looked pained. 'Let's not go counting chickens,' he said. 'The mosque is a bloody strange place to get rid of an MI5 officer.'

'I don't trust him, Boss,' I said quietly. 'I'm sorry, but that's the way it is. Did you hear his crack about me going to Mass?'

He frowned. 'It was a joke, wasn't it? You're not Catholic, Harry. Are you?'

'Lapsed,' I said. 'But my mother was and I got dragged to church at Christmas and on special occasions. So Simon has been checking me out. And obviously checking on DC Nasri, too. Which means he doesn't trust us.'

'Not necessarily, Harry. It's what they do. They check on everybody. And to be fair, Nasri does seemed to have walked into their surveillance operation.'

'Why did he show us those pictures, Boss?'

'He wanted to keep us in the loop.'

I laughed but it wasn't funny. 'Since when have the spooks wanted to share intel with us unless they need someone arresting? He had a reason for doing what he did, I'm sure of it.'

'Well you let me know when you work out what that reason is,' said the Sheriff.

'I'm more worried about how we move the investigation forward. Evans being a confirmed MI5 agent does give us a motive but doesn't really help us identify suspects. And how am I supposed to catch the killer if all I can ask potential suspects is their name, date of birth and if they saw anything at the mosque?'

'To be fair, that's not what Simon said. He just doesn't want you digging too deeply into the background of his assets.'

'Except he won't tell us who those assets are which means we have to treat several hundred potential suspects with kid gloves.' I sighed. 'We're going into battle with one hand tied behind our back.'

'You're worried you might get the blame if the investigation stalls?'

Damn right, I was. I was Senior Investigating Officer and even if I didn't send out the Action detailing what questions were to be asked, it would still be my responsibility. 'I'd be happier if the meeting we had with Simon could be on the record,' I said.

He shook his head. 'Out of the question.'

'I understand that, but I'd want to make a note of the meeting in my diary, who was there and what was said. Just to aid my memory.'

He nodded and the fingers were back steepled under his chin. I reckon the Sheriff thinks it gives him gravitas but really it makes him look like a pantomime villain plotting an evil deed. 'That's your right, of course.'

'I don't want to make a big thing of it, Boss, but I'm going to need some protection if this comes back to bite me in my arse.'

'You think I won't protect you, Harry? You're SIO on the case but it's still my overall responsibility.'

Actually, I did think that if push came to shove, the Superintendent would back me up. He was a copper's copper, which is probably why he'd gone as far as he could up the slippery pole and wouldn't be going any higher. He was five years away from retirement and no one expected him to make Chief Superintendent. Don't get me wrong, he wouldn't go out on a limb to protect and he damn sure wouldn't step in front of a bullet meant for me, but if I was in the right – and I was – then yes, he'd back me up. 'It's just murky when the intelligence agencies get involved, that's all.'

He looked at me for several seconds, then he nodded. 'I'll enter it into my diary, too,' he said. 'A note of the meeting, and what was said, in particular about the Actions.'

'Thanks, Boss,' I said. 'Much appreciated.'

'Just make sure we catch the bastard, Harry, that's all the appreciation I need. And the diary thing – best we don't mention DC Nasri and what was said about him.'

'Agreed, Boss. But do you want me to have a word with him?'

'Up to you, Harry. He's your bag carrier. We haven't been told officially that anything is amiss and you heard Simon, he has no intention of passing the pictures on to Professional Standards.'

'I suppose there could be an innocent explanation for what happened.'

'Do you think?'

I couldn't help but laugh because it would be a stretch. Nasri was definitely taking money from Sameer Siddiqui, and doing it sitting in the man's car. If Sameer Siddiqui was indeed an ISIS financier then it raised a hell of a lot of red flags.

Chapter 28
(Sal)

Porter stepped out of Sherwood's office, his features all scrunched up. He clearly wasn't happy. He shut the door behind him and paused for a moment as though evaluating what had just been said to him. I figured that he'd gotten a bollocking as the case hadn't developed to the Super's satisfaction, but I couldn't be sure. Porter looked up and met my eyes. I raised my eyebrows. He gestured with his head for me to follow him and walked away. I guess I was about to find out.

We used the stairs to get to the canteen and queued in silence before ordering; tea and muffin for me and a coffee and a bacon sandwich for him. He paid for them both without even mentioning it. We passed empty tables and located one at the very end of the hall. I sat opposite him and watched him drown his sandwich with ketchup before taking a large bite and washing it down with coffee whilst still chewing. Yeah, something was on his mind.

'Guv,' I offered him a serviette and mimed for him to wipe the smear of ketchup hanging off the corner of his lip.

'You and I haven't done a real interrogation together,' he said as he dabbed at the ketchup on his face.

'No, Guv,' I said, taking a sip of tea.

'I'm going to tell you what I tell everybody I interrogate, no matter what they've done.' He put down the serviette.

'Guv, you've lost me. What's going on?'

'Just hear me out, Sal, because this needs to be said. It doesn't matter what laws you may or may not have broken, your best option by far is to be totally honest with me and together we'll work out the best way of dealing with it.' He took another bite of his sandwich swiftly followed by a gulp of coffee.

'Guv, I have absolutely no idea what you're talking about.'

'Really? At this point I usually give them a second – and last – chance to come clean. So I'll ask you, what was going on between you and Sameer Siddiqui yesterday morning?'

The question wiped the smile off my face and replaced it with a thump in my heart. There were a dozen questions I wanted to ask off the bat, none the least who had been spying on me but he was right, the only way of getting me out of the hole I was in was to be honest with him. So that's what I did. I told him about my gambling, about my debts, about the money I owed on my credit cards and to the bank, about the heavies giving me a kicking and taking my warrant card, and about pawning my gold to Uncle Siddiqui. He listened without speaking, eating his sandwich and drinking his coffee.

Eventually I sat back, expecting him to tear into me, but he just put his coffee mug on the table and grimaced. 'You must feel like shit, lying to your wife like that?'

I nodded. 'And some.'

'What do you owe in total?'

I shrugged. 'Five grand, Guv. Maybe a bit more. But most of that is to the bank and on my cards.'

He sighed. 'What the hell were you thinking, Sal?'

I was thinking that I was a good player and that I knew what I was doing and that playing poker was an easy way of making money. But I knew I'd sound like an idiot if I said that. I leaned forward. 'I'm on top of it, Guv. I'll get my debts paid off and I'll never gamble again. You have my word on that.'

'It's a bit more complicated than that, Sal,' he said. 'Your Uncle Siddiqui is being investigated by MI5 as an ISIS paymaster.'

My jaw dropped. 'Get out of here.'

'That's why I was in to see the Sheriff. Siddiqui is under investigation and you were seen getting into his car and accepting a wad of cash.'

My head span. I slumped forward and held it in both hands. 'I'm so screwed, Guv. Once Professional Standards get hold of that, it's all over.'

'Maybe not. The spook I just spoke to says he's keeping the intel in-house and there's no reason for it not to stay that way.'

'You trust him?'

'He said he wouldn't be passing it on to Anti-Terrorism or Professional Standards. It's Siddiqui they're after. And their investigation might come to nothing, or they might turn him, there's a whole raft of things that could happen that mean your name would never come up.'

'Guv, I find it hard to believe that he's working with ISIS. It's ... it's ...'

'He's a moneyman, right?'

'Yeah, money and property. I've known him for ten years. Longer. He's a local Godfather, but in a good way.'

'A money-lender with a heart of gold?' I could hear the sarcasm in his voice.

'He doesn't hurt people, Guv. From guys like me he takes collateral, and he's taken houses off people in the past in lieu of their debt, but I know of lots of poor families that he's helped.'

'MI5 don't always get it right,' said Porter. 'But you need to give him the money back and get your gold.'

'Guv, I can't do that. The guy I owe my gambling debt to, he's no joke. He'll come for me.'

'I can help,' he said, 'Give me his name. The guy you owe the money to.'

I shook my head, 'Guv, I can't.'

'Listen to me very carefully, Sal,' He leaned in. I did too. 'You've got your whole career ahead of you. You want to throw all that away?'

'No, Guv,' I said, knowing I had already stepped on that road.

'Okay. Good. Then give me a name.'

I took a deep breath. I didn't have a choice. 'Chottopadhyay. Ray Chottopadhyay.'

Porter took out his notebook. 'You'll need to spell that for me.'

I did, and he wrote it down. 'He's a Bangladeshi, Guv.'

'How much?'

'I thought nine hundred quid but now he's saying eleven hundred.'

'And you're sure he has your warrant card?'

I nodded.

'I'll take care of it,' he said.

I opened my mouth to ask him what he planned to do but he held up a hand. 'Just leave it with me. But you need to get your gold back from Siddiqui. And ideally do it inside so you can't be photographed.'

'Right, Guv. And Guv?'

He looked at me and wiped his mouth again.

'Thanks, Guv.'

He waved away my thanks with his serviette. 'We're cops, we watch each other's backs,' he said. 'That's what we do.'

Chapter 29
(Harry)

I spent an hour going through HOLMES, then went over to Nasri. 'Right, you and me have a job to do. We need to re-interview Nominal 86. Fazal Wazir. There's video footage of him in the vicinity of Sean Evans but he didn't mention it at the mosque.'

'Okay, Guv.'

'He was with his sister. And Ayesha Khan. Neither of them mentioned seeing Evans either.'

'Are we going to re-interview them too?'

'Let's talk to Fazal Wazir first. See what he has to say for himself.'

The door to the CCTV room opened and John Reynolds appeared. He waved to attract my attention. I went over and Nasri followed.

'Nominal 348, Ayesha Khan,' said Reynolds. 'I've got her leaving the mosque.'

'Well done,' I said. 'Let's have a look.'

Reynolds headed into the room and sat down at his terminal. Nasri and I stood behind him. He had frozen the image, showing the back of Ayesha Khan as she left the mosque. We couldn't see her face but there was no mistaking the red headscarf, blue sweater and the designer bag over her shoulder.

'This was at 2.10pm, before the interviewing detectives arrived,' said Reynolds. 'She left the mosque in a hurry, and she was on her own.'

'Going to get the bus back home?' I asked.

'That's what I thought, but no. I checked the council camera covering the road leading to the bus stop and there's no sign of her. So I started checking other council cameras in the area and bingo...' He clicked on his mouse and this time a view of a crossroads filled the screen. 'I found her on a traffic camera at 2.22pm. Heading west, through Kilburn. He pointed at the screen. 'There she is, top left.'

It was definitely her. This time we could see her face as she walked purposefully along the pavement.

'And again, four minutes after that, on another traffic camera in West Kilburn.' Reynolds clicked the mouse and another view filled the screen, this time at a set of traffic lights. After a few seconds Ayesha appeared, waited to cross, and then hurried over the road and out of shot.

'She's definitely on a mission,' I said. I looked across at Nasri. 'It's your patch, Sal, Where could she be going?'

'If she carries on that way, she'll hit the canal,' said Nasri, and we both clearly had the same thought.

'See where she goes from there,' I said to Reynolds. 'We'll be out so call me if you find anything interesting.'

'Will do, Guv,' said Reynolds.

'So you're thinking what I'm thinking, are you?' I asked Nasri as we walked to the lift.

'She knew she was supposed to be interviewed, no question of that. So she knew she was doing wrong by slipping away like that. She's not going home, that's for sure. And she could have something in that bag.'

I nodded. 'Great minds think alike.'

We rode down in the lift.

'Do we re-interview her?'

'Let's see what the CCTV footage shows us first.'

Nasri drove us to Fazal Wazir's home. It was a small terraced house in Wembley in an area where pretty much everyone seemed to be Asian. A lot of the men were wearing thawbs and skullcaps and half the women were dressed from head to toe in black with their faces covered. It wasn't far from where Waseem Chowdhury lived and only half a mile from Gohar Abbasi's home.

I sat in silence while Nasri drove, wondering how the hell he had got himself into such a state that he had borrowed money from a suspected ISIS paymaster. The gambling debts alone would be enough to get him thrown off the force, but the pictures of him in the Mercedes taking a wad of notes could see him being thrown in jail. I've never understood gambling addiction. I've played cards for money and I've placed bets on the horses, but always just for a bit of fun and when I've lost I've just shrugged and written it off to experience. How does anyone get into a five grand hole playing poker? If you're consistently losing doesn't the message sink in that maybe you're not very good and that you should find some other way of passing the time? I get that a big chunk of the debt was interest owed, but even so. Eleven hundred to the Bangladeshi. Another four grand on his credit cards and bank loans. Hopefully he'd learned his lesson, but only time would tell.

Nasri parked. We got out of the car and walked to Wazir's front door. I pressed the bell and off in the distance there was the buzzing of a dying wasp. I pressed it two more times before the door was opened by a small Asian woman in a blue headscarf. I recognised her from the CCTV footage and from the photograph on the whiteboard. It was the sister, Yalina. I gave her my least-threatening smile, showed her my warrant card and introduced myself and Nasri. She kept averting her eyes and had her hand clutched to her throat. I guess she wasn't used to having two policemen appearing on her doorstep so I nodded at Nasri, letting him know he should take the lead.

'Sister, I am sorry to bother you but we need to talk to your brother, Fazal,' he said his voice soft and soothing.

'Fazal went out,' she said.

'Do you know when he will be back?' asked Nasri.

'He didn't say.'

'Do you know where he went?'

'He didn't say.' She stared at the ground. Her right hand was clutched at her neck but her left was on her stomach as if she was comforting herself.

'Are you all right, sister?' asked Nasri.

She shook her head. 'I have been sick today.'

'Why don't you sit down and I'll get you a glass of water,' said Nasri. He gently eased open the door and before she knew what was happening he was guiding her down the hallway and into the sitting room. There was a red and gold carpet that wouldn't have looked out of place in a Chinese restaurant, a large purple sofa with two matching armchairs. On one wall was a massive television screen and another was filled with framed family photographs. Nasri guided her onto the sofa and then sat in one of the armchairs. 'Why don't you get us some water, Guv?' he asked.

I got the message. He wanted to be on his own with her because that would put her at ease. And it would give me a chance to have a quick look around to make sure that her brother wasn't hiding under a bed. 'Good idea,' I said. I headed out and pulled the door shut behind me. I figured if he was anywhere he'd be upstairs so I went up, keeping close to the wall to minimise any squeaking. There were four doors upstairs. One was open. The bathroom. I had a quick look but it was empty. I opened the airing cupboard to be on the safe side, but there were only towels and the hot water boiler.

The first bedroom was clearly Yalina's with a feminine bedspread and make up on a dressing table. I looked under the bed and in the wardrobe. Nothing.

The next bedroom was more masculine and on a bookcase filled with Islamic volumes was a framed photograph of Fazal Wazir with three friends, taken out in the desert somewhere. I recognised one of the men – it was the little shit Waseem Chowdhury. I took out my phone and took a picture of the photograph, then looked under the bed and in the wardrobe. The bed was clear and he wasn't in the wardrobe, but there were more than a dozen empty hangers which suggested he had an excess of hangers or that he'd left and taken some clothes with him. There was a space at the top of a wardrobe that was large enough to accommodate a suitcase. To the right of the wardrobe was a line of drawers and two of them were empty. I'm guessing socks and underwear. By now I was fairly sure that Wazir had done a runner and wasn't going to be back any time soon.

I decided to check the final bedroom just to be sure. I pushed open the door but stopped when I saw an elderly bearded Asian man in a long robe sitting by the side of the bed. He had on thick-lensed glasses and was reading what looked like a copy of the Koran and muttering to himself as he fingered a chain of small beads in his right hand. An old woman, grey haired and wrinkled, lay in the bed with an oxygen mask over her mouth and nose. There was a large grey cylinder with a white top next to the bed. The woman's breath rattled in her throat.

The man looked up and frowned at me.

'Sorry,' I said. 'I was looking for the bathroom.'

I pulled the door shut and waited, expecting the man to come out screaming blue murder but nothing happened and after a few seconds I slipped down the stairs and along to the kitchen. As I poured a glass of water, I looked through the kitchen window into a back yard that was empty except for a couple of old bikes and two wheelie bins.

I took the glass of water along to the sitting room and handed it to Yalina. If she wondered why it had taken me so long she didn't say anything, just thanked me and took a sip.

'I've given Ms Wazir my card and she'll ask her brother to call us when he gets back,' said Nasir.

'Excellent,' I said, sitting down. I didn't believe for one minute that Fazal Wazir would be returning any time soon. 'And did you ask her about her seeing Sean Evans outside the mosque?'

'It was my next question, Guv.'

'Then why don't you go ahead and ask it?'

Nasir turned and smiled encouragingly at Yalina. 'When you were interviewed at the mosque on Friday, you were asked if you had seen the victim. Sean Evans, also known as Mohammed Masood,' Nasri said in his soft soothing voice. 'Do you remember being asked that?'

She nodded. 'Yes,' she whispered. 'I think so.'

'And do you remember what you told the officer?'

'I said I hadn't seen him. He was in the men's prayer room. I was in the women's room.'

'Yes, but you would have been asked if you knew Mr Evans. Mr Masood.'

'I didn't.' She took another sip of water. She was still rubbing her stomach with her left hand. Nervous, perhaps. Or guilty.

'The thing is, Sister, we believe you did see Mr Evans outside the mosque,' said Nasri. Even though he was pretty much accusing her of lying, he did it gently and with a soft smile. 'When you were with Ayesha Khan and your brother. You had words with Mr Evans. Mr Masood.'

She frowned but didn't say anything.

'Do you remember that, Sister? Do you remember seeing him?'

I was starting to understand his use of 'Sister' when addressing her. It was putting her in her comfort zone and making him appear less confrontational, even though he was effectively accusing her of lying. I tend to do the same thing. If you want a nice middle-class gentleman to assist you with you enquiries, a respectful 'Sir' goes a long way. And if it's some scumbag of a sink council estate, calling him 'mate' might get some small measure of cooperation, or at least a fraction less abuse.

Yalina's frown deepened. 'I'm not sure,' she said.

'You were with your brother and Ayesha,' I said. 'One of you shouted over at Mr Evans. He rushed off.'

'I don't know,' she said. 'Maybe.'

'Was it you who shouted over at Mr Evans?'

'No.'

'Your brother?'

'Maybe. Yes, I think so.'

'What did he shout?'

She looked down at the carpet, still rubbing her stomach. 'I don't remember. I'm sorry.'

'Sister, did your brother have a problem with Mr Masood? Were they fighting about something?'

She looked up from the carpet and there was panic in her eyes. 'No. Why would you say that?'

'He must have shouted for a reason. And whatever he said, Mr Masood wasn't happy because he hurried off.'

She opened her mouth to answer but then her stomach lurched and she covered her mouth with her hand as vomit sprayed over her chin. She rushed out of the room, bent double. Nasri stood up and stared after her anxiously. 'What shall I do, Guv?'

'Just let her go,' I said. 'She's obviously under the weather.' I gestured at the ceiling. 'I had a look around and I think Fazal might have hopped it,' I said. 'There were loads of empty hangers and I didn't see any socks or underwear. The parents are upstairs, too. The old woman looks at death's door and the old man isn't far behind.'

'She's been a bit vague about who shouted what to who,' said Nasri. 'Though being questioned by two male officers probably didn't help.'

'She didn't seem fazed,' I said. 'Just evasive.'

The door opened and Yalina returned. 'I'm so sorry,' she said. 'My stomach. Maybe something I ate.'

I stood up and Nasri followed suit. 'We won't bother you any more, Ms Wazir,' I said. 'And please do get your brother to call us when he returns.'

She nodded, clearly pleased that we were leaving. 'I will, I will,' she said. She hurried to the front door and opened it. Nasri and I thanked her and stepped out onto the pavement. The door couldn't have closed any quicker and in my mind I heard her breathe a deep sigh of relief.

We walked back to the car. 'Did you see the way she kept rubbing her stomach, Guv?' he asked.

'What about it?'

'I'm thinking she might be pregnant.'

'She said she was feeling sick. Could have been something she ate.'

'Yeah, but my wife did that all the time when she first fell pregnant.'

'So maybe she is then.'

'But she's not married. For a good Muslim girl like her, that's a big thing. It'd bring all sorts of shame on the family.'

'Maybe,' I said. 'But I don't see how that gets us any closer to finding the killer of Sean Evans.' I didn't like what he was implying. It sounded to me that he was suggesting that good Muslim girls didn't get pregnant out of wedlock but white girls did and that's racist, no two ways about it.

'Let me ask around,' Nasri said. 'Guv, why don't you sit in the car while I knock on a few doors?'

I knew what he meant. If they saw a white cop they'd probably not say anything, but Nasri was one of their own and spoke their language. Another racist statement, but that didn't make it any less true. 'Go for it,' I said.

I got back into the car. Nasri knocked on the door next to Wazir's house. A woman in a black headscarf answered and Nasri spoke to her for several minutes. When she eventually closed the door he walked along to the house on the other side and knocked. This time an elderly Asian man answered and Nasri spent a lot longer talking to him. Then the man opened the door wide and Nasri stepped inside.

I had my radio with me so I made a few checks on Ray Chottopadhyay. He wasn't known to the PNC and other than a few speeding tickets he seemed to be an upstanding citizen. At least he wasn't a bloody ISIS financier because then it would get very messy.

After about fifteen minutes, Nasri emerged from the house and walked back to the car. 'Sorry about that, Mr Buttar insisted on making me tea. He goes to my dad's mosque. Small world.'

'And getting smaller by the minute. So what's the score?'

'Wazir left last night, Guv. A car came to pick him up late evening. The driver sounded his horn, it got Mr Buttar's attention so he looked through his window. It was a blue hatchback.'

'An Uber maybe?'

'Possibly. I'll check with Uber when I get back. Also, Wazir had a suitcase. Yalina went out to the car with him and waved him off.'

'So the sister was lying about not knowing where he'd gone?'

'Looks like it, Guv. I had a long chat with Mr Buttar. He thinks Wazir had fallen in with a bad crowd, as he put it. Gotta be The Faith. Says Wazir used to be a nice young man but that he changed a couple of years back. Every now and then he'd set up a stall in the road with his mates handing out leaflets about Sharia law and how the West was occupying Muslim countries. And he was always hassling women to cover their heads, the normal sort of fundamentalist crap.'

'And Mr Buttar didn't approve?'

'He's a nice guy, Guv. Though I think it was more that his friends kept coming around with music blaring out of their stereo systems that upset him.'

'Waseem Chowdhury lives not far away, and he's got a blue hatchback.'

'You think he picked up Wazir?'

'It's a possibility. Not sure how we'd confirm that, Chowdhury isn't likely to cooperate. The question is, where did Wazir go? Is he lying low or has he left the country? As soon as we get back to the office we need to check ports and airports.'

Nasri started the engine and we headed back to Hendon. I sat in silence again but this time it was

Fazal Wazir who was occupying my thoughts. The fact that the neighbour had seen him with a suitcase suggested he'd gone for good. Was he our killer? From what I'd seen on the CCTV footage, it had been his sister who had been calling over at Sean Evans. But maybe he had been involved. Had there been bad blood between the two? But the thing that was worrying me the most, was why had he chosen just then to run? If he was our killer, why hadn't he left immediately? Why hadn't he gone home and packed his case and left? In fact he had stayed at the mosque and been interviewed there. And he had spent all Saturday in London. If he was going to run, that would have been the time to do it. Why run late at night? On a Sunday? The answer was obvious, something must have happened to spook him. Something must have happened on Sunday evening to have made him realise that he needed to get out of town. So was it a coincidence that only a few hours earlier I had told Ayesha Khan that we knew she had been with Wazir outside the mosque. I hadn't mentioned them seeing Sean Evans or that we had them on CCTV, but she wasn't stupid. Had she tipped off Fazal Wazir that the police were going to be questioning him again? And if she had, did that mean that she was also in some way culpable? Did she and the Wazirs have a problem with Sean Evans? Was that why one of them had been shouting across the road at him? I couldn't tell any of this to Nasri, of course, because that would open up a whole can of worms, not the least being the fact that I had been to the pictures and had a pizza with a woman who now looked as if she might well be a suspect.

When we arrived at Peel House I told him that I was going to be going out for a while.

'Anything I need to know about?'

'Personal time. I'll be a couple of hours. If Teflon or the Sheriff ask for me, say I've just popped out and send me a text. Anything else, Stuart can handle.'

'Right, Guv.'

He went inside as I walked over to my car. I'd thought long and hard about where to confront Ray Chottopadhyay. It was easy enough to get his home address but according to Sal he had seven kids, most of them young, and I didn't want to start getting heavy in front of children. Chottopadhyay's card games were a more adult environment, that was for sure, but I would be asking for trouble confronting him in a room full of shady characters sitting around a table piled high with money. His office was the best bet. I drove to where he worked - a third floor office in a modern block in Grey's Inn Road. I showed my warrant card to an Asian receptionist who asked me to sit on a plastic sofa while she had a whispered conversation on the phone. A few minutes later a door opened behind her and a small Asian man with a bald head peered anxiously at me through round spectacles. When I say small, he really was small, not much more than five feet four inches. He was wearing what was obviously an expensive suit which because of his small stature was probably made to measure, and on his left wrist was a gold watch studded with small diamonds.

'You want to see me, Inspector Porter?'

I nodded and gave him my hard stare. 'I do, yes.'

He looked anxiously at his secretary then back to me. 'Come in, come in,' he said nervously, and held the door open for me. I walked past him into his office. It was big with floor to ceiling windows looking down on the street below. There were paintings of jungle scenes on the walls and several tiger figures around the office including a life size one curled up in front of a desk that was at least six times the size of mine. On the desk were two computer screens and there was a large screen TV on the wall facing his desk showing horse racing with the sound turned down. His chair was massive, black leather and chrome, and it almost swallowed him up when he sat on it.

My chair was smaller and lower so I decided not to sit. It meant he had to look up at me which clearly made him uncomfortable. 'So what is this about, Inspector? Is there a problem with a member of my staff?'

'I'm afraid you're the problem, Mr Chottopadhyay.'

He looked surprised, but I got the feeling he was faking it. 'I'm here about a colleague, Detective Constable Nasri. You probably know him as Sal.'

He nodded slowly. 'Yes. I know Sal.'

'Sal owes you nine hundred pounds, right?'

Chottopadhyay shook his head. 'Eleven hundred.'

'How much of that is interest?'

'It's not about the interest. I'm not a bank. Sal knew what he was doing when he stopped paying me back.'

'Exactly, you're not a bank. You're not regulated by the Financial Conduct Authority. And you're not in the business of lending money, right? Or are you telling me that you are running an illegal money-lending operation?'

'Of course I'm not saying that.' He avoided my eyes, clearly flustered.

I took an envelope from my inside pocket and tossed it onto his desk. 'There's nine hundred pounds in there, in crisp new notes. The way I see it, you can accept that in full and final payment of Sal's debt. You take the cash, the debt is settled, and he never darkens your doorstep again. In the unlikely event that he ever does turn up at one of your games, you just turn him away. That's Plan A.'

He blinked up at me. 'And Plan B?'

'Plan B is more complicated, and less satisfactory for the both of us. In Plan B you refuse to take the money and I walk out of here with it. I then make it my life's work to make your life a misery. Sal, well he's just setting out on his police career. He's a Detective Constable with his whole career ahead of him. Me, I'm an Inspector and I'm coming to the end of mine. I've been a copper for going on thirty years and during that time I've amassed a lot of friends and contacts. Contacts in the Inland Revenue, for instance.

Do you declare the money you make from your illegal games? I'm guessing not. So how would you like to be audited until Kingdom Come, because I can arrange that Mr Chottopadhyay. I can get the FCA on your case, I can have council officials go over all your businesses with a fine-tooth comb to ensure that you abide by all the regulations you are supposed to. You drive a very nice car, too, don't you? An Aston Martin, right? Beautiful bit of British craftsmanship, the Aston Martin. How would you like it if every time you got behind the wheel, there were flashing lights in your rear-view mirror? That would take a lot of fun out of driving, wouldn't it?'

He steepled his fingers under his chin and stared at me, saying nothing. I stared back. I felt a lot more comfortable threatening Chottopadhyay than I did confronting the little shit who had verbally abused Ayesha Khan. Waseem Chowdhury had nothing to lose by standing up to me and threatening me. He'd called my bluff and I'd had to back down. But Chottopadhyay had a lot to lose and I wasn't bluffing. I could do everything I'd threatened him with.

We stared at each other for several seconds, then he leaned forward and picked up the envelope. He took the notes out and counted them carefully and then nodded. 'Plan A is acceptable,' he said. 'Though please make it clear to Detective Constable Nasri that he is never to try to get into one of my games again.'

I smiled and nodded. 'I will most definitely pass that sentiment on to DC Nasri. And I'd like his warrant card back as well. You should know that just having it in your possession could cause you a whole lot of grief.'

He reached into his drawer and took out DC Nasri's warrant card wallet. He had to stand up to give it to me. 'He is lucky to have a friend like you, Inspector Porter.'

'I hope he sees it that way, Mr Chottopadhyay,' I said as I slid the warrant card into my pocket.

He put the money back in the envelope and put the envelope in a drawer as I walked out of his office.

Chapter 30
(Sal)

From the moment this case came our way, we've had nothing but bad luck and obstacles. A new job and a difficult partner didn't help matters. But Porter was starting to warm to me, even though he'd never admit it. Even the gambling debt was weighing less on me, I think talking about it with Porter helped put it into perspective. Family came first with my career not far behind. Whatever happens now with Ray Chottopadhyay, there was no way I was playing the tables again.

Yeah, I was feeling pretty good, for the first time I felt like we were putting a dent in the case and making progress. Yalina had revealed a lot without saying very much, and Mr Buttar, *Mr Serendipity*, had put Wazir in a blue hatchback which could very well belong to Waseem Chowdhury. I added the interview with Yalina Wazir and Mr Imran Buttar into HOLMES as soon as I got back to the MIR. As it was the first time Buttar's name had come up, the system issued him with a Nominal number, 642.

When I'd finished, I called up Ayesha Khan on the system and reread the interview she'd done with Porter. All the information was here, he just didn't say that the conversation had taken place over a curry. I hoped that wouldn't be a problem down the line.

The phone on Porter's desk rang so I leaned over and answered it. 'Can I speak to Detective Inspector Porter?' asked a male voice.

'He's not around, can I take a message?'

'Do you have any idea when he'll be back?'

'I'm afraid I don't. I'm DC Nasri, I work with DI Porter.'

'Okay, this is Dr Balbir Singh, I work at the burns unit in St Mary's Hospital, Paddington. We have a patient who has just been admitted and she has DI Porter's business card in her wallet. The police have already been notified but I thought that DI Porter might want to know what has happened.'

'I'm sorry, who is the patient?'

'Ayesha Khan. She was admitted about an hour ago. She isn't able to talk at the moment so I went through her bag and that's when I found DI Porter's card.'

My stomach lurched. 'What's happened to her?'

'Sorry, yes, I should have said. Someone had thrown acid in her face. She's alive and stable but she's in a bit of a state. I wondered if what has happened had been the result of a case DI Porter had been involved in.'

'There is a case involving Ms Khan, yes,' I said. 'Will you be there for the next hour or so?'

'I'll be here all day and probably most of the night, too,' said the doctor.

'I'll come now,' I said. I put down the phone. I knew that strictly speaking I should tell Porter but he had said he didn't want to be disturbed and I wanted to talk to Ayesha Khan on her own. He said he wouldn't be back until late that afternoon so I had enough time.

The A41 was clear so it took me just under twenty-five minutes to drive to the hospital but it was another fifteen before I could find a place to park.

I found my way to the burns unit and had to wait another ten minutes while they paged Dr Singh. Like most of the doctors you come across in NHS hospitals he looked tired, with dark patches under his eyes and a look of weary resignation as if he knew from experience that his day was only going to get worse. He was in his early thirties and was very colour co-ordinated, with a blue turban that closely matched his pale blue scrubs and there was blue tubing on the stethoscope hanging around his neck. He remembered my name, shook me by the hand and took me over to an observation window through which we could see four beds, all of them occupied. He pointed at the bed on the right. 'That's her,' he said. 'Two uniformed officers came to talk to her not long after she was admitted but she wasn't able to say anything.'

She looked tiny, her head swathed in gauze and bandages, her left arm covered in a dressing and a drip feeding into her right arm.

'Do you know what happened?' I asked.

'According to the paramedic who brought her in, she was walking home and someone threw acid into her face. Probably drain cleaner. He ran off and a neighbour called nine nine nine. The neighbour poured water over her which helped but she's still in a terrible state. She's almost certainly going to lose the sight in her left eye, and she's going to need extensive plastic surgery to get back to anywhere approaching normal.'

'Did anyone have a description of the assailants?'

'I wouldn't know,' he said. 'My job is to take care of her, not quiz her.'

'I'm sorry, I just need as much information as I can get.'

He held up his hand. 'No, I'm the one who's sorry,' he said. 'I'm not having the best of days. The neighbour might have seen something I suppose but it took the ambulance ten minutes to get to the scene so the attacker would have been long gone by then. Like I said there were a couple of uniformed cops here but she was in shock and I don't think she was able to tell them much.' He sighed and shook his head. 'I hope you get the animal who did this.'

'You and me both.'

'This is the third attack like this we've had this month. And across the city acid attacks are up three hundred per cent so far this year. You wonder what sort of person is capable of throwing acid into someone's face.'

'Yeah, there's been a spate of motorcycle thefts where the thieves have blinded the rider with acid. For a bike worth a few hundred quid.'

'The sooner you start giving them life sentences, the better,' said the doctor.

'Yeah, well all we do is catch them,' I said. 'It's the judges who sentence.' I nodded over at Ayesha. 'Can I talk to her?'

'Out of the question,' he said. 'She's on intravenous morphine. She was in intense pain when she was brought in and there are huge psychological implications of what's happened to her, so her being asleep is the best thing for her at the moment.'

'I'm going to need to talk to her,' I said. 'She might have gotten a look at her attackers.'

'That won't be possible today,' he said. 'Tomorrow maybe. But she's going to be very fragile.'

'But she is going to be all right? She's not going to…. '

'To die? No. Her life isn't in danger. The acid didn't get into her mouth or lungs so it's not life-threatening, but she's never going to be the same again. Her life as she knew it is over.' He shuddered. 'The cartilage of her left ear is very damaged, and even if we can rebuild it, it'll never look the same. There's a good chance of partial deafness or more in that ear. Her left eyelid was burned off and even with the best plastic surgeons it'll never look right. Her nose is in a right state and she'll be scarred for life. We can work on the scarring but it'll always be there.'

'She was a very pretty girl,' I said quietly.

'Was being the operative word,' said the doctor. 'Was she married?'

I shook my head. 'No.'

'And probably never will be, now. People are going to stare at her in the street, cross the road to avoid her. It's a life sentence, detective. I wouldn't wish it on anybody.' He looked at me and his eyes were filling up. 'I deal with a lot of burns, but they're usually accidents. But when someone deliberately sets out to harm someone like this, it makes me wonder what the human race is coming to.'

'I hear you,' I said.

'How could they hate so much that they would do that to someone? To anyone. But to a girl.'

I shrugged. It wasn't a question I could answer.

'Why was she involved with the police?'

'She was....' I wasn't sure how to finish the sentence. She wasn't a suspect, she wasn't a witness, she was just a member of the public who had been in the vicinity of a murder. Except she was more than that. She had made an effort to get close to Porter, she had been seen with him in public, is that what had led to the attack? 'She was helping us with our enquiries, that's all,' I said.

Dr Singh was frowning at me. He'd obviously sensed my unease. 'Do you think that's why she was attacked?'

I tried to smile but didn't make a great job of it. 'I doubt it,' I said. 'She wasn't a witness, she was just in the wrong place at the wrong time.'

The doctor's mobile phone rang and he pulled it out and looked at the screen. 'I've got to take this,' he said.

'No problem, I'll leave you to it.' I gave him a business card. 'If anything changes, give me a call.' He nodded, took the card and walked away, putting the phone to his ear.

Chapter 31
(Harry)

It was early afternoon when I got back to the MIR. Nasri wasn't at his desk and part of me wondered if he was off somewhere praying. I grabbed myself a coffee and plate of sausage and chips in the canteen and by the time I'd polished it off, Nasri had reappeared. He was sitting at his terminal and didn't look happy, but I figured what I had to say to him would cheer him up. 'You're all square with Chottopadhyay,' I said.

He frowned as if he hadn't understood me. 'Say what, Guv?'

'I've cleared your debt with him. He knocked it down to nine hundred pounds but I don't think you'll be welcome at any of his games in future.'

I took out his warrant card wallet and gave it to him. He stared at it in disbelief, and then looked at me. 'I don't know what to say, Guv.'

'A "thank you" would cover it.'

'Yeah, sure, thanks,' he stammered. 'So do I give him nine hundred and we're all square?'

Porter shook his head. 'I paid him the money, so you can pay me back.'

'Where did you get the cash, Guv?'

'I got it, don't worry about it. I'm not living in poverty, Sal. My outgoings are low these days. You can pay me back as and when. Fifty quid a week and you'll be clear in less than five months.'

'I'll pay you back faster than that, Guv. I swear.'

'There's no rush. You need to get your other debts sorted first. And get your gold back from Uncle Siddiqui PDQ.'

'I will, Guv. Thanks. From the bottom of my heart, thanks.'

Nasri still looked as if he'd lost a tenner and found a penny. 'What's wrong?' I asked. 'I thought you'd be happier than this.'

'Something's happened, Guv,' he said. 'Ayesha Khan is in hospital. Someone threw acid in her face.'

The news hit me like a blow to the stomach and I actually took half a step back. 'What?'

'She's in St Mary's. She'll live, but... she's in a bad way, Guv.'

'Do they know who did it?'

'The local cops are on it but there were no witnesses. She wasn't able to identify her attacker but she's in shock and she'll be that way for a while. Anyway, Harrow Road are on it. A couple of local detectives will interview her tomorrow. I'll check with them and see if anything comes of it that relates to our case.'

'What is it, some sort of honour thing?'

'I wouldn't know, Guv.'

'Who the hell would throw acid in a girl's face?'

'Guv, you have to realise, there are a lot of morons out there who hate seeing a Muslim girl with a white guy.'

I didn't like the implication of what he was saying. 'Are you blaming me for this?'

'Of course not, Guv. But seeing you with her might have provoked someone. That's what I'm saying.'

I pointed a finger at him, then realised that was a bad idea so scratched my neck. Too late because he'd already noticed the gesture. I tried to keep my voice steady and calm. 'So you are saying it's my fault? You can't have it both ways.'

'Guv, when you were out with her, did anyone give you any grief?'

'Why do you ask that?'

Because it happens. White guy, Muslim girl, sometimes Muslim guys take offence. You said you took her for a meal. Was there a problem there? In the restaurant?'

One of the typists had turned around from her screen and was looking our way. 'Let's go somewhere more private,' I said.

Chapter 32
(Sal)

Bloody right he wanted to chat in private because if he wasn't careful his job was going to be on the line. Interviewing a witness over a curry, a witness who was then almost blinded in an acid attack. And location of said interview not entered into HOLMES. This could so easily blow up in his face.

He found an empty meeting room and ushered me in. There were two tables end to end with a dozen chairs around them facing a large whiteboard on the wall. I sat on one of the tables and Porter stood with his back to the wall with his arms folded. Text book defensive position. He knew he was in the wrong. 'Okay, Sal, here's the thing,' he said. 'The night I interviewed Ms Khan, we had a bit of a problem. A hatchback drove by and three Asians started shouting at her. I got the number and got the address of the owner. It was Waseem Chowdhury.'

'Guv, please don't say you went round there.'

Porter nodded. 'Yeah.'

I shook my head at his stupidity.

'I know, I know,' he said. 'And it didn't end well.'

'What did you think you'd achieve, Guv?' I spoke softly, using the same voice that I'd used with Yalina Wazir.

'I thought I could straighten him out.'

'How, by talking severely to him? Guv, his type aren't fazed by cops. They don't care. And they know there's nothing we can do to them.'

'He'd been smoking cannabis.'

'So a caution. Guv, at most. What were you thinking?'

'I was thinking that three Asians were shouting abuse at a police officer in the street, and that if I fronted him I'd...' He stopped, lost for words. 'Yeah, you're right. I wasn't thinking.'

'You'd have been better going around with a ski mask and a baseball bat,' I said.

'That's what you'd have done?'

'They wouldn't have shouted abuse at me, Guv.'

'So what if some skinheads screamed abuse at you? Would you let that drop?'

'What if?' I snorted. 'It's happened plenty, Guv. But no racist is going to change his views because someone told them he was being a twat. You just have to accept that there are some dumb people out there and move on. Otherwise your life will become one long constant battle.'

'You wouldn't punch them in the face?'

'I'm a cop, Guv. You think I want to go inside for assaulting some fascist racist with a single-digit IQ?' I shook my head.

'I just got annoyed at the way they were abusing us.'

'Yeah, well welcome to my world, Guv.'

'He said he was with The Faith and he threatened me with a group of Muslims going around to my house with knives.'

'What did you do?'

Porter shrugged. 'I walked away with my tail between my legs. It was a stupid thing to have done. I knew it at the time and I know it now. Part of me wishes I'd Tasered the bastard but...' He shrugged and didn't finish the sentence.

'You'd lose your job,' I finished for him.

'Yeah,' he sighed. 'I know. Sal, is it possible that The Faith are behind what happened to Ayesha?'

Of course it was possible. If Waseem Chowdhury and his boys had clocked Ayesha with Porter living it up, no doubt they would have wanted to exact a harsh lesson. 'Anything's possible,' I said.

He finally sat down, slumped more like, on the chair across the table from me. Man, he looked stressed. He slowly ran his hand through his hair, and then again faster, causing his hair to stand up at odd angles.

It wasn't Porter's actual fault that Ayesha was lying in a hospital bed with half her face destroyed; but yeah, I could understand if he was blaming himself.

'So what do we do?'

'Let me ask around.'

A look of pain flashed across Porter's face and I knew that he had something else to tell me. I waited. 'I saw her last night, too,' he said eventually. 'At a cinema in Shepherd's Bush.'

'You what?'

'We went to see a Bollywood movie. I had a few more questions for her and I had to take a picture, she suggested we see a movie.'

I shook my head in disbelief.

'I know, I know.' He ran a hand through his hair again. 'And we had a pizza afterwards.' His voice was practically a whisper.

I shook my head in amazement. 'Guv, please don't tell me you had sex with her.' I was half-joking but it was clear from the way he glared at me that he didn't appreciate my attempt to lighten the moment so I held up my hands in surrender. 'So you're saying a lot of people could have seen you?'

'Yes, but my money is on Chowdhury.'

'I'll talk to him boss. Best if you keep your distance.' Porter nodded and didn't argue. 'Guv, you won't like this but I'm going to have to ask it. Did you talk to Ayesha about the CCTV footage of her and the others shouting over at Sean Evans outside the mosque?'

'Not the CCTV footage, no. I didn't tell her about that. But I did say that we knew she had been with Fazal Wazir. She said she'd forgotten. Which at the time I thought was fair enough.'

'But having learned that Wazir has done a runner, you're re-assessing that opinion?'

He nodded but didn't say anything.

Damn right he'd be re-assessing his opinion. He'd given her information about the case and in all likelihood she had passed that information on to a man who was rapidly becoming our main – if not only – suspect. Said suspect then packs a suitcase and heads for the hills. Plus the fact that Ayesha Khan had gone rushing out of the mosque without being questioned was also a red flag. By rights she should have been brought in to be questioned in a recorded interview, not chatted to over a curry and a pizza. And taking her to the movies? What the fuck was that about?

'I'm going to need your help here, Sal,' said Porter.

'The Decision Log?'

He nodded. Yeah, the Decision Log. Book 194. The record of everything Porter did and why he did it. Except at the moment the Decision Log didn't give the full picture. If Ayesha Khan did become an issue, any senior officer reviewing the case would be going through her statements with a fine toothcomb and it wouldn't take him long to realise that she had left the mosque before questioning had started there. And no Action had been raised to interview her, Porter had done that off his own bat. 'What do you think?' he asked.

What did I think? I think the whole thing could have been avoided if he'd just sent someone else to interview Ayesha Khan, ideally two female officers. It had been a big mistake doing the interviews on his own and an even bigger one doing it socially. But it was fixable. 'The pages are still in the log and there's plenty of space so I can update it fairly easily,' I said. 'We can say that I was going to do the initial interview with you but that I got held up. You went along to her office, it had closed and it was her suggestion to continue the interview at the restaurant. You can say at that point there was no reason to believe that she was a suspect.'

Porter nodded. 'That works for the first interview. What about the second?'

He kept using the word 'interview' but we both knew that both interactions had been more like dates.

'That's a bit harder, Guv. At that point you'd seen the CCTV footage so you knew she'd lied about not seeing Evans and Fazal Wazir.' I scratched my head. 'Okay, how about we say you had your suspicions about her and that interviewing her again in a social situation, one-on-one, might be more forthcoming. You can say that she appeared relaxed in the first interview and that the best way to proceed was another informal interview. And you flag her as a potential suspect.'

He nodded gravely. 'That could work.'

'It's the best we've got, Guv.'

'And what about the fact that she's in hospital?'

'I'll update the Decision Log now,' I said. 'You need to expand the interviews on HOLMES. Once you've done that, I'll update with what I've learned at the hospital.'

'I should go and see her,' he said and I almost roared at him in frustration.

I caught my breath and forced myself to smile. 'Probably not a good idea, Guv. Not just now.'

'You're probably right,' he said, but I could hear the lack of conviction in his voice.

We went back into the MIR. Two of the typists were deep in conversation and they both looked over at us. I was pretty sure they were talking about the Guv. He was going to have to be careful because the support staff are always gossiping.

Alan Russell had clearly been looking for Porter because he strode over as soon as he saw us. 'Harry, we've had some luck with that Ayesha Khan woman.'

I wanted to make some snappy comment about how that would be a first, but decided to keep my smart mouth shut.

'What's the story?' asked Porter.

'We have her on a council camera heading directly towards the canal, close to Homemead Road. Then we have her again about five minutes later heading away, in the direction of her home. We don't have any footage of her at the canal, but putting two and two together…'

Porter nodded. 'We need a dive team in there,' he said. 'Can you arrange that?'

'Will do,' said Russell. 'Are you going to pull her in?'

'It's a bit complicated at the moment,' said Porter. 'Let's see what the frogmen find first. Also, let's get some house-to-house enquiries going, see if anyone remembers seeing Ms Khan on Friday afternoon. Don't use the picture on the whiteboard, see what you can get off the CCTV footage. They're more likely to remember the red scarf and the blue sweater than anything.'

Russell nodded and hurried off. Porter looked at his watch. 'I'd better bring McKee up to speed.'

'Maybe get on top of HOLMES first, Guv,' I said.

He looked at me, eyes narrowing as if he wasn't happy at my second guessing him, but then he nodded. 'Yeah, you're right.'

Almost a compliment. This was starting to become a habit.

Chapter 33
(Harry)

I updated my HOLMES interview with Ayesha Khan, choosing my words carefully to make it look as if the curry and the pizza had been part of a plan to interview her with her guard down. It was still against procedure but hopefully the worst I could be accused of was bad judgement. When I finished I headed over to Ron McKee's office. His door was open. He always liked to claim that his door was never closed which was true enough, but you could always tell from the look on his face whether he was willing to be disturbed or not. When he saw me it cracked into what passes for a smile and he waved me to a chair.

'So how are you getting on with DC Nasri?' he asked as I sat down.

'He's keen. Good operator. Hasn't really put a foot wrong so far.'

'Hopefully he'll stay longer than they usually do,' said McKee. 'But between you and me I think he's destined for higher things.'

'Fast track?'

'He's the new face of the Met, isn't he? Young, university-educated, ethnic, he pretty much ticks all the boxes.'

'Pity he's not a transsexual and then it would be a clean sweep,' I said, trying and failing to keep the bitterness out of my voice. Unfortunately Teflon was right. These days promotion in the Met had more to do with what you were rather than how good you were at the job. Recruitment had gone the same way, and if you were white and male you would struggle to join the Met the way things were.

I could see from the way that Teflon's eyes hardened that he didn't appreciate my attempt at humour so I gave him a smile as if to say of course I'd welcome more LGBTs or whatever the current acronym is. 'So, I've ordered a sweep of the canal, not far from the Westway.'

'I heard,' he said. 'Dive teams are expensive.'

'It has to be done, Guv. We have a member of the congregation leaving the mosque before she could be interviewed, seen heading in the direction of the canal. Her name's Ayesha Khan. She was also in the vicinity of the victim as they entered the mosque.'

'She's been interviewed?'

I nodded. 'I did it myself. She isn't aware that we have CCTV footage of her near the victim prior to the killing or of her walking towards the canal. So I kept it low key.'

'And what's her story?'

'Nice middle class Asian girl, works in the Harrow Road CAB, she was quite helpful in keeping a lid on things at the mosque when our guys moved in.'

'But now she's a suspect?'

'We'll know more if we find the murder weapon in the canal. And we're doing a house-to-house to see if anyone saw her there Friday afternoon.'

'She's not in custody?'

'She's in hospital. Someone threw acid in her face.'

His jaw dropped. 'What?'

'She's in a bit of a state. Not life threatening, but…' I grimaced.

'For fuck's sake, Harry. Do you think it's connected to the killing? She stabs the victim, someone throws acid in her face for revenge?'

'Far too early to say,' I said. 'She's in shock at the moment. DC Nasri went to see her but didn't get anything out of her. We'll interview her when she's more stable.'

'These acid attacks are just plain evil,' said McKee. 'We had five hundred in London last year.'

'Yeah, it's an Asian thing unfortunately,' I said. McKee opened his mouth to protest and I raised my hands. 'I know what you're going to say, but it's a fact and there's no getting away from it. You know as well as I do if there's a shooting in London it's almost always black on black, and if it's an acid attack it's more often than not an Asian involved. It's just a fact and if that fact makes me racist then so be it.'

The Bag Carrier

'I'm not saying you're not right, Harry, but you've got to be careful what you say these days, especially with DC Nasri as your bag carrier. Start making comments like that in public and your feet won't touch the ground.'

'I hear you, Guv,' I said.

'Walls have ears, don't forget that.'

I shrugged. He was right, of course. Expressing an opinion, other than that diversity was a wonderful thing, was a shortcut to the unemployment line. But the simple fact is that the country with the highest rate of acid attacks in the world is Bangladesh. Pakistan also ranks very highly when it comes to throwing acid at people. Where do most acid attacks happen in London? Newham. Which just happens to have the second highest percentage of Muslims in the UK, most of them from Bangladesh and Pakistan. Second highest borough when it comes to acid attacks is Barking and Dagenham where the native British population now makes up less than half of the citizens. The third highest number of acid attacks happens in Tower Hamlets where 35 per cent of the population is Muslim, mainly Bangladeshis. You don't have to be Sherlock Holmes to put two and two together, but there's no way I or any other officer could ever say that, not in public anyway. The Met's top brass loved nothing more than proving that they were no longer institutionally racist and would happily throw me or anyone like me to the wolves.

'Anyway, it sounds like you've got all bases covered.' He leaned back and put his hands behind his head, trying to show me how relaxed he was but he was faking it so I knew he was nervous about what he was going to say next. 'So The Sheriff tells me you had a spook in.'

'Yeah. Said his name was Simon but you can't believe a word those bastards say.' I didn't even try to keep the bitterness out of my voice.

'And the victim was a serving MI5 officer?'

I nodded. 'Yes, recruited at university and tasked with infiltrating extremist groups.'

'So that's the motive right there, surely? Someone found out that he was a spook and stuck a knife in him.'

'Except would they do that in a mosque? They're fanatical about their mosques. Shoes off, women's heads covered, you heard that they moved the body because they didn't want it contaminating their prayer room? It doesn't seem right that they'd kill him where they worship.'

'Do you have any other motive?'

'No, not yet.'

'This girl, what was her name?'

'Ayesha Khan.'

'Any evidence that she's an extremist?'

'None. Like I said, she's a nice middle-class Asian girl.' I smiled and corrected myself. 'Woman.'

McKee grinned. 'Not smitten are you, Harry?'

I flashed him a sarcastic smile. 'She's in hospital, Guv. I'm not sure that's appropriate.'

He squinted at me as if he was trying to work out if I was joking or not, then shrugged as if he didn't care either way. 'So what's next?' he asked.

'See if we can find the weapon in the canal and if anyone saw her there. We're still digging into the victim's background, looking for a motive. The fact that MI5 have an operation ongoing at the mosque complicates things, obviously. Simon said we had to go softly softly with our questioning in case we expose any of his people.'

'You'd think he'd want us to pull out all the stops, it was one of his people that was killed.'

I'd had the same thought. When a police officer was killed in the line of duty it was all hands to the pumps. Everyone would pitch in because it was one of our own. But Simon had seemed more concerned about the viability of his operation than about the death of his man. 'Different mentality, I guess,' I said. 'Spooks tend to look at the bigger picture and not worry about the details.'

'Do you think this Simon knows more than he's saying?'

'I'm sure of it,' I said.

'Just be careful, Harry,' he said, lowering his voice as if he feared being overheard even though we were the only two people in his office and I'd closed the door. 'Spooks can be dangerous bastards at the best of times.'

Chapter 34
(Sal)

I left the MIR at seven while Porter was in a meeting with David Neal, the Action Manager, and Pete Davies, the Receiver, basically checking that everything that he wanted to be done was being done. Neal was a pro and would be on top of it. A large part of any murder investigation – one that went on for more than a few days anyway – was admin. You had an Office Manager making sure that everything ticked along smoothly, a Finance Manager keeping on top of costs and expenses, and the Action Manager and Receiver ensuring that all the detectives were carrying out their instructions. It was all about checks and balances. Neal and Davies checked the detectives, Porter checked them. Teflon McKee kept an eye on Porter and above them all was Detective Superintendent Sherwood, the Sheriff. It was nothing like the nonsense you see on those cosy television dramas where murder is a puzzle to be solved by real-ale drinking detectives getting flashes of inspiration over a pint of Badger's Fart at their local.

The Bag Carrier

I sent Porter a text to tell him I was off, then drove to Maida Vale. I'd phoned Uncle Siddiqui during the afternoon and told him that I'd be dropping his money around and to make sure that he had my gold. He was surprised about my early repayment and told me that he'd still have to charge me interest. I said I was in a hurry and asked him if he'd give me the gold in the mosque. I couldn't tell him that I didn't want to be seen getting into his car again, but he didn't quibble and said no problem.

I got to the mosque just before eight, in time for Isha prayers, the last Muslim prayer session of the day. Isha is a four rak'ah prayer and the first two are said out loud. If you're travelling or pushed for time you can get away with just two rak'ahs.

You learn the rak'ah as a kid and by the time you're a teenager it's ingrained into you and you can do it on automatic pilot. You're not supposed to, of course. You're supposed to concentrate on what you're doing but hardly anybody does. The rak'ah starts when you stand and recite the verses of the Koran. In Arabic, of course. Then you bow low with your hands on your knees. Then you drop and touch your forehead, nose and elbows to the floor, submitting yourself to Allah the most merciful. The last part of the rak'ah is when you chant 'Peace be upon you, and God's blessing' while your body twists to the right but you face left. That's supposed to show that you value those around you, but truth be told it's just bloody uncomfortable.

Anyway, I found a place at the back of the prayer room and did my full quota of rak'ahs. Uncle Siddiqui was at the front, as always, and after prayers I waited for him in the entrance hall. He saw me and nodded, then he walked away and I followed. He took me into an empty office at the back of the mosque. It was clear that Siddiqui had some clout around here and that he could go where he wanted. 'Take a seat,' Siddiqui said.

I sat down behind the desk and watched him walk across to the filing cabinet, open the top drawer and take out a carrier bag. He walked back and placed the bag on the desk, and rather than take the seat across from me he leaned against the desk, looking down at me.

This was at odds with the smiling, friendly, advice sharing, Uncle Siddiqui that I knew. I think he was pissed off that I had come up with the money. He knew the real value of the gold.

I picked up the carrier bag. Inside were the velvet bags. Out of some misguided respect, I resisted the urge to check that it was all there.

'Thanks.' I smiled up at him and stood up, continuing the guise of a man in a rush. I reached out to shake his hand.

'You don't think I see, Salim,' he said, leaving my hand suspended. I dropped it to my side. 'You don't think I feel their eyes on me?'

I didn't say anything. I was still a cop.

'I am blessed, young brother,' he continued. 'I have made enough money so that the children of my children will never be without. And what I choose to do with that money is my business and nobody else. I give, with fierce generosity, to our land, to our war torn devastated land. I don't hide it, my people need resources.'

I wanted nothing more than to walk away from him, from this conversation. The more that he divulged, the more our relationship could come to be misconstrued. I nodded and turned for the door.

'How long have you known, Salim?'

I turned and faced him. 'I don't know what you're talking about, Uncle. I just came to get my gold.'

'You will see Salim, mark my words. They will use all their power to make us the disease.'

I left Uncle Siddiqui and the Islamic Centre. He hadn't said anything that I could use, but he had insinuated. For me the jury was out. Just because Siddiqui was under surveillance, didn't mean anything. It wouldn't be the first or the fiftieth time that the spooks had got it wrong.

For me personally, my life was back on track. Porter had squared it with Chottopadhyay. I had squared it with Siddiqui. Most important of all I had the gold back. Thinking back on it, *the hell was I thinking?* That gold was my family heritage, it would one day be passed down to my daughter. If gambling was a sickness, I swear I think this whole episode was the cure.

I retrieved my shoes and went outside. I'd parked a couple of hundred yards away and as I walked I phoned Miriam on her mobile. I was lucky and the call went straight through to voicemail. It was always easier to lie to voicemail. I tried to sound despondent as I apologised for being late and explained that I had a stack of paperwork to deal with. I said I loved her and asked her to give Maria a kiss and that I'd try to get home before she went to sleep, though I knew that was almost certainly another untruth.

I ended the call and got into the car. I put the gold in the glove compartment, then started the engine and drove to Wembley. My luck was holding up because I managed to find a parking space opposite Waseem Chowdhury's house. It was a small semi with peeling paintwork, loose tiles on the roof and a small garden strewn with litter. The Chowdhury family clearly weren't house-proud. There was no sign of Chowdhury's car so I reclined the seat back and played Solitaire on my phone while I waited.

It was almost ten o'clock when Chowdhury turned up, his arrival preceded by the thumping beat of his car's stereo system. I got out and walked over as he parked his car. I opened the passenger side door and stepped in. 'Boo,' I said.

'The fuck man!' Chowdhury exclaimed, his eyes wide before narrowing, 'Don't I know you?'

'I'll be offended if you didn't recognise me.' I said, shutting the door behind me.

'Yeah.' He slurped his tongue. 'I fucking know you. You were at the mosque, yeah, day Masood got tagged.'

'That'll be me,' I said.

'So, you finally worked out what side you're on?'

'There's no sides here, Waseem. I'm just trying to do the right thing.'

'There's always sides, *copper*,' he spat. 'And you're sitting on the wrong one.'

'Suit yourself.' I shrugged as though it didn't matter to me, but it was something that I had struggled with since this investigation began. Was I a cop first, a Muslim second? No, I didn't think so, but it played on my mind.

'What'd you want? I'm got business to take care of.'

'Couple of things,' I said, noticing that his car was still running. 'First, you threatened a colleague of mine. What was it you said? You were going to take a bunch of brothers from The Faith and wreak havoc on him? Something like that, hot or cold.'

'That old white boy kafir?' He grinned, showing neglected teeth. 'He turned up here, shouting the odds, playing the fucking hero. He wasn't even on fucking duty, clear as day, that's harassment. I could have his fucking badge, mate.'

'We don't have badges. We have warrant cards.'

'Tomato, potato.'

'You threatened him with violence, Waseem.'

'Yeah,' he snarled, 'Says who? I don't see any fucking proof or any witnesses, so you cunts can go take a collective shit.'

'I was there,' I said. 'I witnessed it.'

Chowdhury narrowed his eyes.

'That's right,' I said, getting into the swing. 'I was here, right in front of you, when you clearly threatened a police officer with violence.'

'So that's how you going to play me, brother?'

'Believe me, I play this game a lot smarter than you.'

He took his time rubbing his chin, weighing up his options and realising quickly that he had none. 'Is that it?' he said, finally turning the engine off and slipping out the key from the ignition.

'Whatever happened between the two of you, stays that way. You hold your tongue and I'll make sure I hold mine.'

'Is that it?' he asked, again.

'No, Waseem, that's not it.' I said, and he threw his head back against his seat in frustration. 'Ayesha Khan,' I said.

He turned to glare at me. 'What about her?'

'Did it anger you that much, seeing Ayesha with a white man?'

He closed his eyes and put his head back. 'It killed me,' he said.

'Yeah, I bet it did,' I said. 'So, what you wanted to teach her a lesson?'

'Like you wouldn't fucking believe.' He kept his eyes shut tight.

'Well, she's in hospital, possibly facing losing her eyesight, I reckon she's learnt her lesson.'

His head whipped across at me. 'What?'

'Did you do it? Or was it someone from The Faith?'

'What,' he said. 'Do fucking what?'

'She was attacked, acid thrown over her face,' I said. 'Save the Oscar-winning performance, you had motive.'

'Fucking fools.' He shook his head. 'The fucking lot of ya. Yeah, I was vexed seeing her step out with that kafir, couldn't get my fucking head around it. Ayesha, fiercely protective over her identity, stepping out with a white guy twice her age. The next day, I pulled her to one side, hollered at her. I was fucking furious, but that girl knows how to bat.'

'What're saying? I asked, but by then I already knew what was coming.

'She ain't getting cosy with him, she's pumping him for information about the case.'

Yeah, that was the truth, if ever I heard it. It had never made any sense for her to be getting close to Porter, unless she had an angle. And for Ayesha to be using Porter put her slap bang in the middle of the murder.

Without another word I opened the door.

'Listen up,' Chowdhury said, 'You best find who did this to Ayesha. Because believe me, if we find him first…'

'I'm on it,' I said, 'And you keep away from my colleague. If he gets any more shit from you or The Faith I'll be holding you personally responsible.'

He nodded. 'I hear you.'

'Al-salāmu alaykum,' I said. Peace be upon you.

'Wa alaykum al-salām,' he replied. And upon you be peace. Then he threw in a 'wa riḥmat Allāh wa barakatuhu'. And God's mercy and forgiveness, which might have been meant sarcastically but I let it go. I slammed the door and went back to my car.

CHAPTER 35
(HARRY)

I was up bright and early and didn't even bother making myself a coffee before driving to the canal site where the divers had resumed their search for the murder weapon. When you're looking for something that may or may not have been thrown into a canal, the guys you call out are the Underwater and Confined Spaces Search Team, part of the Met's Marine Policing Unit. The canals are like giant skips, anything and everything gets thrown into them from supermarket trollies and traffic cones to builder's rubble and used syringes.

They had started work the previous afternoon but Stephen Courtney – the Finance Manager – had said there was no need to work through the night. The search wasn't especially time-sensitive and overtime payments went through the roof after eight.

When I got there two divers were in the water while another two were on standby. Two more officers in overalls were in attendance and the operation was being overseen by a sergeant I'd known for many years, Alison Dyke. She was a veteran of the underwater unit and we'd crossed paths dozens of times over the years. 'Harry!' she exclaimed when she saw me walking along the towpath. 'Come to check up on us, did you?'

I grinned and shook my head. I was never sure how to greet her. I was an Inspector and she was a Sergeant but I'd been drinking with her many times and our nights would usually end with a hug and an air kiss. But this wasn't social so we just nodded. 'Wanted a look-see,' I said. 'How's it going?'

'Slowly but surely,' she said. 'We did about sixty feet before it got dark and we've been in for an hour so far. You know the drill, Harry, it all has to be done by touch.'

The canals are only a few feet deep in most places but the divers need to wear full dry suits and breathing apparatus. Visibility is close to zero so they have to use their fingertips to search. It's a slow laborious process and there are no short-cuts.

'Where did you start?' I asked.

She pointed at a marker further down the towpath. 'We've marked a hundred feet either side of where the entrance to the towpath is. Then we started at the entrance and headed west. Once we've reached the marker we'll come back and head east.'

'How long, do you think?'

'We should be done today. That's if we don't find anything, of course.' One of the divers stood up, holding what looked like a hammer. He tossed it onto the towpath and one of the men in overalls put it in a plastic crate. 'We're collecting anything interesting we find,' said Dyke. 'Just to be on the safe side.'

The diver went down again. He was probably kneeling on the bottom, groping forward with his gloved hands. It's not a job I'd want to do.

'So how's life, Harry?'

'It's not getting any easier,' I said. 'This case is a bugger. Six hundred potential witnesses and nobody saw a thing, and unless you come up with the goods, no murder weapon. And no real motive.'

'Awkward,' she said. 'Have you thought of asking Professor Dumbledore for advice?' I gave her a withering look and she laughed. 'Just trying to lighten the moment, Harry.'

'Taking the piss out of my name doesn't help,' I said. 'And it's not even my bloody name.'

'I know, but the way it winds you up always makes me laugh.' She patted me on the back. 'Alan and Paul are further down the towpath.'

I walked a dozen or so paces and around a curve in the canal where I saw Alan Russell and Paul Rees sitting on a bench. Rees was smoking and Russell had managed to get a Starbucks coffee. 'How's it going?' I asked.

They shuffled to the side to give me room to sit. 'Alison reckons she'll be done by tonight at the latest,' said Russell.

'Yeah, she said. Fingers crossed on that. What about the house-to-house?'

A line of houses backed on to the canal and Russell gestured at them with his coffee. 'Paul has four detectives knocking on doors over there. Last night we covered the houses on this side, and on the approaches to the towpath entrance.'

'Who do we have as House-To-House Coordinator?' I asked Rees.

'John Osborne.'

I grimaced. Rees caught the look and laughed. 'Don't worry, Guv. He's off the sauce.'

'You're sure?' Osborne had a fondness for lager and it wasn't unknown for him to go into a pub for a pint or two when he was supposed to be knocking on doors.

'Four weeks now. He was given the red card by the Sheriff and he's doing the AA meetings and being as good as gold.'

'I'll take your word for it,' I said. 'So how's the house-to-house going?'

'Half the residences didn't open their doors so we'll revisit them this afternoon. Of those that did, nobody remembers seeing anything.'

'Ayesha would have been around here at between two and three in the afternoon on Friday,' I said, 'Might be worth having bodies in the street talking to passers by.'

Rees looked over at Russell and Russell nodded. 'Good idea, Guv. I'll raise the Actions on it. Meanwhile, I wouldn't mind your opinion on that.' He pointed at a tower block a hundred yards from the canal. 'The flats on this side get a decent view of the towpath and the approach to it. Everything above the fourth floor, anyway. Paul and I reckon there are four flats on each floor looking this way. The building is eighteen stories high so we're looking at 56 flats. What do you think? Worth knocking on the doors? It's a lot of doors.'

I looked over at the block. There were balconies with washing flapping on lines and a lot of windows with plastic blinds that I guessed were kitchens. He was right, 56 was a lot of doors, but if a housewife had been looking out of the kitchen window or her husband had been smoking on the balcony, they might have seen a little Asian woman wearing a red scarf throw something into the canal. 'I think so,' I said.

Russell nodded. 'Yeah, it has to be done, doesn't it?' He looked over at Rees. 'Can you raise the Actions for it and brief John? Tell you what, get four bodies and have them do the streets on the approach to the towpath from one-thirty to three-thirty and then switch them to the tower block.'

'Will do,' said Rees.

I stood up. 'Right, I'm off to Hendon for morning prayers. Are you guys coming?'

'I am, but Paul is staying here with the troops,' said Russell, standing up, 'I did have a thought, Guv.'

'What's that? And it had better not involve Dumbledore?'

'What?' said Russell, frowning in confusion.

'Forget it,' I said, 'What's the thought?'

'You're assuming that the murder weapon was tossed into the canal. But there's a lot of waste ground and vegetation around. Is it worth a search?'

I looked around. He was right. There were plenty of places that a knife could have been tossed. The assumption I was making was that having walked all the way from the mosque to the canal, Ayesha Khan would have thrown it into the water. But she could just as easily have thrown it under a bush or even buried it in the soil. 'You're right,' I said. 'Can you get something organised?'

'I was thinking of getting half a dozen cadets out, give them a break from lectures.'

'It'll be a nice day out for them,' I said.

'I'll arrange it,' said Russell. 'Any chance of a lift back, Guv, I came here with Alan.'

'No problem,' I said. We walked back to my car, saying goodbye to Alison and her team as we left.

We chatted about the case as I drove us to Hendon. 'So this Fazal Wazir is looking like our best suspect,' said Russell. He was still sipping from his Starbucks coffee.

'He was close to the victim when they went into the mosque and has since done a runner,' I said. 'But we've no evidence.'

'The knife is the key, right? This Ayesha Khan is a friend of Wazir's. And she went to the mosque with him.'

'She's a friend of Wazir's sister. And she says she didn't go to the mosque with him, but admits that he might have been on the same bus.'

'But if the knife turns out to be in the canal, that means she helped him. Or that she was the killer.'

'She's not a suspect,' I said quickly. Too quickly, I realised. I sounded defensive.

'Because?'

The question made me think. Why hadn't I considered Ayesha as a suspect? She had been with the group that had interacted with Sean Evans outside the mosque but hadn't mentioned it, and she had left the mosque before being interviewed, apparently heading for the canal. Was I letting my personal feelings interfere with my judgement?

'Because she's a girl?' pressed Russell.

'Girls tend not to use knives,' I said.

'Housewives in the kitchen do,' he said.

'I'm presuming that the killer brought the knife with him.'

'She had a bag. A nice Louis Vuitton number that my wife would kill for.'

I laughed. 'That would make it premeditated, wouldn't it? And I keep coming back to the fact that if this was planned why would the killer commit the crime with six hundred potential witnesses in the vicinity?'

'And still no motive?'

I grimaced. I wanted to tell Russell that Sean Evans was an MI5 officer who could well have been killed because he had been uncovered, but Simon had made it crystal clear that no one other than the Sheriff, Teflon McKee and myself should be privy to that information. I hadn't even been able to tell DC Nasri. 'None so far,' I said, and hated the fact that I was being forced to lie to a colleague.

'Seems to me that it's most likely to be one of The Faith that did it,' said Russell.

'Yeah, but we keep coming back to the same issue,' I said. 'If The Faith wanted Evans dead, why kill him at their mosque? They could have picked him up at any time.'

'It couldn't have been some sort of suicide, could it?' said Russell. 'He kills himself and someone, that Ayesha woman maybe, takes the knife?'

I looked across at him to see if he was joking, but he seemed serious. 'It's a bit elaborate. A bit Agatha Christie. And what was he trying to achieve?'

'I'm just throwing out ideas,' he said.

'Fair enough,' I said. 'I wish I had more ideas to throw out.'

'It's early days,' he said.

He was right, of course. We were only three days into the investigation. The problem was, it was what we referred to as a low information case. We had little if anything in the way of forensics, and while we had hundreds of statements there was nothing of value in them.

In a case like that the SIO has to ensure that he doesn't start issuing low-quality Actions just for the sake of it. There was a tendency to get men out knocking on doors or re-interviewing witnesses, just to give them something to do but that could be demoralising and tended to clutter up HOLMES with low-quality material.

The most productive thing I could do was to work with David Neal, the Action Manager, to check that all Actions were being carried out properly and effectively. If it continued as a low information case then I might have to consider requesting a formal review, where senior officers would go through HOLMES to check my investigative strategy and its implementation, but that would be tantamount to admitting that I was out of my depth and I didn't think that I was. Not yet, anyhow.

The question that needed answering was WHY it was a low information case. Had something happened to minimise the information available? Had the perpetrator been clever enough to remove any forensic evidence? Were witnesses being interfered with to prevent them sharing information with the police? Material withholding could sometimes happen because of a mistrust of the police, or because there was either loyalty to the offender, or fear of them. That was a very real possibility, of course. It was obvious that most of the worshippers didn't like the police at best, and a high proportion seemed to positively hate us. That would be reason alone for them not to be forthcoming.

But then we had The Faith, a group of young Muslims who were prepared to use violence to achieve their aims. If it was The Faith behind the murder, maybe witnesses were just too scared to tell us what they had seen. Either that or they sympathised with The Faith. It might be worth re-interviewing those worshippers who had identified members of The Faith as having been at the mosque. If they were at least prepared to say they had seen them, with a bit of tactful pressure they might provide us with more information.

We got back to Peel House and headed straight for the canteen. We both grabbed bacon sandwiches though Russell added a sausage to his. 'I heard they might be stopping the bacon sarnies,' he said as we rode up in the lift to the top floor.

'What?' I almost dropped my coffee.

'There are moves afoot to make the canteen Halal. No pork products. There are a couple of Muslims on the canteen staff and they've put in an official request.'

'There'll be a riot if they try to deprive cops of bacon sarnies,' I said.

'It's the way the world's going, Guv. Still, there's always turkey bacon, right?'

I glared at him. 'DC Russell, the words turkey and bacon never have and never will go together. Bacon is bacon. Turkey is just big chicken.' I shuddered at the thought of a turkey bacon sandwich.

'No argument here, Guv.'

The troops were already assembled for the briefing. Stuart Hurley was there, David Judd, Stephen Courtney, Pete Davies and David Neal almost never left the MIR so they were at pretty much all the briefings. Jacqueline Beard was there but as Crime Scene Manager she didn't really have much to do and had already been assigned to two other murder investigations. There were about another ten detectives who were probably in the MIR to update HOLMES, and the Press Officer, Donna Walsh, was sitting next to DS Beard. Press officers didn't usually attend morning briefings so I guessed she wanted something from me.

I went straight into it, telling everyone that we were expanding our house-to-house enquires in the area of the canal and that we hoped to have the search of the canal and the land around it done by the end of the day. I brought everyone up to speed on what we'd found out about the victim, that he'd become a convert at university and that he had been very vocal about his new-found religion at work. What I couldn't tell them was that Sean Evans was an MI5 officer, even though that might well have been the reason he was murdered. Nor could I tell them that any one of the six hundred men and women that had been at the mosque that day could also have been MI5 officers or agents. I'd never been in a situation anything like this before. The purpose of the morning briefing was to keep everyone updated on the status of the investigation but while I wasn't actually lying to my team, I certainly wasn't giving them all the information I had. I was bloody annoyed at Simon for putting me in that position but there was nothing I could do other than seethe. MI5 outranked the Met, that was a fact and there was no getting away from it.

'The closest we have to a suspect at present is one Fazal Wazir. He arrived at the mosque at about the same time as the victim with his sister, Yalina, and a friend, Ayesha Khan. When interviewed, all three made no mention of the fact that they saw Evans in the street. We have footage that shows that they exchanged words with Evans. Fazal Wazir has since left the family home with a suitcase. We have a watch out for him at the ports and airports, but today I'd like to start looking for him in earnest.' I looked over at Stuart. 'Stuart, let's get his phone records and see if we can get a location for his phone. Talk to the banks and see if he's been using his credit and debit cards. I'm reluctant to go public on the fact that we're looking for him but that might be an option down the line.'

Hurley nodded.

'DC Nasri and I spoke to the bosses of the taxi firm that Sean Evans worked for and we have a list of drivers who also worked there. We sent the list to our anti-terrorism people yesterday so can you give them a nudge, Stuart? If any of his co-workers are known troublemakers then we need them interviewed. I doubt that they'll be cooperative but we need them in the system.'

Hurley nodded again.

'We keep hearing about The Faith, the guys who turned up with knives and machetes on the day of the murder. Alan, let's see about compiling a list of members of The Faith and see if any of them have convictions for knife-related offences. Let's interview or re-interview anyone who has been caught in possession of a knife or used a knife. Let's also go through any CCTV footage we have of the members of The Faith who turned up at the mosque after the police arrived. See if we can come up with more names.'

'I'm on it, Guv,' said Russell.

'Right,' I said. 'Does anyone else have any bright ideas, because at this stage all suggestions will be gratefully received?'

I looked around the MIR but all I got was blank looks.

Chapter 36
(Sal)

The phone on my desk rang just as the Guv was winding things up. It was DS Rees. 'Is the Guv there?' he asked.

'Just finishing the briefing,' I said.

'Tell him we've found the knife.'

'You're joking!'

'Well, a knife anyway. We've got it out of the water and in an evidence bag and Lorraine Sawyer is on her way to collect it. Tell the Guv, will you?'

'Just as soon as I can,' I said.

Rees disconnected the call just as Porter was heading my way and he could see from the look on my face that something was up.

'The dive team have pulled a knife out of the canal,' I said, meeting him half way.

He grinned. 'Excellent. Does Lorraine know?'

'She's on the way.'

'Okay. Give her a bell and ask her to send me photographs and we'll take them to the pathologist to see if it fits the profile. And ask her how long she thinks it'll take to get prints and DNA.'

'Will do, Guv.'

He sat down next to me. 'Couple of things I need to run by you for the Decision Log,' he said.

I opened the top drawer of my desk, pulled out a notepad, flipped over to a clean page. Pen in hand.

'I was out at the canal this morning with DS Rees and DC Russell. We're going to search around the canal, DC Russell is going to see if we can get some cadets for the job. We're also arranging for officers to canvass the area around the towpath between one-thirty and three-thirty, the theory being that was the time Ayesha would have been there on Friday. And we're arranging to knock on doors on a tower block overlooking the canal. That's all so far.'

'I've got something for you too, Guv,' I said, lowering my voice. 'Maybe over a coffee?'

'Can't it wait?'

'It's about Chowdhury. I'd rather tell you somewhere quiet.'

We were interrupted by the arrival of the Press Officer, Donna Walsh. 'Sorry to interrupt you Harry but I need a quick word and I have a meeting with the Deputy Commissioner in half an hour.'

'Sure, Donna, what's up?'

'The Press Office had two calls yesterday evening, one from the Daily Mail and the other from ITV news. Both asking pretty much the same question – had Sean Evans been murdered by one of the members of The Faith and were the police treating it as a racist attack?'

'What did you tell them?' Porter said.

'I told them it was too late to talk to anyone on the team but that I'd get back to them first thing.'

'Damn journalists,' I muttered.

'Is it true, was the attack racist?' Walsh asked.

'Hand on heart we don't know,' said Porter. 'Sean Evans was a convert, and from what I've been told, the Muslims love converts.' He looked across at me and flashed me a smile. Credit where credit is due.

'Both the journalists who phoned in also asked if a Waseem Chowdhury was a suspect,' said Walsh.

'Did they now?' said Porter. 'I don't suppose they said where they got that name from, did they?' He gave me another look. No smile this time.

'You know journalists, Harry. They make a big thing about protecting their sources. But it's probably not a coincidence that they both gave me the same name. Is he a suspect?'

'He's a friend of Evans, or at least an associate. They went into the mosque together. I wouldn't say he was a suspect but I wouldn't say he has been ruled out, either.'

'So what do you want me to tell them?'

'That the investigation is ongoing.'

'But do you have a suspect?'

'Between you and me there's a guy we'd like to talk to but he's vanished.'

'I could do you a press release and put out his picture.'

'We want to look for him on the QT at the moment.'

She nodded thoughtfully. 'So I'll say no to Chowdhury being a suspect and that the police are still canvassing witnesses and searching for the murder weapon.'

'That sounds reasonable,' said Porter.

'Thanks, Harry,' said the press officer, and she hurried away.

Porter looked over at me. 'I think I know what you want to talk to me about.'

'Guv' I said. 'You don't know the half of it,'

He nodded and we took the lift down to the canteen and queued in silence. Porter had yet another bacon sandwich – I swear he eats them just to wind me up – and a coffee, while I had an orange juice and a croissant. I waited until we were sitting at a table by the window before telling him what had happened the previous night. The gist of it, anyway. 'So, two things,' I said when I'd finished. 'Chowdhury and The Faith won't be giving you any grief again, I'm sure of that. And he told me that Ayesha Khan wasn't attacked by anyone from The Faith.'

He sat back in his chair with a look of disgust on his face. 'Well, he would say that, wouldn't he?'

'I believed him, Guv. He was very definite about it. Look, I've got something else to tell you, so don't shoot the messenger, right?'

He frowned so hard that his eyebrows pretty much bumped together. 'What do you mean?'

'Guv,' I cleared my throat. I didn't know the full extent of Porter's relationship with Ayesha, and I didn't know how he would react. 'It looks as though Ayesha Khan only went out with you to extract information on the case.'

'Bollocks!'

I held up a hand to placate him. 'I'm just telling you what Chowdhury said.'

'Why would he tell you something like that?'

'Because I asked him if The Faith had been responsible for the acid attack. He said there was no way anyone in The Faith would have attacked her. She's one of them.'

I could see Porter's mind racing as he considered the implications of what I'd told him. 'And you believed him?'

'I did, Guv.' His jaw tightened. I guess no one likes to be told that they've been used. Plus there was every chance that she had tipped off Fazal Wazir that he was about to be brought in, giving him the chance to do a runner. By confiding in her, Porter had jeopardised the investigation.

He nodded slowly. 'Right, thanks for keeping me abreast of the situation,' he said, all professional, but I could tell it had hurt him. 'This interview with Chowdhury? Have you entered it into HOLMES?'

'No, Guv. It was very much off-the-record.'

'In what way?'

'Best you don't know the details, Guv,' I said. 'But trust me, he's not going to bother you again.'

He picked up his sandwich and coffee and stood up. He looked down at me. 'It's a fine line we walk,' he said, and walked away.

'Yeah,' I said to myself. 'It's a fine line, all right.'

Chapter 37
(Harry)

I spent the early part of the afternoon reading through all the witness statements in which Fazal Wazir was mentioned. He was Nominal 86 and he was referred to a total of twenty three times, always by male worshippers. There was nothing significant in any of the statements, he was only mentioned in passing as someone who had been at the mosque. His own statement didn't mention seeing Sean Evans in the street. He told the detectives that he had travelled to the mosque on the bus but didn't mention his sister or Ayesha Khan. He had stayed behind once the body had been discovered because he wanted to know what had happened. He was one of the worshippers who had been outside when The Faith arrived, which meant he could easily have left then. The fact that he had stayed behind was a mark in his favour, unless he had figured that by remaining he made himself less likely to be identified as a suspect.

I found it hard to concentrate because I kept thinking about what Nasri had said about Ayesha Khan using me. Was that what it had all been about? I thought she had genuinely liked me, and when she laughed she always seemed to mean it. I'm a pretty good judge of character and I never felt that she was faking it. There was no reason for Nasri to lie about what Chowdhury had said, though I couldn't help but wonder what he'd said to Chowdhury to make the guy back off. And as it wasn't going into HOLMES, chances are that I'd never know.

At just after two-thirty I received an email from Lorraine Sawyer. There were three attachments, photographs of the knife that had been found in the canal. It was a flicknife, what the Americans called a switchblade, with a pearl handle and a stainless steel button to eject the blade. One of the photographs was with the blade retracted, in the other two the blade was out. There was a steel ruler in all three photographs to give the scale. When closed the knife was six inches long, and it was twelve inches long with the blade out. In the email Sawyer said that the knife appeared to have been wiped clean. There were no fingerprints and swabs were being analysed for DNA but that could take up to 72 hours.

I printed the pictures out but they weren't actual size so I asked one of the typists if she could help me out on the office photocopier. She used the magnification function to get the pictures actual size and

I took them over to Nasri, who was busying himself filling in the Decision Log.

'Get us a car,' I said, holding out the photographs. 'We need to show these to the pathologist. See what she thinks.'

He closed the Decision Log and went off to arrange transport. As he left the MIR, Donna Walsh appeared holding a clipboard. 'Harry, sorry about this but we've just had the Guardian on now.'

I grimaced. The Guardian was one of my least favourite newspapers – if you believed them every London cop was a vicious homophobic racist who liked nothing better than to rough up asylum seekers on their days off. 'What do they want?'

'They've also been given the name of Waseem Chowdhury and want to know if he's a person of interest.'

'They have to know that we can't possibly tell them anything until an arrest is made, and then we can only give them a name and what they've been charged with. Donna, who the hell is putting Chowdhury's name out there?'

'I don't know, Harry, but the Guardian journalist is adamant that the source is good.'

'Well it can't be anyone in the MIR because everyone here knows we're looking for a guy called Fazal Wazir. Chowdhury was interviewed but he's not a suspect. '

'Can I tell her that?'

'It's a woman?'

The Press Officer smiled thinly. 'Yes Harry, there are women journalists.'

'Sorry. It's just when you hear journalist you think male, that's all.'

She flashed me a tight smile. 'You're digging yourself deeper, Harry.'

'Sorry.'

'So what can I tell her? Can I deny that Chowdhury is a suspect?'

'I wouldn't want to rule anyone out at this stage,' I said.

'If we don't definitively deny it, there is a chance she'll still run the story.'

'We'll have to take that risk.'

'She also asked if there was any connection between the murder and...' She looked at her clipboard. 'And an acid attack on a woman called Ayesha Khan?'

I tried not to show any reaction but my mind was racing. How the hell had anyone heard about the attack on Ayesha? And how had they linked the acid attack to what had happened at the mosque? It was possible that the local cops dealing with Ayesha's case had spoken to a journalist, but they wouldn't have been aware of her involvement in the mosque investigation. My big worry was that the journalist would find out that I had been to see Chowdhury after he had verbally abused us in the street. If the Guardian got hold of that nugget of information they would have a field day, especially if Nasri was wrong and

Chowdhury carried out his threat to accuse me of racism.

'Harry?' prompted the press officer.

'The acid attack isn't our case,' I said. 'But the victim, Ms Khan, was at the mosque on the day of the murder and is a witness.'

'A witness to what?'

'I mean to say that she was there. That's all.'

'So there's no suggestion that she was attacked because of something she may or may not have seen at the mosque?'

'No suggestion at all, Donna.'

'Okay, I'll pass that on. I don't suppose you know who is dealing with the acid attack investigation, do you?'

Nasri returned with the keys for our transport so I asked him if he knew who was handling the Ayesha Khan case.

'It'll be the Harrow Road policing team,' he said. 'The doctor I spoke to said two uniforms were in to see her not long after she was admitted, but she wasn't able to talk. You could try Inspector John Holland, he'd know.'

'Thanks, Sal,' said Walsh, writing the name down on her clipboard. She hurried off and Nasri and I went outside to our car. Another Vectra. Nasri drove us to Horseferry Road and we managed to find a parking space in the mortuary's car park. We waited for about fifteen minutes before an assistant wearing green scrubs took us along to where Lucy Wakeham was working. We watched through an observation window as she made short work of cutting the top off the skull of a middle-aged man and popping his brain into a stainless steel bowl and placing it on a set of scales.

'Why would anyone choose this as a career?' asked Nasri, turning away in disgust.

'It's like most things, you get used to it,' I said. 'My dad was a butcher and by the time I was ten I could cut up a pig and not think twice about it.'

'It's the smell that gets me.'

'Pork?'

He looked at me as if I was stupid. 'No Guv, the smell of corpses I'm talking about. It turns my stomach.'

'You can shove some Vicks up your nose, or try breathing through your mouth,' I said. 'I don't find it so bad.'

He grinned. 'Yeah, they say your sense of smell is one of the first things to go when you get old.'

'Tread carefully DC Nasri or I'll send you in there.'

Wakeham spent another five minutes on the corpse, then pulled off her blood-splattered gloves and dropped them into a pedal bin before pushing open the door into the observation area. 'Sorry about that, Harry, we've a bit of a rush on,' she said. 'So you said you've got a possible murder weapon?'

I handed her the photographs. 'What do you think? It was found fairly close to the mosque. We're having it tested for DNA as we speak.'

Wakeham studied the pictures carefully and then nodded. 'It was definitely a knife of this type, yes,' she said.

'What about the angle it went into the heart?' I asked. 'Would you be able to take a stab at how tall the assailant was? No pun intended.'

She laughed dryly. 'Pun very much intended, I think,' she said. 'I'm going to need to look at my notes.'

She went over to a filing cabinet, pulled open a drawer and extracted a file. She spread it on a stainless steel table and studied drawings she'd made at the time of the post-mortem. 'The blade went in horizontally,' she said. 'As if it was held with the thumb and top finger and then stabbed forward. Rather than grabbed around the handle and brought down.' She picked up a pen and demonstrated, first holding the pen in her fist and bringing it down, then holding it in the palm of her hand and thrusting it forward.

'Two very different actions,' she said. 'If it had been held in a fist the blade probably wouldn't have gone through the ribs, but it was horizontal so it slipped through the ribs and nicked the heart.' She motioned for Nasri to step forward and demonstrated with the pen again, showing how the way the knife was held influenced the way the blade would enter the body. When it was brought down in a slashing movement the blade wouldn't penetrate the ribs. It had to be thrust side on and held in the palm of the hand. 'The blade entered the heart pretty much at an angle of ninety degrees, so the attacker was probably about the same height as the victim, give or take a few inches.'

'So not a girl who was a little over five feet tall?' I asked, and I saw the sideways look that Nasri gave me.

'Impossible,' said the pathologist. 'The blade would have been angled up when it entered the heart.'

'Good to know,' I said.

'You were thinking it might have been a woman?'

'We had a potential suspect in mind but from what you've said I think we can rule her out,' I said. I picked up the printed sheets and slid them into my coat pocket. 'You've been a big help.'

'Any time,' she said. She put the file back in the cabinet and then escorted us back to reception where I thanked her again.

'So it definitely wasn't Ayesha Khan,' said Nasri as we walked to the car.

'Not unless she was standing on a bucket,' I said.

'Which means she was disposing of the knife for someone else. Fazal Wazir is looking more likely by the day, right Guv?'

'My thoughts exactly.'

Chapter 38
(Sal)

I was back in the MIR updating the Decision Log when DS Hurley came over. 'Guv, we've heard back from the phone company about Fazal Wazir,' he said to Porter.

Porter looked up from his HOLMES screen. 'Let me guess, his phone has been off since Sunday evening.'

Hurley nodded. 'Afraid so,' he said. 'The GPS shows him at his house and then the phone went off at just after ten o'clock. It hasn't been on since.'

'He's probably dumped the SIM card,' I said. 'What about the call and text records?'

'They're going to email them over,' said Hurley.

'ID all the numbers he contacted, see if we can get addresses. He might have been stupid enough to have spoken to whoever helped him run.'

'Will do, Guv.'

'What about Wazir's bank?'

'They're not as co-operative. They're insisting on all the paperwork before they'll release his details. It's in hand.'

'If he's not using his phone I doubt he'll be using his card, but let's go through the motions.'

Hurley nodded and went back to his desk. I could see the frustration on Porter's face. He'd done everything by the book, pretty much, other than his dalliance with Ayesha Khan, but we were no nearer making an arrest than we were when we'd first arrived at the mosque. Yes, we'd found the murder weapon, but the fact that there were no fingerprints on it suggested that we'd also draw a blank on DNA. And if there was DNA on the knife, the immersion in filthy canal water would almost certainly have rendered it useless. Even if we found Fazal Wazir, we had no witnesses and no forensics, so provided he kept his mouth shut there'd be no case against him.

If I were the SIO I'd probably arrange for everyone to be re-interviewed. I couldn't believe that no one had seen Sean Evans being murdered. There were six hundred people in the mosque and someone must have seen something. My money was on Ayesha Khan. Sure, no one saw her throwing the knife into the canal but there was CCTV footage of her heading that way and walking away. We search the canal and lo-and-behold we find the knife. At least we find a knife. A knife that is a damn-near perfect match to the one that killed Sean Evans. She clearly didn't just stumble across the knife in the mosque and decide it would be a good idea to walk a mile to the canal and toss it in. The chances are that whoever stabbed Evans gave the knife to her, which meant two things – it meant she knew who the killer was and that killer was close enough to her that she would risk breaking the law to help him. Or her.

Porter left at just after six and I called it a day soon after. I got home before seven for a change and I assumed that Miriam would be pleased to see me but I was wrong. In fact she didn't look happy at all and my first thought was that something had happened to our daughter. She was sitting in the kitchen and she didn't get up when I walked in. There was clearly something wrong. 'Is Maria okay?' I asked.

'Of course,' she said. 'She's in front of the TV doing her homework.'

'Who gives a five-year-old homework?' I said.

'It's just spelling. You can test her later.' She bit down on her lower lip, obviously upset about something. I followed basic interrogation technique number one and said nothing, waiting for her to fill the silence.

'Sal,' she said eventually. 'Did you touch my gold?'

'Your gold?'

'My wedding gold. Did you go through it for some reason?'

'Why do you ask?'

She frowned at me. 'That means you did, right?'

She was good. My wife would have made a great detective. Or maybe it's just that she's been with me so long that she can read me like an open book. I looked at her dark brown eyes and felt myself falling into them. I didn't want to lie to her ever again. I hated each and every lie that I'd told her and I knew it had to stop. She deserved better. She was the love of my life and the mother of our child and I had lied to her so many times that I had lost count. I nodded. 'Yes,' I said. 'I did.'

'I knew it,' she said.

'How?'

'My mum was around this afternoon and we got to talking about the wedding. She wanted to see the gold. I got it out, but it wasn't wrapped the way I wrap it. Why, Sal? What did you want?'

'Miriam,' I said. I knelt down and took her hand. 'I can explain.'

'So explain,' she said, holding my hand tightly, desperation and hope in her eyes that I would say the right words.

I couldn't tell her anything but the truth.

She listened without interrupting, her eyes never leaving mine for a second. My back was sweating by the time I'd finished.

'My father worked two jobs,' she said when I'd finished, her eyes brimming with tears.

'I know.' I said.

'Stacking shelves at the supermarket in the day. Then he'd come home, spend time with my mother...and me. Eat with us, read to me and put me to sleep. Then he'd work the late shift loading wooden pallets at the airport.' She smiled sadly. 'His hands would be covered in splinters...You know why, Sal?'

I nodded. 'I do,' I said.

'So that one day his daughter would be married and he'd be able to fulfil his duty as a father and as a man...' She shrugged. 'Old fashioned, I guess.'

'I know, Miriam. I would never have lost the gold, I swear.'

'You don't understand, Sal.' She removed her hand away from mine. 'You're never here. You don't know anything about your daughter. She doesn't even miss you anymore, do you realise how sad that is? She expects it. She expects you to be absent. And me...I sleep alone most nights, running this house and raising our daughter by myself. And I hold down a job. Does that ever cross your mind?'

'Miriam, listen.'

She held up a finger. 'If it was your job keeping you away from us, I'd understand, I wouldn't like it, but I'd get it. But gambling...You'd rather sit in a stinking room full of strangers losing your money, losing our money, and then pawn our gold, our heritage that one day we would pass onto our daughter just as my father did.'

'I've got it back, haven't I?' I said, running a hand through my hair.

'You could have lost it, Sal.'

'Miriam, I screwed up... I'm sorry.'

She stood up. 'You've gone too far this time, Sal.'

'They would have killed me, they could have hurt you, our daughter. I was desperate.'

'You bought this onto our doorstep, Sal. *You did.*'

I grabbed her by the arm but she wrenched it away.

'Miriam... please,'

'Last time, Sal,' She said, softly, her eyes boring into mine making her words gospel. 'You will not do this to me again.'

'I swear.'

She forced a smile and blinked away tears. 'You know, in a way, I'm relieved.'

'Relieved?'

She looked at me earnestly. 'Sal. I thought you were having an affair.'

'An affair? Why the hell would I be having an affair?'

'You're always out late, you don't answer your phone when I call, you're always really disheveled when you do get home and we haven't made love for more than a month.'

'A month? Are you sure?'

She nodded solemnly. 'Very sure.'

'I'm so so sorry,' I said. 'I've just been so tired.'

'Which is why I thought you were having an affair.'

I shook my head. 'I was playing poker. And more often than not I was losing.'

She bit down on her lower lip. 'We can always get more money, Sal,' she said. 'But if I ever lost you I wouldn't know what to do.'

'You'll never lose me,' I said. I reached over and hugged her. 'I swear. I love you with all my heart. I'm so sorry for what I've done. But I'm through gambling. Never again. On my life.'

I hugged her harder and kissed her on her neck. Maria appeared in the doorway and grinned when she saw me kissing her mum. 'Daddy and mummy, sitting in a tree,' she said in a sing-song voice. 'K-I-S-S-I-N-G.'

I laughed and Miriam waved for her to join in a group hug. I kissed them both and hugged them like I never wanted to let them go.

Chapter 39
(Harry)

I got to St Mary's just before seven and it took me ten minutes wandering around the labyrinth of wards and corridors until I found the burns unit and then I had to sit on an orange plastic chair for another ten until they managed to find the doctor who was looking after Ayesha. His name was Dr Balbir Singh, and from the turban I figured he was a Sikh. I couldn't help but wonder if he was carrying a ceremonial knife under his scrubs. 'Inspector Porter?' he said, and he shook my hand. He looked dog-tired. 'Your colleague was here yesterday. Ms Khan had your business card in her bag.'

'How is she?'

'She's awake at the moment and we're giving her morphine to help her deal with her pain. As I told your colleague, she has a difficult road ahead of her.'

'Can I see her?'

'We're outside visiting hours but if it's police business, I don't see why not.' He took me through to her room. She looked tiny in the hospital bed, her face swathed in bandages and gauze. She was hooked up to a machine that beeped softly. 'I'll leave you to it,' said the doctor. 'I'm snowed under.'

As he hurried off, I sat down on a chair next to her bed. Her eyes were covered with pads of gauze. 'Ayesha?' I said softly.

'Harry?'

My heart lurched at the realisation she had recognised my voice. 'Yes. Hi.' Her arms were on top of the covers and I wanted to reach over and hold her hand but I figured that wouldn't be professional. 'I'm so sorry,' I said.

'For what? It's not your fault Harry.'

'Are you sure about that?'

'What do you mean?' she asked.

'Do you think someone got angry with you because they saw us together?'

'Why would you think that?'

'It happens. Honour attacks. Someone takes offence at seeing a Muslim girl with a white guy and they...' I didn't want to finish the sentence.

'That's not what happened,' she said. 'I think it was someone from the Citizens Advice Bureau. The husband of a client.'

'I thought you didn't know who attacked you. That's what you told the police, right?'

'I was confused. In shock. I've had time to think now. It was the husband of a woman I'd been advising.'

'Are you sure?'

She took several breaths as if she was in pain. 'I'm sure,' she said. 'His name's Mohammed Gomastha. He's in his sixties and has been in the UK for twenty years. He came here with his wife but two years ago he acquired another wife in Bangladesh and somehow managed to get her over here. She's barely twenty, Harry, and speaks next to no English. He's using her as a sex slave, pretty much. Anyway, she'd had enough and came to the bureau for advice, basically asking if she can stay in the country if she leaves him. She came in to see me a couple of times and then he found out and he stormed in and started abusing me, calling me all sorts of names and spitting at me and shoving me.'

'Did you call the police?'

'We handled it ourselves. It happens quite a lot. Anyway, he made a lot of threats but he eventually left.' She was talking slowly and I could tell she was in a lot of pain, despite the morphine.

'And you are sure it was him?'

'I was walking home and he was behind me. I didn't think anything of it, but a minute or so after I noticed him I was attacked. I'm sure it was him, Harry. So don't beat yourself up.'

'I'll kill him,' I said, and part of me meant it.

'Harry, don't talk like that. You're a policeman.'

'Fuck that,' I said. 'I will have him.'

'I've never heard you swear before, Harry. Seriously, don't get yourself into trouble.'

'You'll give evidence against him?'

She took a slow deep breath and the exhaled. 'Yes. I will.'

'Then I'll have him arrested tonight.'

'Do be careful of the young wife. Her name's Dina. She married him in Bangladesh and the marriage hasn't been registered here.'

'Don't worry, I'll make sure she's taken care of.'

'Thank you, Harry.'

She sighed, and then winced. 'Does it hurt?' I asked, which I suppose was a stupid question.

'Sometimes, but I feel numb, mostly.'

'I'm so sorry.'

'Please stop saying that, Harry. There was nothing you could have done.'

I sat in silence for a while, hating myself for what I was going to have to do next. Ayesha was horribly disfigured, her life was never going to be the same again, but I had to start treating her as a suspect in the murder of Sean Evans.

'Ayesha, I'm sorry about this but I've got to ask you some more questions about what happened at the mosque on Friday.'

'Oh, Harry, do we have to?' she moaned.

'Something has come up,' I said. 'And before I ask you any questions, you need to be aware of a few things. Your rights. You do not have to say anything. But, it may harm your defence if you do not mention when questioned something which you later rely on in court. Anything you do say may be given in evidence.'

'Why are you doing this?' she said. 'I know my rights. Are you planning to charge me with something?'

'You left the mosque before you could be interviewed.'

'We talked about this.'

'Yes, we did. But you didn't tell me that you went to the canal.'

'The canal? What are you talking about, Harry?'

'We have CCTV footage that shows you leaving the mosque and walking towards the canal. We also have footage of you walking away from the canal.'

'I just wanted some air. There'd been a murder, Harry. Everyone was stressed out. I had no idea where I was going, I was just walking. I wanted to clear my head.'

Her words tailed off and again. The only sound was the beeping of her monitor.

'Whenever I'm in a situation like this, there's something I usually say, and I'm going to say it to you now, Ayesha. It doesn't matter what you've done, it doesn't matter what laws you may or may not have broken, your most sensible option by far is to be totally honest with me and together we'll work out the best way of dealing with it. I can help you. I will help you. But you have to trust me and you have to be honest with me.'

She didn't say anything.

'Ayesha, do you understand?'

'Yes,' she said quietly.

'We had a search team in the canal and they found the knife that we believe was used to kill Sean Evans. Ayesha, did you throw the knife in the canal?'

Her hands bunched into fists on top of the covers.

'I don't think for one moment you stabbed him, Ayesha, but if I am to help you you're going to have to tell me everything.'

She took a deep breath. 'I'm feeling dizzy, Harry,' she whispered. 'I need to rest.'

'Just answer me the one question. Did you throw the knife in the canal?'

'You're going to have to go now, Harry,' she whispered. 'I really can't talk at the moment. It's too painful.'

She was lying. Of course she was lying. But there was nothing I could do. I stood up. I still had to fight the urge to hold her hand. She looked so small and defenceless lying in the hospital bed, but the simple fact was that she was now a suspect in a murder investigation. 'I'm sorry,' I said, and I really was.

I left, but I knew it wasn't the end of the matter. I'd given her every chance to cooperate but she clearly wasn't going to open up to me. That meant the next stage was to arrange a formal interview and I knew that I would have to hand that over to someone else, either to DS Hurley or DS Rees. From what the doctor had said, she was going to be in hospital for a while which meant she would have to be interviewed there, and ideally be videoed. I was sure that she knew who the killer was, and that she was protecting him. Or her.

At some point I was going to have to explain why I wasn't doing the interview myself. Nasri had done a good job tidying up the Decision Log, and initially I would just say that I felt that a change in interviewing officers might produce results. But I knew that eventually someone – Teflon or The Sheriff – was going to ask me why I had interviewed her over a curry and a pizza. I was pretty sure that my explanation that she would be more at ease in a social setting wasn't going to fool anyone at which point the shit was well and truly going to hit the fan. Was it a career ender? Possibly. A lot depended on whether or not she cooperated and gave up the killer. If the investigation resulted in the successful prosecution of the killer of Sean Evans, any hiccoughs along the way might be overlooked. It was a slim hope but just then it was the only hope I had.

I went back outside and collected my car. Before I started the engine I called Nasri and told him that Ayesha had identified her attacker.

'Guv, tell me you didn't go by yourself.'

I could hear the contempt in his voice but I ignored it. 'I need you to talk to the Harrow Road cops tonight. They need to pick up this Mohammed Gomastha and search his home. The way she tells it, Ayesha was advising Gomastha's second wife about her divorce options so it might have been personal, but I'll check him out with the anti-terrorism boys.'

'Yes, Guv.'

'I'm heading home now but call me later to confirm that it's in hand.'

'I will do, Guv.' I could tell he wasn't happy but at that moment I couldn't have cared less whether DC Nasri was happy or not. All I wanted was to get the bastard that had attacked Ayesha in custody and start the process that would ensure he spent a big chunk of what remained of his life behind bars.

Chapter 40
(Sal)

What is it with Porter? He's like a lovesick moth around a flame. Even after I had told him that she was using him for information. Why couldn't he just damn well keep away? He could have just picked up the phone and spoken to the SIO at Harrow Road nick and got an update on Ayesha Khan, but oh no, he just had to turn up at the hospital on his white horse, making promises that he wouldn't be able to keep. And who's going to clean up his mess? Me, who else? No doubt he'll be wanting me to censor the Decision Log, again.

'What's wrong?' asked Miriam, a touch of concern creeping on her face.

I'd been so caught up with Porter that for a moment I'd forgotten she was curled up next to me on the sofa. I had made an effort, had to. From now on, I'll be home early whenever possible. I tried to force a smile, but seeing her face, it came naturally. 'It's nothing.'

'You're not thinking about...'

'No. I'm through with that.'

'I read on the internet that gambling addiction could lead…'

'Miriam,' I took her by the hand. 'I'm okay. It's just work. It's just… Porter. I've got to make a call. Maria's asleep?'

She nodded, then kissed me on the neck.

'Why don't you see what's on Netflix?' I asked.

'Can we watch it in bed?'

I smiled. Watching Netflix in bed was code for not watching Netflix in bed, which suggested I was back in her good books. 'Sure,' I said.

I phoned Inspector John Holland on his mobile and, professional that he was, he actually answered. He's a good copper, old school like Porter but he'd had no problems in adopting modern police methods, which is another way of saying that he's not a dinosaur. I ran through the Ayesha Khan situation and gave him the name of her suspected attacker. He listened as I explained about her possible involvement in our murder case.

'But she's not a suspect?' he asked when I'd finished.

'We think she might have disposed of the murder weapon in the canal,' I said. 'So we're going to need to talk to her at some point.'

'But DI Porter has already spoken to her, you said?'

'Off the record. It wasn't official.'

There was a few seconds of silence and I was starting to think that I'd lost my connection when he grunted. 'Is there something I need to know, Sal?' he said. 'Off the record?'

I'd worked with the Dutchman for a couple of years and I trusted him totally, but now I worked for Porter so I was in a difficult position. 'I think DI Porter has taken a bit of a shine to Ms Khan,' I said, putting it as diplomatically as I could. 'I think he wants to give her every opportunity of cooperating before we get heavy with her.'

'So when she identified her attacker, it was what, just a chat? Not official?'

'Yes, Guv.'

'So Harry wants me to bring the guy in and question a suspect on the basis of an off-the-record chat with a girl he's taken a shine to?'

'Is that a problem, Guv?'

The Dutchman chuckled. 'No Sal, it's okay. Harry and I go way back. And it's not as if we have any other suspects at the moment. I'll have him pulled first thing.'

'Thanks, Guv.'

'So, how are you enjoying homicide?'

'It's challenging, Guv.'

'And Harry?'

I couldn't help but laugh. 'Also challenging,' I said. 'But I'm learning a lot.'

'I bet you are.'

Chapter 41
(Harry)

Nasri was at his computer terminal when I arrived at the MIR. He looked up and nodded as I took off my coat. 'They took Mohammed Gomastha into Paddington Green station this morning and there's a forensics team in there now,' he said. There was an orange juice and a half-eaten croissant on his desk.

'Excellent,' I said.

'DI Holland will be carrying out the initial interview, he says he'll wait until you get there.'

'Right, we'll head out to Paddington Green as soon as we're done with the morning briefing.'

'Guv, are you sure it's a good idea, you sitting in on the interview?'

'Why do you say that?' I asked.

Nasri looked uncomfortable at the question. 'Because it's not our case and the top brass might wonder why you're getting involved,' he said.

I tried not to sound defensive and I smiled as best as I could. 'She's a witness in our murder case.'

'Exactly. But Gomastha isn't. Anti-terrorism gave him a clean bill of health. We can't even do him for bigamy because his second marriage hasn't been officially recorded.'

'Until he's been questioned, we won't know why he did what he did,' I said. 'It might be that this Gomastha is connected to our murder and, until I know for sure that he isn't, he remains a person of interest in our investigation.' I gave up trying to smile.

I could see that he wasn't convinced but he nodded. 'Right, Guv.'

I went to the canteen and got myself a bacon sandwich and a coffee, then spent half an hour going through HOLMES before starting the briefing. There wasn't much to tell, other than that our priority was still to locate Fazal Wazir, our prime suspect. I explained what had happened to Ayesha Khan and that a suspect was in custody. It was all over in two minutes. I asked if anyone had any questions. They didn't. There was a general air of despondency in the room and there wasn't much I could do to dispel it. We'd done all the searching and questioning we could, now we needed a break in the case which in all probability would come down to either dumb luck or Fazal Wazir making a mistake.

Forty-five minutes later, Nasri and I were at Paddington Green, the fortress-like police station on the corner of Harrow Road and Edgware Road. We were able to park at the rear of the station and went in through the back entrance where DI Holland was there to meet us. He was wearing a pinstriped suit and gleaming brogues. The Dutchman always dressed well. Mohammed Gomastha had been picked up in the early hours and had been held in one of the station's underground cells. A forensics team had gone in immediately but so far hadn't found anything. All Gomastha's clothes and shoes had been taken away for analysis and swabs had been taken from his hands and under his nails. So far no trace had been found of any acid.

DI Holland took us to the canteen where we loaded up on coffees before Nasri and I were placed in a windowless room with two TV monitors showing an interview room on the floor below. As we watched, the door opened and a uniformed constable brought in Gomastha. He was wearing a blue paper suit and had paper shoe covers on his feet. Gomastha sat down on a plastic chair and linked his hands together.

'What about his wife?' I asked.

'Which one?' said Holland. 'Apparently he has two.'

'Only one, officially,' said Nasri.

'Dina,' I said, ignoring Nasri's comment. 'She's nineteen or twenty years old. He brought her over from Bangladesh as some sort of sex slave.'

'She was there and I have officers from our anti-trafficking squad with her,' said Holland. He looked at his watch. 'Right, I'll get the interview started.'

'Who's going in with you?' I asked.

'DS Mackenzie. I don't think you know him.'

'You don't have an Asian you can use?' asked Nasri.

'Why do you think we fought so hard to keep you, Sal?' said Holland. 'Guys like you are as rare as hen's teeth. I don't suppose you want to sit in, do you?'

Nasri looked over at me and I shook my head. 'Probably more use watching here,' I said.

'Fair enough, and Mr Gomastha speaks reasonable English,' said Holland. 'Okay, I'll leave you to it.'

Nasri and I sat down and made ourselves comfortable. We watched the monitors. After a couple of minutes the door to the interview room opened and Holland and his sergeant walked in. The uniformed officer left and the two detectives sat down. DS Mackenzie was in his thirties, bookish with metal-framed spectacles and a fringe that he kept flicking out of his eyes. Mackenzie had two digital tapes that he slotted into a recorder, then both detectives identified themselves and asked Gomastha to state his name. He seemed confused and Mackenzie had to ask him again. This time he mumbled his name. Mackenzie asked him to repeat it. Another mumble but clearer than the first time and Holland nodded.

There were two cameras in the interview room, one focussed on Gomastha and the other on the two detectives. Mackenzie did all the talking while Holland sat and listened. Holland was holding a pen and had his notebook out, though he didn't write anything down. I was guessing that the pen would be the transfer signal. If at any point the Inspector wanted to take over the questioning, he would put the pen down on the table. That would tell Mackenzie that he was to take a back seat while Holland took the lead.

Mackenzie asked Gomastha to account for his whereabouts on the evening that Ayesha Khan was attacked. Gomastha said that he was home. Mackenzie asked him what he was doing at home and Gomastha shrugged and said he was reading. Reading what? A newspaper. Which newspaper? Gomastha gave Mackenzie the name of a Bangladeshi newspaper. Did he go out? A shrug but no answer. The question was repeated. Yes, he went to the shops to buy tobacco. When did he go out? A shrug. The question was repeated. Five o'clock maybe.

It was like pulling teeth. Most of the questions had to be repeated at least once, not because Gomastha didn't understand, his English seemed fine, he just seemed to be evasive.

'He's as guilty as sin,' I said, sitting back in my chair and folding my arms.

'Why do you say that, Guv?' asked Nasri.

I looked across at him in astonishment. 'Are you serious? Look at how evasive he is. He doesn't want to answer any of the questions. He's looking down, he won't look them in the eye, when he does speak he's hesitant. His entire body language screams "guilty". I'm surprised you don't see it.'

'Maybe I see it differently, Guv,' he said.

He obviously disagreed. 'Spit it out,' I said.

'Okay, Guv, here's the thing. Mr Gomastha's from Bangladesh. He may be a British citizen now but he's spent more than half his life in Bangladesh, where these things are a little different. You so much as look at a cop in the wrong way and you're asking for trouble. Pakistan is the same. My dad used to tell me some crazy stories about the time he dealt with cops in Pakistan. Trust me. They operate like a gang. Organised and targeting the weak, living off back-handers and placing blame on whoever they don't like.'

'This is London, Sal. London, England. He knows that.'

'You don't think it happens here?' he said, 'Maybe not as much, but it happens.'

I let that go, it wasn't the time or place to be getting into a conversation about police corruption.

'No two ways about it, we, the police have a bad rep,' he continued. 'Especially amongst Asians, blacks. Muslims. Come on. A Muslim in an interrogation room is bound to get jittery. He's from a culture where a cop can slap you around if he wants, where if you don't tell them what they want to hear they'll string you up and beat you on the feet with sticks. There's no PACE, there's no Habeas Corpus, if the cops want you to disappear then that can happen. He's scared, Guv. He's scared shitless and he doesn't want to say anything that might get him into trouble.'

Mackenzie was repeating a question, asking him the route he'd taken from his house to the shop where he was claiming he'd bought the tobacco.

'He doesn't have to be scared,' I said. 'No one's going to beat him.'

'You know that, Guv, and I know that. But this guy probably hasn't dealt with British cops before. And in his community, well, you know we're not exactly flavour of the month. He probably thinks it's open season on Muslims and that we're trying to fit him up.'

I opened my mouth to tell him that he was talking bollocks but then realised that he might be right. I looked back at the monitors. Mackenzie was asking if Gomastha had the receipt for his tobacco purchase and Gomastha was mumbling and shaking his head. Who keeps receipts for things like that? He was asked what route he had taken to the shops, again Gomastha struggled to answer the most basic of questions as though one slip of the tongue would see him behind bars. He just sat there with his head down, unwilling to look the detectives in the eye. Maybe he was just scared.

'Guv, the only evidence we have against him is that Ayesha Khan saw him in the vicinity before she was attacked,' said Nasri. 'But we know she's already lied to the police once. He lives local. He could be telling the truth. The least we owe Gomastha is to hear him out.'

He was going to say more but then his phone started to ring.

Chapter 42
(Sal)

The ringing phone threw me off my rhythm. I could see that I was changing Porter's mindset and his opinion of Mohammed Gomastha. No doubt, the way Gomastha lived his life would raise eyebrows; bringing over a bride forty years his junior. He was old enough to be her grandfather, so what, did that make him a pervert or a nasty piece of work? I don't think so. I mean, wasn't Porter doing the same thing chasing after Ayesha Khan?

Porter wanted Gomastha to be guilty so he was looking for anything that would support that. I'd seen this scenario in investigations many times, trying to make evidence fit a pre-determined theory. But like I'd said, the only reason we were looking at him was because Ayesha Khan had seen him in the street and we both already know that she hasn't exactly been totally honest with us.

I took out my ringing phone. 'Sorry, Guv,' I said as Porter flashed me an annoyed look. I didn't recognise the number. I went out of the room and took the call.

'DC Nasri?' said a voice. I hadn't recognised the number but I recognised him immediately. 'Imam Abdullah Malik?' I said.

'Yes. Can you speak?'

'Yes, Imam. How can I be of service?'

'It is imperative that I meet with you.'

'Okay,' I glanced at my watch. 'I can be at the masjid in an hour or so.'

'No, not the masjid,' he said. 'Do you know the Harrow Cricket Ground?'

'Of course.' I said.

'Can we meet there? Within the hour?'

'I can do that,' I said.

'Just you, DC Nasri,' he said. 'Please come alone.'

'Yes, I will. Are you okay, Imam?' I asked but he had already ended the call.

'Imam Malik wants to meet,' I said to Porter as I walked back into the room.

'About what?'

'He didn't say, Guv. But something's clearly on his mind.'

'We can go and see him after this.'

'Just me, Guv. He was quite definite about that.'

Porter frowned as if he was about to argue, but then he just shrugged. 'Sure. Go for it.'

'Are you okay if I take the car?'

'No problem, I'll wait here and you can pick me up when you're done,' he said.

I understood why he was being so agreeable. He seemed sure that they had the right man in Gomastha and he was probably day-dreaming about breaking the news to Ayesha Khan, so she would be suitably impressed and continue to make eyes at him. Personally, even if they did detain Gomastha, it would never hold. The search of his house and car hadn't turned up any forensics. There was no witness to the attack, apart from the fact that Ayesha said that she'd seen him shortly before the attack. She wasn't exactly a reliable witness. Without a confession, I didn't see how there was a case.

I drove to Harrow Cricket Ground and parked nearby. Harrow Cricket Club used to be my team, this used to be my ground growing up. Demon bowler, right arm, around the wicket, for the under 11's then the under 13's. I looked around the cricket pitch twice before realising the man sitting on the bench by the pavilion was the Imam.

I hadn't recognised him at first because he was wearing Western clothing – baggy trousers and despite the weather, a quilted jacket with the hood up. It looked as though the Imam did not want to be seen. I approached him. 'Imam,' I said, sitting next to him.

'Thank you for coming, DC Nasri,' he said, not taking his eyes off the green of the empty cricket pitch.

'I'm always happy to talk with you, Imam,' I said. 'I'm surprised you wanted to meet here and not at the masjid.'

'I find myself in a very difficult position, DC Nasri.'

I didn't say anything. Better to let him talk. I mirrored his gaze and stared out at the green.

'Ayesha Khan,' he said eventually, his voice a whisper.

I nodded. Obviously he knew. News like that travels fast in tight-knit community. His community.

'It was an abomination. To throw acid into the face of a young woman. How can one be so full of anger and hatred? It goes against every value that I teach. It goes against Islam.'

I noticed him clench both fists on his lap. He slowly relaxed his hands and finally turned his gaze away from the green and looked at me for the first time since my arrival. His eyes were wet. 'I know who did it.'

'Tell me, Imam,' I said.

'You mustn't ever tell anyone that the information came from me.'

'That won't be an issue, Imam.'

'If it was known that I was giving information to the police, I would lose the respect of my people. They would want this dealt with without your involvement.'

I took a deep breath and tried to smile. 'Your secret will be safe with me, Imam,' I said.

He nodded, then went back to staring at the green, taking a moment to compose himself, as though trying to convince himself that he was doing the right thing. 'Two days ago, the day that Ayesha was attacked, I saw someone at the mosque with burns on their jeans and shoes,' he whispered. 'Small spots.'

'Splashback,' I said. He frowned. 'If you throw a liquid, some of it will splash back,' I explained.

The Imam nodded. 'Also there was a large plaster on his right hand, as if he had an injury.'

'When exactly was this, Imam?'

'At Isha'a prayers,' he said. 'He was at the very end of the congregation.'

Isha was around seven in the evening. About the time that Ayesha was attacked. Possible that he turned up at the mosque and tagged himself at the back of the congregation, trying to establish an alibi.

'Imam?' I said.

'You need a name?' he said quietly.

I nodded.

'Abdel-Majed Hassan.' He said. 'A friend of Waseem Chowdhury and a member of The Faith. He was also at the mosque the day of Sean Evan's murder.'

'Thank you, Imam.'

'I do not deserve thanks, DC Nasri. What this man did was wrong. So very wrong. And he worshipped at my mosque. I failed him.'

'It wasn't your fault, Imam. There is no point in blaming yourself.'

He turned to look at me, his face ashen. 'I am supposed to teach people to follow Islam, and to live good, productive lives. This man attended my mosque, he listened to me preach on countless occasions, but somehow I failed to reach him. So I would disagree with you, DC Nasri. This is my fault.' He looked away again.

I stood up. I wanted to reassure him, to pat him on the shoulder and tell him that he had done the right thing, but I knew that nothing I said would make a difference to how he felt.

I walked back to the car. As I left the park I looked over my shoulder. The Imam was still sitting on the bench, his head in his hands.

CHAPTER 43
(HARRY)

DI Holland put down his pen half an hour into the interview and took over the questioning. He did his best but Gomastha refused to confess. He kept pretending to not understand Holland's questions so everything had to be repeated several times. He was doing it to play for time, it was a common tactic and investigators had to be aware of it and not allow themselves to get frustrated. The days of detectives banging on the table or even roughing up a suspect were long gone. I'm not saying that's a bad thing or a good thing, I'm just saying that in the old days, before interviews were recorded, a flash of temper and a threat or two often brought an interrogation to a successful conclusion. To be fair, it also led to a number of unsafe convictions but, you know, swings and roundabouts.

About an hour into the interview Gomastha asked for a legal representative and everything was put on hold for half an hour while a duty solicitor was found. The questioning went much slower then with

Gomastha taking every opportunity to confer with the legal adviser, a grey-haired man in his sixties who kept popping breath mints into his mouth every ten minutes or so. At no point did Gomastha refuse to answer or say 'no comment'. He often had to be asked the same question several times, but he would always answer eventually. And he was consistent. He had left the house about twenty minutes before Ayesha was attacked, he had walked to the corner shop to buy tobacco, and he had walked back and spent the rest of the evening watching Bangladeshi soap operas on his satellite television system.

His first wife had been in the kitchen, the new wife upstairs in the bedroom, so he had been alone most of the time. He didn't remember seeing Ayesha Khan but he admitted that he knew where she lived. Every time he was directly asked if he had thrown acid at her, he had denied it, and denied it vehemently. 'Why would I do such a thing?' he had asked at one point. 'What sort of man do you think I am?'

That was an easy enough question to answer – he was a man in his sixties who had found himself a child bride and resented the fact that Ayesha was helping her to divorce him. The question was, did he resent her enough to douse her with acid?

After three hours Holland brought the interview to a close. He came upstairs to see me. 'What do you think, Harry?' he asked.

'I think he did it,' I said.

'Where's Sal?'

'He had a meeting he had to go to.'

'What does Sal think?'

'Sal thinks the guy's nervous. But that doesn't mean he's not guilty.'

'The thing is, Harry, there were no acid burns on the clothing he was wearing when we picked him up. Or on the clothes he said he was wearing two days ago.'

'He could have been lying.'

'Agreed. But we took away all his clothing and shoes and at first look I didn't see anything untoward. And there was no drain cleaner in his house.'

'Well there wouldn't be if he'd thrown it over her, would there? Look, are you saying you don't think he did it?'

Holland looked uncomfortable. 'I'm saying I'm keeping an open mind. But I don't see that we can keep him in custody, not with what we have. Or rather, what we don't have.'

'You're sending him home?'

'I don't see we've got a choice, Harry. Unless you can talk to Miss Khan again. If she's prepared to definitely identify him as her attacker, we can charge him.'

'She saw him close by, but the acid went in her eyes, remember?'

'I remember, Harry. I guess the question is, how much does she remember? If she can remember him throwing the acid, we'd get a conviction, forensics or no forensics.'

He looked me in the eyes and I got the message. But I wasn't sure that Ayesha Kahn would be prepared to go that far. 'I'm not sure that's going to happen, John.'

He shrugged. 'Then you know my position, Harry. Under PACE, I'm going to have to let him go soon.'

'Keep him as long as you can, please,' I said. 'And make sure the anti-trafficking people keep the girl away from him.'

'Will do, Harry,' he said.

Holland went back to his office and I headed down to reception. As I reached the ground floor my phone rang. It was Nasri. 'I'm outside, Guv,' he said. 'Are you done there?'

'Unfortunately, yes,' I said. I ended the call and headed outside. Nasri was stuck in traffic on Edgware Road and I jogged over to his car and climbed into the passenger seat.

'How did it go, Guv?' he asked.

'Not great, but I'm sure he did it,' I said.

'You might want to rethink that,' said Nasri. 'According to the Imam, one of his worshippers had acid damage on his shoes and clothes not long after Miss Khan was attacked.'

My jaw dropped in astonishment. 'Are you serious?'

'As a heart attack, Guv. And there was a plaster on his hand. The Imam was clearly uneasy about telling me, but the greater good and all that. He's worried that word will get out that he's helping us. But he gave me the name. Abdel-Majed Hassan. He should be in HOLMES. The Imam says Hassan is a friend of Waseem Chowdhury and a member of The Faith.'

I folded my arms and stared out of the window. Had I got it completely wrong? Was Gomastha innocent after all?

'What do you think, Guv?' asked Nasri quietly.

What did I think? I grimaced. I thought that maybe I'd been wrong about Gomastha and that offended my professional pride. 'Let's see what we have on this Hassan back at Peel House,' I said.

Nasri drove the rest of the way to Hendon in silence, and I was grateful for that. As soon as we got to Peel House we took the lift up to the MIR and went over to the boards where the photographs of all the worshippers were posted. It didn't take long to find Hassan. He was in his twenties and he had been photographed at the mosque. Dark skinned with a neatly-trimmed beard and steel-rimmed spectacles.

'Was he with Waseem Chowdhury when you were seen with Miss Khan?' asked Nasri.

I stared at the picture. 'I'm not sure. There was a guy in the back of Chowdhury's car. Maybe. But I couldn't swear to it.'

'How do you want to play this, Guv?'

I looked over at him, wondering what he meant.

Nasri shrugged. 'It's still a Harrow Road case, right?'

'Except that Hassan is on our radar. And Ayesha is a witness and a possible suspect in our case. Let's see what we've got on HOLMES.'

We went over to the terminals and we both logged on. Hassan had been at the mosque at the time of the murder but claimed not to have known Sean Evans or to have seen him. He was down as Nominal 132 and had given half a dozen names of people he knew, all of whom were also interviewed at the mosque. He hadn't given Chowdhury's name. I sat back and stared at the screen. Was Hassan the killer and had he attacked Ayesha because she could identify him?

'Sal, run a PNC check on Hassan. And let's check his phone records, see if his GPS can place him near Ayesha when she was attacked.'

'Will do, Guv,' he said.

I called John Holland and explained what had happened and that we now had a new suspect for the acid-throwing. 'What about the victim?' he asked. 'Did she see this guy hanging around?'

'We'll show her a photograph,' I said. 'John, are you okay if we run with this? It could well be connected to our murder.'

'Not a problem,' said Holland. 'And you're okay with me releasing Gomastha?'

'I don't see we've any choice,' I said.

I ended the call. I went back on HOLMES and got an address for Hassan and went over to Stuart Hurley. I briefed him on what had happened and asked him to arrange a search warrant for Hassan's home.

Lorraine Sawyer wasn't at her desk so I phoned her mobile. It went through to voicemail so I left a message asking her to call me back.

By the time I got back to my desk, Nasri had Hassan's PNC details – two cautions for possession of cannabis and a fine for breach of the peace. He and a group of like-minded individuals had been standing outside an off-licence in Kilburn haranguing customers about the evils of alcohol. 'I've spoken to the phone company, but it'll take time,' he said. 'They're snowed under at the moment.'

My phone rang. It was Lorraine Sawyer, returning my call. I explained that we had a new suspect for the attack on Ayesha Khan, and that we had received a report that said suspect had acid damage to his clothing. I gave her Hassan's address and asked her to get a forensics team ready to move in as soon as we had a warrant. That done, I went over to Paul Rees and asked him to get someone over to St Mary's Hospital and show Hassan's picture to Ayesha Khan. I also asked him to canvass the area where Ayesha was attacked to see if anyone remembered seeing Hassan there before she was attacked. I really wanted to go and talk to Ayesha myself but I figured I'd best steer clear, for a while at least. I caught Nasri glancing over at me and I knew for sure that he was thinking the same.

CHAPTER 44
(SAL)

Porter and I were outside Hassan's house at three o'clock in the afternoon, along with Lorraine Sawyer and her forensics team and an Armed Response Unit just in case Hassan turned nasty. Nothing on the PNC suggested that Hassan would be carrying a gun, but as a member of The Faith there was a good chance he would have a knife and there was also the possibility that acid would be his weapon of choice.

Hassan lived in a studio flat in Kilburn, on the second floor of a Victorian terraced house. There was an intercom at the main door but we didn't want him tipped off that we were coming so Porter rang the bell for one of the ground floor flats. A middle-aged Indian lady in a red and green sari opened the door and Porter explained that we needed to go up to the first floor. She looked at him blankly and he repeated himself, louder the second time.

'Guv, let me have a go,' I said. I explained the situation to her in Urdu and she hurried away down the corridor and slammed her door shut.

The armed cops went up the stairs first, dressed in Kevlar and carrying large carbines. Porter and I stayed at the front door with Stuart Hurley and Alan Russell. The forensic team were doing the smart thing and staying in their vehicle until the area was secured.

We heard the armed cops knocking on the door and then a few seconds later shouts of 'Armed Police' and less than thirty seconds after they'd gone in there was a shout of 'Clear!' and we all went upstairs.

Hassan was standing facing a wall with his hands cuffed behind him. 'No weapons on him,' said the sergeant in charge of the armed unit. 'But there are a couple of nasty blades over there.' He gestured with his gun at a machete and a butterfly knife on a coffee table. The large blade was legal so long as it stayed indoors. It's illegal to sell, buy or import a knife with a blade longer than fifty centimetres, and carrying one in public was an offence, but so long as it stayed inside it was legal. The butterfly knife was a different matter; it was an offence to even possess one. Porter smiled when he saw it.

I noticed a leather holdall on the sofa. It was unzipped and filled with clothes. It looked like Hassan was looking to move in a hurry. I recalled what Chowdhury had said to me;

You best find who did this to Ayesha... Because believe me, if we find him first...

Had word got to Hassan that he was a marked man?

'I ain't done nothing,' said Hassan. 'I ain't got no drugs here.'

'This isn't about drugs,' said Porter, walking up behind him. He pulled back the plaster on Hassan's right hand. 'What do you think, DC Nasri?' he asked me. 'Does that look like an acid burn to you?'

I looked at the wound. 'Definitely,' I said.

'I don't see any splashback on his clothes or shoes, so I'm guessing he's changed,' said Porter.

'I know you,' sneered Hassan. 'You the old guy who was sniffing around our sister.'

'The sister you threw acid over?' asked Porter. 'Ayesha Khan?'

'Guv...' I said, and flashed him a warning look. Hassan hadn't been arrested or read his rights, so anything he said now wouldn't be admissible.

Porter realised straight away what I was getting at and gave me the slightest of nods. 'Why don't you do the necessary,' he said.

'Right, Guv,' I said. 'Abdel-Majed Hassan, I am arresting you for an acid attack against Ms Ayesha Khan on the fifteenth of this month. You do not have to say anything. But, it may harm your defence if you do not mention when questioned something which you later rely on in court. Anything you do say may be given in evidence. Do you understand your rights as I have explained them?'

'Fuck off, Uncle Tom,' sneered Hassan.

'I'll take that as a yes,' I said.

The armed police went out to their SUV and left soon after. Hurley and Russell took Hassan downstairs and put him in the back of a van. We had already agreed that we would do the interview at Paddington Green, so the van headed off. Porter wanted to wait to see what forensics if any Sawyer's team would be able to come up with.

The forensic technicians took all Hassan's trousers, shirts, jackets and shoes and placed them in plastic bags, but a quick look suggested there were no acid burns. There was a rubbish bin in the kitchen area and the contents were bagged. If we were lucky we'd find a receipt for drain cleaner in there. Sounds stupid? Yeah, but then most criminals didn't fare well at school.

One of the forensics team went down to check the wheelie bins at the side of the house. She came back with a Tesco carrier containing a pair of jeans and a pair of Nike trainers. There were small white holes peppered over the legs of the jeans. Porter grinned when he saw the damaged denim. 'Well, I'm no forensics expert but that looks like acid damage to me,' he said. His grin widened when he saw similar damage to the trainers.

We left the forensics team to continue their work while I drove Porter to Paddington Green. We were only a few minutes away when Porter's phone rang. Whoever it was calling him had him grinning like the proverbial Cheshire cat. 'She saw him, in the street,' he said as he put his phone away, and I knew straight away who he meant. Ayesha Khan. 'She recognised him from the photograph they showed her. Didn't know him, but she said she's sure he was in the street.'

'That's good news, Guv,' I said. He seemed to have forgotten how close he was to pinning the attack on an innocent man. Okay, Gomastha is a nasty piece of work and I hope he gets to lose his child bride, but he hadn't thrown acid over Ayesha Khan and Porter was so bloody sure that he had done.

The Dutchman was waiting for us in reception. Porter told him that Ayesha had made a positive ID, and that the forensics team had found jeans and trainers with what looked like acid damage. 'Brilliant,' said Holland. 'Nice work.'

'Nothing to do with me,' said Porter. 'It's all down to Sal. He got the tip.'

'Do you want to do the interview?' Holland asked him.

Porter looked over at me but I didn't have to say anything because we both knew that it wouldn't be a good idea. 'Not me, no,' said Porter. 'But maybe Sal could sit in with you.'

'Sounds like a plan,' said Holland.

'I'll watch on the CCTV,' said Porter. 'You'll see there's a plaster on his right hand. It's covering acid damage.'

'Let's see what he has to say about that,' said Holland. He patted me on the shoulder. 'Good cop, bad cop?'

'Like the old days,' I said. The Dutchman would often use me as the good cop when it came to interrogating Asians. I know, it's racist, but what can you do? The thing is, nine times out of ten, Good Cop, Bad Cop, works.

They had put Hassan in an interview room with a uniformed constable to watch over him. The handcuffs had been removed and he'd been allowed to keep the clothing he had been wearing when he was arrested. Inspector Holland collected two tapes for the recorder and took me down to the interview room. He paused outside the door. 'I'll put my pen down on the table when I'm ready for you to take over. You can ask me to get him a drink or something. Okay?'

I grinned. 'Back in the old routine,' I said.

'Seriously, Sal, we miss you around here. Anytime you want to come back...'

'I appreciate that, Guv, thanks.'

He went into the room first and I followed. He thanked the uniform who slipped out of the door and closed it behind him. I took the seat nearest the door and the Dutchman sat by the wall, giving him access to the recorder. He pointedly ignored Hassan as he unwrapped the cassettes and slotted them into the recorder. I smiled at Hassan and nodded. Good cop, bad cop. He sneered at me but I continued to smile.

Holland placed his notebook in front of him and held his pen. He identified himself for the tape, then I did the same. He asked Hassan to give his name, address and date of birth, which he did. Hassan was sitting in typical gangsta pose, back in his chair with his arms folded and his legs wide apart. Manspreading they call it. He was showing us what big balls he had.

Holland asked Hassan where he was when Ayesha Khan was attacked and he lied straight away, saying that he was watching television at home. Alone. It was a lazy alibi and assuming he was carrying his phone, his GPS would betray him. The Inspector took him through his day, hour by hour, and made notes in his notebook. Down the line he would take him through the timeline again, possibly in reverse, looking for inconsistencies. Holland was firm and unfriendly, and never referred to Hassan by name. He never smiled, and he fixed him with a stare that said he would happily slap him behind bars and throw away the key. Bad cop.

After an hour, he put his pen on the table. My cue. 'Sir,' I said. 'Perhaps Mr Hassan would like a cup of tea. Or a soft drink. He's been here quite a while.'

'It's not a café, DC Nasri,' he said coldly.

I smiled. 'No, Sir. But I'm sure Mr Hassan would appreciate a drink.' Good cop.

'I would as it happens.' Hassan smiled smugly at Holland. 'Coffee. Lots of milk, lots of sugar, yeah.'

'I need a break anyway,' sighed Holland, getting up out of his chair. 'You keep an eye on him.'

'Yes, Sir,' I said.

Holland let himself out of the room and closed the door. I sat back in my chair and raised my eyebrows at Hassan and smiled. It was amazing how many suspects would forget that the recorder was still on.

'Yes suh! No suh! Two bags fucking full.' Hassan shook his head in disappointment. 'What's it like working for kafir cops?'

I smiled. I had him. 'Institutionally racist, the Met, but that isn't exactly the best kept secret.' I shrugged, 'But, you know, I get by.'

He leaned forward and lowered his voice. 'How the fuck can you work for them, bruv?'

'It's a job. And they're not all like him. And sometimes they let me use the siren.'

Hassan snorted. 'I couldn't do it.' He sat back in his chair, unfolded his arms and placed his hand on the table. More relaxed now.

'What about you, you working?' I asked.

'Fuck that for a laugh. I still get paid, though, know what I'm saying.'

'Trust me, bruv,' I said, and then yawned loud and wide. 'I'm beat.'

'Yeah, long night?'

'The longest. Hit the bars up town last night.' I smiled. 'Got a little lucky.'

'Fit?' he asked.

'Like a fucking gladiator.' I looked back at the door to check that Holland wasn't about to burst in. 'She was white.'

'Ah, bruv.' His fist was out for a bump. I obliged. 'White girls go to town on that shit. Believe! Only good for one night, though, yeah. After that, that bitch is expired, know what I'm saying?'

'Of course,' I nodded. 'Out the door with me still dripping out of her.' I said, crudely. It made him laugh. 'Never seen a sister behave like that. Until, you know?'

'What?' he said.

'Ayesha Khan,' I said, lowering my voice.

'What about her?' His face couldn't help but scrunch up in disdain.

'You said earlier, she was knocking about with that other copper?'

'That old copper you were with? Yeah. Like they were on a date or something.'

I shook my head in disappointment. 'I can't believe a sister would do that.'

He pointed at his eyes. 'With my own eyes, bruv. I swear to Allah.'

'I believe you,' I said. 'That would have vexed me, man.'

'One of *ours* with one of *them*. A *kafir*!' He spat out the word as if it was burning a hole in his tongue.

'Yeah, it fucking upset me. I've seen girls like that get punished for a lot less. You feel me?'

'Yeah,' I said. 'I feel you.'

Uncertainty flashed in his eyes, he dropped eye contact, as though he had revealed more than he had wanted. I changed tack.

'You think, maybe, there may have been something in it,' I rubbed my chin. 'Like she was after something? I mean, a girl like that with a guy like that…'

'What'd you mean?' Hassan said, quietly, and for the first time I saw some semblance of guilt fall across his face. I changed tack.

'Waseem must have been livid, right? I hear Ayesha is quite close to him, to The Faith,' I said and watched him shrug feebly. 'Is that why you had a bag packed?'

'No, man. The fuck they be after me.'

'I didn't say they were after you.'

He glared at me and then a smile spread slowly across his face. 'I see what you're doing. You think I was born yesterday? You think I just crawled out of the fucking maternity ward?'

I held up my hands. 'I'm just trying to understand why you did what you did.' I leaned in. 'Honestly, you're better off here than out there on the streets. They're coming for you.'

'Get me a fucking suit. I want some counsel now.'

Hassan was welcome to a solicitor. They wouldn't be able to do anything. The forensic evidence alone would be enough to see him in court, plus during the interview he had revealed his hostility towards Muslim girls that don't conform to his views, and we had it all on tape. Not to mention that Ayesha Khan had placed him at the scene of the crime. It was enough to convince any jury in the land that he was as guilty as sin.

Hassan leaned back in his chair, crossed his arms in defiance, trying so hard to portray a man who couldn't care less. But his legs that were spread wide at the start of the interview were now closed for business, painting an entirely different picture.

I glanced at the tape recorder and back at him. I smiled as I enjoyed the look of fear in his eyes.

'Solicitor?' I smiled, 'As you wish, *bruv*.'

CHAPTER 45
(HARRY)

I drove home pretty much on autopilot, barely aware of the traffic around me. I kept running through everything I'd done so far, trying to see if I'd missed anything on the Hassan case but I felt as if I had covered all the bases. The forensics alone would convict him, the fact that Ayesha had seen Hassan shortly before the attack was the icing on the cake. Nasri had done a first class job with the interrogation but no one had expected him to get a confession. Hassan's outburst detailing how he felt about white men going out with Muslim girls could be shown to the jury so even if he continued to plead his innocence I didn't see how we could fail to get a conviction.

By the time I got home, I was knackered. It had been a long day and I was looking forward to microwaved Marks & Spencer bangers and mash and a can of lager and maybe a Netflix movie before I hit the sack. As I climbed out of the car, a black people carrier with tinted windows cruised along the road and pulled up outside my house. I turned to look at it and caught my own reflection staring back at me. Then the side door slid open and a familiar face looked out at me. No smile, no friendly greeting, but then this obviously wasn't a social call.

'I need you to come with me, Inspector Porter,' said Simon. He was wearing a dark green Barbour coat and brown corduroy pants as if he'd been out shooting or fishing. He seemed to be alone in the back.

I walked towards him. The interior was quite plush with just four large seats around a polished pine table. Simon was sitting facing the driver which gave me the choice of sitting next to him or taking one of the two seats opposite. I took one of the rear-facing seats. He pressed a button and the door slid shut and then we drove off. 'Do me a favour and switch your phone off, Inspector,' he said. 'We're not fans of GPS, obviously.'

I switched off my phone and sat in silence. I knew he was expecting me to ask him where we were going, but I didn't want to give him the satisfaction so I just settled back in my seat and linked my fingers together on the table. He smiled. We both played the 'leave a silence and he'll fill it eventually' game. I smiled at him. He smiled back. I looked out of the window. He looked out of the window. We looked at each other. We smiled. We looked out of the window. He'd obviously played the game before.

We drove to Hampstead, past the Common and through the centre, the bars and restaurants filled with nice middle-class people enjoying themselves. I liked Hampstead. If the whole of London was like Hampstead there'd be a lot less work for me to do.

I looked back at Simon. His smile was wearing thin now that he'd realised I was never going to ask him where we were going. To be honest, I didn't care. I'd find out eventually.

We turned off the main road without indicating, then slowed as we approached a Victorian detached house. A pair of black wrought iron gates opened automatically and we drove into a small paved area where there were three nondescript cars already parked; two grey saloons and a blue hatchback. The gates closed behind us.

The driver brought the van to a halt and Simon pressed the button to let us out.

I got out first and looked up at the redbrick building as he joined me. 'This is what we call in the trade a safe house,' said Simon, as we walked up to the front door.

'Good to know,' I said. I couldn't tell if he assumed that all cops were stupid, or just me.

The door opened as we got close to it. A CCTV camera looked down at us and someone was checking us out through the blinds covering the front window.

It was a West Indian girl who had opened the door, wearing a black suit and scarlet lipstick. Simon flashed her a beaming smile. 'Carmen, thank you so much.'

She nodded and smiled at him, and the smile stayed in place as she looked at me, though there was coldness to her eyes that suggested she was capable of much more than door-opening. There was a slight bulge on the jacket over her hip, not much but enough to tell me that she was armed.

Simon walked along the hallway and I followed him. It looked as if it hadn't been decorated since the Fifties - there was a red and black chequered carpet, striped wallpaper and framed prints of hunting dogs, even a couple of umbrellas in a large wooden stand with an ornate mirror above it. He went by the first door and then opened the second. A television was on. A comedy with canned laughter. He went inside and I followed him.

A young Asian man was sitting on the sofa. He was wearing a blue sweatshirt and had his bare feet up on a coffee table. He looked tired, as if he hadn't slept for a few days, and there was stubble on his chin that didn't appear to be a fashion statement. There was a half-eaten pizza in a takeaway box next to his feet, and a can of Coke. It was Fazal Wazir.

Chapter 46
(Sal)

I started the final chapter of The Diary of a Wimpy Kid, squeezed in next to Maria on her princess themed single bed, which she had long grown out of. My phone vibrated in my pocket and I slipped it out enough just to check out the caller. I sighed when I realised that the call had been withheld and contemplated whether or not to answer it.

'Answer it, dad. It's okay.' Maria smiled, making my mind up for me. 'It could be important.'

'Yeah,' I returned the smile. When did my little girl get so wise? 'Give me a minute.'

I put the phone to my ear as I stepped out of Maria's bedroom and sat on the top step of the stairs. 'Hello,' I said.

'Is that Detective Nasri?' The man asked, speaking in Urdu, but it clearly had an English inflection to it.

'This is Detective Nasri,' I replied back in Urdu. 'Who am I speaking to?'

'A friend,' said the caller.

'Do you have a name, friend?'

'It's not important right now,' he said. 'I believe that you are looking for Fazal Wazir?'

'Yes.'

'I can tell you where he is. But you need to be careful. He is armed and the house he is in, it's dangerous.'

'Dangerous? How so?'

'Guns. Explosives. He is part of an ISIS group that are planning a terrorist attack.'

'How do you know this?'

'That isn't important. What is important is that you stop them before they take innocent lives. I am sending you the address right now.'

Maria opened the bedroom door and sat beside me on the top step. She looked up at me. I shrugged at her and for some reason it made her giggle. My phone vibrated and I scrolled to messages. I had been sent an address in Ealing. If the caller was telling the truth, it was the location of Fazal Wazir.

I put the phone to my ear. 'Hello... Hello.' But he had disconnected the call.

'What's wrong, Daddy?' asked Maria.

'Not sure.' I said, 'Maybe something. Maybe nothing. Maria, pop yourself off to bed, I have to go out. I'll send Mummy up to tuck you in.'

'I can tuck myself in, *dad,*' she replied, incredulously.

I held her close and gave her a kiss before rushing downstairs, trying to figure out my next move.

'Miriam,' I said, entering the living room and grabbing the car keys off the coffee table. 'I have to go out. Work.'

'Again?' she sighed.

I deserved the look of reproach because I'd used the excuse that I was working to get out of the house to play poker so many times in the past. 'I'm sorry. It's that murder in the mosque we might have a lead on where the suspect is.'

'Not poker?'

'I swear, honey. I'm done with gambling. This is work.' I was in a rush, but I knelt in front of her and took her hands. 'I won't let you down again, Miriam.'

She nodded slowly and softly kissed me on the cheek.

I rushed out of the house, my phone wedged in between my shoulder and ear as I struggled to get my jacket on.

Porter's phone went straight through to voicemail. I left a quick message asking him to call me back as I sat in my car. I started the engine and gave some thought about who to call next. I could either go up or down the chain of command. Down meant calling the Deputy SIO, Stuart Hurley. Going up meant DCI Ron McKee. I figured this was important enough to merit a call to the DCI.

He wasn't happy to hear who it was but he soon changed his attitude when I ran through the anonymous call. 'And he said Wazir was armed?'

'Armed and with explosives in the house.'

'Okay, I'll get onto Specialist Firearms Command. Have you spoken to Inspector Porter?'

'His phone's off, Sir. But I've left a message.'

'As soon as he gets in touch, tell him to get out there.'

'Will do, Sir.'

'Good work, DC Nasri.' He ended the call. I appreciated the compliment but I hadn't done a thing. I hadn't recognised the voice of the man that had called me, but I'd given out my number hundreds of times while I was on the Harrow Road policing team. The caller's choice of language concerned me. He was obviously second or third generation Pakistani, somebody who could communicate in Urdu, but the English accent had crept into it. I know, I was the same when I spoke in Urdu. I filed it away in my head to worry about later, for now the priority was to make sure that Fazal Wazir was arrested.

I entered the postcode in my SatNav and headed for the location.

Chapter 47
(Harry)

My jaw dropped as I stared at Fazal Wazir, sitting on the sofa and looking as if he hadn't slept for a couple of days. This wasn't what I was expecting at all. I looked at Simon and could see the look of satisfaction on his face. 'Fazal is our guest for a while,' said Simon.

'He's a suspect in our murder investigation,' is all I could think to say.

'Which is why he's in our safe house,' said Simon. 'Until we get this resolved.'

I shook my head and folded my arms. Defensive body language, I know, but I couldn't help myself. 'The only way this will be resolved is when Mr Wazir is formally charged with the murder of Sean Evans.'

'Please bear with me, Inspector Porter,' said Simon. Carmen had appeared at the door and was holding the handle. 'Can I offer you a drink?' Simon asked me.

'I'm good,' I said. I was thirsty, all right, but I wasn't in the mood to take anything from him.

Simon nodded at Carmen and she went out and slowly closed the door behind her. Simon picked up the remote and muted the sound. 'Take a seat, Inspector,' said Simon. 'There's something you need to know.'

'What the hell is he doing here?' I asked, gesturing at Wazir. Wazir looked down at the floor, avoiding my gaze.

'If you sit down and listen, you'll understand everything.'

'I'd rather stand,' I said. Bloody spooks. I'd had a murder team running around like crazy trying to find Wazir and all the time MI5 had been feeding him Coke and pizza.

'Suit yourself,' said Simon, sitting down in an armchair and crossing his legs at the ankles. He unzipped his Barbour jacket and waved a languid hand at Wazir. 'Fazal, why don't you tell Inspector Porter what happened on Friday afternoon?'

'He's a cop, isn't he?' said Wazir, his voice a hoarse whisper. He was still staring at the carpet.

'Damn right I'm a cop and if I get my way you'll be behind bars where you belong!' I snapped.

'Inspector, please. Put your understandable feelings to one side until you hear what Fazal has to say.' He smiled over at Wazir. 'Fazal, you can speak freely in front of the Inspector. Our deal is sacrosanct.'

Wazir looked up and frowned. 'Say what?'

Simon smiled patiently at him. 'Nothing you tell the Inspector affects the deal you have. Nothing is going to happen to you. Just tell him exactly what went down at the mosque that day.'

Wazir swung his feet off the table and took a sip of his Coke. His hand trembled as he drank. 'My sister...' He started and then stopped.

'Yalina,' I nodded, 'What about her?'

'She's pregnant.'

It wasn't how I was expecting him to start. How was Yalina's pregnancy relevant to the murder?

'Last Friday we were heading to the masjid for Jum'ah Prayers,' he continued, failing to meet my stare again.

'We?' I repeated.

'Ayesha was with us,' he said, meeting my eyes for the first time. 'Ayesha Khan.'

I nodded for him to continue, so far it had tied up with what we already knew.

'Sean was outside the masjid, and as soon as he saw us he tried to hurry away before we spotted him. But Yalina did, she saw him. She called him, shouted over, but Sean ignored her and hurried into the masjid.' Wazir scratched his head. 'If he just stopped and talked to her, I swear, we wouldn't be here right now.'

'Stay with it,' Simon said, sensing that Wazir was struggling.

Wazir sighed before continuing. He was staring at the floor again. 'Yalina and Ayesha entered the masjid around the back. I went in through the front and said that I'd meet them inside.' His voice was barely a whisper.

Wazir stopped talking and took another sip of his coke. He shook the empty can.

'Would you like another drink?' Simon asked, which annoyed me. This was no time to be interrupting the flow. Wazir shook his head.

'You entered the mosque...' I prompted.

'I only just found out she was pregnant,' he said. 'I heard Yalina talking to Ayesha on the phone saying that he was giving her the runaround. He'd told her she had to get an abortion, get rid of the kid. Said he didn't want to be a father. Right?' He looked at me as if he expected me to say something. 'Right?' he repeated.

'Okay,' I said. 'And?'

'So we go into the mosque and that's when Yalina corners him in one of the side rooms. The one they use to store the copies of the Koran and stuff. She's telling Sean he has to marry her, that she loves him, that she wants to keep the baby. Sean is not happy, keeps telling her to keep her voice down. He doesn't want anyone else to know what's going on, right?'

Again he stopped talking. He looked up at me, to see what my reaction was.

'Okay,' I said. There wasn't anything else I could think of saying. I just wanted him to get on with telling the story.

'Okay, so I stand next to Yalina, I can see she's getting upset. Then she loses it and pushes Sean, hard, both hands against his chest. Bang. She's really angry. I've never seen her like that before. And Sean, he loses it, too, and he shoves her, so hard that she falls back and hits her head against one of the bookcases. I saw red. I had a knife in my pocket, I pulled it out...' He left the sentence unfinished.

'And you stabbed him?'

Wazir nodded. 'I didn't mean to.' Tears were welling up in his eyes.

'You didn't mean to stab him? How does that work? You pull out a knife and you thrust it into his chest, and that was what, an accident?'

'Inspector,' said Simon. 'There's no need to be so adversarial. Fazal is cooperating here.'

'It all happened real quick,' said Wazir. 'It was a flick-knife, you know? I pulled it out and my thumb was on the button and the blade was out and I don't know if he stepped forward or if I stabbed him, it all happened so fast. It was over in a second. Look, I killed Sean, no getting away from that. But I swear on all that is Holy, may Allah be my judge, I didn't mean to do it. I swear I didn't plan on killing him. Even when I'd stabbed him I thought he was okay. He walked away. I thought maybe I'd just nicked him.'

'You did,' I said. 'But you nicked his heart. He bled to death.'

'I was as shocked as he was and I pulled the knife out. He looked at me and said it was okay. I swear, that's what he said. He kept repeating it. "I'm okay, I'm okay, I'm okay." Then he turned and walked away.'

'He was bleeding to death,' I said. 'The knife had penetrated his heart. Blood was oozing out with every beat.'

'I thought he was all right.' said Wazir.

'It was an accident,' said Simon.

I shook my head. 'Stabbing someone with a knife is never an accident,' I said. 'What were you doing with a knife in the mosque in the first place?'

'Protection.' He looked across at Simon. 'The job I do... If people find out, I need to be able to defend myself.'

'Job? What job,' I said, directing my question at Simon.

'There's a bigger picture here,' Simon said.

I turned back to Wazir. 'And what happened then? To the knife?'

I knew the answer, but I needed to hear him say it.

He swallowed, and wiped his mouth with his hand. 'Ayesha took it from me. She said she would get rid of it.'

I nodded. All the time Ayesha had been talking to me in the mosque, she had the knife in her designer bag. She had been hiding the murder weapon while she looked me in the eye and smiled at me. The woman must have ice water for blood. Then when the police had moved in she had slipped out of the mosque and taken the knife to the canal. The thought of what she had done sent my heart racing and I glared at Wazir. 'Sean Evans wasn't attacking you,' I said. 'You weren't protecting yourself.'

'He attacked my sister.'

'He pushed her and that was wrong. But what you did was worse.'

'I was angry! My sister is pregnant!' A tear rolled down his cheek. He wiped it away.

'Anger is no defence,' I said.

Simon held up his hand. 'Actually Inspector, I'm not sure that's true. Fazal saw his sister being attacked and rushed to defend her. That is totally understandable.'

'He stabbed an unarmed man,' I said. 'I don't understand why you are so keen to defend him. He killed one of your agents.'

'Sean Evans was an MI5 officer, not an agent,' said Simon. 'And yes, he was one of ours and no one regrets his passing more than I do. But there's a bigger picture here, Inspector.'

'The bigger picture? A man is dead, Simon. One of your men. And you want to give his killer a pass? What the fuck is wrong with you?'

He stood up. 'Why don't we go outside and get some fresh air?'

Wazir put his head in his hands as I followed Simon out of the room and along the corridor to the kitchen. Carmen was sitting at an oak table with a transceiver in front of her and a glass of water. 'We're just going outside, Carmen,' said Simon. 'Can you let the team know?'

As he opened the kitchen door, Carmen picked up her transceiver.

Chapter 48
(Sal)

My SatNav took me to the address in Ealing but two patrol cars were blocking the road, blue lights off so it looked as if it was all being done on the quiet. I wound down my window and showed my warrant card to two uniforms but they were adamant that they had been told not to let any vehicles through. I could walk, but the car had to stay. I found a place to park and then jogged along the pavement. Various emergency vehicles were parked about a hundred yards from the house, including a fire engine, three armed response vehicles, two ambulances and several paramedic vehicles.

I found DCI McKee and tried not to smile when I saw he was wearing his full uniform. He clearly sensed a photo opportunity. He was standing outside a mobile command centre, a dark blue Volvo truck that had been fitted out with state of the art communications equipment and CCTV. 'Have you spoken to DI Porter?' he asked.

'I left him a message.'

'What the hell's he doing?' muttered McKee. 'He's leading a murder investigation, his phone should never be off.'

A Sky News van was parked a few houses down and a camera crew was filming. An Armed Response Vehicle drove up to park next to the three BMW X5s that were already there. Three officers dressed in black climbed out and took their carbines from the gun safe between the rear seats.

'There are four men in the house,' said McKee. 'Our guys are using infra-red equipment to see through the walls. And they're getting a police helicopter up.' We looked up as a helicopter roared high overhead. 'Speak of the devil,' he said.

'No, that's a news helicopter,' I said. 'They got here quickly. How did they manage to get here before the police chopper?' I realised I hadn't called him 'Sir' but the question just leapt from my mouth.

'Maybe the top brass wanted coverage. Show that they're on top of things.'

'Who's running the show?' I asked, forgetting for a moment that the DCI was several rungs above me on the promotional ladder and I shouldn't be asking him about anything.

McKee didn't take offence. 'A Superintendent from SO15. Dave Pilling. He's briefing the SFOs as we speak.' He gestured at the closed door to the mobile command unit. 'He knows that Wazir is a suspect in our murder investigation and he'll let us have an early crack at him.'

Just as he finished speaking the door opened and half a dozen SFOs filed out. From their black uniforms I could tell they were regular SFOs which surprised me because I would have expected them to be using one of the Counter Terrorism SFO teams who had more experience in dealing with terrorism incidents. There are seven CTSFO teams in the Met, each made up of one sergeant and fifteen constables and they wore wolf-grey outfits. They trained with the SAS and were a level above the SFOs, who tended to work in groups of three based out of their BMW X5s.

'Any idea why CTSFO aren't here, Sir?' I asked, but he didn't hear me, he had spotted the Superintendent at the entrance to the mobile command centre.

'We're getting ready to breach the front door,' the Superintendent said to McKee. 'There's an SAS team on the way to assist. You need to keep well away until the premises are secure.' He spotted me and frowned. 'Who's this?'

'DC Nasri,' said McKee. 'He got the tip-off that our suspect was here.'

'Nice work, detective,' said the Superintendent.

'Thank you, Sir,' I said, though again I knew that no credit was due. All I'd done was to answer my phone.

'Get yourself a flak jacket,' he said. 'And keep your head down until this is over.'

Chapter 49
(Harry)

There was a half moon overhead and no clouds and the night sky was peppered with stars. The garden was well-tended with a white gazebo covered in ivy at the far end. Simon headed towards it, taking a pack of cigarettes and a gold lighter from his pocket.

'I thought you wanted fresh air,' I said, following him, my feet scuffing across the grass.

Simon chuckled. 'My one vice,' he said. 'The safe house is classed as a place of work so Health and Safety means that I can't smoke inside.' He offered the pack to me and I shook my head. He shrugged, slid out a cigarette and lit it. He blew smoke up at the moon and put his pack and lighter back into the pocket of his Barbour jacket. 'This is very complicated, Harry. Can I call you Harry?'

'I don't see why not.'

'This is all very much off the record, so I don't see that we need to use honorifics.' He blew smoke again. 'So, Sean was indeed an MI5 officer. Had been since he left university. No one knew, outside of the agency, of course. He was deep, deep undercover, tasked with penetrating jihadist groups. He was a natural, Harry. He was born to it. Fazal Wazir was one of his agents. Fazal is a hardcore Muslim who will do whatever needs to be done to protect his mosque and his religion. But he's not a terrorist and has nothing but contempt for those who are. Fazal is in The Faith, but for him The Faith is about protection, not terrorism. Sean realised that and spent time getting close to him and eventually recruited him.'

'So Wazir works for you?'

'That's putting it a bit strong. He was helping us when he thought it was in the best interests of the mosque to do so. We didn't pay him, he just provided intel through Sean. They were friends. Sean met Fazal's sister and they became romantically involved.'

'Big mistake.'

'Huge mistake,' agreed Simon, flicking ash onto the grass. We reached the gazebo and he sat down and stretched out his legs. I stayed on my feet, I didn't feel like sitting. 'He didn't tell anyone, least of all me. She's a pretty girl, though. You've seen her?'

I nodded. 'Yes, she's pretty.'

'So Sean starts seeing Yalina, in the biblical sense. Why he doesn't use a condom I'll never understand. But he doesn't and she gets pregnant.'

'He told you that?'

Simon shook his head. 'This is all hindsight, Harry. If I had known I might have been able to help him out of his predicament. I don't know what he was thinking. Fazal says Sean wanted her to have an abortion, but it seems she wanted him to do the decent thing and marry her. He started trying to avoid her, but that wasn't easy as he was running her brother.' He took another long pull on his cigarette. 'That day at the mosque, she confronted Sean. She wanted to know when he was going to marry her. Ayesha Khan was there, and so was Fazal. Sean was under a lot of pressure, he was in a very stressful place. If anyone found out who he was, he'd be dead, no question. And it wouldn't be a pleasant death, either. His life was on the line, every hour of every day. And then Yalina confronts him in the mosque, of all places. They argue, and Sean loses it. He pushes her, hard. She bangs her head. Fazal is furious, pulls out his flick knife and instinctively lashes out at Sean.'

'Stabs him. He stabbed him. You heard what he said. He admitted it.'

'Yes, but in anger, not with any deliberate attempt to kill him. They were friends, Harry.'

I held up my hands, knowing that it was pointless to argue.

'Fazal stabbed Sean once, and as he said, didn't realise that the wound had been fatal. Sean staggers away, a dead man walking. Fazal, Ayesha and Yalina don't realise the extent of his injury so Fazal put his knife away and they carry on with the prayers. It's only when the prayers are done and Sean's body is discovered that they realise what trouble they're in. Ayesha takes the knife off Fazal and says she'll dispose of it. Fazal and Yalina stay at the mosque and are interviewed, Ayesha gets rid of the murder weapon. You know the rest.'

'So Fazal came to you, looking for protection?'

'It was an accident, Harry. And Fazal is a valuable asset.'

'So valuable that you'll let him get away with murder?'

'Manslaughter at best, Harry.'

Simon's phone buzzed in his pocket. 'I have to take this,' he said, and he put the phone to his ear. He listened, nodded, and thanked the caller and put the phone back in his pocket. He smoked the last of the cigarette, stubbed it out on the side of the gazebo and flicked the butt into a hedge. 'There's something you need to see,' he said. 'Let's go back to the house.'

We walked back in silence, our breath feathering in the night air. Somebody was watching us from one of the bedroom windows but I couldn't see if it was a man or a woman. An airliner flew high overhead, red and green lights winking.

He took me back through the kitchen where Carmen was looking at her phone, and into the hallway. He opened the door into the room across from the one where I'd seen Wazir. The room was lined with bookshelves except for one wall where there was a big screen TV. There were two overstuffed leather armchairs facing the television, with a coffee table between them. 'Take a seat, Harry,' said Simon. He picked up a remote from the coffee table, switched on the television and flicked through the channels until he found Sky News. He sat down and boosted the volume.

It was an outside broadcast and according to the strap across the bottom of the screen we were watching a siege situation in Ealing, West London.

The camera was focussed on a semi-detached house. Both ends of the road had been blocked by police cars. Inside the cordon were emergency vehicles and four ARVs. Armed police crouched behind the vehicles, their carbines at the ready.

The picture changed to that of an overhead view presumably taken from a helicopter. The house was in the centre of the picture and more police and emergency vehicles could be seen parked up outside the cordon.

'What's happening?' I asked.

'A group of jihadists have been cornered in a house in Ealing,' said Simon, stretching out his legs. 'Four of them, I'm told, including at least one name you've heard of. Waseem Chowdhury.'

I stared at the screen. People were being evacuated from neighbouring houses. Four men dressed in black emerged from a hedgerow at the bottom of the garden behind the target house. There was just enough moonlight to make out the carbines they were holding and the handguns strapped to their thighs.

A newsreader was explaining that police had responded to calls that Asian men had been seen going into the house with guns. The house was now surrounded and a police negotiator was trying to make contact with the men inside. According to police, there was the possibility there were explosives in the house so the street was being evacuated.

'The negotiator won't get anywhere,' said Simon.

'You sound sure of that,' I said.

'I am.' He smiled smugly.

'You've had Chowdhury under observation?'

'We've been watching a lot of the so-called Faith,' said Simon. 'Some of them are just over-enthusiastic kids but there's a hardcore group of potential jihadists, some of whom have been over to Afghanistan for training and others who have fought in Syria.'

'And what are they planning?'

'You heard what he said. Explosives. And guns. So they're clearly up to no good.'

The helicopter went lower and the camera focussed on the men in black by the hedgerow. 'Are they cops?' I asked.

'I'm pretty sure they're ours,' said Simon.

'Yours?'

'SAS. Working for us. A group called The Increment. They're better trained for this sort of work.'

'But what about the negotiator?'

'As I said, the negotiator won't get anywhere.'

The view on the television changed again, back to the camera covering the front of the house. Four more armed men in black were moving across the tarmac. They moved towards the front door. 'Are they going to storm the house?' I asked.

'There's a risk of an explosion,' said Simon.

'All the more reason to try to talk them out, surely,' I said.

Simon shrugged but didn't say anything. Another figure in black moved across the road towards the house. He was holding a wooden frame, like a glassless window. He rushed up to the front door, placed the frame against it, then stepped to the side. A second later there was a flash of light and a puff of smoke.

'A shaped charge,' explained Simon. 'These guys are pros.'

The explosion knocked the door off its hinges and the troopers charged over it, guns at the ready. They disappeared inside the house. There was no sound with the pictures but I could imagine the crack-crack-crack of shots being fired.

The camera stayed focussed on the front of the house. There were flashes in the downstairs room, and more upstairs. Then nothing.

Chapter 50
(Sal)

McKee and I were given flak jackets and told to stay crouched down behind one of the patrol cars. A few minutes later two black Range Rovers with tinted windows pulled up and parked next to the fire engine. Four men climbed out of each vehicle. Like the SFOs they were dressed in black and had guns in holsters strapped to their thighs, but their black coveralls and helmets didn't have any police markings. They had pulled carbines from the back of their vehicles and then trooped into the mobile command centre, pulling scarves over their faces. Superintendent Pilling followed them inside and closed the door behind them.

'SAS,' said McKee, confirming what I'd been thinking.

'Where are our CTSFOs, do you think, Sir?'

'It's possible they're otherwise engaged,' he said, but without conviction.

It looked to me as if the armed cops had been told to stay well back. They made no move to approach the house.

'Did you see a negotiator, Sir?' I asked. McKee shook his head.

The Superintendent reappeared from the mobile command centre and hurried over to the armed cops. They went into a huddle and he was clearly telling them something.

The eight SAS men filed out. One of the troopers jogged over to the Range Rovers. He opened the back of one and took a wooden frame, about the size of a small window. It was a shaped charge, used to blow open doors. He followed the rest of the troopers as they fanned out and headed to the house, keeping low as they cradled their carbines.

'They're going to blow their way in, Sir.' I said, 'Where the hell is the negotiator?' McKee ignored me. It was becoming clear that this was out of his hands and he was only here to serve as decoration.

I looked over at the four ARVs. There were plenty of SFOs around, all armed to the teeth and wearing their Kevlar helmets, but they were staying well out of the way.

The Superintendent jogged over to us. 'They're going in now,' he said to McKee. 'There's another SAS team in position at the rear of the house.'

I wanted to ask the Superintendent why Met cops weren't being used but I was a lowly Detective

Constable so he would probably quite rightly tell me to mind my own business. It did all seem a bit rushed, though. If the nearby houses had been evacuated then no civilians were at risk, and so far there had been no shooting from the house.

I peered over the car. The trooper with the shaped charge had fixed it to the front door. He moved to the side of the house. He had something in his hand. A trigger, I guess. He raised it in the air and his colleagues all ducked down. There was a bang and a flash, and a second bang which I thought was an echo but then realised it was from the rear of the house.

The troopers piled into the house through the ruptured front door. Unlike when the Met's armed police mounted an attack there were no shouts identifying who they were. There was a series of rapid cracks, silence, then more gunfire. Then silence again.

'It's over,' said the Superintendent.

Chapter 51
(Harry)

I stared at the television, trying to make sense of what I'd seen. 'They weren't even trying to negotiate with them,' I said. 'They just went in.'

'They were following instructions,' said Simon. 'They're all dead, including Mr Chowdhury. They were prepared to die for their beliefs, so our guys were happy to oblige.'

'They were told to shoot to kill,' I said, and it wasn't a question. It was clear that Simon had known what was going to happen even before he had switched on the television.

'The men inside were armed and dangerous, and there are indeed explosives in the house,' said Simon. 'Lives were at risk.'

'I see you're not contradicting me.'

One of the men in black appeared at the front door. He stood there with his carbine across his chest.

'If it makes you feel any happier, Harry, they will find the knife that was used to kill Sean Evans. His blood will be on the blade and Mr Chowdhury's fingerprints will be on the handle. Oh, and they will find blood from Sean Evans on Mr Chowdhury's shoes.'

I tried to hide my surprise but it was clear from his grin of triumph that I had failed. 'Chowdhury didn't kill Evans,' I said. 'We both know that.'

Simon smiled thinly. 'Tell me, Harry, in your experience, which is considerable, what is the least reliable evidence in any case?'

'Eyewitnesses,' I said. I could see where he was going but I had no choice other than to let him play his little game. I could see he was enjoying himself.

He nodded enthusiastically. 'Exactly,' he said. 'If you have three witnesses to an incident you will get three totally different accounts of it. In a simple road traffic accident, most witnesses will even get the colour and make of the vehicles wrong. Eyes and memory are unreliable, every police officer knows that. Memories are coloured by experience and expectation. And what evidence is by far the most reliable in any case?'

I sighed. 'Forensics.'

'Exactly,' he said again. 'Forensic evidence. Blood on his shoes. Blood on the knife.'

'The knife that killed Sean Evans was found in the canal,' I said. 'We have it in our possession.'

'No, you have a knife that had the characteristics that the pathologist thinks could have caused the damage to the victim. Blade length and blade width are a good match. But there was no DNA and no fingerprints on the knife.'

'But we know the knife was thrown in the canal by Ayesha Khan after she took it from the mosque.'

'No, that's supposition,' said Simon. 'No one saw Ms Khan throw the knife into the canal. For all you know the knife could have been there for months.' He gestured at the television. 'The knife that will be found in that house is a close match to the one you found in the canal. But the big difference is that Chowdhury's fingerprints are on the knife along with the DNA of Sean Evans.'

'And you know that before any forensic testing?'

His smile tightened a fraction. 'Yes, Harry. I do. And I also know that traces of Sean Evans's blood will also be found on Mr Chowdhury's shoes. It will be an open and shut case, a case for which you as SIO will be able to take the credit.'

'What?'

'You yourself flagged Mr Chowdhury as a suspect very early on. And you raised the Action to have him interviewed. So it is only fair to say that you were instrumental in solving the case.'

'And you've already briefed journalists to expect that Chowdhury will be identified as the killer? Clever. Very clever. Positively Machiavellian.'

On the television, a senior police officer in a flak jacket walked up to the front door accompanied by two armed police in Kevlar vests and helmets. The officer exchanged words with the man in black but the man in black stayed where he was, blocking the doorway. As his face turned towards the camera. I realised the officer was DCI McKee. I frowned, wondering what the hell Teflon was doing at the scene. 'The case hasn't been solved,' I said. 'It's been covered up.'

'We have a killer who arrived at the mosque with the victim, who was at the murder scene at the time of the murder but left before he could be questioned, who is found with the murder weapon and with the victim's blood on his shoes.'

'A so-called killer who isn't in a position to defend himself. Him being dead and all.'

'And doesn't that make everybody's life so much easier? Look at all those messy trials where the defendant is clearly guilty but he insists on maintaining his innocence to the very end. I would say that everybody gains from the death of Mr Chowdhury.'

'Except for Mr Chowdhury himself.'

'He's no great loss, Harry. He and his pals were planning an attack on Oxford Street. A dozen members of his little group were going to start at one end with knives and machetes and see how many shoppers they could kill before they were stopped. What do you think? How many innocent civilians could a dozen angry men kill before they were stopped? Fifty? A hundred? Two hundred? I'll be shedding no tears over his death or the death of the three jihadists who died with him. Trust me on that.'

'And what about Wazir? He walks?'

'He continues to work for us. It was his work that put us on to the Oxford Street plan. He saved dozens of lives, maybe hundreds. That goes some way to redressing the balance.'

'He stabbed Sean Evans.'

'Yes, in a moment of anger after Evans shoved his pregnant sister. He whipped out the knife and lashed out but he wasn't planning to kill him.'

'Everyone who ever killed someone with a knife says that.'

'Do you know how difficult it is to kill someone with one thrust?' said Simon. 'We've got experts who've trained for years who still can't guarantee it. I'm not going to say it was an accident, but when Wazir stabbed Evans that's what he was doing – stabbing rather than killing.'

'Then he should stand trial for manslaughter.'

'And the jihadists plots that he will no doubt expose in the future –what about them? How many deaths do you want on your conscience, Harry?'

'Don't put this on me!' I said, unable to keep the anger out of my voice

'But it is on you, don't you see that?' said Simon. 'If Wazir goes to prison, we lose one of the best agents we have. He's sorry, you can see he's sorry. He's killed the father of his sister's child and he's going to have to live with that for the rest of his life.'

'And that's punishment enough?'

'You just have to look at the big picture here, Harry. And think about the greater good.'

I stared at him in silence for several seconds. 'What about Wazir's sister. And Ayesha Khan?'

'In what way?'

'They saw what happened.'

'Do you think Yalina wants her brother to be locked up? And I doubt that Ms Khan would want to explain why she walked to the canal that afternoon.'

'But what's to stop them telling their version of events?'

'They both understand that it wouldn't be in their best interests.'

'You've spoken to them?'

'Not me personally, no. But they have been approached. And I think it's fair to say that they both appreciate the value of not rocking the boat, shall we say. Chowdhury killed Sean Evans, and Chowdhury is now himself exposed as a terrorist and has paid the price for his career choice. There is no downside to that story being accepted as fact.'

'All's well that ends well?'

Simon smiled. 'Harry, you say that as if it's a bad thing.'

CHAPTER 52
(SAL)

A forensic team went into the house but I didn't recognise them. I'd expected to see Lorraine Sawyer but they were all men and all strangers to me. The guys with guns stayed inside and it was almost thirty minutes before they allowed the police to join them. Well, I say police, but they only let Superintendent Pilling and DCI McKee in. One of the troopers barred my way and shook his head. 'Not you,' he said.

Not me? Not me personally, not me the detective constable, or not me the Asian? I glared at him but I didn't say anything.

'It's okay, you wait outside,' said McKee.

I did as I was told, but I wasn't happy about it. I knew way more about the investigation than either Pilling or McKee, but I guess they were looking to claim the credit.

I paced up and down outside. Eventually McKee came out of the house and strode towards me. He had a puzzled look on his face. 'Your informant said we'd find Fazal Wazir here?' he asked.

'It wasn't really an informant, Sir,' I said. 'More an anonymous call. But yes, Fazal Wazir. Is there a problem?'

'Yes and no,' said McKee. 'The four casualties in there are definitely jihadists, and they were definitely planning a terrorist atrocity. There are guns and knives and God knows what else. But Fazal Wazir isn't one of them.'

'He was quite definite.'

'I'll tell you who is there,' said McKee. 'Waseem Chowdhury. The guy we've been getting journalist enquiries from in connection with the mosque murder. He's one of the four. And they found a knife on him that's pretty much the twin of the one that the divers pulled out of the canal. Forensics are processing the scene, but it's already looking as if Chowdhury is our killer. There is blood on the knife and there seems to be blood on Chowdhury's shoes. If that blood turns out to be that of Sean Evans then we can close the case.'

'I think the feeling was that if Chowdhury had wanted to kill Evans, he would have done it somewhere less public, Sir.'

'I understand that, but maybe he was taking the view that it was better to hide in plain sight. Certainly if it hadn't been for your tip-off, I doubt we would have found the knife.' He shrugged. 'Either way, it's been a good night's work. We've taken out a jihadist cell and with any luck we've got our killer. Still no call from Inspector Porter?'

I shook my head.

'What the hell is he playing at?'

Right on cue, Porter arrived in his Volvo. McKee sighed. 'Bring him up to speed,' he said, and turned to go back into the house.

'As SIO, shouldn't he be at the crime scene?' I asked.

'At the moment it's senior officers only,' said McKee. He walked away leaving me wondering what the hell was going on. Porter was the SIO and an Inspector. Who had taken the decision not to allow him in at the kill?

I went over to Porter and started to tell him what had happened but he put up his hand to stop me. 'I saw it live on TV,' he said.

'McKee and Superintendent Pilling are in there now, they want us to wait outside,' I said. 'That's just wrong, Guv. This is our case.'

'Wheels within wheels,' he said, and I had no idea what he meant by that.

'I got a tip that Fazal Wazir was in the house. But that was bollocks. It was Waseem Chowdhury and three other guys and now they're saying it was Chowdhury that murdered Sean Evans. According to McKee there's blood on the knife they found and blood on Chowdhury's shoes.'

'That's convenient,' said Porter.

'McKee seems sure that the blood will be a match to Sean Evans.'

'I'm sure he's right,' said Porter. He had a faraway look in his eyes as if he was thinking about something else.

Another half an hour passed and then the bodies were removed, put in vans and driven away. Superintendent Pilling came out and addressed the media, with McKee at his shoulder. Pilling gave few details but said that the police were confident they had disrupted a terror cell that was close to committing an atrocity in London, and that they were equally confident they had identified the killer of Sean Evans.

'This is wrong, Guv,' I said. 'This is all wrong.'

He turned to look at me as if seeing me for the first time. 'What's wrong?'

'Just…' I shrugged. 'It's odd.'

'What is?'

'Where were you, Guv?'

'Personal business,' he said. 'What's odd, Sal?'

'There was no negotiator. No attempt at communication was made with the house. They went in. Bang, bang, bang, bang. No shouts, no nothing.'

Porter nodded. 'There must have been an immediate threat for them to storm the house. They know what they're doing. They're pros.'

'Yeah, they do.' I said, 'Only, I was here from the start. I got the tip off. I made the call.'

'You did the right thing. You'll get the credit, don't worry.'

I shook my head. 'It's not the credit I'm worried about.'

'Okay.'

'Guv?'

'Sal?'

'Do you remember when we were handed this case?' I asked. 'When we first entered the mosque?'

'I do.'

'Do you remember what you did?'

'I've learnt my lesson, Sal.' Porter smiled, but there was no humour in it. 'Never enter a mosque with your shoes on.'

'That's right, Guv.' I said. 'Always take your shoes off before entering a mosque.' I shrugged. 'So, how did Sean Evans' blood get onto Waseem Chowdhury's shoes if he was killed inside the mosque?'

Porter didn't have an answer to that.

I left the scene at midnight. They never did allow Porter or me into the house. I drove home. Maria's lights were out. The living room lights were out. Our bedroom lights were out. I knew with all the shit that was knocking around in my head, sleep would not find me so I continued to drive past my house. I knew where I was going and I drove on autopilot.

I parked the car, took a breath and stepped out. I entered the establishment and the bell jingled, signalling my arrival. A man who was standing by the back door nodded and pushed it open. I walked into the small room and without making eye contact with anyone, I sat down, Murmurs of acknowledgement greeted me.

My phone vibrated. I slipped it out of my pocket enough to check the display. A message from Miriam. I didn't need to read to know what it said. I slipped it back in my pocket. Behind me a hand clapped my shoulder, I could feel his hot breath in my ear.

'I knew you'd come back.'

I nodded at nothing and nobody in particular as I felt him laugh in my ear.

'They always come back, Sal,' Serge said with his heavy Russian accent, squeezing my shoulder and placing a thousand pounds worth of chips on the table in front of me.

Betty the dealer licked her lips and two cards flew towards me. I placed my hands on them and smiled without turning them over as that familiar rush of release swept over me.

Everything that had gone before forgotten about, if only for a moment.

About The Author

Stephen Leather is one of the UK's most successful thriller writers, an eBook and *Sunday Times* bestseller and author of the critically acclaimed Dan "Spider" Shepherd series and the Jack Nightingale supernatural detective novels. Before becoming a novelist he was a journalist for more than ten years on newspapers such as *The Times*, the *Daily Mirror*, the *Glasgow Herald*, the *Daily Mail* and the *South China Morning Post* in Hong Kong. He is one of the country's most successful eBook authors and his eBooks have topped the Amazon Kindle charts in the UK and the US. *The Bookseller* magazine named him as one of the 100 most influential people in the UK publishing world.

Born in Manchester, he began writing full-time in 1992. His bestsellers have been translated into fifteen languages. He has also written for television shows such as *London's Burning*, *The Knock* and the BBC's *Murder in Mind* series, Two of his novels, *The Stretch* and *The Bombmaker*, were filmed for TV and

The Chinaman is now a major motion picture starring Pierce Brosnan and Jackie Chan.

To find out more, you can visit his website at www.stephenleather.com.

Short Range

Hodder and Stoughton have published fifteen books featuring Dan 'Spider' Shepherd written by *Sunday Times* bestselling author Stephen Leather. The sixteenth, *Short Range*, will be published in July 2019.

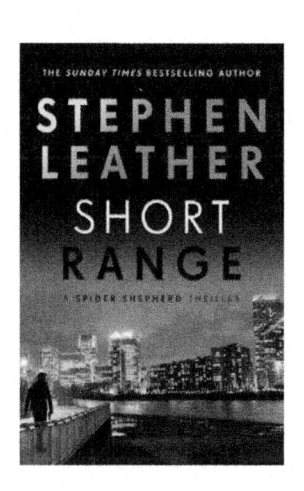

Dan 'Spider' Shepherd's career path - soldier, policeman, MI5 officer - has always put a strain on his family. So he is far from happy to learn that MI5 is using teenagers as informants. Parents are being kept in the dark and Shepherd fears that the children are being exploited.

As an undercover specialist, Shepherd is tasked with protecting a 15-year-old schoolboy who is being used to gather evidence against violent drug dealers and a right-wing terrorist group. But when the boy's life is threatened, Shepherd has no choice but to step in and take the heat.

And while Shepherd's problems mount up at work, he has even greater problems closer to home. His son Liam has fallen foul of the Serbian Mafia and if Shepherd doesn't intervene, Liam will die.

Printed in Dunstable, United Kingdom